PENGUIN

THE
𝒫ERFUMER'S
SECRET

Fiona McIntosh is an internationally bestselling author of books for adults and children. She co-founded an award-winning travel magazine with her husband, which they ran for fifteen years while raising their twin sons before she became a full-time author. Fiona roams the world researching and drawing inspiration for her novels, and runs a series of highly respected fiction masterclasses. She calls South Australia home.

fionamcintosh.com

FIONA McINTOSH

THE PERFUMER'S SECRET

PENGUIN BOOKS

PENGUIN BOOKS

UK | USA | Canada | Ireland | Australia
India | New Zealand | South Africa | China

Penguin Books is part of the Penguin Random House group of companies
whose addresses can be found at global.penguinrandomhouse.com.

Penguin
Random House
Australia

First published by Penguin Group (Australia), 2015
This edition published by Penguin Australia Pty Ltd, 2016

Cover design by Nikki Townsend and Laura Thomas © Penguin Random House Australia Pty Ltd
Text design by Samantha Jayaweera © Penguin Random House Australia Pty Ltd
Cover photographs: Peony: Maximillian Stock Ltd/Getty Images; Roses: Olena Chernenko/
Getty Images; Peony roses: Grant Faint/Getty Images; Town: PhotoAlto/Frederic Cirou/
Getty Images; Woman: CoffeeAnd Milk/Getty Images
Author photograph by Anne Stropin
Typeset in Sabon by Samantha Jayaweera, Penguin Random House Australia Pty Ltd
Colour separation by Splitting Image Colour Studio, Clayton, Victoria
Printed and bound in Australia by Griffin Press, an accredited ISO AS/NZS 14001
Environmental Management Systems printer.

National Library of Australia
Cataloguing-in-Publication data:

McIntosh, Fiona. 1960- author.
The perfumer's secret / Fiona McIntosh.
9780143573814 (paperback)
Love stories.
Family secrets—Fiction.

A823.4

penguin.com.au

MIX
Paper from
responsible sources
FSC
www.fsc.org   FSC® C009448

*This book is dedicated to my photographer,
Anne Stropin. We lost Anne too soon – just as I signed
off the proofs of this novel. Like any gorgeous perfume,
she will linger long in my memory.*

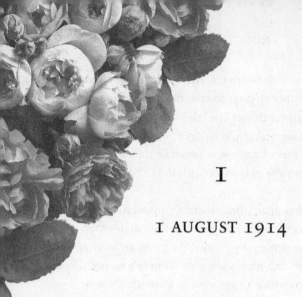

I

1 AUGUST 1914

I loathed the man I was to marry today.

A hand reached across and covered my wrist; it was hairless with blunt, well-kept fingernails.

'Be still, Fleurette.' I hadn't realised how I was fidgeting. 'Collect yourself,' my brother continued. 'Father would want you composed, representing the family so publicly.' Henri tipped my chin through the veil which, though sheer, likely hid me enough to blur my expression of anguish.

Henri's purposeful mention of our genial father demanded I obey. I was nothing if not dutiful. They say we all make choices in our lives, but I was born into a family who made nearly all of life's choices for me. In their defence I had little to complain about. I was the precious daughter to be cherished and admired like treasure.

I had failed to comprehend until recently, however, that this was not simply a charming notion. I was indeed the family treasure and I could be exchanged like a coin, traded as human currency. I was as helpless as a glinting gold sovereign passed from one hand to another: a bargain made, a transaction secured.

And now with the deal done – and just the ritual required to confirm its existence to everyone else – my angst counted for naught. I made another attempt to take the legal position, my last bastion, the only aspect of this vile union I could attempt to hide behind. The war, it seemed, might be my ally.

'Henri, in the eyes of the law, we shall be unmarried. Without that certificate from the mayor, the priest can't legally wed us.' I spoke the truth.

'Don't start that again, little sister. I can assure you that the mayor and his councillors have far more on their minds than a society wedding. I have personally pressed the point an hour ago and not even our name and its weight – or Aimery's or my threats, I might add – can convince his assistant to interrupt the town's war meetings. Besides, the mayor and his adjoint aren't even in Grasse,' he said, sounding exasperated because he knew I was aware of this last fact.

True. We were supposed to have had our civil ceremony yesterday but with France on a war footing, awaiting declaration, no town hall anywhere in the country would have been inclined to concern itself with legalising a marriage, not even one for an elite pair of families such as ours.

'When is the mayor back?'

He lifted a shoulder helplessly. 'Tomorrow, hopefully. The emergency meeting in Nice at the prefecture will likely close today when declaration of war is surely formalised.'

'Can't anyone else —'

'No,' he snapped. 'It is unbefitting that a lower representative would wish to perform a marriage ceremony today with the nation in such flux – even if he were in a position to or permitted to.' I wanted to leap in and press my point here but Henri was ready for me. 'Now,' he continued, cutting the air with a raised palm. 'Enough. It has been hard enough to convince the priest to go ahead but if he has acquiesced, then I suspect you have no higher authority.'

'I have my moral —'

'Let it be, Fleurette,' he sniped, brushing imaginary lint from his trousers. 'We are toppling into war with Germany! These are hardly usual circumstances. Heaven will forgive you – it's just a formality, and it's not as though we won't be having the civil ceremony.'

'When?'

'The mayor has sent word that he will do his best for us – let's hope tomorrow.' He was flushed pink with simmering anger and I watched him run a finger between his collar and neck, grimacing with displeasure at me. 'Now, neither I nor the De Lasset family will ever forgive you if you get in the way of this important union. We can hardly cancel after months of preparation. This town needs this marriage. Plus our mobilisation orders will be through at any moment – let's at least get the church wedding completed. The civil duties can be sorted quietly. I know it's backwards – *I know* – but I need you to tolerate the discrepancy. If our church can, you can. Please think of everyone else . . . anyone else, in fact, instead of yourself for once.'

The rebuke hurt. I was not selfish but I was angry with our priest for bending the rules of our faith, the laws of our land, simply because the wealthiest families demanded it. No doubt Henri or my equally boorish husband-to-be had coerced the priest – the new window for the apse, perhaps?

'Henri, I will be lying with a man who is not legally my husband,' I bleated.

'Not in the eyes of the law, no, but it shall be fixed. What are you hoping for? That we shall cancel because of a piece of paper?' He glared at me. 'Are you going to disappoint the entire town, all of its people gathered to celebrate what is arguably the most important marriage in recent times, perhaps ever, for Grasse? Two of its elite families, formally unified: it's the dream, Fleurette. Don't spoil this dream, this optimism, given that every able man here is about to march off to do his country's duty.'

'Exactly! How can we be sure of the legal paperwork being achieved without Aimery's presence?'

I suspected he had no ready answer – this was my final flag, my last standing post. I was shocked that he was more than ready for me, though, with a voice filled with disdain.

'The declaration will be chest-beating by Germany. We have to observe our mobilisation duties but I suspect we shall all be making our way back to our homes within a week, perhaps two at worst. It will be short-lived and Aimery will be home, but for now he wants to leave Grasse as a married man, potentially with an heir already seeded, and you are going to ensure you live up to everyone's expectations. That's your duty.'

I closed my eyes in revulsion. Now my body was being spoken about like a field, ready to be turned over and . . . oh, it was too ugly to contemplate.

There was no response to my brother's tirade. I was struck mute; I opened my eyes to stare at my gloved hands and the small mound beneath the glove of my left hand, third finger. The glint of crimson winked at me. It was a half-carat ruby set between curves of old mine-cut and rose-cut diamonds. The result was a ring shaped like an eye . . . and it stared back at me from under the lace with accusation in that red eye. Aimery could not engage me for marriage with an heirloom ring; he had nothing of his mother's and I suspected he would have ignored something of hers even if he had it to give. Instead, this had been designed at enormous expense in Paris, but without my involvement, of course. And so it reflected only Aimery . . . flamboyant, no doubt outrageously expensive, ostentatious in its bright colouring – demanding attention. The shape was odd and I already imbued it with a sinister sense that it would always spy on me. I hated it, but then everything about this marriage carried despair for me.

An odd pain enveloped me in the claustrophobic carriage, sharp and nauseating. It was the height of summer and the flowers in my hand and threaded through my hair might wilt; that was the reason given for us not travelling in an open landau. Churlishly, I decided the real reason was more likely Henri's concern for his hair and the carefully applied pomade. The pain deepened; perhaps I was panicking, like the time I thought Felix had chopped his fingers off with a lavender scythe, or the morning of the June picnic when I fell from my horse and everyone's voices were coming from too far away . . . or the day my mother died, which in itself was beyond my comprehension as an infant, yet as young as I was I recall my father's body sagging like an empty sack of rose petals and not understanding why.

I was not prone to being flighty and in my defence those memories belonged to isolated, intensive events that I could conjure authentically. Today's anxiety didn't feel as though it would pass, or that someone would come along to make it feel better; today was the start of a new life I feared. The desire to shrink from it was sufficiently overwhelming that I felt as though I was trying to tear part of myself free . . . me and myself needed to separate in order to get through what duty now required of me.

I looked away from the stone dwellings of the town as we picked our way through the streets, drawing ever closer to the sound of the single cathedral bell chiming our imminent arrival. My gaze fixed on my hands in my lap, which were finally still. The fingers beneath the pearl-studded silken Chantilly lace were straight, unblemished by any hereditary disease like my father had suffered. I tried to pretend the internal ache was coming from their joints, pathetically I suppose, trying to commune with my dead father in a moment when I had never needed him more.

I privately wished Henri the pain of our father in his own

fingers. Perhaps he sensed the curse pass between us as I remembered the physician's description of Father's arthritis. My recall of any event was so reliable I could watch the scene, hear the words accurately replay in my mind.

'Your joints are building their spurs,' Dr Bertrand had observed, puffing on a pipe as he bent to inspect my father's hands, despite his host's muttered protest. 'They're called Heberden's nodes, if you prefer me to be precise,' he said, frowning. Bluish smoke had escaped his lips and moved like a phantom, stealing around the room, scenting it with top notes of the whiskey I smelled in my father's decanter and the dry leaves I threw on the campfire that my brother and I set the previous winter. I reached hard and could still conjure the taste of tea and a gentle hum of what I thought might be vanilla. Father would have waved a finger in appreciation at my observation.

Ah, those crooked hands; they had taught me everything from how to ride a horse to how to pluck a tiny, delicate flower at dawn without touching the fragile bloom, a necessary ability in our family business. The only skill I could think of in this tense moment in the carriage of misery with Henri was that the only talent my father's hands had not physically taught me was gifted through his blood. I had known even then, as a beribboned child with a black kitten making a nest in my lap while Dr Bertrand mused over my father's arthritic fingers, that my heightened sense of taste and smell was emerging in tandem with my twin brother's equally strong talent.

Our elder brother Henri had known too that, once again, he was different to his siblings. And he could not cheerfully regard this talent we'd acquired as a blessing; even now it sat between us as an invisible presence, taunting him despite its silence. Henri had learned how to ignore it but never to disguise the impact it had on his constant desire to impress our father.

The Delacroix twins had 'the Nose'. The divinely bestowed

gift of olfactory superiority allowed us such a heightened sense of smell we could distinguish aromas beyond the average person. Thus our ability to develop complex fragrances with depth and skill made us gods of our industry. Except I had the misfortune, I suppose, to be born a woman. Had I arrived into any other family, I suspect my prowess would have lain dormant. As it was, only Felix was taken seriously as the upcoming perfumer of the family but I was permitted to contribute my thoughts as a sort of invisible consultant to Felix and my father. It was enough – it had to be, for I had no choice in this. However, more obvious than my passion to use my skills was that the inherent ability had bypassed the heir, and so Henri found creative ways to punish us for this fact. I realise now that most of the time even poor Henri wasn't aware of just how deeply angry he was to lack this highly prized skill.

It was unusual for two such closely related family members to possess the flair that for most felt unattainable. Oh, indeed, recognising bouquets was a skill that could be acquired with a workmanlike diligence. No, what I'm referring to is a sixth sense. An inherent aptitude for deciphering dozens – no, scores – of elemental tastes and smells, even when jumbled together. As a youngster Henri's wrath tried to trip us up; he'd blindfold us, demand we perform like circus animals. What he couldn't realise was that denying us the sight of the source only heightened our proficiency. If he'd paid more attention, he would have recalled that whenever Father smelled a perfume, or even a single flower, he would close his eyes as if to be deliberately blindfolded from any visual cues.

I couldn't touch this exquisite pain I was feeling in my fingers now. I couldn't soothe it, or send it away. I had no idea from where it emanated: my departing soul, I thought, and I knew Felix would scoff at the dramatic notion.

I would give anything for my father's gnarled hands to reach out and hold mine now; he would know what to say, would know

7

how to quell the pain. He would cancel this pantomime and counsel all involved that he wished a happy rather than a dutiful marriage for his only daughter. He had never favoured Aimery for me, wouldn't hear of it when it was first proffered several years back. In fact his horror had matched mine. I'd had a reliable ally until now; why hadn't he stated in his will that I should marry whom I wanted and not have my marriage arranged? My mother, rest her soul, might not agree. She herself had been forced into a union of duty demanded of her aristocratic English family. Fortunately for Flora St John, the man on the other end of that bargain was Arnaud Delacroix. I doubted she could regret her family's agreement, hammered out in Paris, as I understood it, between the two heads of the household, for it had been a wise and – luckily for her – a blessed one. Although no one could have known that, surely, at the time. The agreement would have been made purely on the suitability of his and her families' combined financial clout. I wish I'd known my mother longer than two brief years and could ask her now how it had felt to be sold on.

I gathered from others in the household that she had been a golden-haired beauty with a milky complexion and pale eyes and was treated like a goddess by my father. She roamed my memory more as a line-up of senses. I could recreate her preferred fragrance simply by closing my mind and thinking on it: honeysuckle, jasmine and rose would linger in my thoughts. I could dimly recall the sound of her gentle voice; I could also latch on to a memory of her hugs and kisses, but her physical presence was not easy to conjure. She was like a ghost who drifted through our house in photographs or the portrait in my father's salon; she was real only through her possessions – jewellery, clothes, her ivory comb and hairbrush – but I couldn't miss her because I didn't know her. We lost this fragile woman to complications from her pregnancy when we twins were just over two years old.

My parents' life together was short but I am constantly, almost deliberately, assured by others that it was filled with affection. She had loved him completely, according to our old nurse, who was like a mother to mine and a grandmother to me. She told me how Flora St John had wanted to run down the same church aisle I was approaching in her hurry to become a Delacroix of Grasse. The name counted for so much, not just in the south-west but in all of France and England too, and now I was giving up that fine name for an even more powerful one.

Except I did not want it.

The person who did desire it for me cast a look of smug pleasure my way as we rounded the corner to crest the incline to where my future beckoned. 'I think the whole town has turned out,' he remarked in an airy tone, tapping my hand in a proprietorial way. 'You should feel honoured. Look how happy they all are for you, for us.'

'Father would not approve of your decision,' I said, finding the courage to throw down one final challenge. 'And you know it. It was discussed years ago and he told you then he would not sanction it.'

Henri looked back to the adoring townsfolk, cheering and clapping as we passed. I recognised many of them. I should have been smiling, waving to them. I did neither.

'His last breath was about wishing he'd seen you in your wedding finery.'

'He'd approve of my gown, Henri, but not of the person you're forcing me to wear it for. It's not that he didn't like Aimery; even you must know he behaved oddly around him, as though there was something about him that made Father's hair stand on end. I can be specific, though – I don't like Aimery.'

It was stale debate. Henri did not trouble himself to argue it again. Instead he sighed at me as one might an insolent youngster. 'You will marry Aimery De Lasset today because it is an excellent match for our family.'

9

'For you,' I whipped back, living up to the label of a petulant child.

'As head of this family I am tasked to make the decisions,' he said in a voice leaden with forced patience. I could tell Henri was schooling himself not to be baited today.

'As eldest by a mere five years,' I said, feeling a pathetic glimmer of victory at qualifying his status, 'you may have the power to make decisions, Henri, but it doesn't capacitate you to make good ones, as you are ably demonstrating today. It's simply an easy one – solves a problem in your mind that doesn't exist in reality. If you would only wait, I would help you to make a brilliant decision on this matter and a prosperous one too. Trust me, Henri, I know my role. This is the wrong choice and definitely the wrong time.'

His irritating smile widened indulgently. 'I'm sorry you feel this way on your wedding day, Fleurette, because frankly I believe twenty-three is an ideal age for marriage. Who knows when you might decide the perfect lifetime partner has walked into your life? No, little sister, we shall not wait for an emotional readiness of your choosing that could be years away and thus miss the chance at this union of our two houses. Between us I think our father indulged you too much; his zealous refusal to consider a marriage between a Delacroix and a De Lasset bordered on fanaticism.'

'Do you think our father was mad, Henri?'

'Don't be ridiculous. You're twisting my words.'

'In that case, you're saying he possessed a genuine and fundamental objection to our houses joined in blood.'

'I never understood it and he never bothered to explain it. We all know the bitter rivalry of the past but as both fathers got older their blood cooled, plus of course they were both so successful there was no need to keep fighting one another. Until you grew up there was no reason to discuss marriage, and I'll admit I remain perplexed as to why our father didn't feel inclined to pledge you to

De Lasset, if just to keep our perfume empires strong, but he always did indulge you. Nevertheless, he's not here now and he's not the one looking to the future of our family, whereas I am, and I do not share his views. I have no reservations for this union because it makes every bit of sense to me. Furthermore, neither Aimery nor I am prepared to wait any longer. You're in your prime now; you will never look more beautiful, your skin will never glow as much, your body will never feel or move the way it does now.'

My value was now being reduced to the youth of my flesh and I wanted to accuse him of having no knowledge of my prime – or any other potential bride's prime, come to that – but he lectured on, trampling my thoughts.

'Be grateful for your charmed life, Fleurette. You belong to the second-wealthiest family of Grasse and your marriage into the town's richest family is surely a rite of passage; the timing is perfect and you know it ensures strength for the town as well – the whole region, in fact.'

He was so transparent with his manipulation I felt a momentary pity. Henri had always lacked subtlety. It was only I suppose in the last year or two that I'd come to understand Henri so fully, with his odd sense of inferiority. He had so much in his favour simply by being the eldest – that special status of being entitled – but still he envied his siblings, hungered for what we had.

If my father treated us all with what felt like identical affection I suspect my mother held a special and deeply embedded compassion for Henri. I gathered this from the old nursery maid who helped raise us. Henri was Flora's firstborn; the celebrated arrival of a son and heir made him her most beloved. It also helped, I'm sure, that he echoed her family with hair the colour of the sunbaked beaches of our childhood. He must have looked like a little angel as an infant; the grainy photos attested to this. Now, though, that once shiny hair was thinning and looked less like straw and more like wispy gold thread. His hairline had receded to reveal wings of shiny scalp that made his forehead seem a little too large. He compensated with a wiry moustache, ostentatiously curled so its tips flew north. And a newly grown beard offered the added benefit of making him seem older – the air of the patriarch he was aiming for. He trimmed his gingery beard to a point, like an exclamation to end a debate and prove he was, at twenty-seven, virile and capable of growing hair.

Meanwhile, Felix and I were the antithesis of Henri; we were a pair of midnight sentinels to his once angelic gold. Our fluff of infancy darkened quickly and by five we sported the lustrous near-black hair of our father's ancestors and we knew we would turn first moonlight silver before we became white as our predecessors, while Henri continued the march into bland baldness. The dissimilarities continued. Where Henri was slightly built with sloping shoulders hidden by skilled tailoring, our brother was strapping and I too was long-limbed, wide of shoulder, and both of us glowingly healthy to Henri's somewhat wan appearance. He routinely took 'herbal inhalations', gargled with salt, had taken to the waters at Lourdes for several years in an annual pilgrimage . . . anything to keep the feared infection at bay. He sniffed eucalypt and had rubdowns of tonic of menthol as he worried incessantly that he might contract the same disease as our mother. He would often ungraciously claim that she'd bestowed weak lungs upon him. Perhaps if he gave up smoking his expensive cigars from Cuba, it might help . . . but who was I to question our family's head any longer? Soon he would no longer be head of my family. I would belong to another man, another head of household, another controlling son who strived to live up to his ancestors.

Another bully.

The horses drawing our carriage slowed and paced out a wide circle on the cobbles sprawling in front of the cathedral before we finally lurched to a halt. We'd arrived at the place where one half of me would likely give up on life. The other half would bear witness to that surrender but hopefully remain safe, hidden, alive and dreaming of better luck for us both.

'Marriage, family, duty is everything our father stood for,' Henri finished, as though wanting to slam the book shut on any further discussion about the suitability of this marriage.

I insisted on aiming to have the last word, though. 'Well, as you're selling me off like a stud horse, Henri, you really should take into account my fine teeth!' I said, my voice finally breaking as my body felt itself sundered. It seemed as though only a shell now remained inside the carriage, dabbing quickly at her eyes, while the spirit version of me shrank and surely floated outside, finally free, to await on the church steps for the Delacroix bride to emerge from the froth of white inside the closed carriage.

'Do your duty,' Henri urged in a clipped tone. I watched his face betray the sneer that was close to the surface. Henri had no time for girlish tears. 'A wise and solid marriage is the only contribution demanded of you . . . that, and some heirs. You can manage that, surely?'

'Duty?' I heard my voice squeak on the word. 'Henri, we're potentially going to war and you're more troubled by a strategic marriage arrangement and —'

He made a condescending tutting sound. 'Hush now, Fleurette. It is not your place to discuss politics.' I could almost see myself blinking in disgust opposite him. 'Besides' – he smirked – 'this is why young women should not focus on men's business. You may claim otherwise, Fleurette, but you are as emotionally vulnerable as the next girl. Let me remind you of the shared blood that runs in the veins of the German Kaiser and the Russian Tsar. They are hardly going to prolong any bad feeling against each other. War may well be declared . . . yes, words, but it likely won't amount to much fighting.'

I couldn't be bothered arguing otherwise. Henri's tactless hint at the next duty of horror I would be required to perform was suddenly crowding me, smacking in my mind as one might swing at a fly with a swat. He was not a deliberately cruel man but I could almost hear the snapping sound in my thoughts, almost feel the sting of his taunt.

And I replied in a similarly cruel vein, although I was ashamed of myself for stooping this low. '*You* should marry him, Henri. You've always had a fondness for Aimery.'

His glare was ringed by invisible rage. I could feel it wanting to reach out and grab me by the neck as he used to when we were little and he was up against both of us. Because Felix was bigger, stronger, Henri picked on me instead, even if he wanted to fight back against only my brother. I was never a match physically but Felix had schooled me in how to use my wit instead. But I had failed him today. Today my tongue was a blunt instrument, clubbing Henri with the only weapon I had against him.

His secret had always been safe with us. We were brothers and sister. No matter our differences, we shared the name of Delacroix and nothing stood between that and the rest of the world. Except now. Now the brother I had protected was casting me adrift into a new world I did not want . . . not yet.

I was his chattel. In that moment I hated him as much as Aimery and if not for Felix's sympathetic grin from the top of the cathedral stairs as he spotted our arrival, I may have faltered. But the glance from Felix told me to bear up. I looked at the male version of me; we had shared our mother's womb during the same thirty-nine weeks, emerging within a minute of each other. I was born first and took regular delight in reminding him of this. Everything was shared, often our emotions – especially today – and I knew he was losing his best friend in a way that most couldn't understand and everyone would underestimate.

'I will forgive you for that insult, Fleurette, though I'm sure I don't know what you mean by it,' he lied. 'Catherine also would not appreciate your sentiment.'

I might have liked Catherine in any other situation and I would be a welcoming sister to her if she married Henri. However, her family's driving need for her to be a Delacroix at all costs was surely out-muscling her instincts. If only she'd met Aimery first and they could have married, then I wouldn't be facing my trauma; maybe I could blame poor Catherine for this dark pathway I now had to walk?

'Fleurette?' His tone this time was surprisingly gentle.

Yet I responded as if he'd hit me. 'Yes!' I clenched two fists in my lap in a bid to contain my fury. 'I know, Henri, I know . . .' I gave one last sniff. 'Let me gather myself.'

'I want to say something meaningful to you.'

'Don't,' I warned. People were hushing around the carriage, and the coachman was waiting as a footman put down a stool for me to step onto.

Henri held the door closed a few moments longer.

'Make it work, little sister. This is a match unrivalled in our family history . . . or theirs. It is one made in heaven.'

'Or rather one on paper, using arithmetic with a lot of French franc symbols.'

'Fleurette, you are a beautiful, young woman with an intelligence to match. Learn how to use those gifts amongst the others that have been bestowed upon you to get what you want.'

The words drove into me like the chilling blast of the mistral blowing ferociously in November, roaring through my mind, taking with them my haughty resentment and perhaps even the arrogance that I should have the right to choose the man I marry. It was not so for any of my friends. Why should I be different? I was a romantic fool. Felix regularly accused me of wanting to script my life when it would be controlled by seniors, or take its own merry path and would likely throw up obstacles to clamber over, or throw down challenges to fight through. A slit of comprehension opened for me like a shaft of dawn's sunlight breaking over the hills of Grasse.

Henri's revolting choice for me would indeed ensure the success and wealth of ongoing generations. 'Keep it in the family of Grasse' had been one of my father's favourite phrases and no doubt that philosophy was one he had wanted to apply to our unions. I couldn't be selective about when his advice was relevant. It never stopped being relevant. Protecting the industry of Grasse, protecting the family's interests and its ongoing success, was my job too, and part of my job was to marry strategically.

Love was irrelevant – a lucky by-product, if it occurred.

'We have to go, Fleurette,' Henri said, and his tone was even kinder.

The door to the carriage was opened and the sounds of the people who lined the courtyard and some of the narrower alleys that fed into the cathedral square hurried in. Henri stepped out first to applause that turned wild as I emerged to take his hand with as much grace as I could muster.

'You have never looked more gorgeous,' he whispered. 'If I were Aimery, I would consider myself the luckiest man on earth.'

I looked into his earnest expression and saw no guile. Poor Henri. He truly believed this was for the best. In which case, I should do the same. Accept my lot now and get on with it. I could hardly complain that I wanted for much.

I braced, took a slow, deep breath and found a smile for my brother. 'Walk me down the aisle, Henri.'

Women sighed, thrilled at the sight of the first Delacroix bride of the new generation to step out, ready to take her wedding vows at the cathedral of Notre-Dame du Puy. Others, mainly boys, hung from windows, whistling and vying for my attention – a little smile, a sideways glance, perhaps. I gave nothing but hoped they'd all forgive me, imagine me a nervous bride, desperate not to trip or stumble. I began to understand, feeling their collective surge of pleasure. How impossible it must have seemed to my brother and his partner in this transaction, to consider cancellation or postponement.

These might be the last smiles for a long time and although war had yet to be officially declared and we prayed it might still be averted, I think we could all feel its press. This wedding was needed to keep everyone optimistic for the future.

Henri and Aimery had forgone the age-old tradition of the man calling at the house of his bride and then walking with her to the church, gathering a long procession of townsfolk behind them. Henri considered it beneath us and it troubled me that he saw us as different from the townsfolk in anything but privilege. Each of us children had been born and raised in this town and our father had come here from Paris as a boy. We were locals. Perhaps the word Henri didn't utter but heard in his mind was 'peasants'. Either way, I had to forgo what might have been the only fun of the day for me, to walk with the people I loved and perhaps channel their joy into mine. It seemed they'd all proceeded to the church anyway, just without the main couple.

I noted their sense of celebration had not been dampened and they were determined I still follow some of the ritual. Each stair to the cathedral was flanked by two children who belonged to the workers of our fields – I knew each by name. Between each pair they'd stretched a white ribbon. Normally, I would have been required to cut those ribbons intermittently on my journey from my home to the altar, but they seemed happy enough to make me cut the ribbons on the stairs. The first boy, Pierre, son of one of the violet growers, solemnly handed me some tailor's scissors that looked cumbersome in his small hands.

'Mademoiselle Fleurette,' he said, bowing sweetly.

I could hardly refuse. '*Merci*, Pierre,' I whispered, touching his curly head, before I cut his ribbon and the crowd cheered.

I lifted the hem of my gown, which was made of transparent embroidered silk covering the palest ecru satin. The elbow-length, gently ruffled sleeves of sheer Flanders lace had been fashioned from my grandmother's bridal gown. We were a superstitious lot, we Delacroix. The overall colour effect seemed to match the marble of the shallow exterior stairs of the cathedral we were ascending, and I wondered how many happy brides – like my mother – had wanted to run up this short flight towards their intended. I had walked these smoothly worn stairs most Sundays of my life and never dreaded them as I did now. From within the womb of the cathedral's stone walls I could hear the echoing sounds of people restless in their pews – coughs and the drone of men's voices, the light laughter of women – before the organ's soft background hum became louder, turned into official wedding music, and hushed those tones.

The pain had left me. I was no longer whole, though. I genuinely believed in this moment that part of me had escaped and now observed my other. I reminded myself that when Henri let go of my arm, my twin would be standing alongside the groom to keep me strong, get me through the trial of agreeing to be Aimery's wife without shouting my true feelings. Felix had already disappeared into the cathedral, no doubt quieting anyone who hadn't realised I'd arrived at the gateway to misery. I imagined his crooked smile with that glint of mischief in his eye, urging me to be strong.

The thought encouraged me and I turned once, reaching deep to find a glimmer of a smile for the still applauding townsfolk outside. They loved the old families, loved what we did for the town; they especially loved my father for how he looked after everyone who worked for the firm of Delacroix. It didn't matter whether they picked the flowers, worked on the factory floor in the distillation process or drove the carts that would make deliveries – they were all viewed as vital, valuable and worthy of his smile, his care, his kindness at all times.

We were the European chieftains of this industry. We were the royalty of Grasse, beloved old families of France.

We are the Perfumers to the World.

Perhaps it was this thought that warmed up my expression as I turned to lift a hand of appreciation to the townsfolk for their welcome when I helplessly locked on to the searing gaze of Graciela Olivares. She seemed to be standing on a low wall, for her shoulders were easily visible above even the tallest townsfolk. This gave her a clear pathway of sight to burn her fury towards me. I wanted to assure her I was as helpless in this event as a tethered lamb. It had never occurred to me that she wouldn't be Aimery's wife. If only I could explain that the talks between the two heads of household happened in private and were announced without me having any say in the agreement, that my pain matched hers . . . but Henri was dragging me into the shadows of the cathedral porch, where the heat of day and Graciela's fire were instantly chased away by the cool.

I took one long last draught of freedom and on the air I tasted my beloved Grasse, picking out its flavours with ease as though I was pointing to each on a store shelf. They were imprinted on my memory and I could select them as I chose, and yet when they reached me fresh of a morning it was as though I smelled them for the first time.

The sun-coaxed honeyed lusciousness of rose came first, tumbling on the soft thermals rising from the valley to the summit where I stood, soon to take holy vows. I reached for the waft of violet . . . there it was, syrupy and haunting, before it was pushed aside by woody, camphorous rosemary and the earthy yet elegant thyme that was never far away. They were using essential oils we'd distilled months earlier. Right now we were approaching jasmine harvest but the sensual jasmine would come into its own tonight. Even so, more flavours crowded; I wished I could linger to pick out more, but Henri was guiding me into the shadow of the vestibule.

People were clearing throats, glancing around, standing. Children were staring. I couldn't bear to meet the glance of anyone; instead I fixed my gaze on the dark stone of the church walls ahead.

Henri touched my fingertips, which clasped his arm loosely. 'Ready to do battle?' he whispered in the strange language of our mother's tongue.

It seemed timely given what Europe was facing but it was an old jest from childhood and nearly undid me. However, I embraced the affection he'd hoped he could elicit with that question.

'Tally ho,' I whispered, using the familiar yet odd response that none of us children had ever understood.

He grinned and I saw her in him and a fleeting echo of our father's smile. And then we were walking, our steps matched to the solemn music; underfoot I crushed fresh rose petals, dropped by the small child chosen as flower girl for the ceremony. Blanche was the daughter of one of our staff. I wondered if she was imagining her own wedding day. I wished Blanche a happier union as the fragrance of roses once again lifted and cradled me in its familiar scent, which I had known throughout my life. It reassured, and I held myself straighter to the organ's sombre music, which Henri had also chosen.

Eight hundred years of memory and knowledge embraced me. I knew this former cathedral, now simply called our church, almost as well as I knew my own home with its crooked stone pillars soaring to the vault of the gothic ceiling and strengthened by iron girders. Simple, grey marble tiles underfoot echoed its inherent modesty. Cold stone surrounded me and for now suited my heart. I noted some crumbling in the dark grey walls.

'We should contribute some money to restore our church,' I whispered. It was inappropriate – a useless comment – but I needed to have a reason to talk to Henri or I would be forced to acknowledge the beaming audience come to bear witness. Maybe that was the bribe offered to coerce our priest into overlooking the necessary paperwork. He was a sweet, elderly man, no doubt intimidated by both the Delacroix and De Lasset chieftains.

'It's fine,' Henri said, patting my hand as he might an obedient pet. He surely knew what I was thinking.

I shifted my gaze from my hem towards the high windows near the ceiling. It had always intrigued me that all but one of the windows had clear glass. Perhaps Henri was right to leave the cathedral be. The sobriety made that single, richly stained glass window all the more beautiful for its presence.

We were nearly there and I finally had to look ahead to the cluster of men awaiting me: priest, husband-to-be, twin. Felix glanced over his shoulder, flashed me a devil-be-damned grin and whispered something to the man he stood next to. But the groom did not turn; he stood patiently, as he had waited all of his life for me to grow up and be old enough for him to steal me from my family.

Henri and I drew alongside. I stood nearly shoulder to shoulder with Aimery but he would never see me as his equal, never recognise me as my own person; from today my role was to support his every need and, above all, deliver him the heir he now required . . . and perhaps a few as spares.

Only months ago I'd listened to the men talking about war, but the conversation had a distant quality as though even they believed it couldn't ever happen. The news filtering through newspapers and various reports suggested the shared royal blood of Queen Victoria's grandchildren may not be enough to save Europe from dragging itself into all-out war because of the troubles between Austria–Hungary and Serbia.

I'd switched off from the conversation. Our father had been too old to be physically involved in the Franco–Prussian war and my brothers yet to be born. Germany's hostility remained buried in alliances. I knew only what I'd learned at school and, despite being fed a regular diet of war propaganda, politics interested me only marginally more than marrying Aimery. My inspiration, the reason I would wake and smile for the day ahead, was to help my father and Felix to make perfume. The rest of the world held little interest for me other than where we might discover new plants, new elements.

Although I could demonstrate the gift, I was not permitted to be known as '*le nez*' but my advice was sought, indulged; I was part of the family apparatus that had delivered the exquisite and popular *Minuit*. I had even chosen the name of midnight. More recently our *Coeur de Printemps* had created an avalanche of orders and to achieve that sense of spring's heartbeat we had combined a dazzling eleven notes so finely balanced that I remember how we argued down to the last minuscule drop of vetiver. We had hotly debated whether to include anise or leave its broody presence out and whether iris stayed plush enough after the first joyous whiff had dried away. Felix and I had disagreed about lavender, sat on opposite ends of the table over grapefruit, suffered angst over the inclusion of ambergris.

My mind was always full of combinations. I felt I had no room for the drama of when the Kaiser had offended Russia, and Germany's neighbours had suddenly unified against it in shared resentment of Berlin. Britain – my mother's homeland and a naval titan – had become alarmed at Germany's build-up of its seafaring might. I had the awareness that Europe was suddenly divided into two opposers – ourselves with the Entente, Germany with its allies – that we identified as the Central Powers but it was not truly impacting on me yet. I can remember my father talking to that same doctor,

Monsieur Bertrand, that war across Europe seemed inevitable.

Aimery apparently agreed and this was why he had pressed for the marriage – to get his line established, get sons born to carry the family name and business forward, no matter what. And as I stood there, staring at the single stained-glass window that radiated colour around me like divine ornamentation on a neutral scene below, I had a moment of dawning that Henri would be next. He would marry urgently now to achieve the same aim. He had no intention of risking leaving the Delacroix future in the hands of a woman, even one with the sublime talent he knew I possessed. He was so rigid, he would rather risk birthing a male heir without the skill so long as the family had a Delacroix man at its head. And there was always Felix . . . the family 'nose' was intact through him – he could guide the new heir as he grew.

I gave our priest a look of accusation and he had the grace to avert his gaze, filled with guilty remorse. We were all too far down this path to turn back now and I knew this lovely man would have been outnumbered, outmuscled by the heads of the foremost families of the community he served. I hoped that he had at least put up a good fight for me on moral grounds. The priest asked a question and I heard Henri answer formally and yet couldn't determine the words for the sudden alarm in my mind that things were moving fast now – I had only moments of Delacroix freedom remaining to savour. Every ounce of my body was denying progress but duty was the lead in my feet. Contrastingly light of heart, Henri was beaming as he nodded at Aimery, delighted to unload the burden of the spinster sister. I didn't want Henri to leave me – a rare feeling – but he was unclasping us and handing me over to the new owner of his property.

Only now Aimery turned. He blinked. I saw satisfaction in his expression and I had to look away for fear of picking up my skirt hem again and bolting from the church.

2

With the haunt of our grandmother's favourite plain violette essential oil that I had worn scenting the air around me, I was married to Aimery, and became Madame De Lasset. By the time the cathedral bells gave their triumphant clangour and we moved from the depths of the nave into the sunshine of uproarious cheering, I noticed Graciela had left.

I couldn't blame her. I would not linger to see the man I had believed myself partnered with married to another. Aimery's elbow was crooked around mine as rice and barley were flung into the air to offer us fertility and prosperity throughout our married life.

I moved through the later celebrations at home as if in a trance, smiling, accepting the compliments and the kind wishes, thanking guests for gifts that were so plentiful they were being stored in a separate series of chambers in our house to be catalogued and properly acknowledged later. I could see days ahead spent writing letters, finding new and creative ways to express the same sentiment so that each recipient felt valued.

In the meantime I had to publicly be seen eating the five white

24

dragées, softly scented with violet, in another symbolism of health, wealth, happiness, longevity and, of course, fertility. My ability to produce a De Lasset heir was on everyone's minds, especially Aimery, who kept glancing my way with a wolfish look.

People had gathered to watch us cut our cake and just as we all took appreciative sips of effervescing champagne to toast, an ominous sound rang loud through the clear summer evening. People gasped, looking around at each other, alarmed. Champagne flutes remained suspended halfway to open mouths, shocked expressions changed to concern and a murmuring of 'War . . .' erupted but was muted rather than loud. Earlier in the day the bells had pealed joyous celebration of marriage but now the sound was a mournful tolling; it was the tocsin that would mobilise the men of our town to go to war.

A frigid hush fell across us all. I noticed Henri's valet whispering to him, but it was hardly necessary as we all knew what the ringing meant. Aimery and Felix joined them and they spoke for just a few seconds. The valet bowed and retired. The thought shuddered through my mind that surely they would stop the wedding feast, but it would mean Aimery taking me 'home' all the sooner.

Aimery was the first of the trio of men to move, raising a hand of calm, the other still holding his fizzing champagne.

'Friends, I am assured that the President has ordered the army to mobilise so it seems that this could be our last night together for a while.' Our guests began to murmur again but he hushed them with a soothing sound. 'We don't know what the future will bring, but I am sure I speak for all of us here when I say that the thought of war against Germany is not going to dampen my spirits. Somebody get me my sword and a fresh bottle of champagne – I need to start practising my swing, it seems!'

His jest provoked a roar of applause and cheering. I wanted to escape but Aimery fixed me with a stare to ensure his adoring bride waited nearby to watch his next playful trick as he performed the ritual of sabrage.

I didn't think he would be able to wield a sabre so adeptly but I'd misjudged him. After brandishing the weapon in a casually arrogant manner, swiping at the air to the gasping appreciation of the women in his audience, he had accepted the new bottle of champagne to be popped. I was invited to stand nearby as his adoring bride.

'For you, my beautiful wife,' he announced.

Balancing the bottle expertly against his long, outstretched fingers, his thumb buried in its dimple at the bottom, I watched him swipe the blade the length of the glass and I admit to feeling as surprised as Felix looked when the glass collar flew off the bottle while still attached to the cork.

This act won loud applause, especially as the spuming liquor exploded in orgasmic style from the shaft. There was another symbolic message there, which I know everyone comprehended but I chose to appear ignorant of. The real act was going to be frightening enough without buying into this theatrical build-up.

As though threat of war was momentarily forgotten, Aimery poured some of the fizzing nectar into one of our family goblets to represent *le coupe de mariage* to toast our union. It was Catherine who stepped up with the tiny cube of toasted brioche and dropped it into the cup.

'Let us toast to a healthy life together,' Aimery announced. Flutes were raised in response as he insisted we sip together from the goblet to appreciative oohs and aahs from his worshipping audience.

As soon as I could I excused myself and fled. Older people smiled with that indulgent glimmer of knowing. Was I as nervous of my wedding night as they believed I should be? Of course I was. The solemn vows in our family's sacred place had been an emotional challenge, but the one ahead was all physical and I was responding with a fresh bout of nausea. Apart from the fear of ignorance, the very thought of Aimery's clammy hands on my skin . . . private areas . . . was making my heart drum a powerful new rhythm of fear that clubbed so loudly in my chest I wondered if I might need to retch soon. Best to distance myself.

I had managed so far to lock away tightly that it would be smug Aimery who had the pleasure of taking my virginity, but as the time closed in on me, the horrible thought escaped my internal jail. Like Dr Bertrand's smoke, it moved wraith-like through me, prodding here, nagging there, reminding me the last hour or so was ticking down. If only there was another man I had loved romantically . . . even an older man I had a crush on, I might have given up my virtue to deny Aimery the main jewel of his transaction. But I had even failed there.

'How are you, Ettie?' Felix had found me at last; I knew when I fled the ballroom it would only be a matter of time before he left our guests, wandered through the small gate at the far side of the property and followed the winding path to the playhouse our father had built for our fifth birthday.

I gazed down from our cliff-top perch, which jutted from the side of the hill at the top of Grasse. It had always felt like the box our family took at the ballet, from where we and similarly affluent families looked down upon the less wealthy . . . and, of course, at each other. I couldn't see Aimery's house, soon to be my prison, from here. I considered this for the best. For maybe just one more hour I could still call this home, and so cherished this opportunity to look down into the picturesque valley of our homeland.

I didn't answer my brother immediately. My gaze was fixed rigidly on the terraced gardens, all of them crowded with centifolia rose bushes, down to the patchwork of fields below where other scented flowers stood in neat rows. The rose bushes were bare of blooms because we'd stripped them during spring, but summer was at its zenith right now, showing off its power, boasting of the regeneration it could coax from the previously frozen ground of winter. This year some of our precious rose bushes had been left resplendent in their deep pink of petals, richly golden at the centre of the flower so that they could be included in my bouquet and on the feast tables. The annual generous yield of these fields had paid for the decadent celebration of my marriage, which I was sitting here in the twilight feeling so ungrateful for.

And in spite of the glorious rose, integral to our family's wealth and success, its importance, its lifeblood, it was in this cool of evening that I could detect the note of muguet clinging to the terraces beneath the trees. Our mother called this lily-of-the-valley, which I always thought was a far prettier name. It gave up its narcotic-like notes to steal upwards, find me and calm me. Such a poisonous little plant and yet so dainty, with its sweet white bells, that I had carried it in my bridal bouquet because of the clear beauty it brought to scent. How would I describe it? Demure, I think. To me it represented a delicate woman of taste, of perfect manner and sophisticated dress. In perfume terms, if the royal line-up was rose as queen and muguet as princess, then the king was, without doubt, jasmine. This headily scented flower was like a pillow of opulent velvet – it was all about night and sensuality. My mind was wandering.

'Ettie?'

'How do you think I am?' I finally replied, lazily coming back to attention. We both hated it when someone answered a question with a question and made a point of using that ploy to niggle at each other. He was better at it than I was, but only because Felix knew how to amuse with his pettiness, rather than irritate.

Except Felix didn't react in his usual manner. Instead he glanced sideways with a look of sympathy. I wished he didn't feel sorry for me, but maybe it wasn't regret; maybe it was pity. Felix never took offence and forgave me every gruff comment over our two decades together. Best friends do that.

'I, of all people, understand why you're here but apart from avoiding wellwishers, how are you justifying your absence from your guests?'

'Scent waits for no man . . . or woman. I'm busy gathering a new perfume in my mind,' I said, trying to sound lofty. 'You just walked in and ruined the middle notes.'

'Well, I'll allow that creativity doesn't work to schedules. So, for my benefit, describe its fragrance in a word.' Felix smiled. I knew he was indulging me but I was in no mood this evening to be managed by my brother's knowing way.

'Sorrowful,' I replied.

'Oh, Ett—'

I shrugged. 'It's true. The scent is sad; jasmine will be my foundation.'

He played along. 'Enlighten me, so I can smell it.'

This was a game we played. It had always fascinated my father the way one could give clues in words and our other half would close his or her eyes and be able to smell the fragrance, taste its individual parts and then, like a symphony, play all those notes to form the music of perfume. I don't know if it was because we were twins or simply because we had both inherited a sublime talent, but we were good. No, we were wizards at it.

'Jasmine for the dormant sensuality, not ready to be broken into.' I watched his lips purse; it was not Felix I wanted to hurt with my dark thoughts. 'And a hint of sandalwood and clove.'

'Exotic.'

'More like night,' I suggested and saw him nod as the sky darkened from its tender blush, as though the angels had just splashed a pipette of ink into its ocean. Soon it would be as though a tap had been turned on, this time flowing with darker ink – that English blue-black that I learned my mother had liked to write with – to flood the dome of night and herald my fate.

'Go on,' he urged, as though he knew what I was thinking and was trying to distract me.

'Over the jasmine comes black pepper, juniper, lavender, geranium.'

His eyes snapped open. 'Aggressive,' he noted.

'Because I'm angry.'

He gave me another sad smile. 'Finish it.'

'I don't know yet,' I replied, looking back over Grasse, the fields now in deep shadow. 'My mind tells me this perfume would need some gentle sweetness, that rose should have wandered into its base, but my heart wants no tenderness in this scent. Maybe clementine and some lime?'

'Fresh,' he remarked with surprise.

'Like a slap,' I said, and he gave a gust of a laugh and I helplessly joined him.

'What would you call it?'

'*Morne*.' At his haunted expression I lifted a shoulder of regret. 'Mournful is how I feel.'

'Listen, Ettie.' He shifted closer and covered my hand with his large, dry palm. 'The spectacle of the townsfolk showering you with rose petals was not only mesmerising but a poignant symbol. In that moment, as I watched their joy, and even though I know you don't want to hear this, I believe Henri made the right decision.' I swung around but he held a hand up. 'Perhaps not for you, darling sister, but for the whole town . . . This is your moment to find the grace our father always spoke of.'

I swallowed as he echoed what I'd been hearing in my mind. Graciousness was missing from me today and it was time to stop putting myself ahead of what was expected of me.

As if he needed to lance the boil, let all the poison flow out, Felix continued, cutting into the gloom, adding more pain but it was necessary, no doubt, to cleanse the toxic mood. 'As to the legality, mere paperwork that will be fully signed tomorrow, hopefully before —'

'Is the mayor returned from Nice?'

'He's not up at the house, if that's what you mean.'

I grimaced.

'The point is, no one really cares at this tense time because they want this marriage more than they want to prevent it over a piece of paper. Threat of war changes everything. From the people's perspective, you are the most beautiful bride they've ever seen and they are all deliriously happy that two great families have come together.'

I knew it and still I needed reminding. I stayed silent and let him say it all; given that I couldn't take the advice of my own sensibilities, and that I refused to pay attention to Henri's, there was only one person left who might get through.

'Make it work with Aimery. He has looked me in the eye and promised me he will revere you.'

'Do you trust him?'

'He was a vile child but boarding school and Paris were good for him, I think. Surely he has told you about his travels?'

'Yes. I envied him. What about his brother?' I frowned. 'We never hear anything of him.'

He shrugged. 'We were far too young when his mother left. I don't even know if Sébastien was born then.'

'Why did she go?'

'I don't really know. Unhappy, probably. I heard that the people of Grasse were told she was returning home to England to have her second child, and then, to recover her health, was going on that grand tour. She took him with her by all accounts and I suppose never returned. I'm sure I heard through Father that they visited some exotic ports in Africa, India . . . . I think Sébastien sent back santal from Australia to Aimery.'

'Australia. I wish I could see it for myself. He lives in England now, is that right?'

'Father told me a couple of years ago that he's more English than French, as that's been their home for the past two decades. Although I really rather hoped he might return for the wedding, you know, bury the hatchet; not that the two brothers know one another to have a genuine grudge.'

'Prodigal brother. A good chance to build bridges,' I mused, knowing we were both enjoying this conversation as a means to avoid the inevitable.

'Perhaps he doesn't care sufficiently for his brother to be bothered. They would be perfect strangers to each other.'

'Then we are kindred spirits,' I said, smiling at Felix's look of dismay that he'd walked into that trap.

'I wonder if Madame De Lasset is still alive?'

I nodded. 'The last of the quartet.' That's how the two great families of the previous generation had been known. The Quartet of Grasse. Their parents had begun the empire but it was our father and Aimery's who had built its wealth. 'She would probably be in her mid-fifties now, disinclined to travel for her eldest son's wedding.'

'She hasn't worried about him all of these years; I can't imagine she would be overly troubled now about whom he has chosen to marry.'

I gave him a glare. 'Why not? The quartet remains intact through this marriage, even though the boy she didn't like sufficiently to raise is being forced upon a bride who doesn't want him.'

He shrugged, clearly bored of the repetitive nature of my argument. I was tiring of hearing my own groans. 'Ettie, I think you have to remind yourself that you've married a man, not the boy we recall.'

I sighed. I wasn't convinced but I needed to keep those thoughts silenced now. 'Do you really trust him, Felix?'

'I trust his promise. It was made gravely within the hallowed walls of our church.'

'I have no choice.'

'No, you don't.'

'Is that what you were sent to tell me?'

He nodded. 'But I only came because I believe it.'

'I truly dislike him. When he looks at me it's as though he's undressing me. I even hate the way he smells.'

Felix chuckled but he looked sad for me. 'You'll need to get used to it.'

'What if I can't?'

'You won't be the first wife who feels repulsion at first but you have to find every small redeeming factor and build on each to find a level of admiration that can help you to feel affection.' His reply was honest as always but tinged with sorrow for me.

'How am I supposed to be intimate with someone I detest?'

Felix put his arm around me now. 'It will be over quickly, I promise.'

I couldn't help the sound of disgust or the accompanying shudder.

'You're not the first bride to go unwillingly to her husband's bed.'

'I don't know what to do!'

'I can —'

'No, please don't,' I said, halting his words with a shove. 'I couldn't bear you trying to conjure the right instructions – it's all very well for you. You've certainly sown your wild oats far and wide.' Felix made his eyebrows dance suggestively and we dissolved into soft, sad chuckles, snickering helplessly. Nervous laughter, no doubt.

'Fleurette, you'll have to fake it, or smarten up and find something to focus on that you do enjoy about him.'

'Like what? His enormous chin?'

'Perhaps you'll discover he has an enormous —'

'Felix!' I cackled, and covered my mouth to hush the screech but now we were both loudly laughing.

'I was going to say "enormous and hidden sense of humour",' he lied.

'We both know that's about as probable as me calling down a dragon and riding away on its back.'

'Well, how about his money?'

I snorted with contempt. I didn't need his money.

'All right, then. How about the doors that his connections will open for you? Keep an open mind. If you can't love him, learn ways to bond with him. He's hardly stupid and he's not ugly either.'

'You do remember him pulling the wings off butterflies and traumatising us?' I snapped.

'We were eight.'

'You and I haven't changed much since then. I doubt he has either.'

He slow-blinked, had fallen into my new trap, but I was no match for Felix. 'That's because we're a partnership. He doesn't even have a Henri in his life. He's grown up without a lot of parenting as you well know: his father never cared much and his mother abandoned him. Anyway, I think you might just be the person to smooth those hard edges.'

I folded my arms defensively.

'You're going to have power and status now, Ettie. You'll be running your own household.'

'I run ours now!'

'Yes, but only from beneath the shadow of Henri, and once Catherine gets that ring on her finger, you'll likely feel like a scullery maid when the power for decisions is wrested away. Find all the positives, Ettie. Take the power being handed to you and use it. Rise above the imagined gloom and give Aimery a chance. Let's not forget you will be mother to his sons. That is where the real power lies, my darling sister. Influence your children, guide them on everything you and I have discussed over the years about growing plants – heaven knows you think creatively in that regard. And even though you've met a blank wall with Father and Henri on those ideas . . . perhaps with Aimery, or potentially through your sons, you can pursue those dreams.'

Felix wasn't playing me. From anyone else I would have felt manipulated but this brother, the twin beat of my heart, understood my passion, and he knew what drove me. He was giving me hope where I felt none existed.

'And should I have daughters?'

'They will be as fearless as you. Teach them all you know about perfume notes but in the meantime be the best wife you can be so you gain power and influence early. Handle Aimery right and you might be able to mould him to your way. I can assure you that most men are helpless in the hands of a beautiful woman.'

'The thought of him touching me makes me ill.'

'You may learn to enjoy it.'

I shook my head. 'I want to be in love. Like our parents were. How do I achieve that when the man I must lie with makes me feel cold? I want to dream up perfumes about passion, not despair.'

My brother looked back at me unhappily.

'I know, I know,' I said, resigned. 'It's not my place but it doesn't stop me wanting to make perfume.'

'You've got a new life unfolding. Make it work for you and in the process continue to influence perfume. Ours could not have been crafted so exquisitely without you. And I'll be here, just down the road. We can visit daily.'

I nodded, knowing everything he said was right.

'Do you believe what's going on with the military is posturing or are we facing prolonged war? I haven't paid enough attention. But I know you have.'

I knew Felix wouldn't be surprised by my shift in conversation; I also knew he wouldn't treat me as though I lacked mental capacity in this regard purely because I was female. 'Yes,' he replied, instantly gloomy. 'It's why the mayor and councillors have been holed up most of the last day. I suppose we'll know as soon as the decree filters down from Paris.'

'I still keep hoping we might avoid all out war.'

'I doubt it. Our army is already gathering. Britain thought it could broker the peace conference last July but that only inflamed the Kaiser. He felt it was condescending.'

'You're saying he feels obliged to declare war?'

'I understand Germany not wishing to scuttle to Britain's foreign secretary's orders despite their cordial terms,' he replied with patience. 'I also understand Germany said it would always support Austria–Hungary. But I just don't understand why everyone who says they don't want Europe in conflict is taking every measure to ensure we all march to war.'

'And —'

The bells stopped. I imagined the bell ringers perspiring with the effort and suddenly being told they had to finish, go find their uniforms. I halted before I allowed my easily distracted mind to wander. The fresh silence seemed more poignant and haunting than the tocsin.

Felix looked around in the quiet and checked his watch. 'It's time to go back in, Ettie.' He sounded weary, as if talk of war had exhausted him. 'You need to rejoin the festivities.'

The sigh at being forced back to my duty was out before I could stop it.

'Come on,' he urged. 'Matters of state aside, it's also time for you to leave our childhood playground behind.' He offered an elbow, which I gratefully took, and we began the stroll back to the house, which was lit by lanterns, with music enchanting the hillside, and laughter sounding from within its happy walls. Felix gave a sigh. 'You must grow up tonight. Please him, no matter what it costs you.'

'But war, Felix,' I appealed. 'None of this matters!' I said, flicking at my flouncy lace. 'Besides, I won't know what to do.'

'He will.'

'Did you see Graciela Olivares?'

'No.' He sounded intrigued. 'I can't imagine she was a guest.'

'Not a guest. She was at the church.'

'With the townsfolk?'

I nodded. 'The only one not cheering; her glare was like Greek fire. She launched it across the heads of all the townsfolk.'

'It's that Hispanic blood in her. You couldn't blame Graciela, though.'

'I don't, but I wish she'd blame him, not me.'

'Maybe I could offer to soothe her wrath?' He winked.

Back inside the villa and out on the verandah where people were feasting anew at small tables, I mulled over the false jollity and eavesdropped on conversations. It seemed the older folk were eager to avenge the Franco–Prussian disaster of the previous century while our younger guests were filled with bravado and equally eager to taste war. Aimery left me alone while he guffawed with his army cronies, no doubt whipping them up into a frenzy of arrogance that they were all invincible. I wasn't unhappy for the hours to pass in this way, but it all did move before me while I watched in a sort of daze. Food and drinks seemed to flow faster as though hurtling me towards my destiny but it wasn't until the mayor arrived, newly from Nice, making apologies for his lateness, that I became fully focused. I heard Felix chuckle nearby and cut him a slit-eyed look but he came up and linked arms.

'I'm going to war, dear sister; I don't want my last memory of you to be sour-faced and frightened.'

Aimery appeared before I could answer Felix, Henri trailing him.

'Ah, here she is,' Aimery said in a jolly tone but I heard the false note. 'Hello, my darling,' he said, pulling me free from Felix. It was a deliberate act that was not lost on us. 'I've been wondering where you'd got to.' He kissed my hand. 'From now on I shan't let you out of my sight.'

I felt a trill of fresh despair pass through me. 'I was just saying goodbye to everything familiar,' I ventured.

'You're only moving up the road, my sweet. I promise you shall visit here regularly but I do look forward to you making my home your home from this evening.'

He stared at me and I heard the words *make my bed your bed* whisper through my mind.

'Aren't you worried about war, Aimery?'

'Not right at this moment but I promise I shall give it my full attention soon enough,' he said, shutting me down with his condescension. It seemed I was the only person putting the terrifying prospect of war ahead of the only slightly less terrifying prospect of climbing into bed with Aimery.

'Is it time to leave?' Felix said, saving me a response. 'It's nearing ten.' He wouldn't be able to save me from here on so I squared my shoulders and did my best to take control.

'It must be,' I said, catching an enquiring look between the plotters who hatched this terrible yet brilliant union. I wanted to say, *Let's get this over with*. Instead I feigned a smile. 'Shall we make our farewells, Aimery?'

His eyes glistened with intent. 'Indeed. Come, my darling, I think we have to live through one final teasing ritual.'

'Oh no, can't we just run for it?' I said, hoping to prompt a moment of shared wickedness. It was an empty hope as the humour was lost on him. His look of dismay said everything.

'Heavens, no, girl, the guests expect to formally perform *le charivari*.'

Girl? There it was, damning proof of how my new husband viewed me. The final evidence I would gather in about an hour. I glanced at Felix, who was moving, refusing to look my way, already letting go of his twin self, as he and I both knew he must.

'Come along, Fleurette, bear up,' Aimery urged. I noted he didn't disguise his vexation sufficiently when he waved his hand impatiently at me.

Henri had the grace to slide me a sheepish look but I couldn't be tempted to glare at him. In truth I couldn't bear to hold his gaze, for I'd left behind the warmth of our family bond in the church when I had noticed him share a glance of deep satisfaction with Aimery as the priest pronounced me wed.

In that moment of shared smugness, I hated them both.

3

Le charivari was a predictably boisterous affair. The mocking sere-
nade was achieved on instruments that ranged from pennywhistles
to the banging of saucepan lids and the clanging of pots with olive
wood stirrers. This was one French custom I had hoped to avoid but
it seemed the champagne had flowed fast and strong, encouraging
our normally well-behaved guests to find their sense of the ridiculous and join the waiting townsfolk for the final public spectacle.

The townsfolk began it and I knew it was meant with affection, particularly as they'd not been allowed to accompany me on
my way to the church. They were not going to miss out on accompanying me to my new husband's bed.

Off we went, supposedly happy arm in arm, laughing for the
benefit of our guests and the people of Grasse who wanted this rare,
important marriage to work. We were to walk up the hill to the De
Lasset family mansion where the last fragile tendrils of my hold on
the Delacroix name would be broken as determinedly as I was sure
Aimery intended to break into me.

The cacophony gave a solid sound to the noises in my mind,
which only I could hear, and followed us through the grand

entrance into the reception hall, up the magnificent staircase and another flight to the landing on the floor of the house that we would now share.

Tonight I would be in Aimery's room but I knew that by tomorrow morning I would be shown to a wing on this level that would house my private chambers, including my boudoir and bathroom, a salon and sitting room for greeting close personal friends. Tomorrow felt a long way away, though, when Aimery hushed the discordant music of our trailing guests – mainly the young – and obliged by picking me up to cradle me in his arms as he chivalrously carried me into his room, slamming the door in their faces.

This prompted loud applause and we waited for the cheering to die away finally as people left us behind.

'They've likely attached cowbells to the mattress,' he warned as I did a slow and full revolution to take in my new place of torture. As I did so, a new lament erupted; this one urgent and demanding. The eight bells of the Cathédrale de Notre-Dame de Puy began tolling once again, and I wondered if the old priest was now hanging on the end of one of the ropes with the choirboys. 'I can't believe we're really going to war.'

Aimery looked back at me nonchalantly and even took a moment to slip off his jacket, loosening his top button. 'Indeed, war has found us, Fleurette.'

Aimery blinked slowly as if working hard to remain patient. 'Would you like me to do it? I'm probably faster.'

I'm sure you are. 'No, Aimery, I can manage,' I said as politely as I could, but I was still in shock from the bells announcing the mobilisation of the men of Grasse while my new husband insisted on enjoying his conjugal rights. I knew I was struggling to undo my straight front corset because of trembling fingers, and although

I tried to convince myself otherwise, I suspected he could see my nervousness too. I had practised this in private – could have it undone in a few heartbeats – and yet that newly acquired skill had deserted me in the moment of need.

I worked at it a bit longer and finally the ties came free and the palest of pink corsets, designed to go beneath the ecru of my gown to achieve that perfect 'S' figure, fell away.

My husband gave a sigh of exasperation. 'Well, thank heavens for that. You can hear how impatient the war is, my dear,' he said, gesturing towards the open window where the sound of the bells coursed through with a relentless energy. I noticed that Aimery's gaze was resting on the flimsy, narrow petticoat that was now my sole modesty, save the lace inlaid stockings that I was quickly rolling down.

I gave a thin smile as his little jest forced him to visibly sigh.

'Let's have a cognac together, shall we?'

'I don't dri—'

'I don't care, Fleurette. The cognac will relax you.'

He unbuttoned his shirt further, took off his cravat and flung it carelessly aside. I heard his jewelled cravat stud tinkle as it hit the glass of the dish at his bedside table. He moved around to the marble mantelpiece, rolling up his shirtsleeves.

It wasn't cold but I shivered before I nodded at his suggestion, resigned. I watched him symbolically place the rose that he'd worn at his buttonhole on the dormant fireplace, which was made up but would not be used for another three months. I would be expected to pluck a rosebud from my bouquet to lie next to his bloom and they would be lit with the first fire of winter and signal a long life and many warm winters together. Try as I might to be open to the idea, he couldn't stir my internal flames. I simply didn't like Aimery. Others considered him handsome . . . I didn't.

A balloon glass was handed to me containing a syrupy slug of liquor. I sipped as Aimery sniffed his theatrically.

'Ah, the finest of Charente,' he mused. 'Do you know the Dutch used to call this burnt brandy?'

I shook my head as the fumes cleared my nose.

He talked for a while about the cognac. I wasn't paying attention but I sipped quietly, giving myself all the help I could to dull my senses. The cognac must have mixed with the small glass of champagne I'd managed to keep down and a great drowsiness was pushing on my shoulders. I may even have yawned. Aimery smiled but it was one of hunger.

'Why didn't your brother come to our wedding?' I asked in a sleepy voice.

'Sébastien?' He smiled. 'On his way, apparently.'

That surprised me. 'I was hoping he might. I'm sorry he missed it.'

Aimery shrugged. 'Really? I don't know why. You've never met him and I don't even know him. What would he be now? A couple of years older than yourself but as English as I am French because our mother divided our family, which I shall never forgive her for, and why she was not invited to our wedding.'

'Oh, Aimery, grudges are hard work to hang on to. Whatever happened occurred a long time ago. She's old enough now to have regrets. Maybe she'd like to see you, explain her absence?'

'I don't care to hear it. To tell you the truth, Fleurette, when I look back upon my childhood I realise that it lacked the motherly love others talk about. She left me; I've never understood it.'

'Oh, stop,' I began, but he held up a warning finger.

'Why is truth hard to hear? There's no need to cover up my reality. I'm perfectly resigned to my situation. My father did his best by me despite being a cold-hearted man, and no amount of wondering or recrimination would bring her back. I used to blame myself as a youngster, but now I blame her and wouldn't welcome her back if she tried to re-enter my life.'

I winced, never believing I could ever imagine something so cruel about my parents.

'As for Sébastien, well, he missed out on a father. I wasn't even sure I wanted to share the news of my marriage with them.'

'Clearly you did, though, and that's a good step,' I offered.

'I sent a telegram as a formality. And my brother, clearly odd, replied with a telegram from Paris yesterday begging me not to go through with the service until he'd arrived.'

'Pardon?'

Aimery gave a cynical laugh and downed his cognac with a satisfied sigh. 'Oh, I suppose he wanted me to wait. You know, the favoured prodigal son returning to steal the show.'

'I can't imagine he'd want that. Did he mention your mother?'

'Dying, apparently. The cancer has her in its grip.' He raised his glass as if saluting the disease.

'Aimery!'

'Hmm?'

'That's callous . . .'

'Is it? Why should I care about someone who does not care about me? One more burden gone from my life. She'd better not make any claim on the family's empire – we built it without her.'

'Where is she?'

'London. I also received a telegram from her. She insisted I hold off for Sébastien.'

I frowned but said nothing, waiting for him to add more.

He obliged. 'And I was right not to delay. He isn't here, even now, and frankly why would I? For her? I don't think so.' Aimery put down his glass. 'Come and sit on my lap, Fleurette.'

I shuddered inwardly. Outwardly it must have appeared to him as a coy tremble of anticipation and I could see just how much it teased him. His rising excitement matched my escalating horror. The cognac was doing nothing to quell the loathing.

'Aimery, apart from the obvious desire to link our families, what do you find desirable about our marriage? I really didn't think you felt affection for me.' I hadn't moved to join him, hoping to distract him a little longer.

Mercifully the jangle of bells ended; the priest had probably collapsed.

Aimery seemed in no hurry, which troubled me even more. 'Well, now,' he said, playing along, reaching to light a small cigar next to his empty cognac balloon. I watched him suck and puff at the tobacco. He blew out smoke and there was something about the way he held his head to one side that shockingly reminded me of my father in that moment. I caught my breath, hating the notion, and then it was gone as he grinned from beneath his gingery moustache. What would our children look like? Redheads? Freckled on their arms, like Aimery? I had to conceive the children first, and this prompted another silent intake of breath.

'I've always found you somewhat fascinating, Fleurette. You've been indulged from birth.'

I opened my mouth to protest but he tsk-tsked at me.

'I don't mean spoiled by your family money, although frankly you've never wanted for anything, never had to fight for anything, never had to look for affection or wonder about how loved you might be. You have been adored like a little princess for all of your life. And in being adored in this manner I know your father has given you freedoms that I wouldn't afford our daughter, for instance. You can be a bit wild; you have opinions and you're not afraid to air them. You've also been allowed to be involved in the family business in ways far more inclusive than I consider appropriate for a woman.'

'I wouldn't have thought you'd find any of those qualities endearing.'

He smiled wider, blowing out smoke as he did so. 'I don't. But I do find you a challenge. You're not simpering, you're hardly doting, you're very beautiful, of course, but then I would not choose a woman otherwise.' I tried to cover the sneer at his condescension, quickly rearranging my expression to remain interested.

'No, of course not,' I murmured.

'You will make life interesting and frankly, Fleurette, you demonstrate strength. Of all the qualities that I find tricky about you, I do like that one most of all because I suspect it will serve the family well and I'd like to think that this part of you will shine in our children. Strength of mind is important, although perhaps I need to break what I see as wilfulness in you.' He sniggered at my soft gasp of shock. 'Wilfulness is certainly neither attractive nor desirable in a woman. So yes, to answer your question,' he finished airily, 'it is, I suppose, your strength of character that attracts.'

'I see.' It was a backhanded compliment even if it was all but grudging.

He continued, not looking at me, but staring moodily into his cognac. 'My mother ran away when life got too challenging. I don't wish for that weakness in my wife.'

'Do you know why she left?'

He sucked back on his cigar. I watched the cylinder of leaf glow as his breath was drawn through it. I had perhaps another two minutes, maybe three, before it would be ash and my time would arrive.

'My parents didn't care enough for each other. Lack of affection, I suppose, drove her away. She used to cherish me – I know I'm not making that up – and then she was gone and I had no mothering at all for the rest of my life, save hired nurses. I can remember her voice, though, her affections, but I also remember the day my father returned from somewhere they'd been without me. He sat me down in front of him – I think I was about four or five – and he told me my mother had left us, pregnant with Sébastien too.'

'He gave you no reason?'

Aimery shrugged. 'I was an infant. Why would he bother to explain?'

'And you never asked more as you grew up?'

'I did but I was fobbed off. She was ailing; she was with family in England; she was travelling . . . all manner of odd reasons were tossed carelessly at me, so in the end I gave up asking and decided she hated us – or why else would she leave her firstborn? And so I hated her.'

'Maybe she wanted to take you with her. I can't imagine she'd willingly leave behind a young child.'

'Well, if she did, I was given no sense of that. Besides, he wouldn't permit it. My father couldn't do much about the unborn child, but knowing him I suspect he'd rather be damned than let an heir be carted off around the world, or made British.' He gave a moue of disdain. 'Whatever the reason, they were never suited, I'm sure.'

'Because they were forced to marry,' I offered innocently enough but he heard the challenge all the same.

Aimery fixed me with a pale stare. 'Our marriage is a glorious union, Fleurette. Bear me heirs, be faithful, do not challenge me and the world is yours. I will provide everything you need. I will give you jewels, property, a wardrobe the envy of anyone in France. We will travel and you will meet other wealthy folk. Truly, what more could a woman want?'

His condescension made me seethe. 'And what about those freedoms you mentioned earlier? The ones my father afforded me.'

He tapped off a clump of ash into the tray nearby and I watched it fall apart soundlessly. It felt like a symbol of my life disintegrating and I had no voice in it. 'I'm afraid a married woman does not have so many freedoms as a spinster.'

'Aimery, you know that I have the talent, don't you? I have the Nose. I can create new perfumes that people haven't yet imagined possible.'

'So I'm assured by your twin. But you are a woman, my dear, and no wife of mine is going to be playing in a laboratory when she is supposed to run my household, care for my children and fulfil her wifely duties.'

'You will ignore my greatest gift? So few are bestowed with it!' I tried to keep my despair under control.

'I'm glad we're having this chat now,' Aimery said, his tone amiable but firm. 'I don't wish you anywhere near the De Lasset perfume factory. You may spend time with the growers and our gardeners – I know you love your flowers and I'm happy for that; it is comely for a woman to be near flowers – but no, Fleurette, it is not a woman's place to make perfume. We have our perfumer, Monsieur Planque, and he has no need of another assistant, especially his employer's wife.'

It was like a prison sentence being passed on me – no, a death sentence. I couldn't live happily without being allowed to create. Aimery knew very well what having the Nose meant. This was not a conscious choice and while subtle aspects could be learned, the gift of being able to discern different smells – dozens and dozens of them – was divine, and could not be acquired. He was effectively sneering at what was part of my soul. 'May I then at least have some input in the Delacroix range?'

'No. Fleurette, your family's business is under the captaincy of Henri. We remain rivals, albeit friendly ones, and indeed family now. Nevertheless, I do not wish any crossover at this stage when it comes to our respective perfume empires. Maybe in time . . .' He made a tutting sound as though it was all laid out neatly now and should be set aside. 'Now, settle yourself down into running this vast house, the prospect of motherhood, and I'd very much like you to take on some charitable duties. You might care to start planning the Christmas lunch for our workers. It's only a few months away.'

'Aimery.' I pointed uselessly off towards the terraces somewhere in the blackness of the Grasse night. 'All those workers are marching to the drum of war. They're not going to be attending the De Lasset Christmas meal.'

He smiled in a patronising way. 'Nevertheless, the planning would be good for you, even if it is academic. This sort of skill can never be overlooked or overestimated. It's excellent practice for the future.'

I wanted to scream.

'Now,' he said, and I realised this was his favourite condescending opening to any sentence, 'let us forget about perfume, war, or anyone else for a short while – let's begin our own private offensive here in this room. I am going to bed my wife and I hope in the next short while we shall make our first child.' He gave a tight grin as he crushed the life of the last embers of his cigar and my hopes. 'If not, we shall try again . . . and again.' Aimery's patience with me had petered out. He stood and began undoing the last two buttons of his shirt. 'Get into bed, Fleurette, and let me show you what I wish you to do for me.'

I looked away as he began to undo his trousers. I felt the urge to run and yet my feet were leaden, weighted to the floor in a helpless lack of mobility. I had nothing to say. I couldn't think; I knew this was it. I had to let it happen and stop hoping against hope that —

Aimery cursed aloud as I swung around at the sound of banging on the door. 'What the hell?'

'Monsieur Aimery?' The voice sounded familiar. It was his housekeeper, Madame Mouflard.

I reached quickly for his dressing-gown and with an urging expression helped him into it. It was obvious he was furious by the way he pushed his arms into the sleeves and carelessly tied it at the front. Aimery flung the door open only just giving me time to hurriedly pull on a gown for my own modesty.

'Madame Mouflard, what is this?' he demanded with unconcealed rage.

She quailed beneath his fury. 'Forgive me, sir, forgive me,' she pleaded, casting me a beseeching look. 'The bells say it all, Monsieur,' she said, trembling.

'I am highly aware of them, Madame, and what they mean,' he snarled.

I gently pushed him aside, a calming hand on his arm, and was relieved he permitted me. 'What is it, Madame Mouflard?' I asked more gently. I eased into the little space left at the door's threshold.

'Captain Louis Drevan is here to see you, sir,' she said, returning her attention to her employer. 'He needs to speak with you.'

'My captain?' He spoke this title in a reverential tone. 'Well, well . . . the decree has been signed, no doubt.'

'We shall be down immediately, Madame Mouflard,' I said. 'Please offer the captain some refreshment.' I closed the door on her before my husband could explode. 'It's the formal announcement of war,' I said, more to myself than Aimery. 'What else could it be?'

'It better be, or I shall start one of my own,' he snapped, tearing off his dressing-gown and re-buttoning his trousers. I was relieved to note his ardour had deflated with his mood, although I secretly wanted to kiss Captain Drevan for the intrusion.

I'd rearranged my silken dressing-gown and stepped into satin slippers. It was time to embrace my role as woman of the house, even though it was nearing midnight. 'I'll see you down there,' I said, after checking my hair was still neatly pinned.

'Fleurette!' I halted at his shout, my hand on the door handle, looking over my shoulder. 'You're not going downstairs like that?'

'Why not? It's a ridiculous hour. It's my wedding night. Why on earth should I worry about how I appear?'

His mouth pursed and I was reminded fleetingly of Henri for some odd reason.

'Well, dear wife, mainly because I forbid it.'

I think I began mouthing the word *forbid* silently, as though I needed to understand what he'd just said, but he was talking over my shock.

'Not only are you not going downstairs in that garment, but you are also not meeting a captain of our army at all. May I remind you that the captain has asked for me, not my wife. This is men's business.'

Now he sounded like Henri.

'War is —'

'I will inform you with the rest of the household. For now, please let the men discuss men's issues.'

I don't know why Aimery didn't just walk up to me and take a full swing to punch me in the jaw. My mouth went slack with dismay as he strode to the door, which he closed behind him. I remained rigid with the horrific understanding that my role in this house may have a title, but it held little weight.

Nevertheless, I defied him in a small way. If Aimery was refusing to let me join him during this most emotional of moments, then I would join the staff; I needed to be with others and share the worry of war. This was not about our wedding, me suddenly being his property or abiding by his rules; we were facing a much bigger problem and I had no time for Aimery's chauvinism. I hurried downstairs and then deeper still into the dark belly of the De Lasset mansion to where it felt as though the entire household staff had gathered in tense expectation.

Distantly drums were adding new urgency to the bells as the town was coming to terms with what the call to action signified.

'Oh, Madame!' Madame Mouflard exclaimed, looking aghast to see me.

Everyone stood, chairs scraping back, hair pulled away from faces, all conversation ending abruptly. The aroma of cooked food mingled with the smell of working men, the sudsy freshness of washed dishes and the inevitable tobacco. A fog of smoke hovered above their heads.

Almost tiptoeing onto the flagstones, I could still hear my footsteps it was so instantly silent, save the tick of a clock in the corridor. I looked around at the staff's dazed expressions and felt as lost as they appeared.

'Please, everyone. Forgive me for intruding,' I began. I could tell now it was a significant mistake to defy Aimery. I felt ridiculous with all of them fully clothed and me in garments clearly of the boudoir, and of a wedding night. It was unseemly of me and they averted their gazes but I had to press on now. 'I am feeling as bewildered as you but I'm sure my husband will tell us what he has learned soon.' I smiled to encourage them.

'Madame De Lasset, we are so sorry that this has occurred on tonight of all nights,' Madame Mouflard said, doing her best to ignore my silken-clad presence, instead glancing around at everyone who murmured agreement. 'The mayor received the telegram from the prefecture and Captain Drevan came over to inform Monsieur De Lasset.'

I smiled to reassure but there was little humour in my gesture. 'I think our nation's security is entitled to win my husband's attention. The message will surely go to my brothers next. I don't suppose there's any coffee left?'

My request and casual manner seemed to snap them out of their spell. Making noises not unlike a hen, Madame Mouflard, whom I found myself liking in spite of all my worst intentions to hate everyone in the De Lasset home, fussed until a mug of sweetened milky coffee was pressed into my hands by one of the young women. Despite the warm night, it was exactly what I felt like after those few sips of cognac.

'Thank you. What is your name?'

'I am Jeanne, Madame.'

'And what do you do in the house, Jeanne?'

I noted the young woman look to her elder and Madame Mouflard gave a curt nod. 'I am training to be your lady's maid, Madame.'

'Ah, that's right. Madame Mouflard did mention this. You're new, aren't you?' They hadn't needed a lady's maid in so long, it was clearly a novelty.

'Er, yes, I am new. I began only a few days ago so I am feeling a little unsure.' She blinked, wondering if she'd said too much but after another glance at her senior she continued. 'I wanted to help you this evening but I was nervous and Madame Mouflard said you would probably appreciate privacy.' She blushed, suddenly embarrassed she had referred to something she should not. I smiled to ensure she knew I'd taken no offence, despite the stiffening back of Madame Mouflard nearby. 'I am not yet ready but I will be.'

I glanced at our housekeeper. 'Let Jeanne start immediately. We can teach and learn together.'

She blinked. 'Very good, Madame.' She looked at Jeanne to say that was enough conversation. 'Madame, perhaps I might introduce you to the rest of the staff here tonight?' she offered. Like me, she was looking for anything to ease the tension.

'A lovely idea,' I agreed. 'Please,' I gestured.

'Please meet Madame Clothilde. She is head of our kitchen.'

'Madame Clothilde,' I repeated, nodding at the flushed, round-faced woman watching me from small eyes. She curtsied, which set a trend.

Names were cast my way and I received nods of heads in polite bows from the men while the women gave a brief curtsey. My memory delivered each into its own compartment in my mind; I knew, even if I wanted to, I wouldn't forget them. Even though I did not need to, I politely repeated their names with a smile to each.

'I'm sure you will not remember all of us,' Madame Mouflard continued, and I chose not to correct her.

The uneasiness thrumming around us was intensifying. 'Please sit,' I urged, and people gratefully shuffled back to corners of the room or returned to their seats. 'I'm sorry you are all up so late,' I began and this was greeted with shrugs and tutting sounds that it didn't matter. It didn't, and neither did my weak apology.

'Do we know anything?' I wondered aloud, desperately feeling as though I needed to lead the staff through this uneasy time. And yet I was one of the youngest people in the room, with little experience of such adversity. All I had was entitlement and authority; it would have to be enough.

'We're hearing that our boys are already mobilising,' said a man, looking dejected. He was nursing a wine.

This was news to me. 'Do you have sons, Pierre?' He had been introduced as the head gardener and I didn't need to look at Madame Mouflard to know she was impressed by my recall of his name.

He nodded. 'Two, Madame. One is nearing twenty-three, the other turned twenty-one in May. He's at the beginning of his active duty. They're both marching now, eager to be part of it even though they don't have to formally depart for another nine hours,' he said, sinking a gloomy swallow of his wine to drain the glass.

I couldn't blame him. Already my thoughts were turning away from Aimery and towards my brothers. Felix had only completed his conscription service last year and I knew this meant he would be called up. As would Henri. The notion that my only living family would march off to war against Germany made spangles of fear explode like tiny bombs of nervous energy in my belly.

The cook's maid, Marie, offered to top up my coffee but I declined. 'Too much excitement already for one day,' I said in a hollow excuse. She nodded, smiled, and moved on to the next person.

'Oh, Madame.' The housekeeper suddenly startled me. 'I meant to mention that a small trunk arrived today for you.'

'For me?' I was puzzled. 'From whom?'

'From Monsieur De Lasset, the younger,' she said, eyes glittering.

'Sébastien?' I sounded the disbelief I saw reflected in her gaze. 'Is he here?'

She shrugged. 'We received a telegram to expect him but no, we have not sighted him yet and now I doubt we shall.'

I put down my half-drunk cup of coffee. 'Perhaps you could show me the trunk?' I was intrigued but, dressed in my night attire, I mostly wanted to be away from the escalating tension of the servants. They surely didn't want me around as my presence only added to their discomfort. 'Definitely just for me?' I asked as we moved to the door.

'Oh yes, Madame. Only your name is attached with it. He sent a separate parcel for your husband.' She gestured for me to go in front of her. 'I was going to have it carried up to your room tomorrow, but if you're sure. . .?'

'I am.' I turned. 'Thank you, everyone. Please take heart. We're all in this together.' Again, bland, empty words, but what was one supposed to say at a time like this? I had no experience to draw upon. And I did say it with sincerity. I hoped that part came across genuinely. People stood, nodded, curtsied again. 'Goodnight,' I said, even though it was far from such a thing.

'*Bonne soirée*,' they echoed in a miserable chorus because none of us believed we were going to have a good evening at all.

I breathed in and sighed. 'I wish I could say something to lift their spirits,' I admitted to the housekeeper as I followed her silent footfall across the flagstones. How did she achieve that, while I clicked behind her, despite my best efforts to tread quietly? I didn't mean to sound forlorn, but I was certainly feeling it.

'You are here. That is enough for all of us who have wished a happy marriage for Monsieur De Lasset. Soon the sounds of children's laughter will echo – it is everything our staff looks forward to. This marriage will help our household to remain optimistic through all of this upheaval.'

It sounded wonderful as a concept but I felt entirely dislocated as one of the main players of that theatre. I would have to start now, train myself to overcome my revulsion of Aimery if I was ever to give heirs to the De Lasset family.

We'd arrived at a storeroom. 'Forgive me, Madame, for not telling you about this. There really wasn't an ideal time today.'

'No, it's quite all right. I'm glad to be distracted, frankly. Oh, is that a letter with it?'

'Yes. I signed for this. It is marked for your personal and private attention.'

I picked it up. It was slightly gritty from its journey but the hand that wrote on its front looked firm, the ink scrawled in a flourish of unexpected purple like a missive from the Pope. I recognised it instantly as the expensive ink from J. Herbin in Paris; I'd seen this colour, had been permitted to test it, writing wet and so fresh against a white page. I had visited this shop with my father on the rue des Fosses Saint-Germain. Father had purchased *la Demi Courtine*, a particularly shaped squat bottle with a tiny shelf near its stopper to rest his pen, and within it he'd chosen a single ounce of a deep *rouge caroubier* he favoured for personal letters, and another ounce of the *perle noire* he preferred for formal writing.

I could remember being fascinated by the smells alone in the shop and wondered why Monsieur Herbin had not considered a scented range. I could imagine lavender for the blue pigments, rose for the warmer colours and earthy, forest scents for the greens. I had been convinced that Monsieur Herbin's dark blue ink should smell salty, as though of the ocean, or was I being fanciful in childhood, having been told Herbin was a former sailor? And now I stared at the darkly sensual purple ink of Sébastien's. If not for Madame Mouflard's presence, I might have held the letter to my nose because I so desperately wanted to sniff the handwriting . . . it should be scented with violet, surely?

I smiled, slightly embarrassed, as I realised Madame Mouflard awaited. 'Forgive me for holding you up. Um, maybe I can look at the contents of the trunk tomorrow and just take the letter for now.'

'Of course,' the housekeeper said with a friendly frown of concern. 'There is no need to rummage through it on your wedding night. We shall bring to you all of the hundreds of wedding gifts gradually and you can deal with them in your own time and with an assistant.'

'Can Jeanne write?'

'She can read; I don't know about her writing . . . er, yes, Jeanne?' she said, glancing past me.

'Madame De Lasset?'

I swung around to see Jeanne looking wide-eyed and panicked. 'What is it?'

'Your husband is searching for you,' my new maid stammered.

I shared a brief look of concern with the housekeeper.

'Thank you, Jeanne,' I said. 'Where is he?' But Madame Mouflard was already moving briskly and I fell into step, pushing the letter into the deep pocket while picking up the hem of my silk gown and hurrying upstairs after the housekeeper, wishing I'd had the forethought to change.

4

I found Aimery in the front salon. The captain was still present. Muted reintroductions were politely mumbled while I blinked with expectancy, looking between both men, ignoring Aimery's thunderous glare at my attire; he clearly couldn't say anything humiliating to me before his superior.

'So, France is officially mobilising for war?' I said, deciding to be direct and breaking into the brittle atmosphere.

'I'm desperately sad to confirm this, yes, Madame De Lasset,' the captain admitted, clearly with bigger matters on his mind than my inappropriate garments. Just last week he had been full of genial wit, kissing my hand and offering congratulations for our impending wedding. Now he wore an expression like a man going to his execution and although the veins on his nose traversed the journeys through many bottles of champagne in his time, his pallor was grey, draining the cheerful red I recalled.

'I was called away to the prefecture in Nice today; please forgive me for not being able to attend your celebrations.'

Aimery moved past his focus on my clothes and instead of looking ashen at the news, appeared instead flushed with excitement.

'I shall leave tonight, sir. Immediately, in fact.'

'I suspected you would, De Lasset. It sets a good example to the men.'

The mayor arrived now, still flustered and full of apologies and hand waving. The three men shared a tight exchange before the captain departed and I presumed he would go to my brothers next, although he was gone before I could ask.

My thoughts fled to the mundane. 'Er, what about our marriage certificate?' I said into the quiet.

'It will have to wait, dear friends,' the mayor bleated. 'I have no idea what Monday will bring. I will likely be called away again.'

Aimery rescued him with a noise of exasperation. 'Fleurette, half of the councillors are waving off their sons to war, the other half are marching towards it. Stop fretting over trivia. We can sort that out as soon as I have leave.'

I blinked at his public admonishment, which no doubt carried some heat about my defiance, but I was offended by his belief that the legality of our marriage was trivial. I couldn't wait to see the back of him.

'Anyone of my age is a Reservist. Most of the men of Grasse will be leaving.'

'So you're all leaving tomorrow?'

The mayor nodded, his expression filled with despair. 'It is already tomorrow, Madame,' he said, glancing at the watch he pulled from his waistcoat pocket. 'Those are the orders from the prefecture and those orders come direct from Paris. All of France's army is on the move; even the Reservists are being mobilised, as your husband notes. Come, look.' He and Aimery led me to the front door, where I stepped out onto the porch and noted once again that the stillness of the night had gone. It was as though a full working day was in progress. 'Men are departing now,' he added.

'Aimery,' I breathed, but couldn't think of anything to say, so

I shared what was really on my mind. 'I must farewell my brothers.'

He nodded, distracted. 'I could use your help getting my things packed. Our housekeeper and my valet will know what to do.'

'Yes, of course,' I agreed, feeling instantly abashed. 'I'll find Madame Mouflard.' I looked to the mayor. 'Please excuse me. I should change,' I said, glancing at Aimery, but keeping my expression neutral.

'Of course. Please excuse *us*, Madame De Lasset, for ruining your happiest day and, er . . . night.'

He looked mortified, lost for what else to say. I couldn't blame his presumption and rather than make him feel any more awkward, I lowered my gaze, even squeezed Aimery's arm in a moment of bright sadness. 'Leave the arrangements with me.'

He nodded, barely paying attention. As I left I heard him excusing himself, muttering about not knowing in whose hands to leave his company, given that all the men who worked for him would be marching alongside him, no doubt.

I closed the door on their farewells, my mind fleeing to Felix and Henri as I spotted the housekeeper hovering in the shadows at the entrance to the main corridor. Madame Mouflard had already removed the small ruff of lace at her neck to leave her uniform of midnight black, stark and sombre, as though already in mourning. Her keys clanked gently on the end of a leather plait that hung from her belt.

'Ah, Madame De Lasset, there you are,' she said, hurrying towards me.

I was feeling unhappy with such unfamiliar austere formality; if ever there was a time for us all to cleave more closely and be as unified and friendly as possible, it was now. I would lead the change in this lofty villa, where the divide between upstairs and downstairs was so severely delineated. 'I'd like you to call me Madame Fleurette when it's just us. Would that be all right?'

The housekeeper, out of the shadows, her face now looking more ghostly in the lamplight for its pale colour against so much darkness, appeared momentarily unnerved. Then she forgot herself and smiled. 'Why not? You will surely bring change to this household, Madame. What can I do?'

I explained with haste about Aimery's possessions.

'Yes, I have already asked Monsieur Blanc to help. That's Monsieur Aimery's valet.'

'Excellent. Where is he? Should I supervise?'

'Only if you want to. He is in Monsieur De Lasset's rooms . . . er, where you . . .'

'All right, thank you. I know where you mean.'

'Can you find your way back to your own rooms? Should I send Jeanne up?'

'Good idea. I want to make sure everything's in order for my husband and then I'll be walking down the hill, so I need to change out of this first,' I said, flicking at the silk.

'Madame? At this time?'

'I've been running around these streets since I was a child; the dark does not disturb me. However, the threat of not saying goodbye to my brothers does.' At the fall of her expression I dug up a reassuring smile. They would all be counting on me now. 'It will feel like harvest with all these men on the move.'

'Yes, Madame. This is why I feel it is unwise.'

I looked at her, feeling perturbed by what she wasn't saying. These were the men who worked for our two families, men who had known me with plaits in my hair, who had lifted their caps as I rode by on my bicycle over the years, who revered our name. These were the men of the town I loved . . . my greater family. Her frown deepened and I realised in that moment she hadn't meant anyone might interrupt me; instead her disapproval confirmed that Felix had been right. This was a time to embrace the notion that I must behave as a highborn woman of the town, with certain protocols now forbidding me to act in the carefree, almost childish way I always had. This was surely what Aimery had been getting around to discussing earlier. I nodded. 'I understand. I shall take Jeanne with me.'

Madame Mouflard's bearing changed. Her shoulders relaxed and her lips loosened. 'Very good, Madame. I shall send Jeanne up to you now.'

Upstairs, I changed hurriedly into similarly sombre clothes as our housekeeper's. I was head to foot attired in simple charcoal and made my way to the chamber of our wedding night. There I found a different man in the bedroom where less than an hour earlier had been prepared for a night of lust. Guilt at shaking myself free from Aimery's hook crowded low in my throat. I knew resounding in my mind were cheers of happiness that I'd escaped my great fear of his body pressed against mine, in mine. But at what cost? I could hardly blame myself for war but the fact I was inwardly celebrating at the perfect timing of mobilisation of French villages was sickening me. A nervous laugh warbled just above the guilt.

'Pardon, Madame?' the valet said, his moustache drawn thinly across his lip.

I cleared my throat. 'I was wondering if there was anything I could do to help? It's Monsieur Blanc, isn't it?'

He clicked his heels and gave a brief nod. 'Yes, Madame. I am Monsieur De Lasset's valet. I have been in his employ now for ten years and three months.'

I nodded, impressed.

'It is best I pack his clothes.'

'Of course,' I murmured, understanding his need to freeze me out of not only the world of men but his territory.

I walked around the bedpost to stand opposite, noting that the valet had swept all the rose petals of our wedding bed to the floor.

I was treading on them, could smell their sweet perfume being released. There was something symbolic about us stomping over the rituals of marriage. Another press of guilt clogged my throat.

I touched the shiny buttons on Aimery's blue serge cape. It looked new, had seen no action, of course. I looked up at the squeak of leather being rolled up and noted the cumbersome belt and pochette that Monsieur Blanc was packing. He was frowning in concentration and I could tell from his demeanour that he willed me gone.

'Monsieur Blanc, I wish to put something into my husband's belongings.' I deliberately didn't phrase it as a question. He glanced at me and I saw the flash of irritation disguised quickly as he cleared his throat.

'Of course, Madame.'

I smiled to thank him. 'Excellent. I shall be back shortly.' I fled, picking my way back to my suite of rooms where presumably Madame Mouflard had already been earlier that week to unpack my trunks of garments and belongings. I walked from wardrobe to dressing table, trying to imagine what might be meaningful. There was a photo of me but it was taken with Felix. Hardly romantic and romantic was what I was reaching for, even if it didn't apply to him; I needed Aimery to understand what it was that drove me. I looked for the romance in everything, whether it was the pretty picture of a laundry maid hanging out washing against the backdrop of flowered terraces or the rush of joy at smelling the year's first harvest of violets. Violets. Yes. My wedding perfume.

I would send him with that. Not my grandmother's vial. But Felix had made up some bottles of violette toilet water that I could scent my boudoir with, my linens, my personal belongings from pillowslips to handkerchiefs. It was a gently sweet smell . . . a favourite of childhood. I knew it didn't summarise me and that wasn't the intent, but it did prompt a romantic notion and perhaps that would be the companionship Aimery, new husband, denied his wedding night, might appreciate.

I found the smallest bottle and scribbled a note to accompany it.

Aimery. I couldn't find a single affectionate way in which to start the note so I kept it simple. *I hope this reminds you of me while we are apart. Come home safely. Affectionately, F.*

It was with a sense of sinfulness that I wrote this note to him because of the insincerity that was mocking me from the corner of the room. Heaven knew that I quietly worshipped the realisation that we were not to be forced together tonight or any night soon. But that sin came with a wish not to hurt Aimery. I was married to him now. I had given a vow and whether I wanted to be his wife or not, this was my lot and I had to make it work, as Felix had urged. So it felt important at this moment of high tension and deep despair, which would be rippling through all the marriages of France, that I offer affection and support, if not love. What else could any of us women do tonight except hug our brave men fare-well, wish them courage and safety, and hope their lives would be blessed?

This resignation didn't stop me screwing up the note, disgusted with not being true to myself, and writing anew.

Aimery, my husband.

May this remind you of Grasse while you are away from her sweet embrace. Come home safely.

That felt better. It offered tenderness without me feeling a hol-low liar.

As I walked back to Aimery's rooms at the other end of this hallway, Jeanne met me.

'Madame?' she enquired.

'Fetch us cloaks, Jeanne. We're on foot to the Delacroix house as soon as I deliver this to Monsieur Blanc.' I was impressed that I didn't say *my house*.

She didn't hesitate, nodding and dashing off to my rooms.

I tapped on the door this time. 'Monsieur?'

'Ah, Madame, I was just about to close the locks,' he gestured.

'It is only small,' I said. I'd wrapped the bottle and note in a scented lace handkerchief. He let me tuck it into the trunk. 'Thank you.'

'Goodnight, Madame De Lasset.' He clicked another bow and I felt dismissed. I wondered if he'd read my note. I didn't care if he did. All I cared about now was getting to Felix and Henri.

It felt like a railway platform in the main lobby of the house. Servants were moving in brisk motion, frowns creasing their expressions, mouths set tight with the tension of getting errands run, duties complete. It was mainly women because the men were no doubt hurriedly digging out their Reservist uniforms. The atmosphere was weighted by fear, as though shadowed monsters crouched in corners, waiting to leap out and trap the unwary. Gazes darted, never settling long enough on anything or anyone. I felt useless.

Jeanne caught up with me. 'Have you heard, Madame?'

'What is it?'

'Even Pierre, Guy, Fabian, they're all going!'

'The older men?'

She nodded, looking terrified. 'All the Territorials have been called up too. We thought it would be only the Reservists but the mayor has confirmed it's nearly everyone except the very young and very old.'

My life, which at the beginning of this day felt miserable, was now feeling out of control. I had never been consciously aware of what people called 'the fear of the unknown' but I believed, in this moment, I was experiencing it. We were all involved and our way of life was now under dark threat. Suddenly, my wedding gloom, my problems, felt minuscule . . . even my life was unimportant as I finally grasped the scale of what was now underway and horribly real. 'I must speak with my husband,' I breathed, not waiting for her answer, and scurried away. The man I had wanted to avoid was now the one I searched out. Though curious to confront, I had to admit that in these rushing moments of search my heart was genuinely worried for him. Conflicting emotions raged with the fear; Aimery was now my husband, after all. We'd taken a solemn vow in our church; we'd made oaths before the priest to each other, to our families. My husband, the father to our children; I certainly looked forward to being a mother and that couldn't happen if my husband was off to war, and might be injured, maimed, killed. He might never be able to father children, which meant I'd be left with him in a dry, barren marriage.

Again, I was making this about me, I realised, and admonished myself. My father would be ashamed to listen in on my selfish thoughts, which now quickly rearranged themselves to focus on what was truly important.

Felix might be hurt . . . Henri too. They could be killed: a stray bullet, an unlucky shell, disease, starvation . . . If I could take back all my sourness and loathing of today, I would. If absorbing it, reliving today with a smile and glad heart might change this evening, I would accept that burden in a heartbeat and romp into bed with Aimery, if it meant the declaration of war might change.

Why was I bargaining like this? What a useless waste of energy.

After stopping various staff, I found my husband in the side courtyard delivering brisk orders to the youngest stablehand. 'Aimery?' My voice was noticeably tender and I could see him register it as new from the way he swung around.

He gave the reins over to the nearby stable lad and strode up to me, placing his hands on my shoulders. I can't say I felt affection, but this was a step up from earlier. I was in a neutral state with my affections but my emotions were escalating. It meant I couldn't find the right words for this moment. What was I supposed to say? Lie and tell him I would miss him? Or remain impartial and utter placations like 'Stay safe'? My hesitation left it to Aimery to fill the awkward pause.

'I have to change into uniform and leave, Fleurette. We're gathering at the barracks but leaving in the early hours and we have plenty to organise in between now and then. My *fascicule de mobilisation* strictly requires me to leave.' He pulled a watch from his fob pocket.

Perhaps I gave a look of doubt.

'As an officer,' he reinforced, 'I set the example. Imagine how it looks when their superior leaves on his wedding night; it shows my commitment and will inspire them to follow their duty as rigorously.'

How heroic, I heard myself in bitter thoughts. This was clearly about how he might appear and how he might inflate a legend around himself. Nevertheless it saved me from what I most feared. He was waiting for me to say something. I blinked. 'You're riding to the barracks?' Nothing quite so irritating as stating the obvious.

But Aimery was more caught up in his courageous act. 'No coach drivers,' he qualified.

And it will look so brave, of course, I thought, if you arrive at the station urgently, cantering loudly across the cobbles on your steed, having deserted your marital bed on your wedding night. 'Monsieur Blanc has packed for you,' I blurted. 'He seemed to know what he was doing.'

Aimery gave a wolfish grin. 'Froze you out, did he?'

I shrugged. 'It's his world. I've only just arrived. Best I let everyone get used to me.'

'Wise girl,' he admitted and kissed the top of my head.

Curiously, I found that show of affection more endearing than anything Aimery had ever said or done. While none of his theatrical exhibitions of today had impressed me, this simple, private peck felt sincere.

'Aimery . . .'

He waited.

'I'm sorry.'

'The war —' he began.

'I don't mean the war. I'm sorry that I've been' — I wondered what the right word was — 'reluctant,' I settled on. 'I wish I could change it, but . . .'

He seemed to understand and pulled me close. I wanted to feel love – even a trickle of fondness might have helped in this moment – but I felt nothing other than relief that I didn't have to lie naked beneath him tonight.

'I don't plan on getting killed, Fleurette, so let's start again when we can. We're married. No one can take that away.'

'The civil ceremony —'

'Yes, unfortunate. But we haven't consummated our marriage, my dear, so spiritually you can feel smug. I shall attend to that paperwork the moment I can get some leave. Perhaps the war is well timed.'

'What can you possibly mean by that?'

'Well . . . I probably frightened you this evening too. I haven't been sensitive. I suppose I'm used to —'

'Graciela?'

Aimery's eyes glowered from the pale of his face, darkness surrounding us like a shroud. We both seemed to shift effortlessly from polite exchanges to warning growls in a heartbeat.

'Don't speak of her,' he muttered.

But I wasn't to be put off easily, even though this was neither the time nor the place to be having such an earnest conversation. It spilled from me. 'I wish you'd married someone you loved. You should have married Graciela.'

His hand squeezed my arm. It wasn't painful but I felt the pressure enough to snap open my eyes to attention. 'I married *you*,

Fleurette. And you know why. Become resigned to it. Your apology meant something just now but what I feel for Graciela is not your concern. Please do not utter her name again.'

Now my arm was hurting; I refused to show it, though. Years of growing up with brothers had taught me to fight back. Years of knowing Aimery to be a bully reminded me to never to be fooled by even a moment of unguarded emotion. And that's what his fleeting kiss and embrace had been – a heartbeat of weakness.

'So we have a business arrangement, is that what you're saying, Aimery?'

'If you wish. Let's just not pretend there's any great romantic love lost between us.'

I opened my mouth to say more but he gripped my arm harder and the words died.

'That doesn't mean we can't find a level of tolerance, perhaps even fondness, and it doesn't mean that I don't enjoy the fact that the Delacroix girl is now Madame De Lasset. I am prepared to treat you lavishly, Fleurette. All I ask is that you behave as a wife should in every respect.'

'And that I never utter her name again,' I said. My tone was bitter deliberately.

'Exactly. Fast learned. Excellent, Fleurette. Now.' He loosened his grip, running his palm down the length of my arm until he held my hand. Anyone observing, including the stable lad, would have seen nothing but a tender moment between new husband and wife, as Aimery bent over my hand and kissed it gently. 'Hug your husband farewell and hurry off to kiss your brothers goodbye too.'

'What about your brother?' I asked, defiance dancing in my voice. 'He sent me a wedding gift.'

He ignored that fact. 'I gather from a curt telegram that he couldn't reach us because he was stopped at Gare de Lyon railway station in Paris by the same news that is mobilising us. I presume he'll be scuttling back to London as fast as he can. I'm glad. I had no desire to lay eyes on him anyway.'

I didn't mention the letter. The way Sébastien had scrawled *Private* on the front and back suggested he wanted only me to read it. I'd get to it when I could. 'So where do you go?'

'Well, unlike your brothers in the No 24e, who will have to gather at Villefranche, I have the convenience of the local barracks,' he said, moving towards his horse. 'Nevertheless, the 23e will have a long journey to make later today.'

I frowned. 'Will Sébastien fight in the French army?'

'Who knows? I imagine he will claim British status, but if I see him,' he said, affecting his most dry and cutting tone, 'should I offer my best wishes?'

'Please do,' I replied in a cringingly polite retort. Newly wed, our wedding night unfulfilled; I should have been hanging on to him, weeping, while he bravely unfurled my fingers from his arms. Instead I effected a stoic countenance for the purposes of onlookers. I was aware of my seesawing emotions but while I did not wish Aimery any harm, I still felt nothing akin to romantic affection towards him and his attitude only helped me in that clarification. 'So, you're headed to the station?'

'Yes, once we've packed up ammunition, ration packs and the like at the barracks.' He held up his papers. 'Acts as a railway warrant as much as my orders. I gather some of the orders to move will be staggered to avoid a bottleneck but I certainly shall be gone on the first available train as mine is a two-hundred-mile journey.'

'Goodbye, Aimery,' I said, sounding brave.

'Farewell, Fleurette. You should invite some of my female cousins to stay – two will surely want to escape Paris and it will stop you feeling lonely.'

How could I tell him that I'd rather not make that invitation, but it seemed he didn't require a response, continuing his thoughts.

'The first leave I get I shall return to our unfinished business.'

He winked and the pit of my stomach opened up and fresh dread was released. How could I have felt that tender compassion a few moments ago when now all the loathing was back?

I watched him swing easily into his saddle to seat himself, straight-backed and proud in his uniform. He glanced at me and then his gaze cut away. 'Lead on,' he said to the stable boy, who was swinging a lantern to light his master's way. The boy skipped ahead and I watched Aimery knee his horse forward. A message had obviously rippled through the staff that the remaining member of the De Lasset family was departing.

However, it was now only women who lined the gravel drive, some holding candles as if to illuminate their master's heroic moment. The festivity of our marriage hung around them in white bows and flagged bunting, at odds with their collectively grave expression. Hands were clasped in a solemn, funereal manner, and their heads bowed as Aimery triumphantly paraded by, walking his horse slowly so his audience could feel the full drama of his departure. I joined the women – what else could I do, except go along with the display of reverence for the time being?

He would be gone in moments and then I could run . . . no, flee, to my real home, and the men I really loved.

———

I wasted no time and pulled on a shawl and scampered like a carefree child back down towards the Delacroix villa. Jeanne hurried alongside as we wound our way through the familiar lanes to the villa where similar activity had been underway, which would ultimately leave our family home feeling silent and deserted. However, I could see a light glowing in one of the rooms and all but ran there, knowing both of my brothers would have waited, would have known I would come.

I burst through the front door with barely time to pause and hug a moist-eyed Madame Girouard, who looked after our family as fiercely as a mother might care for her brood.

'They're in your father's salon,' she said unnecessarily. 'They wouldn't leave without seeing you.'

I gave her a smile that said we must all bear up and threw an introduction over my shoulder that this was Jeanne, my new personal maid at the 'big house', as we'd always termed it. I didn't bother to knock, flinging the door open theatrically, because I was in a hurry, I had to see them, hug them . . .

'Fleurette!' It was Felix, moving quickly to scoop me up and twirl me around in a hug before placing me back on the firm floor, with an Aubusson rug between my boots and the parquet. Why I noticed its pale prettiness of creams, greens and pinks of luxuriant flower bouquets in this moment, or how it felt out of context in my father's richer-coloured chamber, I don't know. My father had told me it was our mother's and he knew how much she adored it, so he liked to keep it close. Father would also want me close now – it was right that I was here.

'Thank you for waiting,' I choked out. Suddenly all the emotion of the day seemed to collect into an arrow point of this tinglingly frightening moment, which felt as though it was piercing my heart. 'Aimery's gone to the barracks to organise everything.'

They nodded together, sadly.

'Presumably he'll see you before he leaves Grasse so that you and . . .' Henri began but seemed to think better of it. I couldn't tell him I wanted nothing more than Aimery gone.

I eyed Felix. He squeezed my hand. 'We don't have much time.'

'Are they not staggering the mobilisation? Won't there be bottlenecks all over France if everyone leaves in the same moment?'

Felix laughed. 'Our orders say we must be with the 24e regiment at Villefranche within ten hours of the declaration. That's now. We're risking being late. Won't do for officers.'

I think at any other time I might have shed some tears but right now, staring at my brothers, feeling lost and rudderless, those tears felt redundant and my eyes remained dry. I was glad of it, for it seemed to hearten the only family I had left.

'We shall have to count on you to run the house in our absence,' Henri said. He looked to be still in a state of shock. 'You do it with ease anyway.'

'I shall run both. Don't think on it again, Henri,' I assured. 'It's safe in my care until you return. Have you seen Catherine?'

He nodded, looking on the verge of tears. Henri cleared his throat, perhaps reaching the same conclusion of wasted emotion. 'Briefly. Everyone's getting family away. There's barely time for the others we love in our life.'

'Her brothers. Yes, of course – both going?'

Henri nodded miserably. 'Her family seems to think because I'm an officer in the same regiment I can wave a magic wand and keep her brothers safe.' Henri stood, running a hand carefully through his receding hair, and shook his head. 'None of us is safe.'

'Don't be bleak,' Felix warned. 'Come on. We have to go.'

'Can someone explain why every man of the town seems to be walking out?' I demanded. 'I mean, isn't anyone considered "essential services"? I thought the fact that you'd done your two years' ordinary training would mean you wouldn't be called up immediately. Aren't there enough men already in their two years' service?'

Felix swung on a thick cape that was part of his regiment's uniform. 'Not enough to match Germany's army, apparently. The prefect reminded us that because of the conscription law passed in 1905, it's now possible to call up every able man as a *"pantalon rouge"*, including us Reservists. Gendarmes are promoting the message all over France, calling men to their colours.'

'But how are we to run our township?' I asked, already hearing how selfish that sounded when people were marching off to put their lives on the line to keep our borders safe. I had remained frozen to the rug and bizarrely thought of how my leaden feet would make no impression upon it because it famously had no pile. No genuine Aubusson did. In that empty-headed mindset of shock, meaningful words deserted me. 'Anyway, you both look very fine in your uniforms.'

Felix raised an eyebrow. 'I am merely thankful that we are Chasseurs. You realise, dear sister, that apart from being trained to operate in mountain conditions, on skis or showshoes, and being hardier than our fellow soldiers not trained in alpine conditions, we wear blue?'

I didn't want to smile but Felix was doing his utmost to amuse.

'I do not envy the poor old infantry their scarlet trousers one bit. Always stand next to a man who makes an easier target, I say.'

Both Henri and I gave him a look of exasperation.

'What?' he said, looking injured. 'If there was ever a time to make a jest, it is now, when we feel at our most vulnerable and fearful. That's when laughing, even sadly, helps. We may never stand in this room together again.'

'Felix!' I said in a muted half-scream.

'Be realistic. And if it is the case that this is the last time I shall hug you, darling Fleurette, then I should like to do so with a smile.'

'I'm afraid your gallows humour is lost on me, brother,' Henri said. 'What is going to happen to our family business? We start jasmine harvest shortly. What shall happen to our fields?' he wondered aloud, staring around our father's room, now his own – but we all still thought of it as Father's . . . even Henri.

'Given that everyone is sharing the same trauma, you could say we maintain a status quo,' I tried, not really believing it, feeling disturbed afresh that our flowers, watched over with such care, would wither on the stem this year . . . and possibly the next.

'You're probably right.' Henri cheered somewhat. 'If we all miss out this year, then there's simply no new perfume circulating out of Grasse.'

'Not necessarily,' I murmured. When their gazes slid quickly to me, I shrugged. 'I mean' — and I wasn't really sure what I meant — 'Um, I mean, not everyone has someone in the family left behind who can manage or indeed run the business.'

Felix snapped me an amused wink. Next to him Henri bristled.

'Fleurette, we have a manager in place,' he cautioned.

'Yes, but you need someone above Monsieur Bouchard who can make decisions. It's harvest, Henri! And how do you know Monsieur Bouchard hasn't been called up?'

'He's past fifty,' he snorted.

I lifted a shoulder. 'We don't know what's going to happen, so we shouldn't speculate. But I am capable and if you forbid me, fine. I'll just put my efforts into taking the De Lasset brand onwards.' It was a cruel threat and I felt mean watching my elder brother blink in surprise. 'Forget I said that. I'm nervous and frightened. You know I will do everything I can to protect the whole region's business, not just ours.'

Henri straightened. 'The truth is, Fleurette, your role is now to consider De Lasset before Delacroix.'

'Never,' I said.

Madame Girouard was back at the opened door but not crossing its threshold. We all looked at her, expecting the worst.

'Yes, Madame?'

I was impressed Henri's voice sounded granite-steady.

'The Senateur has returned, Monsieur Delacroix.'

Henri glanced at Felix, who in turn cut me a look. This was it.

'Until we see you, Fleurette,' Felix said carefully, reaching for me. 'You may need to send on some trunks for Henri. You know how he needs so many pomades and toiletries.'

I chuckled. Felix was right. It did help to cut through the tension, even though the humour felt sad.

'Oh, do be quiet, Felix,' Henri growled with mock disgust but we all knew he was right to not allow us to become maudlin. 'Fleurette, I'm sorry your day has been marked by . . .'

'I know, Henri. But it doesn't matter. What counts is that you and Felix stay safe and come home soon.' I suppose I should have added Aimery's name into that mix but I was too busy hugging my eldest brother fiercely so he knew I meant it, and all those dark words that had passed between us earlier today were forgiven, forgotten. I loved Henri . . . I just sometimes found it hard to admire him.

Meanwhile, admiring Felix was easy. I moved my affection to him with a squeezing embrace. 'I shall miss you every moment,' I murmured. 'Don't die, Felix.'

His eyes glittered at me when we pulled away. 'I shall try not to. Besides, I'm an officer,' he added, as though title alone would keep him from the bullets.

'No heroics,' I warned them both. 'Just do your duty and come home.'

And then they were gone, greeting the Senateur who stood inside our hallway, stiff and silent. He gave a small bow of respect as he spied my brothers. Perhaps the politician had called at the De Lasset villa too out of similar respect and discovered Aimery already departed. I wondered if he also would be clambering into uniform soon enough. I followed like a loyal pet, walking behind the men, hearing every squeak of their leather boots and crunch of those same boots on our gravel path until we'd reached the gates of the property, where the household staff had gathered. Some of the younger women were weeping. I noticed Felix kissed each of the staff on both cheeks. He knew they were sad to see the family sons walking off to war but there were also their own sons, husbands, fathers, going. What would our prickly family do without Felix's charm? I wondered, as I noticed the women brightening for him, finding smiles, even a sad gust of a laugh from the housekeeper.

'Go on with you, sir,' I heard her admonish, with a gentle tap on my brother's arm. She'd been with our family since before Felix and I were born.

'No further, Fleurette,' Henri warned. 'The prefect says it's chaotic out there.'

I didn't need him to tell me. I could hear the cacophony of men's voices, marching boots, yells and squeals from women in the distance, presumably bestowing weepy farewells. I knew he'd want me to remain composed, represent our family well. On impulse I hugged him. 'Take care of yourself, Henri.'

'Don't worry about us,' he said, but I could see the concern like a shadow behind his bravely set expression. It danced in his eyes, which seemed slightly glassy in the lantern light. Henri turned to address the staff, gave them an uplifting talk that I barely heard because my mind was wandering, considering whether this was the last time I'd see them together. Was this the last moment of innocence in our lives, where hours earlier we'd been sipping champagne and toasting my good health? Were we saying farewell forever?

If not for the way Felix turned and flashed me one of his signature grins, I might have faltered. Instead, I watched them fall in with the rest of the men from our neighbourhood who had respectfully gathered outside our villa – they were all part of the Bataillon de Chasseurs Alpin. Our alpine light infantry had a reputation for being reliable soldiers, brave and willing. What more could you ask of any man? I thought, feeling a rush of sentimentality as I watched the huddle move as one away from us in the low light.

They began to sing. It was a French lullaby I recognised: something my father would hum as he soothed us off to sleep as infants.

And with their song came the ancient, enchanting fragrance of jasmine that was first cultivated in the Middle Ages in our region. It was now synonymous with Grasse, imprinted on my memory as richly as a photograph captures a moment. Full of opulent sweetness, *Jasminum grandiflorum* could be picked out with its fruity notes. But this moment belonged to its sister, the evening-blooming *Jasminum sambac*, which rose through the warmth of the night like a ghost of our childhoods to remind us of home, where our hearts lay. Brooding and animalistic, it swept like a wild, invisible creature past me, moving nimbly over the top of the hill to stalk the marching men to their destinies.

5

It had been over a week since Aimery and his 23e Chasseurs had left the town but Henri and Felix were still forming their companies at Villefranche. No visitors were allowed, I was informed. Despite a certain secrecy, it soon became common knowledge that their battalion was going to leave on August 10th. I understood there was nothing to be gained from making the trip down from Grasse other than inevitable pain should we catch a glimpse of each other. Nevertheless, I joined the throng of women to tearfully wave off our men as they proudly marched down to the train station for transportation to La Vésubie.

I gathered that my brothers – two of more than two dozen officers – were on their way to the north, where the Germans had already invaded Belgium. I didn't see Henri, but Felix I could sense, and I would not let that column of men march past me without one final glimpse of my twin. I scanned the familiar faces, expressions now set grimly as if hammered from stone, eyes forward, following their orders. There was Etienne, perhaps our most trusted chemist. He was nearing forty with a family of five children. I picked out Jean-Paul, a violet grower; Alain, one of our foremen; Hercule, a giant of a fellow who could coax muguet from our fields to be as sweet as I knew his nature to be. On his heels was Stephane, who worked in the distillery – an only child, as far as I could recall.

And there he was, grinning for me. Or, at least that's what I told myself. Felix was hailed as not only the most handsome bachelor in the town but the most eligible. I was aware of his reputation amongst his peers of his female conquests and I also knew directly from Felix that he would never marry someone from Grasse.

'Too much history, Ettie. We've all grown up together.'

'Not all of us,' I'd remarked.

'Well, those who didn't come from our side of the bed have watched me grow up and I've probably . . .' He had stopped and I had given him a sideways look. 'Well' — he'd continued with a sigh that said *Let's say no more about it*, 'you understand.'

'Yes, Felix, I do.'

He wore the same slightly lopsided smile now as he had then and while I convinced myself it was for me, because he had broken orders presumably to look directly at me, I heard various women call out his name. He winked and my heart hurt. Felix was so full of mischief, so full of affection for everyone, and was adored in return. I was admired but not adored like my brother. I waved, blew him a long kiss and barely registered the tears until a soft breeze made the moisture cool on my cheeks. I mouthed, 'Where's Henri?' but Felix could only give a slight shake of his head. They'd look after one another.

I had no idea where Aimery and the 23e had been sent from Grasse but I imagined he'd send news soon enough so I could stop shrugging, looking blank or making excuses whenever anyone from the town asked me.

Opposite me, through the column of marching men, I caught a glimpse of Graciela again. Was she looking for my husband? Did she not know he had already left the immediate region? As far as he'd told me, his regiment, though assembled at Grasse, had left during the same day he'd left me. I was yet to learn where the new barracks were. She looked even more anguished than she had on the day of the wedding.

'Madame De Lasset?'

I swung around, my thoughts interrupted by one of the women from a family of growers. 'Yes? Oh, hello, Soline. Surely your father is not marching?'

She shook her head. 'He would if he could. I don't know if my father will see out the year.' She sighed, but did not dwell on that hurt. 'No, my two cousins are leaving with this regiment.'

'They look resplendent, don't they?'

'I suppose. They're both so young.'

'Everyone's too young to go to war,' I replied, just short of being dismissive and sounding like one of our elders. Did marriage do this to people? One day riding a bicycle through puddles and shrieking with laughter, the next behaving contemptuously of single people, as though being wed brought vast wisdom? 'I'm sorry,' I followed up quickly. 'That was condescending of me. I am a believer that war is pointless, even if you do hail yourself the winner. The ruin of people, families, livelihoods, land, finances feels too costly.'

'What's the alternative, though, Madame? I admit I have no desire to learn German.'

She had a point and I conceded it with a sad nod.

I looked back and Graciela had effected one of her amazing disappearing acts and Felix was already advancing out of my immediate sight. At any other time I would have chased the column, calling his name. Now I was expected to behave with grace. It would be unseemly but it didn't stop me standing on tiptoe to maximise my full height. I caught a final glimpse of his beret, worn just a smidge more rakishly than his companions.

And then he was gone. Lost to the blur of brave blue. What were they marching into? I didn't want to think on it and yet it was all I thought about over the next few days.

6

If I was asked to write down what I'd done in the week following the wedding, I don't believe I could scribble anything of note. It was a grey haze of confusion . . . Not only were we all taking on new duties, sharing as much of the burden left by the men as we could, but I was moving around as if some giant puppeteer was in charge of me. There was no conscious thought that I could recall. My actions were being performed either by rote or simply memory. Nothing was achieved, it seemed, while we all came to terms that our men were gone. This was the first time I could remember not having one family member within speaking distance. I was alone, entirely in charge of myself, two households and a team of women and old men across both villas. Everyone was waiting. I wasn't sure what they were waiting for, but it began to filter into my consciousness that they were waiting for me to make decisions.

And it was my good fortune the weather had been contrary enough that the harvest would run late and we didn't look out across our fields to see spoiled flowers.

I'm sure I'd only emerged out of this state of almost frozen bewilderment because I found the letter. I remembered now that I'd hurriedly stuffed Sébastien's missive into the pocket of my silk dressing-gown when Aimery and I had been interrupted on our wedding night. In the chaos, I'd forgotten about it and I'd left the dressing-gown at the De Lasset mansion. For the past few days I hadn't returned, preferring to set up my family's household first on its new war footing before I walked back up the hill to be Madame De Lasset.

This is where I found myself now, seated in my boudoir of my marriage home for the first time, and so resplendent it was that I felt insignificant. We'd discovered the letter rustling quietly when I'd undressed this evening.

'Madame?' Jeanne had said, as she'd taken out my silk gown from my trousseau, untouched since my wedding night. Presumably, the housekeeper had hung everything up in my absence. I knew I'd left the room in an untidy state. Jeanne held out the unopened letter with a look of enquiry. Yes, indeed, who did leave sealed letters in their dressing-gowns?

'Oh, my. I forgot about that. It arrived the night of the mobilisation.'

Jeanne smiled and I was glad she didn't recognise the writing. Then again, potentially no one would, given that Sébastien had not been glimpsed in Grasse's small world.

'Would you like me to fetch your letter opener?' she offered.

'Er, no, I'll read it later. It's just well wishes,' I dismissed. 'Not in the mood for those right now.'

She set it down on the dressing table and we both stared at it for a moment before she picked up the brush and began to polish my hair with sweeping strokes of the boar bristles. I busied myself dipping my fingers into a pot of lavender-scented cream from Haute Provence. The luscious cream was made with the oils from its olive groves, and I took my time smearing the gently fragranced balm onto my hands and arms.

'May I, Madame?' Jeanne gestured at the pot.

'By all means,' I said, thinking she meant to try some on her skin, but she dipped just a single fingertip into the cream, then warmed the small globule between her hands, coating them, before she ran glistening fingers through the dark waves she had been brushing. I smiled as she began again and my hair started to feel slippery-smooth.

'This will nourish it, Madame.'

'Who taught you this?'

'I used to work in the household of Madame Graciela Olivares.'

I couldn't hide my surprise fast enough and she could see my shocked expression reflected in the mirror.

'Oh, forgive me. I thought Monsieur De Lasset had told you this.'

'No. Perhaps he thought it would feel odd that I would be attended to by his former lover's maid.'

It was Jeanne's turn to look shocked. 'No, no, Madame. I was no such thing. I was the sister of her maid and I simply cleaned in her home. I had very little to do with the family itself.'

'I see.' I began imagining Jeanne as a spy for Graciela. Perhaps she guessed this because she blushed.

'I am not here to pass on information, Madame. I promise you I will demonstrate my gratitude by being your loyal servant.'

As children we had been taught to accept people as they presented and only judge them when cause was given. While I was now helplessly suspicious, Jeanne had given me no cause; she could have hidden the truth and yet had spoken it seemingly without guile.

'I hope I am placing my trust truly,' I answered. Using one of my father's phrases deliberately prompted a sense of needing to live up to his expectation. I don't think I feared anything more than disappointing my father. 'Plus, I have nothing to hide. If you are a spy, there is no secret to pass back.'

'I am no spy, Madame.'

'I know you will prove that, Jeanne. Trust is earned, is it not?'

'Yes, indeed.' She started brushing again, frowning. 'Sometimes, though, trust is blindly given.'

'Husbands and wives?' I said, in a slightly ironic tone.

She smiled and nodded thoughtfully, but her frown deepened. 'Children, too.'

'To parents, you mean?'

'For example,' she answered.

'But that's the purest form of trust, surely?'

'I suppose. My parents let us down, though. My father had affairs; my mother drank herself to death.'

I felt immediately sad for Jeanne, knowing how secure I'd always felt with my father and brothers.

'Then there's our men of the town going off to war, trusting their superiors, our government . . . But we all know some of them aren't going to return, despite that trust.'

'Jeanne, I'm sorry I haven't asked you this before, but do you have a sweetheart?'

She gave a coy smile. 'I do. His name is Errando.'

'Is he Basque?'

'Proudly, yes. He's been living in Lyon. He arrived two years ago to help with the harvest and never left . . . until now.'

'Will you marry?'

'I hope so. We agreed we would wait for his permission to come through for leave.'

I didn't mention that Felix had got word to me through one of the gendarmes left in our town that no leave was being granted in the immediate future. 'Well, then, I shall help you as soon as you know more,' I offered.

'Really, Madame?'

'Of course. We can prepare a celebration lunch in our gardens here if you wish.' I might as well demonstrate my trust now.

It would be up to Jeanne to earn it.

'Only women would be present. And the priest.'

'All you need is your bridegroom and a bed,' I offered, affecting a wicked glint that Felix would have been proud of.

'Madame!' She giggled. 'You are so lucky. You managed to marry just in time and have your wedding night.'

So the household believed Aimery and I had consummated our marriage vows . . . I would let that belief remain intact for now, if it kept everyone happy.

'So what is Mademoiselle Olivares like?'

'I barely said more than two words to her in my time at the house.'

I smiled conspiratorially. 'Oh, come on. Your sister must have revealed something.'

'Not really. I am not very close to my sister. I do know Mademoiselle prefers to be called Senorita behind closed doors, and I know she possesses a fearful temper too.'

'Really? Spaniards are known to be fiery.'

'She is more than that, though, Madame. Mademoiselle Olivares struck me as being spontaneous.'

It was such an odd word. Something in the tone of Jeanne's voice made me believe she actually wanted to say unstable.

'Do you mean unpredictable?'

She shrugged. 'I think her actions ebb and flow with her emotions.'

'Don't we all?'

'No, I think the senorita lives off her spontaneity. She could slap a servant or cuddle a child in the same heartbeat.'

'Truly?'

'I saw her sweep a fully dressed table clear of everything so that food spilled everywhere because she wasn't happy with the chilindrón stew.'

'Surely not?' I asked, aghast.

'I do not jest. It was horrifying. She was having guests. Such a mess. All because she claimed the paprika tasted stale.'

'How old is she?'

'I think she is past thirty, Madame.'

'Not a happy age for a spinster.'

'A rich, unhappy one.'

'Why here?'

'I don't claim to know. Her family had to leave Spain, I believe. Her father was immensely rich; her brother died, her parents were killed in an accident at sea, I believe. She's been alone since her early twenties.'

'What a tragic tale. I think, Jeanne, she believed she would marry the man I did.'

Our gazes met over my head in the mirror. Jeanne blushed.

'Aimery and I have discussed it. I am sad to think she carries a flame for him.'

Jeanne had the grace not to respond. If she knew more, she wasn't saying at this stage and as she tied back my hair with a satin ribbon, I sensed it was the end of our conversation about Graciela for the time being. However, I felt better – more powerful for having been first to bring the subject into the open.

'Thank you.'

'Is there anything else I can do for you?' she offered, reaching for the lamp.

I smiled. 'No, you get off to bed too. I'm going to enjoy my first full night in my new bed.'

'Shall I turn off the light?' she said, looking hopeful.

I nodded. Electrical lighting was still a novelty. Our rich town enjoyed electrified street lighting from the turn of the century and our villa, along with the wealthy families like the De Lassets, joined the new world of lighting in every room. Our staff and the general population were still carrying around oil lamps at home, however, so I could understand her pleasure that at the pull of a cord light magically came on or switched off at her command. Plus it was clean and required no additional work so I could imagine how much easier that made her life in the big house.

As Jeanne left the room I was plunged into a moodier atmosphere that was illuminated now by a single lamp at my bedside. I picked up Sébastien's letter and carried it to the bed so I could read it properly. It popped open easily enough and I withdrew two small sheets. The purple ink once again trapped my attention because it was such a rare colour in nature and yet it was so thoroughly symbolic of Grasse, with its purple spring violets. Purple . . . the colour of royalty and also of mourning. And unlike most, who might cite scarlet or crimson first, I considered purple to be the colour of the romantic. It was, without any doubt, my favourite colour, and I was arrested by its rich beauty on the thick cream paper and wondered if the hand that wrote this felt the same way about the colour as I did. Sébastien's handwriting, though flamboyantly looped, flowed on neat, straight lines.

> *My dear Mademoiselle Delacroix,*
>
> *No doubt you will think it odd that I choose to write suddenly, given that we do not know one another. However, we are connected strongly through our families' past friendship. I must ask you to forgive both my candour and brevity, as I am taking this precaution of sending you a letter should anything prevent me from reaching Grasse in time to, in person, prevent you from marrying Aimery.*

I caught my breath, stopped reading. I could feel myself blink with consternation at his blunt words. I had to scan them again to be sure they did in fact say what I thought I'd read.

No, I hadn't misread or misunderstood it . . . *to prevent you from marrying Aimery.*

Fresh shock trilled through me at the bald statement. This felt entirely different to the alarm of Jeanne's revelation of her connection to Aimery's lover; this felt sinister, full of threat.

I read on, hardly daring to stir the pages before me by breathing.

> *I will explain more as soon as I see you, and my deepest apology for disrupting your life with such a dark instruction. Yet, I feel sure you already accept that I would not make such a traumatic suggestion in jest. I am honourable in my mission to ensure this marriage is not made and there is solid reason for it never to take place. Make any excuse, Mademoiselle; make yourself ill if you must, but do not take a vow of marriage to Aimery De Lasset.*
>
> *I implore you not to ignore this edict that comes from our mother.*

I had been gobbling these words with widening eyes and an escalating pulse but now I paused. 'Edict. . .' I heard myself repeat in a whisper. She didn't know me, as her son said, but we were connected. How could Aimery's mother possibly have such a strong feeling against me when she knew of my family, our links, our importance to the town? As much as it galled me, I was privately and helplessly claiming the perfection of our match. I set aside my disgust and continued with the letter.

> *I am in haste to get this away to you. The gifts are a ruse to carry the letter. It is likely wise you do not permit my brother to know of this communication; I am assured he has a famous temper that may emerge. I have sent him a separate parcel so that he suspects nothing.*

*There is something urgently important I must tell you
both but it needs to be said in person rather than in writing.
It is a message from our mother and Aimery must be
convinced of her sincerity and that can only be achieved
face to face. Unfortunately she's gravely ill, and I have
the unenviable choice of either being with my mother as
she dies and thus traumatising her by not following her
instructions to return to Grasse, or returning to Grasse
to deliver her instructions and not being at her side as she
passes. I am damned either way but, as a dutiful son,
I am carrying out her demand.*

*Needless to say, the information my mother wishes to
share will explain much of our strange life that I've led with
her, which I now finally understand.*

*Again, forgive me for the cryptic nature of this message
and that I cannot say more now; it is necessary to leave
it unwritten in order to protect us all. I shall be with
you shortly. Trust me, please.*

Yours,

Sébastien

Except he'd never arrived. I sat back on the edge of the bed with my
heartbeat drumming a pounding rhythm in my chest so hard that I
felt nauseous. I breathed out at last and, moving with confusion
and disbelief, hurried across the room to fling the windows open
further. I gasped my disbelief at these instructions.

The night was still, lights were winking off across the town
below and the scent of jasmine hunted me. In fact, I lost myself to a
few desperately grasped moments of clarity while the ethereal scent
of white jasmine gave up its sweetness to the starlight and I could
taste the makings of a new scent on the rim of my senses. Here, in
this place of fragrance and beauty, was truth; life felt pure and

uncomplicated. I understood it, I trusted it, but knew I couldn't remain in this world; life awaited me. I had to confront the darkness that the letter had introduced into my thoughts.

What did Sébastien need to share? I was trembling at his direct manner but, of course, he was rushing to get the note to me so he'd had no time to construct a polite letter that gently led me to the shock he had in store. I blinked in vexation. What possible reason could there be for Aimery and me to withhold our marriage ceremony? Why the great secrecy? I felt a tingle of fresh relief that Aimery and I had not shared a bed yet, but that came with a pinch of anger that someone was now trying to prevent it. I knew my thoughts were at odds with my feelings towards Aimery but I was truly weary of men exerting control over me. Whether I liked it or not, Aimery and I were man and wife now. What could possibly trump that?

Clearly Sébastien's plans to arrive at Grasse in time had been interrupted by the declaration of war. I wondered if Aimery already knew the information that Sébastien was so determined to give us; surely he would have shared it with his brother by now. What would it mean?

Sleep would elude me now until I addressed this dilemma. I refused to see a new sunrise being mute and unresponsive to this drama; I needed to do something that addressed it. In a burst of energy I turned my room lights back on, pulled out my new writing compendium – a wedding gift from Felix – and began a letter to my husband.

> *Dear Aimery,*
> *I am convincing myself that this letter will find you cheerful of spirit, if not happy to be where you are. I know you will be setting a fine example for your men. We are all very well here although life is certainly quiet – near silent – in the town.*

Thank you for my beautiful suite of rooms – I can see some trouble has been taken with the decor to echo my favourite colours in a restrained, tasteful way.

I didn't think it was necessary to tell him this was my first night here. I also didn't think it wise to hedge. Honesty was required, and I couldn't pretend, no matter how heartfelt the entreaty, that I had not heard from Sébastien.

Unfortunately, this letter to you leaves me confused. I have received a note from your brother. Sébastien asked that we postpone our marriage until he could arrive with some news from your mother. He doesn't say what, but was emphatic. Do you have any idea as to what he might be referring to?

I left it at that, preferring not to remind him that our wedding may have gone ahead but that we remained man and wife in name only.

On a brighter topic, harvest begins tomorrow and can you imagine we shall be distilling by week's end? The two households and staff will do the families proud. I know it will help everyone to keep to our routines, keep the fields turning over, the warehouses busy.
I will write again shortly. For now, stay safe, dear Aimery, and I shall watch for your letter to arrive.
Fondly,
Fleurette

I sealed it to prevent me from wanting to change anything. I stared at the envelope with its plain black ink. Next to it sat Sébastien's letter, like an accusation. I was betraying him but I consoled myself that I didn't know him and that I hadn't asked for his trust. I kept imagining a younger version of Aimery, which hardly thrilled me. He didn't sound like Aimery, though; his letter, despite its demanding nature, sounded respectful, affectionate almost.

I switched all lights off to close the matter and took my time getting comfortable in a new bed, with its high pillows. The sheets felt shockingly yet deliciously cold against the warmth of the room and I slid gratefully between their satiny quality, kicking off the eiderdown and staring up at the canopy of blue toile that hung majestically above, cascading down each of the four posts.

I lay there, pretending my thoughts were still. In fact they roamed, first to Felix, wishing him a safe goodnight, then to Henri to do the same. Curiously it was to Sébastien my mind stole next. I tried to imagine what the situation must have been when his mother shattered the quartet of our two families and left Grasse.

As I decided I must learn more about this elusive woman, sleep must have mercifully tiptoed up and claimed me because I fell into that drowsy plane of being neither awake nor asleep, and not conscious but dulled to the point of no thought. I felt comfortable from my safe haven in Grasse, knowing France would heroically fend off the Germans, and that our men would be home soon enough. From this vantage I was tipped softly into sleep, little knowing that a storm was stirring, readying itself to blow through my life – all our lives – and render them changed forever.

7

In an effort to be seen mixing with the other officers' wives, I attended a coffee morning at Catherine's house. She was in a bright mood, having heard from Henri yesterday – as had I – and although his letters were brief, we knew from reading between the lines that my brothers were probably fighting in Lorraine or Alsace. Two of her other guests whom I knew, but not well, had husbands in Aimery's regiment and they seemed to know more than I did: that the 23e had also left the Italian frontier and was also already in the north of France.

I politely sipped coffee, although I would have preferred tea, and leaned close to Catherine as she squeezed my arm.

'It seems to be going well for them.'

I nodded. Henri hadn't said as much in his letter but then he hadn't really said much at all beyond the hint of being close to the border and that he'd forgotten to pack books and would I please confer with Monsieur Bouchard about whether we have sufficient lard for this year's enfleurage. I suppose I drew some comfort from the banal nature of his letter because there was nothing at all in it to alarm me.

'Yes, Henri and Felix will look out for each other,' I assured. 'You're not to worry.'

She shrugged. 'You're so lucky to have been married before the men left.'

'Am I?'

She looked at me, perplexed.

I quickly adjusted what I'd meant. 'I mean, now that I'm married, I have reason to worry too much, I suspect.'

Catherine's nature was to be sweet to everyone. She gave me a sisterly hug. 'Your Aimery will be a hero, I'm sure.'

I smiled thinly as she turned to the person next to her to fall into a discussion about bolts of cotton and silk newly arrived from Italy. It would be the last for a while, I imagined, feeling a trite bored but desperately trying not to show that I was far more interested in the jasmine harvest than the latest fabrics. It wasn't their fault that I felt awkward, and I realised I would have to try harder to fit into groups of my peers, because with Felix gone I was going to be lonely if I didn't make the effort.

'I hear all our men from Grasse are now united in the north – is that your understanding, Madame De Lasset?' My neighbour chuckled, but didn't let me respond. 'Oh my, it's so odd calling you that instead of Mademoiselle Delacroix.'

I kept the smile steady. 'I am yet to be used to it,' I agreed.

'Oh, I think you're the luckiest woman in all of Grasse to be married to that dashing officer of yours.'

I suppose they would all believe this. 'Thank you,' I said as graciously as I could. 'We didn't have much of a chance to share being man and wife.'

She tittered again, obviously hearing the innuendo I hadn't meant to convey. 'Oh, I'm sure he'll make that up to you as soon as they get some leave. My Giraud believes that will occur soon. He thinks it will all be over by Christmas. There are towns already repatriated, according to a newspaper, my father says, so maybe Giraud is right.'

'Oh, yes, done by Christmas,' another officer's wife assured, joining our conversation as she reached for a tiny sponge cake laced with syrup.

'Let's hope so,' I replied.

'Will you spend the summer in Grasse this year?' she asked, biting neatly into the cake, and then answered her own question. 'I suppose it's not wise to be going anywhere at present, although I for one could do with a change of scenery.'

'It's jasmine harvest,' I said, masking my surprise that she would question how a Delacroix or a De Lasset might spend her August.

'Oh, but you have people for that, surely?' she said, sounding vaguely appalled that I might concern myself with it.

'Not this year,' I reminded and smiled evenly, disguising how much I couldn't wait to be amongst the flowers and the workers and the real life I loved.

––––––––

It was stifling and it wasn't yet midday as I stood in the factory warehouse, where scores of kilograms of jasmine flowers were being tipped gently out of sacks. These fragile blooms I was taught had probably come first to Spain via Africa from the exotic Orient of Kashmir and Persia. The Spanish had brought this most royal of our flowers with its incomparable fragrance to our region. It was precious in so many ways, not least in the manner it needed to be harvested, with the trained hands of specialist pickers. These female pickers who might pluck six, maybe seven kilos of roses in May, might only gather three-quarters of a kilo of jasmine during the same number of work hours in August. It was tedious, exhausting work requiring concentration and speed. Nothing could kindle my father's anger faster than a sack of bruised or spoiled jasmine petals, which, I used to jest, turned brown if you looked at them the wrong way.

Pickers had begun at first light and I had been out in the fields with them, sharing the workload, as dawn broke gently over Grasse. Normally the women would sing as they walked to the fields of flowers, a soft sea of luminous white, but this day we had kept silent, all of us thinking of the war unfolding at our border.

I'd received a communication from Felix via the local barracks explaining succinctly that despite being sent to guard the Italian border, the 24e would be sent to Lorraine to take part in the initial advance into Alsace. It all felt too real, too frightening, and I was glad to lose myself in the repetitive work of picking and the world I understood.

———————

Leaving the fields nearly an hour ago, I gave myself just enough time to down a slim tartine and a shallow bowl of sweetened coffee before moving across to the warehouse. I didn't want to miss a moment of the critical next stage.

Breathing in deeply, I savoured the fresh, creamy smell of our most prized bloom, which couldn't be macerated or steam-distilled. Instead we had to employ a technique known as enfleurage, and that was already underway with a team of women busily at their chassis, which I had called 'windows' since I was a child. With a nod to the supervisor, a fearsome former picker now dressed in the familiar all-black of management and taking her new role seriously, I strolled away from the idyllic scene of workers tipping out the sacks of gathered flowers and moved to the enfleurage area to oversee the progress. I knew Madame Aurelie would run a brisk yet fair schedule for the workers, especially as she knew the toll the work took on their bodies. She would ensure regular meals, breaks, stretching out their bent spines, even if the old supervisor, Monsieur Planque, was less forgiving.

'Good afternoon,' I called out as brightly as I could to the fifteen or so women.

'Good afternoon, Madame,' they said as one, to make me smile.

'How are your hands holding up?'

'Not so bad,' one elderly woman admitted.

Hers looked like the claws of an eagle and yet they moved with gentle dexterity. I watched, marvelling at her expertise as she took a fresh pane of glass that was framed in timber. It had been smeared with lard; I could tell from the smell that it wasn't tallow this year – definitely pig fat. Working fast yet deliberately, old Adelie embedded the petals of jasmine into the layer of lard with a tenderness one might handle a newborn with. No petals, fat with their luscious, precious juices, ever spoiled in Adelie's hands. Over the next few days that perfect scent of night would diffuse. She and her companions would work for the next few weeks, replacing those petals every three days until the lard reached what my father called saturation, when the fat could take on no more of the fragrance.

'There you are, Madame Fleurette,' Adelie said, finishing yet another chassis. 'You will have your pomade before you know it.'

I smiled my thanks. We all knew this was our region's wealth. This was the moment, the main month in which we made our money. Outside of May – rose time – August was critical, and why I insisted that we set aside our fear for our men and show that we could bring in the harvest with the workforce we had available. Given that this part was mainly women's work anyway, supervised by men, I was confident we could achieve our 1914 harvest and make our men proud.

I wouldn't attempt to sell our enfleurage wax – pomade, as we called it – as our two families had on various occasions. Given we were at war, I wouldn't know how to begin such negotiations. Instead it was my intention that we wash out the fat and absorb the scent molecules into alcohol, which our chemists could then evaporate to leave me with an enviable resource of jasmine absolute. This viscous, yellowy liquid possessed the very spirit of those powerfully scented flowers of the night. It would carry their delicate scent onwards.

'Marvellous work, ladies. Keep it up!' I said with as much enthusiasm as I could push into the words, and they chorused a farewell. Everyone was doing their best to remain cheerful but the lack of men around us and the knowledge that guns might already be firing on our borders skulked like a gloomy shadow in the corner, threatening to saunter out and intensify its presence whenever we dared to enjoy the happiest time of year.

As I left the enfleurage area, my gaze was once again drawn to the mountain of dewy jasmine petals, calming in their coolness, laid out at the other end of the warehouse. I began to do the sums in my mind, astonished at the numbers. Each fluid ounce of absolute would take approximately one quarter of a million flowers – maybe another five million or more to achieve a saleable amount – which meant hundreds and hundreds of picking hours. Staggering! At least half of Grasse's fields were carpeted in jasmine; could we get that frightening number of plants harvested with the available workforce of women? This was not a problem our families would have encountered previously; it was certainly not a matter I had ever even had to think about. The labour force was Henri's domain, had been for many years, and it was hardly a difficult juggle for him – not only did the entire working population of Grasse traditionally get involved with harvest, but we would normally have an influx of itinerant workers. Other travelling French men and women would come in from various provinces but also workers from Spain and

Italy. With a sense of alarm I made a mental note to have a meeting with the council – whoever was left, anyway – to discuss a formal announcement of the task we were up against. We would need every woman, young or old, to pitch in to help keep Grasse's economy moving.

Drifting on the scent of the flowers as I moved away from the main warehouse, I began to unconsciously break down the intoxicating flavours I could taste. Definitely greener this year, I felt, yet its opulence was intact to achieve that heady sensation so inherent in 'the king of fragrances', as Felix called it. I smiled, remembering how he would describe rose as female, jasmine as male. What I smelled in our jasmine was a curvy lusciousness that I knew from experience and from my imagination required only a minute amount to lift a perfume into a new level of beauty. This was my skill, my divine gift. Flowers could have anything from fifteen to several hundred individual components. I teased out a few as I walked towards the De Lasset laboratory. Today I picked out a note resonant of apricot softening down the slightly grassy flavour that I sensed was stronger this year. It would challenge the traditional way we tended to think of our jasmine. When I used it I would need to adjust that freshness if I wanted to keep it in that darkly sensuous quarter. My father had always leaned towards the exotic with perfume of jasmine, paying homage to its origins; one of my favourites was one of his earliest. He had made it for my mother as a wedding gift and it was a heady mix of sandalwood, vanilla notes, cinnamon and cedar, with jasmine looping through them, tying them together like an ethereal, invisible ribbon that made sense of the parts to form a whole. A majestic night scent he called *Immortelle*.

I wore a dab of it today in honour of the jasmine harvest and of my father . . . and to remember our mother in this time of families scattered and in strife. I smelled my elbow – an old habit – to rid myself of all other thoughts of fragrance, and then my wrist. As I inhaled at my pulse, my father's noble face shimmered into clearer focus in my mind but, more importantly, the presence of my mother was instantly more tangible. It was as though her spirit had been called down in that heartbeat and she stood before me now. I couldn't see or hear her in my mind as I could my father, but she was present nonetheless. That was the power of fragrance; it transported one. Time had no distance or age where smell was concerned. I halted at the surprise of being catapulted back to infancy and that sultry aroma that lived in my soul.

It was in this instant that I knew what I needed to achieve. It was a task I was setting myself . . . a dream, a goal, an aspirational milestone that would clear a path for my future.

I was going to design my own perfume. The average person in Paris could detect maybe twenty different smells. Felix could hold at least two and a half thousand, my father a fraction more, but I had been endowed with a sense that could discriminate just over three thousand. Felix had counted them once, to be sure that I really could eclipse his talent. Not that either of us cared, for the Delacroix brand was like the fulcrum – my father on its point, and the pair of us balancing either side. We complemented each other's talents in myriad ways, from the obvious of male and female to the more subtle of Felix's grasp of the chypre family of smells that encompassed citrus to grassy or fruity. In this regard his talent was superior to mine, whereas when it came to fougère – the more smoky, woody, spicy notes – I had no equal. Together we could be formidable but my father hadn't been dead long enough to hand over the laboratory entirely to his twin children. We'd stuck to the more conservative pathway of providing raw materials or fully formed fragrances for other houses in Paris, London, New York or Milan to present as their own. Felix and I had possessed a dream since our teens to develop a range under our own brand of Delacroix.

Why couldn't I begin this summer, in the depths of our misery, to lose myself in the design of a new perfume? Why not indeed? At its heart would be jasmine, in minuscule amounts, but there nonetheless as a final nod to my parents and the start of a new era.

The De Lasset chemist was an old man: he had to be sixty and his assistant, the only one left that I could see, perhaps a decade younger. They both looked startled to see me arrive in the hallowed chamber of their laboratory. They were surrounded by bottles of all shapes and sizes containing liquid of varying shades of yellow through green to brown. Some bottles were an opaque chocolate colour to house the more fragile oils; the clear-glassed bottles gleamed jewel-like at me. I never failed to be seduced by their potential.

Both men halted in their activity as though they'd been caught in mischief. They had been working near two large chunks of dull grey ambergris. This waxy regurgitation from the digestion of whales had lost its primitive, faecal quality and had aged to offer up its earthy, sweeter aroma. I had never lost my fascination for this vital element of the perfumer's craft. Since my father had explained its origin, I had come to favour it as an anchor flavour in perfumes. Felix had read somewhere that once expelled – by only the sperm whale, he assured me – it took years to form, floating endlessly on the ocean to wash up on beaches. Its rarity was profound, its price akin to gold. Our guild treated it with enormous respect, used it in tiniest amounts, and yet I felt myself mesmerised by the pair of enormous boulders of this uncommon material.

'Madame De Lasset!'

'Oh, do call me Madame Fleurette, please,' I urged. 'Good morning, Monsieur Planque. You must be missing your brother,' I said, proud of my memory. 'He is surely missed in the warehouse.'

'Philippe will write when he can to assure us of his whereabouts and safety,' he said, stiffly. 'Madame, may I present Monsieur Boucard, who works alongside me.'

'Monsieur Boucard,' I repeated and smiled, nodding in polite salutation.

The man looked appalled to see me in the lab and merely bowed, clicking his heels.

'How are you getting along, sirs?' I was determined to circumvent all the formality but suspected it would be an uphill task with these gentlemen.

'I am perfectly well, Madame. And your good self?'

'As you find me. A bit wearied from the picking but otherwise brightened because of it, given the mood of our town.'

They both stared at me as though I was a new life form.

'What are you working on, Monsieur?' I said, trying to get a conversation started.

'Er . . . it's a blend for an English perfumery.'

'Yes? Good, and what is the brief?'

The men shared a glance. 'Base notes of leather, Madame. It is to be used in a range of toiletries.'

'I suspect it will be years before that client pays, under the circumstances.'

He nodded, still looking stunned. 'I expect you are right, Madame.'

There was an awkward pause.

'How can we help you, Madame De Lasset?'

'Actually, I came to offer some help, see if I might be of service.'

'Pardon me, Madame? In what regard might that be?'

I couldn't tell if he was being deliberately obtuse.

'Well . . . I am every inch my father's daughter,' I tried, hoping to clue him without sounding arrogant. But Monsieur Planque just looked back at me, perplexed. 'I mean, I have the Nose.' It sounded so pompous and yet the boast was out and parading between us – the one my father had reminded me as he had died that I was not to air.

'How can something be boastful if one is only speaking the plain truth?' I had asked him.

He had given me an indulgent smile. 'Let those around you discover all your talents for themselves. Someone who needs to impress others is someone suffering insecurity. Do not be that person, darling Fleurette. Be strong but understand you are a woman with a gift that only men believe they should possess and in a time when they will hate you for it.'

'Then I'm going to change the world's attitude. I am going to become a leading perfumer.'

'I hope you do, but you must demonstrate your talent, not talk about it . . . and you must tiptoe this idea into their lives, let stealth be your friend, my girl.' He'd paused for a coughing fit and when recovered, sucking air as though each breath might be his last, he had continued. 'They must turn around one day and realise a woman perfumer is in their midst and by then it will be too late to deny you.' His voice rasped, sounded wheezy. Soon one of these sucking breaths would indeed be his last, I recalled thinking with deepest dismay. 'But if you show off or push your dream too hard before them, they will resent you and work against you. A man must be permitted his pride, Fleurette, never forget that. The day of the woman perfumer is surely coming and I hope you lead that charge, but you must arrive quietly and not make your male peers feel any less for that arrival.' My father had died the following day but I could now hear his caution, which I'd ignored.

'Congratulations, Madame Fleurette; that is a rare and enviable talent. Yes, I had heard of your special prowess.' He made a good fist of trying to disguise his mocking words.

I had to go forward, though; it was too late to back away. 'I thought, given that we are living through these unusual times, that I might offer some involvement.'

'Really? In what way?' He managed to make himself sound entirely self-effacing and innocent, but this was the type of man my father had referred to . . . and all like him. They came from a previous generation and a previous century because the leap I was trying to make here required him to jump his thinking forward in the most luminary of ways.

Perhaps it was the assistant who cut Planque a sideways glance of amusement that got my ire up. I could feel the very beast that my father had warned against waking up inside. 'You are aiming to achieve a masculine fragrance, am I right?'

They both nodded. Clearly neither had overlooked the fact that I was their employer's new wife and they had to indulge me.

'And you think men want to smell as though they've just staggered out of the woods, having wrestled with a bear for hours?'

Monsieur Planque blinked rapidly. 'I'm not sure I understand what you mean, Madame.' His tone had eased into polite now. Soon he might even hit charming.

'How can I make this easier for you to grasp, gentlemen? A man uses scented products to add to his grooming, yes, but essentially he does so to appear attractive to others, especially women. I can assure you that in order to achieve resonance with women, you need to lift your fragrance with some scents that will round out that almost boar-like aroma that you've achieved.'

Planque looked as though I'd slapped him. 'Madame! Surely you don't mean to —'

'But I do. Perhaps you forget that I am the reigning figurehead of both families now while our men are away fighting a war, Monsieur Planque.' The unspoken accusation that he wasn't there at the Front with them was nonetheless felt. I saw him flinch beneath its sting and although I felt ashamed, I couldn't stop now. 'If you are aiming for that horsey, fresh-from-the-barn smell, then it needs to be balanced so that a woman doesn't simply get the impression of a sweaty rider who has fallen and rolled in the loam or perhaps even a cow pat. Do you understand my direction?' I didn't wait for his answer, especially as Planque set off with another series of astonished blinks. 'Now, I love a scent that brings to mind the picture of a stable: a handsome, powerful man in his long boots and all-weather coat, the creak of leather, hay, rider and horse gently perspiring from an early morning gallop through the mist. Yes, I want it underpinned with the tobacco flower's absolute. And of course I can smell quite rightly your addition of musk amber, white birch, juniper, oakmoss, patchouli, the woodiest of lavender, but give me a hint of this man's humour, his romantic side, Monsieur Planque. Give me some bergamot, coumarin, the soft promise of rose . . .' I gestured behind me in soft exasperation. 'A shadowing of jasmine will make me helplessly think of a starlit night and its promise in that man's arms.'

Both men gasped and I felt myself blush.

'Forgive me.' I cleared my throat but a fresh wave of indignation came into that silence. 'The point is,' I said, desperately hoping I could make one, 'the point is that blending the more masculine aromas, especially the civet and musk I can smell, with a softening of the feminine does make the perfume more instantly attractive to the very women you're hoping to impress. She smells the primeval, the hunter, but she knows he will not hurt her,' I finished, hoping my storytelling was working.

Mercifully, Monsieur Planque nodded and I hoped I wasn't imagining the brief eruption of respect I noted in his expression. 'How about some olibanum?' he said.

'Perfect, of course. It remains woody but strikes a citrus chord so that freshness will ride through the smokier flavours, and if you do decide to use the fresher bergamot, then the olibanum will modify it. It will of course enter the realm of the exotic with the addition of olibanum resin.'

'Because it echoes frankincense,' his colleague offered hopefully, trying to rescue us from the brink we'd been leaning over.

'Indeed. And I for one can't wait to smell that fragrance. May I offer some further feminine intuition?'

They nodded helplessly.

'Perhaps a greener smell with some water hints might also work?' I breezed, hoping my fresh enthusiasm felt like a blast of orange or lemon into sandalwood. And my new mood worked. Suddenly we were back on the level footing of gushing new bride and the older, indulgent male.

'Well, thank you, Madame,' Planque said, infinitely more sincere in his tone than when I'd arrived. 'You have given me something to think on.'

'Any time, sir.' I left it at that, although words backed up behind my closed mouth. I was finally taking some of my father's well-intended advice. *Say less, listen more* was a favourite adage of his. I looked at my watch. 'Good afternoon, gentlemen. Thank you for your time. I suppose I should be ensuring all our workers get to their midday meal,' I said, hoping the reference to more womanly work would appease. 'I will look forward to smelling your finished perfume, Monsieur Planque.'

They both bowed and Planque's assistant did another polite click of his heels for my benefit. I hoped I'd climbed back out of the pit I'd dug for myself. Perhaps I would take Aimery's advice and stay away from his laboratory. I refused, however, to stay away from ours, not now that I'd made a decision to dream up my new perfume. I would defy Henri, and yes, I would even defy my father. Nothing was going to stop me using the envied, inherent skill I possessed. I was going to be a perfumer at any cost.

8

23 DECEMBER 1914

Months had come and gone, the weather had turned on its wintry chill and the fields would now lie dormant until next spring. The only aspect of our lives that was not quieting were the guns and bombs of the Front. News came sporadically but letters were censored; I think Felix had given up writing because he hated all the regulation and Henri was not one for putting pen to paper unless there was something vital to pass on. I suspected that both of my brothers had made a pact not to frighten their sister with tales of the war.

Aimery had never responded to my letter about Sébastien. I wondered if he had anything to hide, but I couldn't know any more until I saw him as he was clearly ignoring the query.

There was a knock at the salon door and Jeanne peeped in. I threw a glance across one shoulder and noted she looked unsettled but I didn't dwell on it.

'Yes, Jeanne?' I said, turning back, fully distracted.

I had been busy all morning arranging a swag of holly and herbs over the mantelpiece in a sudden flurry of activity to achieve some sense of the festive season. It had taken me hours of wrestling with the various leaves as well as some hellebores – or winter roses, as we called them – affixing them to the string.

'Do you think it's too much?' I wondered to her, as I stood back to regard my handiwork, gloved hands on hips, staring mainly at the holly. Normally, I loved the architecture of its prickly leaves and the sensual darkness of their waxy, green texture, but the scarlet berries, so jolly, reminded me now of drops of blood – as though suggestive of Grasse's men and their lives being squandered.

I had intertwined rosemary – symbolic of memory and remembering our men – which we protected in pots in a small greenhouse through the winter. Its resinous, slightly astringent smell was being heated by the fire and I could smell its perfume on my fingers, together with the aromatic clover-type scent of dried thyme that I strung into the wreath. I'd added some tarragon as well because it symbolised strength and no good French household cooked without its anise flavouring. Right now I was tasting a spicy licorice that I knew was coming from those freshly dried leaves, which were warming up in this room. It all served to comfort me when I was most missing my brothers.

'Oh, no, Madame. That looks magnificent. It brightens the room significantly,' she admitted.

'I have a length spare. Perhaps the staff might like a similar swag in the parlour?'

'I know they would appreciate that. It would help lift the gloom.'

I peeled off my gloves. 'You wanted me?'

'Senorita Olivares is here to see you.'

'Graciela?' I could have reeled off six dozen names I'd have guessed more likely my visitor might be. She nodded once. Now I understood her pensive manner. 'Did she say why?'

'She said she would like to pay her respects.'

'I see,' I said hesitantly, wondering immediately about Aimery, whether this constituted mentioning her name and how angry he would be if he knew I was meeting her. This wasn't my choice, though. 'Well, she's certainly early but it would be churlish of me to do anything but welcome her in. Will you send up some coffee and perhaps some petits fours, please? I presume it's just her?'

'Yes.'

'All right,' I breathed out, relieved. 'Please show her in.'

Jeanne left and I hurriedly pulled off my apron, aware of my simple sage-green skirt and lacy cream shirt. I wore no jewellery, save my wedding band, as I hadn't expected any visitors today. I'd counted myself safe in the knowledge that there would likely be a steady stream of local wellwishers who would call by all through tomorrow, Christmas Eve, right up until we all walked up the hill to the cathedral for midnight mass. It would be a lonely affair this year but at least we could all pray for the souls of Grasse together. But Graciela! How awkward this was going to be.

Again the knock at the door and I took a deep breath, nervously smoothing my skirt and straightening the buckle at my waist. 'Come,' I said, aiming for a breezy tone.

Jeanne opened the door and beside her stood the petite yet fiery elegance of Graciela Olivares. I probably stood a head taller than she and yet she appeared unfazed by my willowy presence. And why wouldn't she? By comparison I stood dressed in neutral colours like a church mouse while Graciela was graced loudly in crimson theatrically matched with black accessories of boots, gloves, fur collar and muff. Her hat was fur-rimmed and her lips were painted to match the silk of her garments. She was dazzlingly colourful, heedless of the unspoken sobriety of war that had sent most of us scurrying for darker, sombre colours to wear.

'Mademoiselle Olivares,' I gushed with as much welcome as I could infuse into those two words as she crossed the threshold.

She eyed me carefully and we both understood our smiles were affected, not ones of genuine friendship. We went through the motion of kissing each other's cheeks without actually touching.

'This is a surprise,' I admitted, wondering if she'd ever been inside the De Lasset villa before.

'I wanted to pay my respects, Madame De Lasset,' she repeated for my benefit in her husky tone. 'It is usual for me to do this during the festive period, although it is unusual not to be paying my respects to Monsieur De Lasset.' Ah, so she had visited previously. Her Spanish-inflected French meant that her words came in a storm of syllables, which my mind had to first untangle to understand.

She blinked while my brain caught up. I finally smiled brightly.

'Of course, and it is most generous that you've come. Thank you, Jeanne. Can I offer you some coffee?'

'You may. I like a sip of port wine with my coffee, Madame.'

I felt a ripple of admiration for her daring. She clearly didn't care for convention or what others might think of her taking liquor with her coffee like a man. I glanced casually at Jeanne, as though I wasn't in the least disarmed by such a request, to fetch the nip of port and she curtsied.

'Here, shall we sit near the fire?' I gestured to an armchair.

She began to pull off her hat and gloves. Perhaps she hadn't agreed to do so in the entrance hall because she was unsure of what her welcome might be. I watched her, fascinated to see my husband's former lover up this close. Dark, thick but perfectly groomed eyebrows crescented above almond-shaped eyes the colour of licorice that were framed by the blackest of lashes and then dramatically heightened by the use of kohl. They flanked the top of a long, straight nose that ended in a pouting mouth of full lips. Her rich, near-black hair was piled up, almost carelessly behind her head but lighter, chocolate-coloured wisps escaped and she didn't feel the need to tuck them back. It gave her a wanton, sensual look I envied.

Her gaze cut sharply to mine and I felt like a rabbit caught, squirming in a metal trap. Those dark pools for eyes glittered at me with equal fascination. 'Have I made you feel awkward?' she asked, her candour unnerving.

I decided only truth would do. 'Yes, as a matter of fact.' I cleared my throat softly. 'You're a day early for visiting,' I added disingenuously.

She smiled with soft cunning and her scarlet-painted lips stretched easily to give me a glimpse of small, even teeth. She had a beauty mark, to the right of her top lip. I wondered if Aimery found it attractive. She jangled as she spoke too, with jewellery at her wrists, neck, earlobes, gold gleaming against skin the colour of nutmeg. I found her endlessly watchable.

'Visiting hours?' She gave a smoky laugh. 'Forgive me. I do so hate to be predictable,' she admitted. 'So I miss out on seeing your yule log in its glory,' she said, casually glancing to the hearth where this year's big log, which would burn until the new year arrived, sat in readiness for tomorrow's lighting. I wasn't going to follow that ceremony this year but Madame Mouflard and I decided the German hostility had already taken too much from us. It would not deny us our domestic rituals.

Nevertheless, Graciela's wry comment struck me as slightly heartless, given that the welcoming of this new year might carry some special hopes of all who dwelt in this household.

'Never mind,' I said, matching her tone and ignoring her jest, 'we have some Three Kings Cake to share.'

She waved a hand carelessly.

'Oh, no, but you must, or it brings bad luck to the household,' I lied, 'and you wouldn't want that, surely?'

'Aren't you cutting that early? Surely it's a treat for Epiphany?'

I shrugged. 'Nothing in these days of war is unusual. I felt we needed some early cheer.'

Graciela smiled as though impressed that I would flout the age-old traditions.

Jeanne's timing was impeccable, arriving at that moment to prevent my guest having to answer.

'Ah, here we are,' I said as Jeanne laid down the tray between us.

'May I, Madame?' Jeanne asked.

I nodded as Jeanne began to pour out two cups of the brew I favoured.

Graciela gave a smirk, as though impressed. 'That's a rich roast, Madame De Lasset.'

'I like my coffee with deep chocolate flavours,' I remarked.

'Your port, Madame,' Jeanne murmured as she set down the tiny crystal glass. 'It's a tawny *porto*,' she added softly.

Plates of miniature meringues decorated with shards of almonds and petite sponge cakes iced with fondant were placed silently either side of our coffee cups. A small fork accompanied the food.

She picked up the glass and swirled the berry-coloured liquid. 'My mother was Portuguese,' she said, by way of explanation, I suppose. She sipped and nodded. I presumed it was acceptable. Our guest hadn't acknowledged my maid, barely giving her eye contact, and returned her attention to me as I expressed my thanks to Jeanne, surprised by the snub. Perhaps she thought Jeanne might be sharing secrets. The door closed softly and we smiled at each other over the 22-carat-gold-painted rims of the Delacroix Limoges porcelain that I'd had brought up from my family's home.

'What charming little cups these are, painted so festively with holly and berries,' she remarked.

'They're my mother's,' I admitted. 'I have had a soft spot for them since childhood because their Christmas theme meant I only glimpsed them a couple of days of each year, and yet they're so exquisite. I also thought Limoges to be more loyal than using the De Lasset Meissen porcelain.'

She chuckled in that throaty way of hers. 'Patriotic to a fault.'

I could feel her judgement simmering behind her gentle barb. She considered me sugar-sweet conventional.

'Do you blame me, with two brothers and a husband at the Front?'

'I don't blame you at all,' she said, watching me carefully.

'Don't you?'

How had we arrived at this point so fast? What was I thinking in baiting her so blatantly? I couldn't take the words back. I couldn't pretend I had meant something else by them; I wasn't that adept at hiding my feelings. I watched with escalating tension in my chest as she slowly returned the Limoges cup, with its gilded edges and exquisite rendition of barbed holly that seemed to suit her, into the tiny depression of its saucer. I thought she might sit back, knit her fingers together, but she surprised me by curling her delicate fingers around the stem of the crystal and raising the small glass with its angled sides to best bring out the aroma of port. All of this was done in silence and I held that silence as effectively as I held my breath, waiting for her response. Her lips dipped again into the dark amber syrup and she sat back, closing her eyes momentarily.

'Nothing matches the wine of the Douro Valley,' she murmured in a sighing satisfaction at the taste, and I could imagine the memories whirring through her mind of her mother. Few knew better than I the images that taste could provoke. I waited, unsure of whether to make that attempt to correct myself, or to see what my honesty brought out.

Her eyelids snapped open and I was impaled by the dark gaze that was tinged with amusement.

'I appreciate your bluntness, Madame.'

'Do you?'

I forced myself not to swallow, desperate though I was to push back my nervousness.

She nodded, looking as relaxed as I was sure I must appear hesitant. 'I think this Grasse society spends too much time talking around subjects rather than discussing them directly.'

'Is that what we're doing?' I wasn't sure how to proceed here. I was leaping from question to question rather than providing answers.

She grinned lazily and her teeth gleamed momentarily as she saw right through me. 'Relax, Fleurette; enjoy your coffee before it cools.' She now used my first name as though we were long-time friends. 'I have no fight with you.'

I hated myself for being pathetic enough to feel the river of relief that flowed through my body. Fortunately, I held on to my haughty tone. If I didn't impose my status, she would trample over me, I was sure of it. 'Indeed, you should not. I can't imagine how I am to blame for anything in your life. I barely know you, Graciela,' I countered, using her name as easily as she had used mine.

She nodded sombrely. 'This is true, for if you did know me, you would pronounce my name in the Castilian way of my birth. It is *Grathiela*,' she enunciated. 'I think you barely know your husband, either . . . but I know him very well.'

I gave myself away by licking my lips; Felix had warned me off this habit but I clearly hadn't conquered it yet. 'What would you have me say to such a claim? That I'm aware you were lovers?'

'Not were, Fleurette,' she corrected, eyeing me with a dangerous glint.

'I see. Given that he left on our wedding night, I can't imagine it can be anything but past tense.'

'Have you heard from Aimery?' Even the way she spoke his name was filled with sensuality, putting emphasis on the final consonant, rolling that sound in her throat as though tasting it.

'I have, of course,' I replied, sounding vaguely offended by such a question.

'And what has he told you?'

I frowned. 'Really, Graciela,' I said, doing my best impression of the way she wanted her name spoken. 'That's a little intimate.'

'Is it? Here,' she said, dipping into the small fabric bag that had hung off her wrist on arrival and now sat in her lap. She withdrew an envelope. I recognised it immediately as Aimery's stationery.

'I don't think —'

'No, it's not appropriate, but I think it's important. Please, glance through. You have my permission.'

I didn't want to read it; it felt dangerous to take the envelope that was surely meant to bring harm.

'A wife should know these things,' she pressed.

These things?

I reminded myself that if Aimery had only married his Spanish lover, all would be well in his life and mine. Perhaps this meeting could release me from my wifely duties. Maybe this was the start of a process of escape for me? I slipped the letter from the envelope and was aware on the rim of my consciousness that Graciela reached for her port again. She was sipping with studied pleasure as she watched me open the pages. It was dated recently; I read only the opening paragraphs before I folded the pages up and returned them to the envelope.

'My dear, you are blushing,' she observed.

'I'm embarrassed for you, actually, for sharing that with me.' It was a tart reply and she rightfully grinned at the sourness in it.

'You're not jealous, surely?'

I shook my head. 'Bitter, perhaps, because I must contain the anger at being humiliated. Graciela, you do know I didn't want to marry him, don't you?'

'I do, but I hated that you did all the same. Can you not tell even from the few lines you read how he feels about me?'

'How could I fail to? I didn't know Aimery could be so . . . so . . . '

'Lascivious?'

I shrugged. 'Affectionate.'

She tipped back her head and laughed. 'Affectionate? You're so proper but I do like you, Fleurette. You're innocent. I know that your marriage was arranged. I just wish you'd had more spine.'

I turned on her now, flinging down the letter that had opened with lewd and carnal suggestions but with an affectionately witty tone I'd never heard from him in all the years I'd known Aimery. 'I would give anything not to be married to him. But I was cornered by both families and a long history of duty to the family name.'

'You're pathetic!'

'And you're despicable.'

'Why? Because I am not afraid of my sensuality?'

'No, because you mock me for being polite, welcoming. You're openly my husband's lover and I should treat you with the same hostility you treated Jeanne just now and still I accord you respect. You are no match for my name. You have no status in Grasse other than as Aimery De Lasset's plaything. You may be wealthy but you should not sneer at me, Graciela,' I warned.

She clapped her hands, delighted. 'That's more like it, Fleurette, spitting and snarling like the little cat you are. This is how you should have been. You should not have allowed the men around you to bully you into marrying a man you have no feelings for.'

'I wish he'd married you!'

'So do I! Do you know why?'

I shook my head.

'Because I love him. No, I worship him. I detest how weak he makes me feel and yet I can't breathe without him in my life.'

I swallowed hard. I'd never heard anyone speak so passionately about another. And I wished I could see what she saw in the man.

'I become animalistic in Aimery's presence.'

I blinked with shame for her revelation but she laughed again at me.

'You see, I will debase myself for him . . . even before his chaste wife. Did he hurt you?'

I stammered, making no sense.

'When he took you the first time, did he injure you? Aimery has unpredictable moods. You should beware of that. He can be rough, like a lion taking what he believes is his. No man can stir the primitive in me as Aimery does. I have not been with any other man since I met him. I will never love any other from now on.'

'I hate him,' I said, my voice small and overawed by her raw admission. 'He did not bed me.'

That shocked her, her amusement quelled. She stared at me as though searching for guile. 'Why not? You are young, magnificent.'

I gave a rueful smirk. 'The bells of war tolled to save me.'

'So you are still a virgin?'

I opened my mouth, dumbfounded. It was embarrassing to admit and yet I couldn't deny it.

'No need to answer,' she said, waving a hand at me. 'How interesting.'

'Happy?' I snapped, needing to bite back somehow.

She shrugged. 'Yes. How about you? I suspect you are relieved, no?' She gave a disarmingly soft smile and it changed her persona to friendly . . . even to the point of making me feel conspiratorial.

'I would be lying if I denied it.'

Now Graciela laughed genuinely. 'Oh, Fleurette. Are we not a pitiful couple? You are married to the man I love and you hate him. I feel sorry for both of us.'

'Do you hate me?'

'No, I never did. I pity you. He is not an easy man.'

'And you can still love him?'

'I told you. I have no free will in this. I am guessing you have never been in love?'

I shook my head, feeling even more pathetic.

'When you do, you'll understand how it consumes you. It's like a fire burning out of control. Each time you think you have it contained, a new spark erupts to burn brightly and reignite all the feelings you thought you had corralled.'

I gave her a nod of approval. 'I wish I knew that sort of love. I don't think I ever will.'

'It shouldn't be, but just sometimes it can be harmful.'

'Like yours?'

'Yes. We suffer for our bond. He loves me but he is not allowed to do so properly, openly. I will only ever be his mistress, never allowed to declare how I feel publicly. When he married you, my world collapsed. I wished you to be barren so he was also touched by the same pain.'

I glanced up, surprised how hurtful her words were.

'Forgive me. How else could I strike back? I knew he married you simply for an heir. I knew he wanted the pedigree that you offered. He could not have half-Spanish children.' She sneered. 'My breeding is not ideal for him. Yours is impeccable.'

I nodded sadly. 'And we all end up miserable,' I finished.

'Perhaps one day you will experience the love I describe but with someone your heart beats faster for.'

'How can that occur?'

'By permitting me to remain as Aimery's mistress.'

It was so direct, it took my breath away.

She held up a finger. 'Before you leap to an answer, just remember, I can save you a lot of anguish.'

I frowned. 'And by that you mean?'

'Aimery has his particular tastes when it comes to sex.'

My attempt to go toe to toe with her candour failed. I blushed at her frank manner.

'I fulfil all of his needs. Can you?'

I breathed out silently to steady myself. 'I don't even want to.'

'Precisely. Whereas I do, and a man must have his . . . well, shall we say, release?'

Despite hoping I could avoid it, I was clearing my throat with embarrassment before I knew it.

She smiled. 'I apologise for being forthright. My artlessness is sometimes disarming.'

I liked her use of language, and not using her native tongue only impressed me deeper. Graciela was not only strikingly attractive but she had intelligence and wit to match. I could see how any man could fall in love with her but I wondered about Aimery; I wanted to understand the subject he warned me off.

'No, I appreciate your honesty,' I replied as she waited. 'Though it's uncomfortable at times.'

She laughed. 'I have been told this time and again.'

'By Aimery?'

'Aimery, yes, especially . . . others too, over the course of my life. It's why I have no real friends. I don't enjoy the thrust and parry of social etiquette. I prefer to speak plainly, act transparently.'

I reached for my cup again, to take the final sip or two. 'And you don't think sometimes it's important to protect another's feelings by treading more carefully?'

She waved a hand airily. 'The problem is I'm not good at it. At least no one will die wondering what I meant.'

This struck me as witty and she timed her remark as I swallowed. I coughed my amusement back at her.

'Perhaps we could be friends?' she wondered, laughing with me.

'And share Aimery?'

She nodded and I saw her guard drop – there was a held breath of hope in her chest.

'He's all yours,' I said and didn't mean to sound disparaging. 'I had no choice in the marriage, as I explained. I will not stand in the way of your relationship so long as it does not publicly humiliate me or my family. You will have to remain pointedly discreet. It is the only way.'

She smiled and I could almost visualise her sincerity reaching across to shake my hand over a deal. There was no guile here.

'I wish I understood what you see in the man,' I finished.

She lifted a shoulder. 'I have learned not to analyse love. This is not something that can be controlled. One can fight it, one can restrain from confronting it, one can avoid it perhaps by leading a solitary existence, but when that one person crosses your path, one cannot ignore the feelings. It's like a dormant and separate animal that lives within us, Fleurette . . . it is primitive, carnal, never satisfied; it always wants more.'

'Sounds dangerous,' I quipped, imagining a snarling beast.

'Love is dangerous. It's a drug as addictive as opium and you won't know what I mean until love snags you in its maw. I don't know what it is between Aimery and me because love is invisible. I met him six years ago; at twenty-three it was an eligible age for marriage but I convinced myself his reluctance was that I was new, different. And then I came to the understanding that I was not considered good enough for marriage but that enlightenment came too late . . . by then he had become my drug and I had become his. We are dependent on each other. I've not had the family affection you've experienced in your life . . . in fact, I have run away from Barcelona to escape family and problems I won't go into. Aimery is all I need and I know I provide what he needs, not just physically but I think I have filled a particular emotional need in him too. We talk, he makes me laugh.' I couldn't imagine it as she said this. 'We make love and pretend we're married. In my arms he feels safe, can be himself. And if the only way I can enjoy him is as a mistress, then so be it.'

I knew I liked her even more for showing me her vulnerability and I felt genuine sympathy that she admitted to few friends. Her revelation even gave me a grudging empathy for Aimery. It was reassuring to learn that he could feel a tenderness and fondness for someone.

'Graciela, we are friends from here on and Aimery will never hear from me that we had this conversation. I will also never ask him about you because I am no longer curious – I have no reason to be because you've been so honest. I'm sorry you can't have more but you know how I feel, or rather what I don't feel, and so you never need fear my presence. We are man and wife out of necessity, you could say – nothing more.'

She stood, picking up hat and gloves. She held out a hand. 'I hope you will find love one day soon, Fleurette. I think you deserve it.'

My soft snort conveyed how imprisoned I felt, even though I responded politely. 'Thank you.'

'Oh, look,' she said, bending down to stare at the plate that contained her slice of Three Kings Cake, decorated with the candied fruits of Provence. 'I believe I have the bean,' she said, pointing with a manicured finger at the untouched cake. 'In Spain we call this *rosca de reyes*,' and I enjoyed hearing her native tongue. 'In Catalonia it is known simply as *tortell*. We use a figurine of the holy child as the trinket.'

I smiled. 'You have the bean – that makes you royalty for the day.'

'You've made me feel like a queen today, Fleurette, thank you. Who knows, maybe Père Noël will bring love to you this Christmas?' She arched an eyebrow to make us both laugh.

We kissed farewell as new friends, much to Jeanne's surprise as she opened the door to Mademoiselle Olivares. Curiously, though, as I watched her carriage leave, I felt lonelier than I thought possible. Even Aimery was taken from me now – I'd handed him over, effectively – and even though I was relieved that this was the case, I had now isolated myself completely, and married life was stretching before me as an unhappy, soulless existence.

9

29 DECEMBER 1914

Christmas had come and gone quietly. We had attempted our *gros souper* with as much cheer as we could and, as a special treat, I insisted we lay our table in the grand dining room and all the servants were to cook and then break bread together. It was here that Jeanne and I had modestly decorated a small Christmas tree. We lit candles, in keeping with the festival and for the light we knew our men probably ate by most of the time in the trenches. I sat in Aimery's place as host and the women and few older men around the table, though overawed to be dining in this room, made a good fist of gentle celebration, particularly toasting our loved ones away fighting for France.

The kitchen staff presented a small but delicious supper with the seven courses for the seven sorrows of Mary. The servings were tiny but more than enough by the end. I urged them to enjoy the cod and the snails in garlic butter. Upon my enquiry I was assured by Madame Mouflard that the snails were shelled using a new carpenter's nail as a reminder of the crucifixion. We had vegetables and salads with the finest *courge violon* I had ever tasted. Pierre shrugged modestly when the staff accused him of growing the best pumpkin in the district for this festive tart. We all clapped when he brought out three small bowls of wheat that had been sown on the fourth day of December for Saint Barbe; these he had dutifully kept moist to germinate and grow in time for our big supper on Christmas Eve so he could place them on the three pristine napkins. As we applauded I think we all felt relief that Pierre's three bowls, representing the holy trinity, meant we would now have a good harvest for next year. More rose and jasmine and violets . . . the cycle of life made me feel anchored and safe in that moment.

I had been brought back to the present with the smell of the *fougassette* scented with orange blossom. Having been taught in childhood that the seven holes of the flattish bread represented the seven orifices of the face of the holy child, I was careful when given the task by Madame Mouflard to tear the bread apart. I knew that to cut it would bring disaster to us all.

Jeanne had arranged a huge platter of nougat, chocolates twisted in wrappers and some fat prunes and she amused me by explaining that each of the dried fruits represented the colours of the religious orders. We had never done this in our household and I wondered if she had helped with preparations in Graciela's home, which presented dried figs for the Franciscans, raisins for the Augustinians, almonds for the Dominicans and hazelnuts for the Carmelites. We'd all tossed our clementine peels into a bowl because Madame Mouflard intended it as potpourri for the holy crèche in our hall that Pierre had dutifully assembled.

Some hot waffles and fried beignets completed our sweet courses and with hot, spiced wine we toasted the single empty place left deliberately at the other end of the table. I was never quite sure whether our tradition in France was for an extra place for any welcome visitor or whether it harked back to ancient Roman times to honour one's ancestors. I did, however, feel certain that our toast this year was every inch dedicated to our absent loved ones and that empty seat represented all of those from Grasse who were not in town to share their family's suppers.

We'd then headed off to spend hours at the church praying for our men before returning to light the yule log and know that solstice had passed.

I had arrived at the strangely twisted logic that not hearing from either of my brothers meant they were safe. Most would think the opposite but, if I were honest, I didn't look forward to the post arriving and hearing one had been wounded. I dreaded even more the sign of any official telegram, which would mean so much worse. Curious though it was, my conclusion was to feel blessed by the silence . . . a sort of status quo, although I had heard from Aimery via two letters. Not once over the course of those had he enquired after my state of mind. I forgave him; I suppose this was because I didn't love him so his lack of care mattered little to me. If it had been Felix not asking after me, I know I would have felt deep injury.

So here I sat, writing a stilted letter to Aimery, desperately trying to convey a sense of affection I didn't feel. For inspiration I turned to his first letter, dated mid-August, and read through it again, feeling slightly soured from the opening line. I heard it only as condescending in my mind as I couldn't lose the memory of the night he left, when he made it clear our marriage was strategic. I had no right to feel offended – and didn't – but I did feel imprisoned.

> *Fleurette, my dear,*
>
> *At last I find a moment to pen a few words to you.*
> *Of course you will be wondering how I am after all this time and the answer is that I am very well and in high spirits.*
> *So much has happened these past few weeks. I must not bore you dreadfully with our daily life for much of it is tedious and no wife needs to share the mundane world of men.*

I had to close my eyes with irritation and take an audible breath. I believe my father, from a previous generation of chauvinists, so loyal to France, was more welcoming to a woman's point of view than Aimery likely could ever be.

> *I suspect you keep abreast of news through the newspaper and no doubt all the womenfolk in Grasse will have been heartened to read how our glorious regiments from the south were fanfared from their home towns with bands playing, the townsfolk cheering and the children waving flags.*
>
> *Sadly our men were required to almost slink out of Grasse with none of that festivity but everybody rallied to the barracks quickly and I don't think there was a shirker amongst the recruits. The boys look marvellous in their dark-blue attire and everyone is rightly proud of our Chasseur heritage. The colonel gave us a splendid and rousing speech before we embarked on our first short journey towards the frontier. I'm happy to say I led the first rousing chorus of 'La Marseillaise' and to sing our anthem made us all feel united and fearless. The Allebosche will rue the day they decided once again to invade our sacred land.*

Allebosche. I had not heard this term for the German invaders but it seemed inevitable that nicknames for the enemy would emerge. I wondered what the Germans called us French, but here again my mind was wandering. I continued reading, searching for the right tone of response that a dutiful wife should aim for.

> *As soon as Italy showed that they were not siding with our enemy we were moved north. Perhaps you cannot imagine how many trains it takes to move our battalion, but again*

*I risk boring you. As I am amongst the officers, we have
some comfort but the poor old Chasseurs are mostly
consigned to wagons that are supposed to transport horses.
But the enthusiasm is not diminished for all that and the
lads continue to sing and play cards.*

*I cannot believe it took us two days of constant travel to
reach the Front. It is an enormous boost to morale to note the
columns of red trousers at every platform and every station.
Truly, France is sending her finest to beat our hated foe.*

*Women and old men, young lads cheer and clap and
offer us all sorts of local delicacies. We shall not want
for fine food, I am sure. An old lady offered me a roasted
chicken for my journey. As our train pulled out on its slow
shuffle north we left joyous people behind wishing us well
and crying out, 'To Berlin!' Our destination reached, we
formed ranks and began our long march.*

I noted he didn't tell me where that destination happened to be, and
presumed this was part of the censoring process.

*We have had rain and are thus grateful for our capes, which
I am certain protect us better than the greatcoats of the
pantalon rouges. I have a room in a deserted house that I
share with one of my brother officers, older than I, called
Louis from the Isere. He is a most amiable chap and I feel
sure we shall become close friends. He has intimated that
if I make my mark in the coming battle, then promotion is
always possible in time of war.*

*I imagine people will be wondering, especially yourself,
but there is no leave being granted even in the distant future.
I have not the faintest idea of when I shall see you again but
I trust you will manage the households in our absence.*

*Soon we will be going into action, and I am convinced
of our success. I may even whistle 'Au claire de la lune' as
I lead my men triumphantly forward.*
Ever yours,
Aimery

I should have felt proud. I should have felt uplifted. But my sentiment was essentially sorrow because I could tell that Aimery was
actually enjoying the whole theatre of war. He clearly felt invincible
while I suspected he was overplaying how the rest of the soldiers,
who would bear the brunt of suffering, might be faring. I wondered
how many men might fit into an eight-horse wagon and inexorably
began to imagine the smell of such a wagon: what was left behind
by its former user and how it now smelled with perhaps a couple
score of men crushed into it, with their food and cigarettes adding
an arresting medley of odours.

To add to my distraction, while I had been reading Aimery's
prose my gaze had kept helplessly flicking to the violet ink scrawled
on the envelope of his brother's note that I kept in my writing
bureau. Only I had the key; the letter still felt explosive and yet I
was no closer to discovering the truth than I had been the first time
I read it.

For the time being I experienced only curiosity rather than
fear; now that Aimery had confirmed no leave was being granted I
didn't have to concern myself about imminent wifely duties in the
bedroom. I did need to find out, though – and soon – what Sébastien
was hiding. I returned to my letter and tried to make the daily routines in Grasse come alive for Aimery through my writing. I figured
even the dullest duties would surely lift his spirits, as I had learned
from his most recent letter that he was dug into the mud of winter's
early weeks in a trench.

I unfolded that second letter – surely something in here would help me to construct a bright note back to lift spirits and let him know that we had him in our thoughts – but I was reminded that this was a less spirited note from him. The enemy had been engaged by now and even Aimery's grandiose manner had been dampened by the realities of war. Harsh though it seemed, I was relieved that he'd been reduced to a more realistic vision of what he and his fellow soldiers were up against. I hoped it would prompt caution.

> *Fleurette, my dear,*
>
> *I am as optimistic as one could hope for under the circumstances and your welcome letter helped to cheer. It arrived impressively fast and I must congratulate our French postal system, which is obviously functioning remarkably well on its war footing.*
>
> *Your questions regarding the business will have to wait and I am cautioning you now to be wary of those who may offer advice. This war will soon be over and I shall be home to make all decisions.*

My stomach dipped to read that line again.

> *Are you keeping up with the news? They are making appalling references about our 15th Corps. The fiends who write such lies should be here at the Front to witness our valiant soldiers as they fall in the line of duty.*
>
> *Our own battalion underwent their baptism in this war, storming the Boche, who fled before us.*

I noted the new nickname for the enemy.

> *I led my boys forward along a valley towards our objective. I know all in Grasse would have been as proud*

*as I was to watch how they did not flinch in the face of such
ferocious enemy gunfire. They would follow me into hell,
I am sure of it, certainly determined to follow me wherever
I go here at the Front, and I don't want you to fret on my
safety – it is obvious to all that I lead a charmed existence.*

I had to put the letter down. Aimery's self-belief, however, could
only be admired and I reminded myself that if this alone kept him
brave for his men and free from injury, then I should be grateful,
rather than contemptuous.

*The Boche's artillery found our positions after an initial
valiant thrust and our cowardly enemy hides in its trenches,
behind its guns, and cut us down terribly. Do you recall my
fellow officer Louis? I am saddened but proud to say that
he is one of the fearless who found glory on the field of
honour.*

*Myself, I have a slight wound to my shoulder but I have
waived a visit to the hospital tent. It will heal. My servant
makes a fuss and busies himself to ensure my comfort,
but I am more concerned with us getting our trenches dug
out nearby to the forest so we are less exposed and more
able to play the Boche at his own game. Our position does
mean we do not want for firewood and can keep warm
during these winter months as the early hours have become
somewhat chilly.*

I shook my head. Was his understatement deliberate or was he unaware of just how unbearably irritating his restraint was sounding?
It was as though his deliberate attempt to make the suffering seem
trivial would somehow enhance his munificence.

The English shall be arriving soon, to be alongside us as we fervently take back what has been stolen!

My dear Fleurette, I urge you not to believe all that you read in the newspaper. Be assured that your heroic boys hold the line. Their guns may be all powerful but the Boche is no match for a Chasseur.

Ever yours,
Aimery

I was well aware that I was rapidly losing interest in responding today; lacking in inspiration for the right words, my treacherous thoughts were already drifting away from my husband. The jasmine harvest had been successful; the women of the town in particular had found new depths of strength and determination to fill the role their men had previously. I had supervised the production of what might arguably be considered near to our best yield of jasmine absolute, if not the best. I wouldn't boast; it would not be seemly to do so in the absence of the men to make them feel any less heartened. Nevertheless, I suspected Henri would be thrilled with my news because it was all about the extra francs into the coffers and I'd already written to him and Felix about the Delacroix production for 1915.

I stared at my pathetic attempt. I was past the initial salutation, my gush of admiration for the bravery and steadfastness of the Chasseurs. Perhaps I could plunge into telling him about how Monsieur Planque and I were on good terms, that the yield for De Lasset might well eclipse previous years – although I wasn't privy to those historical details – and that I was especially looking forward to keeping on top of the supervision of the violet and rose fields as they developed through late autumn. Soon the fields would sleep as winter spread its frosty chill across our landscape. But these exquisite spring flowers would be readying themselves for their explosion into colourful bloom as the thaw arrived: first the violets at the end of April, then the roses would come in.

I could conjure the scent of both in my imagination by just picturing them. I knew the exact fragrance on the wind of a field of our spring violets and I had just closed my eyes and lifted my chin to reach for the perfume of our roses when a knock sounded at my salon door.

My lids flicked open and I cleared my throat, picking up my ink pen again. 'Come,' I said, pretending to be busy at my letter writing.

One of the maids entered and curtsied, glancing at my bureau scattered with pages. 'I'm sorry to disturb you, Madame,' she began in a tremulous voice.

I know I was frowning, which I'm sure wasn't terribly reassuring. 'Where's Jeanne? Madame Mouflard?' She looked intimidated by my query. 'Oh, never mind, they're obviously running errands. What is it?' I welcomed the intrusion, to be truthful.

'I am Elise, Madame.'

I did recognise her now.

'M – Monsieur De Lasset is returned from the Front,' she stammered. 'People are very excited. He's been followed by some in the town up to the house. He looks exhausted.'

I dropped my pen in surprise. 'What? Why didn't you say earlier?' I admonished, leaping up as if stung. It was a stupid query; she'd hardly taken her time but the expression came by rote in my alarm. 'Quick! Help me out of this,' I commanded, tearing at my working clothes. Aimery home? Why wasn't he striding upstairs, calling orders? Elise had said he was exhausted. Perhaps he was too weary to move from the fireplace? He would surely want to see me looking less dreary than this, even though I preferred to move around in a simple navy day dress that was far more forgiving than the more delicate fabrics of my other garments and infinitely more comfortable. I suppose appearing prettily groomed was the least I could do for him. Appearances were everything in a household such as this one. My mind was scattering. Within a minute I had been hastily buttoned into a simple outfit of long mauve-grey skirt and short, plum-coloured bolero jacket over a fine lace high-necked blouse that was more cheerfully befitting of a wife greeting her husband back from war. I reached for the long strand of pearls that cinched with a diamante clasp just above my waist – a touching wedding gift from Henri.

'You look wonderful, Madame,' my companion breathed.

'Thank you, Elise. Forgive my abruptness but I'm rather shocked that he's back so soon.' A fresh, worrying notion occurred to me. 'Is he hurt?' I suddenly asked my helper, glancing at the mirror as I tucked away a stray curl of hair. I pinched my cheeks for good measure.

'He is, Madame.'

I swung around to fix her with a startled glare. 'How badly?'

'He breathes with difficulty. And his hand – it's bandaged. He's bleeding still.'

Ah, that would explain his reluctance to come and find me himself. 'Right,' I said, and hated myself for instantly feeling relief that he was presumably in no shape to demand his conjugal rights. His brother's unresolved warning, which just moments ago was no immediate threat, now loomed largely in my mind.

Sébastien's letter! I turned back and locked my bureau, tucking the key I had taken to wearing on a chain from my belt safely into deep pockets.

'All right, let's go. Where is Monsieur De Lasset?'

'The morning room, Madame Fleurette.'

In my urgency I all but ran past Elise and swept into the morning room, bursting through the double doors. 'Aimery!'

A stranger swung around from where he'd been standing by

the window looking out onto Grasse falling away down the hill-side.

My mouth opened, then closed, and I think opened again in consternation at the dark-haired, dark-eyed man who surely stood a head taller than my husband. How could anyone have confused the pair? It would be like comparing aromatic lavender to sweetly spiced orange blossom, they were so different. Aimery was light-haired, squarely built. This man was lean-hipped, tall, his thick hair looked to be forced against its inclinations into a neat wave across the top of his head from the parting I was sure would be lost by day's end. I must have appeared as a fish gasping to be back in water.

'Madame,' the man said, turning in obvious physical pain but finding a smile that cut through the shock to warm my heart.

'Who are you?' I murmured. 'I was told Monsieur De Lasset was home.'

'He is,' he said softly. 'Well, I suppose this isn't really home, although a lawyer might say it is.'

'Sébastien?'

He nodded.

I turned at the shuffling at the doors behind me. 'Elise, er . . . this is my husband's brother.' I returned my gaze to our guest. 'I'm sorry, it must have been like excited Chinese whispers up the hill. We were under the impression that Aimery had returned.'

He gave a nod of understanding. 'Yes, I should have been more specific. The whispers travelled faster than I could, I'm afraid.'

'You're most welcome here,' I said as magnanimously as I could so he didn't feel any more awkward than he already did. 'Let's organise some refreshment after your journeying. Can I offer you some coffee?'

'I don't suppose you have any tea, do you, Madame?' he wondered with enthusiasm.

I smiled. 'We're family. Please call me Fleurette. And I'm sure we can offer tea.' I glanced at Elise, who gave a slight nod that we had plenty. 'Personally, I like gunpowder tea,' I said. 'How about you, Sébastien?' I presumed he did not wish me to remain formal about how I addressed him.

'Black tea with milk would be quite simply extraordinary, Fleurette, as it's thin on the ground where I've come from,' he said. His French was just short of perfect. I detected the odd lilt that I couldn't place but it struck me as though his French was learned rather than owned.

I nodded at Elise, whispering for her to hurry. She curtsied, closed the doors and presumably scurried off to do my bidding. I hadn't moved and now felt ridiculous standing so rigidly at the door.

'Forgive me,' he began, taking the responsibility away from me for leading the conversation. He shrugged. 'I had no choice, though. I had to nominate somewhere to come. Look, do you mind if I sit, or I may just pass out?'

I finally gathered my wits and my manners. 'Oh, I am sorry.' I gestured to the sofa.

'For what? You are the most beautiful sight in a long time. I already feel healed.'

I surely blushed. 'Do you need help?' I wondered aloud, transfixed by the enormous bandaging around one hand.

Sébastien grinned. 'Just a seat and the tea is fine for now, thank you.' I noticed though that he grimaced as he limped to the sofa, using a walking stick to support himself. 'Please forgive the poor shape I present myself in.' He still didn't sit.

'I'm glad you came here.' I walked over and kissed both his cheeks, feeling the rasp of his scraggly beard. He smelled of soap and yet his uniform had an unpleasant hum; I was assaulted by smells of blood, earth, gunpowder and disinfectant. But haunting my taste, beneath all those less pleasant tangs, I smelled one lovely note. I focused on that. 'You smell of lavender.'

'Thank heavens. I thought I must smell as bad as I look, although I have bathed, I promise, but my uniform . . .'

'Please don't worry. I'm glad you're safe.'

'It's the . . . the antiseptic.' He gestured with his bandaged hand. 'The lavender oil is good for the skin burns we suffer. I meant to buy some fresh clothes, but . . .'

I clasped his unbandaged hand and gave him the best convivial smile I could. 'Family,' I said, to stop him worrying. 'We meet at last. Welcome . . . or should I say welcome back?'

While we had moved apart from each other I noted he didn't let my hand fall. 'I don't believe so. I have never been here other than in my mother's womb, I gather.'

We both smiled sadly at that. The letter hung between us, our linked hands the bridge I knew I must walk across shortly, but I needed to get the preliminaries out of the way.

'Have you heard from your mother?'

He lowered himself gingerly into the armchair, breathing hard. 'From her niece. My mother died soon after I left for France.'

'Oh, no,' I bleated, hoping to stop another apology escaping but too late. I would just have to sound annoyingly repetitive. 'I'm sorry for you.'

'Don't. She was ailing. I also believe that with me departed to war and the world gone mad, she was more than happy to limp off this plane.'

I nodded, understanding.

'Speaking of limping, I'm embarrassed to arrive on your doorstep like this. It's not my legs, actually, but a chest wound I'm recovering from.'

'Oh, my, I can hear you struggling to breathe. How recent is the injury?'

'Ah, well, there's a date I won't forget. It happened on 31 October. I was working at the Hooge Château, just to the east of Ypres. Both 1st and 2nd Divisions' commanders were using it as joint headquarters.'

I nodded, fascinated by all the strange names. 'That's Belgium?'

He nodded. 'Generals Lomax and Monro were involved in a conference. It was about one o'clock, not long after, anyway, that the German artillery began shelling and scored direct hits.'

I visibly breathed in; this was both macabre and exciting – my first real glimpse of the fighting, as Felix protected me from reality, sharing only amusing snippets in his letters. How he found humour in war is beyond me, but he managed to make me smile and cry at the same time. Henri meanwhile had only written once, mainly to ask for some extra socks and to answer a couple of questions about business queries I'd posed.

'Did you say both generals died?'

'No, both were injured and I'm not convinced General Lomax will recover, to be honest. Lots of us were wounded, a few killed.'

'What were you doing there?'

He gave a sheepish grin. 'Bit of a long tale.'

'I'd like to hear it while we wait for the tea.'

'All right, but you'll have to forgive my raspy breath.' Before I could protest against him straining himself, he was continuing. 'I was on my way here, in fact, to see you and Aimery.'

I nodded – who could forget – and I was sure we would come to the letter shortly; it would be impolite to jump in now.

'War was declared by France and I found myself trapped in Paris. I was travelling on English documents, but of course my French background could be proven. I offered myself at the town hall but I hadn't done my two years' obligatory training. Frankly, I don't think I was French enough for them.' He smiled. 'I considered the French Foreign Legion but I thought they might laugh at a chemist trying to join up.'

My heart leapt at that. 'How intriguing that you are involved in what your father's side of the family does.' Something in his gaze told me this was not coincidental.

'I was in touch with the embassy, of course, and it was while dining at the ambassador's residence that I received the telegram of my mother's death. From that moment life felt to me as though it was all out of control. There was no point in heading back to England, knowing our army would likely be mobilising. Besides, it would have been impossible, I suspect. It was pandemonium in Paris. Britain declared war on the fourth, and then it was on for young and old. It was the ambassador, via another friend who worked at the embassy, who proposed me as a linguist.'

'Inspired.'

'Well, it didn't require military training; my credentials were solid and I guess it helped I was so well connected, and my family name . . .' He lifted a shoulder.

'Spoke for itself?' I offered in a wry tone.

He smiled. 'Having a bluish enough tinge to my blood meant I could get through on the most rudimentary security check. There really was no point in going home when I could get on with my war immediately and be of some use.'

'So they threw you straight into Belgium?'

'Heavens, no! Nothing as exciting. I was sent to Boulogne-sur-Mer for a few months. Port work, helping all the Brits who were coming through to make sense of the French they were dealing with.'

I laughed. 'That bad?'

'Well, I think the army that was flowing through mainly from Folkestone needed as many interpreters as it could lay hands on. Anyway, to cut this story short, I had a chance meeting with a second cousin of my mother's family. He was a senior officer on his way to the Front and I bleated about the tedium of my work and he got me assigned to a higher formation, as they call it. Before I could blink I was on my way east with more action than most would hope for. On the day I was injured I was working as a translator; it was mainly French troops in Ypres but the Brits were there, plus men from around the empire were answering the call to arms, so my job would have expanded quickly to Australians, New Zealanders, Canadians, Indians, Africans . . .' His sentence petered out into a small coughing fit.

'Australians . . . how far they have travelled to fight for their king. And I'm not sure I even know where New Zealand is,' I admitted.

He laughed and that provoked another raft of coughing. 'Nearer to Australia than us, you could say.'

'Other side of the world, then,' I said, not fully hiding the longing in my voice to see these faraway places that I knew Sébastien had.

'Wonderful people, frighteningly tough men who seem to laugh a lot . . . at each other, particularly. I recall I was relaying a British message in French when the shell hit.'

'And so you've been hospitalised since then?'

'Yes, I was at a French Military Hospital just outside a place called Poperinghe, alongside the railway line and railhead. The chest injury wasn't severe enough to require me to be repatriated, but it's enough that I'm no good to anyone for a while. Plus I caught an infection, and when it turned out that I had reduced lung capacity, needed to breathe some fresh air and stop holding up doctors, nurses and a much-needed bed, they took my offer. You see, I'd taken the great liberty of suggesting that I might recuperate in France with my family in the south.'

I raised my eyebrows and he hurried to assure me.

'It was a fib . . . just a white lie, but it got me here. I was feeling like such a burden. I hope it wasn't too forward . . .?'

'No, not at all. Have you seen Aimery?' I'm glad I remembered to ask. 'Or is that a ridiculous suggestion, given the situation? I can't imagine what you have all lived through because no one will tell me.'

'It's best you remain ignorant, to be honest. I have only heard about Aimery from others. I gather he's being extremely' — he searched for the appropriate word — 'inspiring to the men.'

'You must feel proud.'

His bottom lip plumped and slipped forward in a typically French gesture of doubt. 'Not really, though you should, I suppose. We are brothers only in blood . . . and barely that. We have never met.'

'That's so odd, isn't it?'

'Indeed.'

'I'm surprised you've never visited Grasse in all this time.'

'I wanted to, but doubted I was welcome. I feel more English than French and yet that French part of me is very strong. I want to explore it.'

Before I could say more the doors opened and Madame Mouflard was in tow this time, bustling in to supervise the laying out of the tea tray. 'Ah, you're back,' I said in a gust of brightness to overcome the sense of dread regarding the invisible and yet tangible presence of Aimery's and my marriage sitting between me and our guest; I felt the small talk was done and we needed to broach the letter. 'Madame Mouflard, this is Sébastien De Lasset, my brother-in-law.'

'Oh, sir,' she said, bowing her head. 'How wonderful to meet you.' She sounded slightly awed. 'Forgive me, Madame,' she followed up, instantly guarded. 'Er, the town is buzzing with your arrival, sir.'

I imagined poor Madame Mouflard must have hurried home

as fast as her legs could move her when she heard the news.

'Welcome to Grasse, Monsieur Sébastien. I . . . I served your mother . . .' She seemed to lose faith in what she was trying to say and looked down. I thought I might have to leap in and cover an awkward pause but the housekeeper returned her gaze and smiled. 'She is missed, sir, by all of us who worked for her in our youth.'

He beamed. 'Thank you. I should tell you that regretfully she passed away recently.' He talked over her soft gasp. 'She was too young to go but the cancer took her. She left us while sleeping, I gather. I know she would be pleased to be remembered, though,' he replied with great charm. 'It was fast. There was minimum suffering,' he assured.

'Thank you, Madame Mouflard, I can pour,' I offered.

She bowed once and both servants were gone. I smiled at Sébastien and he blew out a breath.

'This was never going to be easy,' he wheezed. He looked up and brightened. 'However, this is a treat after hospital tea,' he said, ladling in a generous spoon of sugar that was likely hard to find where he had been. 'The French aren't particularly fond of tea and aren't sure how to make it.'

'That's not a complaint, is it?' My tone was light with humour.

He put up both hands, his bandages almost comical because of how large they made his left hand appear. 'No, not at all. Tea in England is an institution, though; I'm sure you know that.'

'I do. I'm glad I learned to drink it, but I do favour the delicate Orientals. How about some food?'

'Later, perhaps. Thank you,' he said, leaning his walking stick against the chair, and took the cup and saucer I offered with his good hand. Then he smiled and I burst into horrified laughter again.

'Oh, I am so sorry. Here,' I took the tea back, placed the saucer on the tray and returned the cup to his hand. 'Is that easier?'

'Much. I've forgotten the pleasure of drinking from porcelain.'

He sighed and sipped, then smiled, closing his eyes to taste the tea. 'This is so delicious; what is it?'

'I suspect you've been served Russian Caravan, a blend of black and Chinese tea.'

'Thank you,' he murmured, eyes still closed.

'How bad is it for our men?'

His lids snapped open to reveal the woody green of his eyes, lit by the winter sunshine that slanted into the morning room to trick us into believing its golden light might warm where it fell. 'You can't imagine it and I don't have the right words to describe the horror. I think the fires of purgatory that most were threatened with as children would be easier than the living hell of the trenches.' He shook his head in memory. 'Rats, endless mud, relentless shelling, water up to your knees . . .'

'I'm sorry,' I offered. We drank in silence for a moment or two. 'I'm glad you came here,' I repeated deliberately.

'That's reassuring. I have to report in. They need to be sure I'm not malingering but I'm never going to get well unless I can get my lung working properly again. I'm sure at first they thought I'd "caught a blighty".'

'A blighty,' I repeated, leaning forward with intrigue. 'What is that?'

'Oh, a substantial wound of the non-fatal kind. Those get you home, you see. I'm sure most of the men would dream of catching a blighty. There are some soldiers – and perfectly understandable it is too – who would rather shoot their own limbs and hope to be sent home for hospitalisation than spend another day at the Front. But the hierarchy has caught on. Anyone suspected of it is put on trial, could be shot as a traitor. We've already executed some.'

I stared back, open-mouthed.

'Even the medical treatment is done in different tents for traitors; I gather the doctors and nurses don't even feel inclined to treat them with much kindness – and again, I understand their perspective too – but only someone there can fully comprehend an otherwise brave man taking this path.'

'But they've cleared you?'

He gave me his crooked, self-effacing grin, which I was learning was always at the ready and I found helplessly attractive. 'Yes, but not before I was interviewed rigorously, as someone decided that I, as a civilian, could have been coerced into giving away the location of our headquarters. Ridiculous, but everyone is suspicious these days. Anyway, I was exonerated and it helped, I suppose, that the 23e BCA arrived into the region in mid-November.'

'Aimery's regiment.'

'Indeed. I did send a message but he didn't visit. I am now convinced he's avoiding me.'

'My brothers? They're with the 24e, but I think the two regiments have joined with the same battalion.'

He nodded. 'They have. But I didn't see them – I'm sorry. I didn't think to look for the Delacroix boys but also I wouldn't know your two brothers to see them.'

'Of course,' I said, hiding my disappointment. I refilled his cup and he added a dash of milk but no sugar this time. 'We must get those bandages changed. How badly hurt are you beneath all of that?'

He waved his injuries away with his good arm and tasted his tea again with a greedy urgency. 'There are soldiers in far worse shape than me but I'm not much use to anyone right now until I've healed. It's a burn. I'm only using this wretched stick because I refuse to be aided in walking.'

'Your hand is seeping a bit,' I noted rather obviously.

'Yes, poor manners.' I looked back up at him, blinking, wondering if he thought I was admonishing him and saw only another grin. I had to laugh with him.

We sipped like mirror images for a moment in a pleasant silence that felt vaguely dangerous because of the way the light now flickered in his gaze that was fixed firmly on me.

'Aimery chose incredibly well.'

I shifted with discomfort. 'He didn't choose. Aimery had a lover and I think he is deeply attached to her. Your brother and my brother, Henri, made a strategic decision with me as the ball they tossed between their negotiations.'

'I wish I'd been here to catch you.' When I cut him a surprised look, he smiled. 'Just playing along with the ball metaphor.'

I chuckled cooperatively. He reminded me increasingly of Felix. There was something similarly disarming and sardonic about him. 'Your French is excellent.'

'My mother went to some length to ensure it was as readily available to me as the mother tongue I was raised with. She employed a teacher from Paris who became as close as an uncle to me. He lived with us, travelled with us, grew old with us. I have spoken French every day of my life since I began to talk. In fact, we only speak French at home.'

'My goodness, she was determined.'

'Yes. But her motives were perhaps not as honourable as you might think.'

'What do you mean?'

'I mean that my mother had every intention that I make use of half of the De Lasset empire.'

It felt as though my throat had just been squeezed. 'I see,' I said tightly, recalling now that French law did not allow for children to be removed from a will.

'I suspect lawyers were regularly at work and in contact across the sea that separates our two nations long before his death.'

'So you're here to make a challenge against Aimery?'

His expression clouded with disappointment. 'First, let me

reassure that financial gain is not why I'm here, Fleurette. I don't share my mother's motives. I don't care about the greater De Lasset coffers, even if half is mine – I'm certainly not chasing it.'

'You're a chemist,' I interjected, as though three words exploded any myth he was surrounding himself with.

'Yes, I am. But I shouldn't be damned for it. I was interested in medicine, to tell you the truth.'

I shrank inwardly for being too quick to judge.

'Look, my mother's family is wealthy and I am the only male within it, so presumably in my absence I have already inherited substantially.'

'So why did she maintain her commitment to the De Lasset empire on your behalf after being estranged for two decades?'

'Punishment, I suppose.'

I mouthed the word silently back at him. 'To whom?'

'My father. It's an old wound of hers.'

'Why pursue Aimery, then? Her husband's dead.'

Truth sat like a tense guest nearby, demanding to share our conversation. I desperately wanted it to be introduced but somehow understood that Sébastien preferred to present the newcomer at his own pace. He was trying to paint the background for me, give me the history, no doubt believing my understanding was vital before he exploded the real bomb. Good manners precluded me from throwing my arms in the air in exasperation; so did the tightness of his kind voice, the sorrow in his soulful glance. I couldn't find an ounce of likeness between him and Aimery. He did, however, remind me of old Monsieur De Lasset around the firm jaw, and the dimple, when he smiled, I had recently seen reflected in family photos around the De Lasset home. There was no doubting his lineage but how he and Aimery fitted together was curious; Aimery must look like his maternal line but given not a single photograph or painting existed of his mother in the villa, I could not know.

I straightened.

'I'm presuming you were raised to loathe your father.'

He nodded.

'And do you despise him deeper now that you've learned more?'

'No. I hate my mother for harbouring her secret for so long and now sharing it with me, making it my responsibility, my burden.'

I nearly spluttered as I sipped my gunpowder tea. 'Pardon?'

'You did not mishear me. I have learned the truth of the past. In fact, while I am horrified by him, I can fully appreciate my father's actions of twenty years ago.'

I realised we were now at the precipice of why he had urged us not to marry but I needed to let him tell me. I must not push him over that edge. I could see from the set of his mouth, the pain in his expression, that it was creating deep angst for him to confront it. 'Does Aimery know any of this?' I asked.

'Aimery knows none of it yet.'

'Why?'

'Because this is not a topic one explains in anything but face to face! Suffice to say he grew up despising me. I was the child who took his beloved mother away.'

'Beloved?' I couldn't believe him saying that. 'Your mother deserted him.'

'And worshipped him for every moment they were apart. She loved him far more than she ever could or did love me.'

My hand shook as I put my cup and saucer down. 'But you were to come for the wedding, weren't you? Why would you come for the brother who hated you, secret or no secret?'

'I wasn't coming for his sake. I was coming for *yours*!'

I had read somewhere that fear is an emotion we experience almost always in relation to future events. I understood that notion now fully. Whatever dark knowledge Sébastien was bringing with him this day I did not want to share it.

He continued, sensing my fright. 'But I did the polite thing and let him know I was arriving so he could prepare himself.'

'You also sent gifts.'

'Mere cover, as I explained.'

'No more,' I whispered. 'No more skirting this. You must tell me.'

He nodded. 'It is the most unpleasant task I have ever had to face. Worse than shooting dead a man I did not know and had no personal argument with. It was either him or me but I would fire that gun again if I could avoid having to tell you this.'

'But it can't be avoided, so unburden yourself, Sébastien, because I fear my heart will not take this tension for much longer.'

He turned to me with a tender gaze. 'None of this is your fault.'

'None of what?'

'Fleurette. Aimery is . . .' He blanched.

'Say it. Aimery is . . .?' Bizarrely, the notion that Aimery had already married Graciela arrived. I dismissed it with a blink of irritation. Aimery might be a boor but he was a proud and dutiful one. He might bend the law as he did with our marriage papers, but I doubted he would break it.

Now, with effort, his brother stood, moved to sit beside me and took my hand. His skin was warm and dry against mine and I had the thought breeze through my mind that whatever he said, I might never feel safer than in this moment. I watched him swallow.

'Dear Fleurette . . . Aimery is your half-brother.'

10

A cold tremor, like a waterspout suddenly opening within, flooded me, filling me until I felt I was drowning. I was sure I took an age to speak, as though Sébastien had to hold my hand gently for hours, patiently waiting for my response.

'Sébastien,' I whispered, searching his features, so angular and opposite to the blunt facade of Aimery. 'How can that be?'

He took a slow breath. 'My mother and your father —'

'No!' I cut him off angrily, flinging his hand aside, uncaring of how it threw his body and caused him to flinch with pain. 'You dare not speak of my father in this way. You neither know him nor understand our family. You're not even French!' I was blathering, desperately withdrawing from his words. He wasn't going to let me go, though.

'Listen to me,' he growled, his patience thinning, overriding his fear of sharing his dreaded secret. 'This must be laid bare. I have proof; all you need to do is look at old photographs to see family likenesses or, better still, let's use Landsteiner's science and test our bloods.'

'Test blood? Whatever are you talking about?'

'I've read about it. There are several blood types that cannot be argued. It was discovered more than a decade back. I suspect you and Aimery will share some commonality in that regard because of —'

I ignored his science; his explanation was blurring my mind. 'You have proof?' I snapped, aghast. 'What sort of proof?'

He found fresh patience with me, showing no offence at either my tone or being interrupted. 'My mother kept letters. They're from your father. But there are also hers sent to him – he returned them; I suppose he couldn't bear to destroy them. The point is these letters offer not just incriminating but absolute testimony to what occurred between them. There are hospital records, too, and —'

'Stop it, please stop!' I think I covered my ears like a child but he talked through my protest and I couldn't fail to hear. He reached to pull one hand down from the side of my head and I didn't fight him.

'Fleurette, I do not wish to shatter the illusion you hold of your family. I am aware of the high regard in which you hold your father especially.'

'Then say no more,' I pleaded.

'I cannot remain silent. It is too terrifying for you to ignore me. You have wed your own brother.'

I dry-retched. I had to close my eyes and he mercifully remained silent while I enforced my will over my shock. He must have taken my hand again because I became aware of the scuffed, damaged fist that cupped mine tenderly as one might a baby bird.

'Breathe,' he whispered. 'Deep breaths.' Sébastien counted as I inhaled; he kept counting softly until he'd reached ten. His voice, with its attractive rasp in it, anchored me. 'Any more and you may feel dizzy,' he warned.

'I wish I could fall unconscious,' I ground out.

'It would wait for you to wake up,' he replied and there was pity in his tone that I'll admit I found assuring, as though we were both in this together. He'd had more time to stew on the horror but it was undoubtedly repulsive nonetheless for him. 'Let me say it all. Hear it, in its nakedness, and then we shall work out a plan together. Please remember, this is neither your nor Aimery's fault. Guilt lies with our four parents who hid it.'

'Say it, then,' I commanded, surprising myself.

I watched Sébastien's abdomen expand as he took a deep breath that wheezed through his upper chest sounding like an old piano accordion that had a hole in it. He was of the age of me and my twin but while he stood as tall as I did, he was of a slim build. Felix was taller still and imposing through his broader presence and yet there was something undeniably powerful in Sébastien's darkly quiet manner. In a roomful of men that included my handsome brother, Sébastien would hold his own attention and not go unnoticed, certainly not by me. This realisation prompted an unwanted heat to erupt and I knew it must be showing itself, although I hoped it kept its creeping treachery beneath the neck of my blouse. My mind was wandering, no doubt trying to escape the horror of his revelation. I knitted my fingers together, forced my hands still in my lap and tried to focus.

'My mother adored your father,' he began. 'As I understand it, the feeling was mutual. My mother explained to me on what turned out to be her deathbed that her arranged marriage with Arnaud De Lasset was detestably unhappy. She had not met him until they were to be married here in Grasse, but on paper, via his letters, and from the perspectives from others their union was altogether favourable. But when she met him just eight weeks out before their formal marriage, she discovered little to recommend them as a couple. She told me he struck her immediately as being haughty, arrogant and dismissive of her and her English heritage, even though she had a proud Norman French bloodline. She should have fled back to England but I suppose one didn't do those things in her generation – one faced adversity head-on and coped. I got the impression that her family wanted this union very much and would not have supported her return anyway.'

I watched Sébastien sigh, running a battered hand through his hair to disturb its order and give it permission to go its preferred way.

'Of course I only have Mother's perspective to go on but according to her, Arnaud treated her with disdain in private, and kept a mistress. It made their relationship feel sour before it even formally began.'

I felt as though he could be describing Aimery. In public, though, it was my impression that old Monsieur De Lasset was charming and in company he was a good conversationalist, an interesting man. Sébastien must have sensed where my thoughts ran.

'If that is not your view of my father, I suspect age smoothed his edges, though not his desire to take his revenge. Your parents and my parents were great friends. My mother says they were known as the royal quartet for a few years after their marriages. Their two family lines of course were impeccable and ancient.'

'My father?' I needed to hear it.

He nodded, he was getting there and clearly wanted to lead me to the worst of it as gently as he could. 'Mother admitted to me that she had been instantly and helplessly attracted to your father, whom she met on the day she arrived in Paris. Her mother was English, her father half-French, but she had no family here at all, despite her French-sounding name of Marguerite Beaumont. It was your father who was asked by my father to escort her to Grasse. It is my belief that she fell in love with your father before she took vows with mine. As to your mother, it is my understanding that he had not yet met her, did not know of her.'

I lifted a shoulder in answer; he waited and that forced me to respond properly. 'Er . . . they met by accident, the story goes. My father was in Paris, visiting relatives, my mother visiting friends, and as she and her companion were walking out of their hotel the wind blew her parasol out of her hands. It was a blustery winter's morning, my father recalled, and he rushed to her aid, retrieving the parasol, which had turned inside out and had been stomped on by several horses by the time he chased it down rue Saint Lazare.' I smiled sadly. 'It was love at the first glimpse of each other, in the rain, as I understand their romantic tale to be. I know the date they met was January 1885; they wed in spring . . . my mother a May bride. Henri was born the following year.' I shrugged self-consciously at his surprised expression. 'I'm good with dates,' I admitted.

'And I'm not here to change any of that, but if you want to know what I believe, then I suspect your father and my mother were lovers but they knew they couldn't be together. Society wouldn't permit it, their families would be outraged, given my mother was already promised and the wedding preparations under-way.'

I felt bludgeoned by his words. They fell upon me like dull thuds of pain.

'Your parents probably did fall for each other on sight and their love was likely pure but he'd had to relinquish my mother by then; he had to get on with his life, find a woman to share his life with, give him his family, even though he'd fathered Aimery almost exactly three years earlier.'

'He used to visit his aunt and uncle in Paris each Christmas,' I offered pointlessly.

Sébastien nodded in a kind gesture, as though he knew it required this tenderness to help me work through the pain, accept this reality. 'Their affair began in late December 1882,' he said, closing the gap between us to talk as softly as possible. 'Aimery was conceived at the end of that year, my mother assures, although their tryst continued through January 1883. My parents married in February.'

'It would have been snowing! Certainly frozen,' I remarked, hoping this was my way out – no Grasse bride would agree to a wedding in the depths of winter.

He knew this, sensed me reaching for the escape. 'My mother said it was quite a battle to convince Arnaud to agree to a winter wedding. She knew she was pregnant by then; she knew she wanted the child of Victor Delacroix, the man she adored, and would keep that secret of their child's illegitimacy, raising it as a child of her marriage. She told me that children were born early all the time and no one would query her.'

'My brother and I came early. But they must have been terribly careful not to be seen enjoying one another's company?'

'Indeed they were. My mother spoke of this. Your father was her chosen escort so they could hide behind that permission, if you will, but in public they were extremely cautious. She was living in his house with a set of female servants he employed for her but even so, it wouldn't have been that hard to navigate time together . . . alone.'

I didn't want to think on that. It sounded so ugly, so vulgar: stealing time, stealing kisses, stealing into each other's beds. My father! I gave a shiver of what could have been disgust but more likely was my own despair.

'So he knew Aimery was his?'

He nodded. 'No doubt at all. The letters they shared attest to that knowledge, including my mother admitting she wished she'd had the courage to call off the marriage. But she was young, terrified of what had occurred, of what her family would think of her, of what it meant for both families' reputations if the truth found its way out. Your father loved her but he was bound by her decision to marry Arnaud De Lasset . . . and once she did, he had to keep her secret and get on with his own life. It couldn't have been easy for either of them in such close proximity to each other.'

'And then he met my mother,' I added.

'Yes. Three years later, a wayward parasol brought him together with someone he could find love with again, could enjoy having a family with.'

'But won't you accept that Aimery could be Arnaud's son?' I tried to hold his gaze, pleading silently that he may agree.

'My mother suffered the pregnancy nausea from before she married. She knew but couldn't reveal anything to anyone.'

'No family with her?'

'None. She was alone in France to be married off – the last of three daughters: her father too frail, her mother caring for him as he slipped away. Her brother had agreed to give her away – which he did, I'm told – but he only arrived days before the wedding. Her sisters were either pregnant or nursing new infants, so both indisposed. Apparently Gerald – that's my uncle – was furious to be dragged into the freeze of a Grasse winter when he had anticipated a spring journey.'

'What did she tell everyone?'

'I never asked her that but given she's clearly demonstrated her ability for subterfuge, I suspect Mother claimed she was so keen to marry Arnaud she wanted it to happen sooner rather than later.' He bit his lip, showing me that although he was speaking candidly, it was not easy for him to injure me in this way. 'Imagine it,' he continued. 'The early 1880s.' He pursed his lips deliberately in an elderly maiden-aunt sort of way and I felt a nervous tremor of laughter bubble but I killed it off before it arrived. I was living through a nightmare and while nervous laughter was likely acceptable, it wouldn't do. I needed to hold this anger if I was to survive what was surely coming at me. Sébastien was talking.

'If it's even the smallest and most hollow consolation,' Sébastien urged, 'my mother admitted that she had never known a happier time than the weeks she spent living at your house before the wedding. I'm getting the impression you didn't know she lived at your family villa.'

I shook my head. 'I've never heard that before.'

'No. Well, I guess it was too painful for all of them to admit. Your father was especially generous towards her.'

'Too much, it seems,' I cut in viciously.

'No doubt. Your father was charming, gentle, magnanimous to all he met, especially women, she told me.' I felt tears sting but refused to weep over this. I knew what my father was; I didn't need a stranger to tell me. 'Mother also described him as unspeakably handsome,' he added.

I gave a sad nod. 'I've seen photos of him as a young man. He looked in those as Felix does now.'

'Mother had a close-up photo of him. He looks like you in male form. It's from him that you get your dark beauty.' His voice sounded croaky, his gaze too deep. The helpless pull towards him that I was feeling intensified.

'You'd better go on.'

He nodded, looked away and sighed. 'I think it's important I reinforce and you accept that he fathered Aimery *before* he married your mother and while still single, not even promised to anyone.'

'If you're trying to shift blame, I'm afraid that doesn't help,' I said in a hard tone.

'No, but it doesn't tarnish your parents' relationship. My mother was an unfaithful fiancée but your father – whatever you now think of him – was not unfaithful to your mother. Aimery was born before your parents married, before your mother became pregnant with Henri.'

'But he was faithless towards Arnaud. Whatever your opinion of your father is, he and mine were friends. If your story is right, my father behaved in a shameful way.'

'Love is blind, and often cruel,' he offered.

I gave a sneer at such romantic sentiment. I was not going to let our two offending parents off that easily. 'So was it your father who discovered their affair?'

'Yes, years afterwards. Aimery must have been turning four and my mother was nearing her term with me – I was due in six weeks, I gather, when it all came out. She wouldn't explain how it erupted . . . I guess none of us will ever know now, as they're all gone, but I gather it was ugly. She told me he hit her, raged at her for several hours, then finally spat on her and the family that had first approached him regarding their marriage. She was banished and left with me in her belly. It was then – obviously – that the acrimony between our two families began. Friendship was severed. The race for supremacy in business became brutal for a while and then simply became a personal hatred between the two men.'

'Understandable.'

'Completely. And still they managed to keep it all secret.'

'I'm astonished by that.'

He nodded. 'You must believe it. My mother said not a single servant to this day knows that Aimery does not have De Lasset blood running through his veins. And the only reason she was forced to spill the near three-decade-old secret was because of your marriage.'

'What about the argument that erupted? Did no one else over-hear, share in any way?'

'Handled with my father's usual aplomb, I'm assured. Conducted in a summer property we have in the high country. All servants sent on a picnic so that my father could inform my mother that he knew her secret and it was then he also explained to her, heavily pregnant and lying bruised from his blows, that no one would ever hear the truth.'

My expression twisted; my father had never raised a hand to anyone, least his wife.

He nodded, clearly ashamed of this admission. 'He had made all the arrangements before he told her of his discovery; she was taken that evening away to Nice, then to Paris, and back to London.'

'And no one guessed?'

'He was strategic about where he hurt her. I suppose we should be grateful that he didn't stretch to injuring me, the child she carried. She certainly wasn't going to tell anyone and incriminate herself or your father. Who knows what she and Arnaud agreed to, but she was sent away without a centime of his fortune, without a backwards glance, and only the clothes she stood in. She was forbidden to even say goodbye to Aimery.'

'He wouldn't hurt a child, though. You were his.'

'I was supposed to be a girl. I think my mother somehow convinced him of this in order to make it easier for him to let her leave with her unborn baby safe. I think she feared he might imprison her until I was born and then he'd keep me too.' He shrugged.

'Nevertheless, you were true De Lasset. I wonder how he might have behaved had he learned of the affair earlier and it had been Aimery in your mother's belly.'

'It really doesn't bear thinking on. It's appalling enough that he raised a hand to her.'

I would never condone violence of any kind towards a woman but I couldn't admit to Sébastien that I might understand how an unstable person, filled with rage, his manhood called into question, his family name potentially tainted, might be provoked into striking out. 'The story we have all lived with is that she left to go travelling, became estranged and never came back. It was always very odd but not talked about by my father.'

'My father sold the story very well that she was travelling to take the healing waters at Bath through a difficult pregnancy. Then that I was a sickly boy – a lie, I might add,' he said with a pinched smile. 'And because of that she had to remain in Britain and was taking me to clearer air up north to continue her love of painting watercolours in Scotland. There was a host of reasons peddled and presumably accepted simply because my father said so. No one would defy him here in Grasse, I gather, least of all your father, the villain of the piece. It broke your mother's heart, of course, to learn the truth. That's why she ended up taking her life.'

'*What?*' It came out as a shrieking whisper, my eyes wide with the horror of his words. I caught sight of myself in a mirror that hung above the buffet; enormous and gilded. I looked like a spectre in its reflection. My complexion had turned ashen, my lips drained of their colour to appear near bloodless; I felt as though there was nothing solid left.

'Oh, dear. Fleurette . . .' His fallen expression reflected only embarrassment at his revelation.

'My mother died of pleurisy,' I muttered, biting off each word to ensure its clarity, as though I could make it truth by sounding so definitive. He was shaking his head slowly. I needed to protest; I couldn't give in this easily even though somewhere deep and dark I knew he was speaking the truth. He had no reason at all to walk into my life with this lie. 'No, that's what my father told us,' I insisted plainly, my voice finding its normal, if wavering, timbre. 'He —'

'He lied, beautiful Fleurette. What else could he do? The truth was too painful and he agreed with my parents to keep the secret that was Aimery. Your mother wouldn't – couldn't . . . I think she loved her husband so much she simply wasn't able to accept the truth of his past, or more to the point, the reality of her closest friend's betrayal, I suppose. Mother wept, still feeling it more than a quarter of a century later, that your mother viewed the whole affair as treacherous even though she was not in your father's orbit at that time. Mother believed it was the keeping of the secret that killed her, rather than the secret itself.'

'I doubt your mother could ever see it from my mother's point of view. But she kept their terrible secret all the same,' I said, shaking my head with disbelief.

'That's not correct, actually; she refused to do so. Instead, while she chose not to let their quartet down, your mother stepped aside from her knowledge of the affair and Aimery's parentage in the most final way she could. She was newly pregnant with you and Felix when the truth came out. You were born earlier than you should have been, as you know; my mother said it was probably the shock of the news. I gather from her you were born at eight months and it was all very tense and traumatic as to whether one or both of you might live. You pulled through and your mother gave it time to be sure that both of her new infants would survive, hopefully grow to be healthy.' He stopped, looked down.

'And then?' I knew I was visibly trembling.

He drew a breath. 'Then she invited your father to a picnic. In a way she was mimicking my father in how he treated his wife except your mother was less robust, far more emotional about discovering the betrayal.'

'Don't say that as though it wasn't one,' I warned in a shaking voice.

'A betrayal by your father of mine, perhaps, but not of your mother. I remind you, he did not know her when the affair occurred.'

I shook my head as if denying his rationale. 'They lied, Sébastien – for years. Aimery is their lie.' I knew he was only trying to make it easier on me. 'Finish the sordid tale, please!' The news of my mother's suicide made my breath feel as though it was passing over jagged glass to reach my lungs. It was hurting to breathe – we made a fine pair in the glamorous De Lasset drawing room: Sébastien with his croupy wheeze and my pain-laden inhalations.

'They went into Provence, into the alps, and in front of him she threw herself from a cliff. Your father fashioned the story she was in terrible pain and confusion from complications from her twin pregnancy and the subsequent childbirth . . . and that she slipped and fell from that cliff top. The family doctor was presumably coerced into agreeing that your mother had issues following the birth of her twins; there was no doubt she showed signs of melancholy and people attributed this to her mood post-pregnancy rather than her being unable to cope with the discovery of her husband fathering a child with her best friend. Servants corroborated the apparent fall and the town accepted the account of the tragic incident. It became truth but it was always a lie. She killed herself to show your father the depth of her despair.'

I stared wordlessly at him. I didn't want to believe it but so much of what he was saying was beginning to make sense and resonating in a way that it seemed pointless to keep hoping he might discover his mistake.

'Before you ask,' he said, 'my mother knew all of this because your mother wrote to her and explained what she was going to do, and blamed her . . . they were the best of friends and now the worst of enemies. She made sure my mother felt responsible for her death, the fracture of our families, all the bitterness and acrimony.'

'Do you blame her?'

Sébastien's tone remained even. 'I lay no blame anywhere. I think, Fleurette, only our two sets of parents know what it was like – only one of them has the right to lay blame, feel blame.'

'That's generous of you, Sébastien.'

He took the blow without flinching. 'I've had longer to

consider what a precarious position each of them was in. We can't truly imagine it.'

'I think I can! If all that you say is true, then I can never consider my father in the same way again.'

'You mustn't —'

I stood abruptly, swinging round to face him. 'Don't presume to tell me how to react or to think! I'm so tired of men believing they know best where I'm concerned.'

He hung his head. 'Forgive me. I just believe it's easy to cast stones.'

I walked to the window to stare out at the terraces, stripped of their colour but nonetheless starkly beautiful in their naked winter appearance. 'I disagree in this instance,' I snapped, my breath now clouding the pane I looked out from. I turned back to face him and saw that he watched me intently from beneath his bruised expression. 'They knew what they were doing was wrong and now we see the results of their selfish lust – your life ruined; Aimery with a lifetime of hate for his mother, never knowing she loved him; my mother's life squandered through heartbreak; my marriage now needing to be annulled . . . but I'd like you to consider how I go about telling Aimery why! Their keeping of this secret is now reverberating through this generation and can potentially threaten the next.'

'I know you're angry but what would you have me do? Let you go ahead and have a child with Aimery?'

I felt dizzied by the revulsion those words prompted and couldn't reply.

He pressed his point. 'I have seen the letters. I have seen the letter from your father to my mother telling of his grief at losing your mother and the way in which she was lost, his terror at being left with three young children – two babies – to raise.' I was still pointlessly moving my head from side to side, denying him. 'I have read his letters because, believe me, I needed convincing too.'

'It could be a lie.' I sounded so ridiculously desperate, but who could blame me?

'Who do you imagine was lying and for what purpose, Fleurette? Financial gain? Hardly. No, these were deeply emotional letters of despair. His relationship with my mother was one of help-less passion, chemical attraction, if I might reduce it to that. He adored her and she him. But when your mother came into his life he found the stability of true love, I could almost believe . . .' He shook his head as he hesitated.

'What?'

He gave a sound of regret. 'I was going to say I could almost believe my mother let my father find out the truth.'

'Why, for heaven's sake?' I had to dig my nails into my own palm beneath a balled fist to prevent myself from screaming this at him.

Sébastien's lips flattened into a line of pain. 'It's obvious your father was a charming, highly desirable man to women. Perhaps she'd hoped she could live without him but ultimately it turned out that if she couldn't have him . . .'

'My mother couldn't either?'

I watched his shoulders slump. 'It was a tragedy. If it was because of her machinations, then I think she lived to regret her impossible love for Victor Delacroix, her part in your mother's sui-cide.'

I felt my bile threaten to rise once again at that word. I had to run away from it, force him to move on with his evil story. 'Then what happened after your father discovered the truth?'

'Well, as I explained, he banished my mother the day he con-fronted her and she admitted making a cuckold of him. But he exacted a harsh punishment. He kept Aimery. He was not going to let my mother walk away from Grasse with a cherished memory of your father and their lust; plus he was not going to permit anyone to deny him of his heir, even if the heir did not share his blood. He wanted the infant boy, gave him everything, raised him as his own. Let's not forget he'd loved Aimery for several years as his son before he knew the truth. He didn't care that she was heavily pregnant with me; she convinced him I was a daughter and a daughter was useless to him. My father wanted an heir.'

'Wait . . . wait!' I stood and began to pace as the only way to keep the rising nausea down. I had to open the window to suck in cold air to shock me out of wanting to expel my breakfast.

'Fleurette,' he called softly. Suddenly he was behind me, limping carefully across the rug to hold me. It didn't feel wrong. I turned in his arms and let him hold me briefly in a shared communion of despair. 'I'm so sorry,' he whispered.

Sébastien guided me back to the sofa as though I were an invalid; I certainly moved like an old woman suddenly, and the war, my marriage, my life, all felt very distant as he began to tell me everything else he could that he had learned from his mother as she lay dying.

We sat in silence, bonded through the horror of his words: not one but two dreaded secrets revealed. I was suddenly, glad all our parents were dead, but the burden was now upon our own shoulders.

'Sébastien, I did receive the letter from you on the night war was declared but I wonder if I would have trusted it.'

'I gather it arrived too late anyway.'

'I'm afraid so.'

'Did you . . .?'

'No,' I said briskly, understanding his tense question before he asked it. 'Mercifully, no! Orders came through for mobilisation and Aimery being Aimery couldn't miss out on his opportunity to lead the charge to war. Not even a new bride could keep him from his uniform and saddle, I'm relieved to say.'

'His self-aggrandising inclination is our blessing, then.'

'It was a close call.'

'Do you love Aimery?'

It was not a question I expected from him.

'I . . . what an odd query you pose.'

'I'll take that as a no, shall I?' He irritated me by the hint of amusement in his gaze over the rim of his cup. The tea was long cold.

'You'll do no such thing. That's a terrible presumption.'

'Is it? I thought we were going to be truthful.'

'Perhaps there's been too much honesty for one day between strangers.'

'Yes. You're right,' he said. 'I've brought plenty to upset you,' he observed rightly and leaned awkwardly to set his cup down. With slightly pursed lips I gave in and helped.

'Here, let me,' I offered.

He smiled tightly. 'Thank you, and once again, I ask for your forgiveness. I'm behaving ungraciously.'

'You're behaving like my twin brother, actually. Felix finds humour in everything, even grim situations.'

'I like the sound of him.'

'You'd get on well. But there are times, when you're dabbling in people's lives, that amusing yourselves is inappropriate.'

His gaze darkened and his forehead creased with concern. 'Sometimes, Fleurette, humour is used as a defence rather than an attack.'

I nodded, knew Felix often reverted to making fun because it was easier than confronting reality. 'However, this is my life, Sébastien, and I do feel under attack.'

'I had to protect you.'

'So you said in your letter.'

Now our most awkward pause since we met stretched tautly between us.

He pulled himself to his feet with a soft groan and a cough. 'I'll take your leave, Fleurette. I'm so sorry but I couldn't let it sit a moment longer. I'm just glad I got to you before . . .'

I stood as well. 'But now you've handed the burden to me. All of that bleak truth is mine to bear.'

'He will want an heir.'

I closed my eyes and breathed out. 'You brought the letters?'

'You surely don't plan to —'

'I most certainly do. Dark claims are besmirching my father's name and you're asking me to annul my marriage. I have only third-party words. I imagine you didn't come unarmed without the proof you claimed.'

'I have the letters.'

'Good. And how do you come by letters that surely belonged to my father?'

'I suspect he kept them out of sentiment.'

I noted he was careful about his wording, obviously not wishing to suggest that my father carried a flame for his mother long after their parting.

'And then due to that same sentiment he returned them, for her to make the decision about destroying them.'

'Then I require them.' I matched his gaze as directly as his fixed mine. 'I will not tamper with them in any way. I want to see my father's handwriting, hear his voice in my mind as I read his words to your mother. That's fair, surely, given the damage your news brings?'

'It is fair but it will hurt you more.'

'How can I be hurt any further than learning that my mother killed herself? She chose death over life with her children. And how can I possibly be more upset than learning the father I worship lived a lie?'

'He didn't —'

166

'He did, Sébastien. He knew Aimery was his son. And now I know why whenever the topic arose I had an ally in my father. For as long as he was alive, he wouldn't tolerate the notion of marriage between our families when all others except me agreed it made perfect sense to heal old wounds, bring two grand families together and protect our region's wealth. I thought it was connected with our rivalry – historical bad blood of business. Now I know it is genuinely about bad blood.'

I hadn't seen the satchel that he limped over to now. He'd set it down on a far table before I'd walked into the morning room. He undid it and lifted out a large envelope. 'These are your father's letters. There are only three. The last was sent after your mother was buried.' He handed the envelope to me. 'I've also included the one from your mother to mine.'

I swallowed. 'I will return them, of course.'

'They are your proof. Your way out of the marriage.'

I straightened, feigning a smile. 'You must stay here while in Grasse.'

'Perhaps it's best if I don't. My only aim in lying to my army superiors was to reach you before Aimery had leave. I shall head back into —'

'I won't hear of it, Sébastien. You're our guest . . . you're a De Lasset; you have every right to stay in your family's home. I won't hear of you staying anywhere else.' I moved to the fireplace and drew on the embroidered fabric that would ring for service at the back of the house. 'I know Madame Mouflard will be delighted to make up a room for you.' I walked over to him and kissed him gently on both cheeks, helplessly enjoying the bristly feel of his beard pushing through against my skin. 'Good day, Sébastien, and will you excuse me, please? I feel a headache coming on.'

I I

Before I read the letters, I smelled them. Yes, it was odd, but I am a woman of perfume. Every aroma, while not an object in itself, has provenance because it originates from the solid, the real. Thus smells have their stories to tell me and 'tasting' them is my way of seeing the world in the first instance. I only look after I have derived my uncommon perspective.

I smelled first my father's letters. These were written on his signature mauve-blue paper and I knew before I raised the envelope to my nose that I should smell violets. It was a curious choice for a man to scent his stationery with such a delicate fragrance but I had been raised with it, and never thought to question that feminine note that clung to his salon as a delicate counterbalance to the tobacco he inhaled. I had always presumed he chose it because of his mother's scent – her name was Violette. And I don't doubt the origination now but I found myself questioning whether the scent had come to mean something precious between the two of them.

Could I still smell it on the paper? I sniffed deeply, fancifully reaching for that private commune with the man I thought I knew, the one man I had trusted as being entirely without guile. Perhaps only someone with our family's heightened awareness of smell could find it after years of dwindling potency and deterioration from handling. But there it was . . . tender, slightly powdery, a hint of sweet virtue that made mockery of what my father and Marguerite were sharing. Above all, as I closed my eyes once again and inhaled even deeper so the breath ran over my tongue and down my throat, I smelled that hidden note of melancholy. Was there a sadder fragrance than violets? I doubted it. To stand in a field of violets was to smell the promise of sorrows – a wistful sweetness that was as gentle as a kiss, but was nonetheless mournful. To me the scent of violets, if I could encapsulate it in a word, was forlorn.

I opened the letters and I read.

Words – powerful ones of infatuation as much as love – entered the slipstream of my thoughts and because of who I was I knew I would never forget them. My father, the most precious teacher and guide in my life – a giant in my mind – was reduced to a simpering shadow. It shouldn't have been this way, I suppose, but reading his words of affection to Marguerite somehow reduced him, and I felt an increasing sense of appall and desertion. I wanted to look up to him, not have this helpless adoration for a stranger lessen his stature.

Mostly, I hated that he had loved her. Childish, selfish it may be, but I felt it as a personal betrayal, as though his fondness for her stole from what should have been available only for us.

Marguerite, of course, was desperately in love. I had no doubt about that. While my father's few scented letters were built on fond placations and soothing reassurances, hers were lovelorn and pulsing with the trauma of her lacklustre marriage and finally the physical separation from being able to glimpse my father after her banishment: '*I would gladly live with the pain of seeing you with Flora than not at all.*'

In earlier letters she spoke tenderly of Aimery, moments of resemblance to my father, and then later how the love for her estranged son made her feel still so very connected to her love for my father, even though a sea separated them by then. She expressed her fears for how she might raise the forthcoming baby, due in just days at that time. I was surprised how convinced she was that this child was a girl. Perhaps she willed it in order that her brutal husband would feel less interest in his offspring. In all the letters she didn't mention her shame at their behaviour, or how her family reacted. It was as though she was living in a bubble of her affection for Victor Delacroix and only he, she and Aimery mattered.

She surmised . . . *and he will grow up a De Lasset and sadly with a cruel model of a father to follow. Arnaud will teach him to be proud, vain, ruthless. These are not qualities I cherish and I pray that blood may override those who nurture him for I know there is not a vicious bone in your body.*

By comparison, my father, whose gentle, playful voice I heard all too clearly through his responding letters, seemed to avoid discussing Aimery – certainly in the letters I had before me. I flicked back through the one I was holding to check the date and, yes, it was written almost directly after the birth of Henri. So, by that time Victor Delacroix had not only moved on from his bachelor days to find new love in the arms of my mother but he now had a legitimate child . . . a son . . . the all-important heir to the throne. His new chieftain-in-waiting had arrived to usurp all other affections . . . even those for his illegitimate child and the bleats of love from another woman. She no longer had the same impact, not with the glow of Flora St John shining around him. I had so little recollection of our mother but if she was as pretty in reality as the few photographs and the portraits in the villa of her attest, then my father must have been entirely seduced . . . mesmerised, in fact. That would account for . . . what was it? Not flippancy, but I sensed him distancing himself from Marguerite. And perhaps it wasn't deliberate but he was a married man and a happily married family man at the time. Meanwhile, Marguerite was wallowing in a lost love, a past love that no longer existed, not from my father's perspective anyway, it appeared. In her mind it was still so vital but I suspected that my father was steadfastly and deliberately moving on and away from her, perhaps hoping her letters would dry up.

And then the one I dreaded came to hand in the small pile that had been bound with ribbon. I caught my breath. Different handwriting this time, different paper, dated more than two years after Felix and I were born.

> By the time you read this, Marguerite, I will be dead and I accuse you now as my murderer. Oh, your hand may not have slain me but my blood shall be on your hands all the same.

It was an assault of words. The beautiful, fragile woman whom I had been taught to accept as my mother had poured out enough scathing wrath to surely make even Arnaud De Lasset proud if he'd been privy to it. Who needed to offer bruising blows when you could rain down sentences of such blunt force? I read her letter through the blur of tears, her looping handwriting trembling before me as my eyes watered. Essentially she told Sébastien's mother that she was not strong enough to bear the pain of the deceit of the two people she loved most in the world.

> I have seen my precious Felix and Fleurette into healthy infancy and I suspect now they will thrive as I surely wither. It is time to snuff the candle that has tried in vain to light my way through an overwhelming darkness. But I wish you this, treacherous Marguerite. I wish, unlike me, that you live

*long and miserably in the knowledge of the suffering you
have caused.*

It was vicious. I flung the letter aside, not wanting to feel the pages
with their horrible sentiment against my skin. I felt unwittingly
drawn into the hate, touched by the shame and the lies; I owned
them now, forever to roam my memory. Aimery was still clueless
but the ramifications for our marriage and my life were huge.

This time the bile rose with angry determination and I couldn't
stop its explosive rage.

———————

Feeling better for the purge, a bath and even a rest – fractious
though it was – I emerged some hours later into the gardens.
I needed air despite it being so chilled that the grass felt crusty
underfoot. But I was rugged up against the elements and determined to feel a wind against my face, as if it could blow the demons
from my mind.

There was a tension in the villa and I suspected the servants
were watching me, wondering how the meeting with the prodigal
son had gone. No one could know what terrible information he'd
brought but word had surely run rampant around the household
and I wouldn't be surprised if the fires of gossip weren't already
being fanned around the town to outlying villages. The De Lasset
family was too well known and important for news of the estranged
son returning to the family home not to be causing excited gossip
and providing the perfect subject for heated discussion over morning or afternoon coffee in other wealthy homes. I had no doubt
many women were already reaching for their pen and paper to
extend invitations for morning coffee to the newcomer in our
midst – he would be intriguing, he would be a catch . . . he was male
company, of which we were all in desperately short supply.

Right now I didn't want anyone to be observing my mood or my expression so I walked as far from the house as the garden permitted until I was in a small walled herb patch where not much at all was growing. My companions were some scruffy-looking thyme, its friend a spiky rosemary, which appeared to be clinging on, and some toughened rocket.

Given the size of the estate I was surprised to see the object of the gossip leaning forlornly against the far wall. A thin shaft of dying sunlight lit him as though the angels in heaven had taken pity on his outcast status and bathed him in their warmth as no one else would. No doubt Aimery's brother had gone in search of fresh air and isolation as well.

Despite his dejection and slouch, bandages and walking stick, he managed to look dashing, especially now, seemingly freshly bathed and out of his bedraggled uniform. His medical dressings made him appear heroic rather than beaten, while his downcast expression helped me to feel less inclined to blame him for the pain he'd brought with him – it was clear he was suffering much the same. I expected to see him smoking a cigarette but his good hand was plunged deep into a pocket.

He heard the gravel crunch beneath my tread and he looked up. There was so much grief in his gaze that I felt a surge of guilt and desire to make it right between us.

'Fleurette. How are you?'

'As you'd expect,' I said evenly, approaching. 'You look freshened, though. Is everything to your satisfaction?'

'More than I could hope for. Your maid, Jeanne, demanded my uniform for cleaning.' He tugged at the suit jacket he wore. 'I have no idea where these clothes came from. Are they Aimery's?'

I shook my head. 'Aimery's shorter and bulkier than you. These are my brother's . . . Felix's. I hope it wasn't presumptuous?'

'Not at all. I'm extremely grateful. But I will wear my uniform as soon as it's laundered.'

'It may have to go through the process a few times,' I quipped. 'How are you feeling?'

'Sore.'

'Can we get you something for the pain?'

He grinned.

'Did I say something to amuse?'

Sébastien gestured at a bench nearby. 'Shall we?'

I didn't want to be seated but I obliged. I preferred to extend every courtesy while retaining control. He sat at a respectful distance.

'Did I mention I was a chemist?' He said this in a tone of irony because we both knew he had. I relinquished with a grin. 'I can take care of my pain. I only wish I could take care of yours. Did you read them?'

I nodded this time; words clogged in my throat.

'I would like to have spared you.'

'You tried.'

'I should have tried harder.'

I let out a deep sigh. 'What am I going to do?'

He surprised me by covering my hand and there was something poignant about his injured hand, trying unsuccessfully to squeeze mine through his bandages in an effort to console. I noticed his fingertips poking out from the top made him appear all the more damaged.

'Your fingers look blue,' I remarked.

'I had no idea how cold it gets here. I thought we Brits were hardy enough.'

I gave a snort.

'You've come out in just a shawl, though, like you possess some sort of inner endurance. Meanwhile I shiver like a weakling.'

'Sébastien, you were released to convalesce from a serious

injury. I am healthy, you're far from it. Let me take care of you,' I offered, surprising myself with how easily the suggestion came.

His dark eyes, which I now realised were not truly green but the stormiest of greys, like a restless sea in winter, had lost their amusement. 'You can take me anywhere you please,' he said, his voice gritty.

There was so much earnest intensity in his gaze I had to look away. 'Well,' I began, affecting a jolly tone to cover how disconcerted I suddenly felt. A thrill of unexpected pleasure flashed through me, and then exploded deep in my belly like one of the showers of colourful fireworks that Aimery had organised on our wedding day. In my surprise at the sensation I lost whatever words were coming. Annoyingly Sébastien didn't fill the gap as I searched for what to say next – if anything, he seemed to understand my sudden discomfort. He let me suffer in silence.

'Let's begin by finding you a proper overcoat and planning some healing soups,' I finally offered. 'My father always maintained that a chicken broth has magical healing properties,' I added, inwardly appalled at my babble.

He chuckled, sensing my tumbling emotions. 'Listen, Fleurette, I'm here for you. I'm not going to let you face this alone.'

'Thank you.' I meant it. 'But I don't really see how you can help.'

'I won't let him bully you.'

'Perhaps you shouldn't presume . . .'

'He's grown up walking in the footsteps of my father. Anyone who beats a pregnant woman is a bully . . . and that's putting it mildly.' He held a hand up. 'I'm not for one moment condoning my mother's behaviour. I'm ashamed of her, although let's keep in perspective that both of our villains were unmarried when their liaison occurred. Their error was in not owning up to it.'

'And the fornication?' I sounded like such a prude but my

mother killed herself over this. I felt I had a right to feel affronted – and prudish!

He fixed me with the wintry sea gaze again. 'That's a harsh word. I'm sure neither of our parents saw their helpless attraction in that light.'

'They were wrong. Look at the pain they've caused, surging down a quarter of a century to hurt all of us.'

'I'm sure if they could have known the repercussions, they would have spared you.'

He was so calm and generous to all in this melodrama that he only made me angrier.

'What is your point, Sébastien?' I snipped, removing my hand abruptly from beneath the rough feel of his dressing and felt ashamed at his flinch. I'd hurt him but he made no sound.

'My point, I suppose, is that until anyone has walked in their shoes they cannot know what it is to feel such passion.'

'I would never behave like that.'

'You can be absolutely sure of this?'

I glared at him. 'Certainly, I can!' I could hear the saintly conviction in my tone and didn't enjoy it. 'I suppose you can imagine a world where this sort of behaviour is appropriate?' Now I just sounded cornered, as though I was looking for a way out.

He raised dark eyebrows above features that were not perfect in symmetry and it was this ever-so-slight crookedness that allowed him to achieve a look of almost constant bemusement or, like now, deep sadness.

'I can envisage a world where someone falls helplessly for another and perhaps lacks judgement and indeed a clarity of thinking.' He cleared his throat. 'Have you ever been in love, Fleurette? The sort of love that makes you feel irrational, irresponsible, irrepressible?'

The question stole up and alarmed me. My head rocked back. 'No.' I spoke the truth and felt self-conscious that I was able to answer so categorically. I struck back, though. 'How about you?'

He frowned, took my enquiry seriously rather than as the attack I intended. Finally, he shook his head. 'Until now, no.'

I swallowed. 'What do you mean "until now"?'

He hesitated, then fell back on a Felix-style grin that stretched thin across defined lips, as though an artist had drawn them with great care. 'I mean, taking into account all of my life to this moment, I can honestly say to you I don't know what that heart-stopping sense of falling in love with someone that others write poetry about feels like.' He shrugged but I thought his explanation too long and I don't think I was imagining a slightly curious new tension reaching between us.

And my even odder way of addressing that tension was to attempt what I thought was an adroit change of subject. 'I know what's troubling me – you have no beard, no moustache.' I remarked, wishing in that heartbeat that the walls of this herb garden would just fall in on me and save me humiliating myself any further.

'No facial hair in the British Army allowed. All soldiers to be clean-shaven. Gone are the lustrously hirsute chins of yesteryear,' he said with a flourish of his unbandaged hand. I found myself smiling as the former awkwardness mercifully dissipated. 'I suspect your brothers and Aimery are bald-chinned as well.'

I couldn't imagine it. 'Felix won't be thrilled with another chore. He'd want to transfer instantly to the navy, even though he sickens in a rowboat.'

Sébastien smiled, rubbed his chin, and I could hear the rasp of his scruffy beard pushing through. 'I must shave; I could be court-martialled for this alone,' he remarked.

I knew he was jesting. I stood. 'So, let me organise some warmer clothes for you and some of that healing soup.' And now I had to offer a proper invitation or appear churlish. 'Will you join me for dinner tonight, Sébastien?'

'I would be delighted to.'

'Right,' I said, wondering why I was feeling guilty and as though I was on dangerous ground. 'I shall see you this evening. Madame Mouflard will make all the arrangements.'

He nodded, took my hand again – this time with his uninjured one – and laid a soft kiss at my knuckles as he murmured a polite thank you. I felt flustered and when I became flustered it regularly amused Felix that I had a tendency to say the first thing that came into my head.

'Did you crush some thyme?'

He laughed aloud this time at my oddity. 'Yes, moments before you joined me. You can still smell it?'

'Of course. I smelled it as I arrived. It has sat between us throughout our conversation.'

'Really?'

'Yes, I can smell soap lingering in your freshly washed hair, I can smell the tea we shared on your breath, the —'

'Wait, Fleurette. What is this trick?'

'No trick.' I shrugged. 'I can't play the piano very well; and I know my teacher despaired of my inability to sew without tying myself in knots; my cooking needs lots of work, although my taste is highly developed . . . however, I have inherited my father's talent.'

'You have the perfumer's gift of the Nose?' he said, sounding awed.

I pushed my nose up comically with a finger, surprising myself at such a playful gesture with a stranger. 'I do. So does my twin brother. But his being the male makes him *le nez* and me simply . . .' I gave a twist of my mouth, looking for the right words. 'Well, helpful to have around, shall we say.'

His face was full of consternation as I spoke but his expression evened and he brought us back onto less controversial ground.

'And so do you like thyme?'

'With food or do you mean in perfume?'

He considered my question. 'The latter.'

I nodded, feeling happier to be on familiar territory that I felt stable on; the previous discussion had felt momentarily dangerous and I didn't think it right to reveal my inner desire to Aimery's brother. 'Indeed I do. In perfume it has an earthy yet somehow sparkling quality . . . a high, green note that speaks of the hillsides and of more ancient forests. I think it has the capacity to form one of the brightest bases to a cologne for men without dominating it.'

He was paying attention despite his smile. His brow knitted. 'Why men's?'

I looked to the sky, taking the aroma of crushed thyme inward again, drawing it through my memories. 'Because it has a woodiness to it that complements a man's smell.'

'Is that why it goes well with meat?'

'Possibly,' I said carefully.

'How do I smell to you?'

'Like a hunter. Straight from the forest.'

Sébastien tipped back his oval-shaped head and laughed before howling like a wolf.

'I'll send some shaving equipment for you too,' I added as a means to take my leave before I spun on a heel and forced myself not to scurry.

I supervised the cooking of the evening meal, even helping out by picking leaves of herbs into the pot, although I could tell Clothilde would have preferred me not to be in the kitchen.

'And you, Madame? What will you be eating?' she said, trying to disguise what was presumably her sense of feeling crowded.

'I'm happy with soup too, and perhaps some of your delicious bread I smelled baking early this morning.'

'Of course, Madame. We French eat bread with everything, no?' she said with a shrug, as if I needed to see a doctor for such a comment; obviously my attempt to compliment had fallen short.

'Is there something wrong, Clothilde?' I couldn't let her get away with being rude to my face. Heaven knew what she said behind my back. I saw her flick a glance at a purse-lipped Madame Mouflard and she shook her head.

'Forgive me, I have just not seen thyme in my chicken soup previously.'

'I like thyme, though,' I countered. Now, why was I blushing? Had she noticed? 'Er . . . and there are few herbs to choose from this time of year.'

'Yes, but I have some parsley in the greenhouse, Madame. I suspect that works better.'

'Just trying something new,' I offered as airily as I dared. 'Smells intriguing, don't you think?'

'Intriguing, Madame?' she repeated with feigned innocence.

'I'll leave you to it,' I said, smiling for her and the kitchen hand. Madame Mouflard had her back conveniently to me.

'Dinner for seven?' Clothilde checked.

'Dinner for two at seven, yes, please.' Well, I thought it was an amusing play on words to farewell them with but clearly the kitchen was in no mood for jest. 'Thank you,' I said and dismissed myself to hurry away and cool my cheeks upstairs.

What a buffoon! And why the heat at the mention of thyme? I could try to convince myself it was the heat of the stove but the memory of Sébastien's lips touching my knuckles . . . perhaps made all the more sensual somehow because of the leather gloves that divided us. It was an entirely permissible gesture – a polite one, a kiss between in-laws – so why did it feel like it was inappropriate and that his kiss, amidst thyme-scented air, was somehow stolen?

Ancient civilisations revered the benefits of the Mediterranean shrub with its elliptical curl of leaves and tiny lilac flower. I'm sure I read in one of those dusty books from my father's botany library that it was one of the first holy herbs. That's right, I could remember that passage now. It was connected with a recipe of medieval days in which thyme was supposedly a key ingredient 'to achieve a state to see the elves'. That had amused me then and still did, but did not detract from the elegance of its scent, which the pharaohs were embalmed with, the Romans purified their living quarters with, and the crusading knights were given a sprig of as an emblem of their courage. This delicate plant that grew in our gardens around Grasse, often wild, hid a surprisingly robust aroma . . . with its faint aftertaste of clove that was a mainstay in culinary uses, especially in our herbes de Provence, but was also an important ingredient in our family's perfumes.

It was a feminine smell at first because of its freshness and yet, I believed, deeply masculine with its complexity of wooded spiciness. It would now always remind me of Sébastien, I suppose. As thyme was one of the few antiseptics on the battlefield, there was little wonder that even his bandages gave up the faint smell of it. His eyes were the colour of thyme too: indistinct darkish green like its leaves, which were a metallic grey on the underside. Yes, if a plant was required to summarise Sébastien, then thyme would serve him well . . . in its fragrance – not brash and boorish, but with a softer, more feminine side. In its colour. In its variety of uses. In its presence . . . important in so many aspects and yet never shouting its own praise; like the thyme of any herb garden, Sébastien let the showier plants announce themselves with more colour, bigger leaves, louder fragrances. And yet it was to thyme that the bees flocked. It was historically to thyme that men of the spiritual, medical, ritual turned. And thyme, seemingly plain and quiet, upon scrutiny was the most beautiful of herbs . . . with its whorls of tiny flowers.

I smiled to myself. I didn't want to think on a plant that encapsulated Aimery but the notion that the leather represented my husband as a barrier between me and his brother was amusing for a single heartbeat before I gathered myself. The attractiveness of Sébastien was not a point I could allow myself to dwell upon further. Having these feelings, I told myself, was akin to lechery and bordering on adulterous. What a pity he had not been around before now! Marriage to Sébastien would have been far less problematic and infinitely more agreeable to me. I cooled my cheeks with my hands, annoyed with myself for even thinking such a thought.

I needed a distraction. Everything was quiet in the warehouses. The oil we'd distilled was gathered, silently deepening its flavours, while the enfleurage frames were now washed, fully dried, scrutinised for cracks or breaks and were likely right now being stacked away for next summer. Even all the main work in the fields was done. The soil was icy hard and resting and the two factories understandably quiet with their main tasks complete and their men gone to war.

It was nearing four o'clock. I would take a walk; into the town square would be best. I could check for any post, as the woman who had the job of delivering our mail was far older than me and quite slow on her bicycle. I could save her a trip up the hill to the villa, if anything had arrived from my brothers. It would clear my head too. I rang the bell and within a minute Jeanne was at my door.

'I thought I'd walk into the town.'

'Of course,' she said and entered to gather the right coat and accoutrements. 'Would you like me to accompany you, Madame?'

I slipped my arms into the coat that she helped me to shrug on. 'Thank you, no, I shall be fine. I just thought I'd take a quick stroll. I've been cooped up in the house for too long. I'd go to the Delacroix villa, if it wasn't so lonely and closed up for winter.'

'Yes, don't go. I always think a house with dustcovers is depressing.'

I smiled at her. 'Just until my brothers return.'

She gave me a look of sympathy. We all tried to keep each other's spirits up but in doing so we were hiding our constant worry that those we loved would never come home from the Front.

'Have you heard from your fiancé?'

She shook her head, smiling bravely as she tied my scarf neatly. 'I am taking the view that it is better to have no news than a telegram, Madame.'

'Yes, that is a wise approach.' I was fast developing a knack of speaking words and saying nothing of value when it came to reassuring the women, not just of the house but of the town as well. It didn't matter that I was young or without much experience, I think my new status as married elite meant I was now expected to have the composure to inspire. The sad truth was that I was as anxious as the next person and the shadows around my eyes that lurked like bruising attested to poor sleeps, worrying about Felix in particular.

I left the villa, crunching over the gravel drive, and felt immediately better to step onto the worn cobbles of Grasse's narrow, walled streets. Warm salutations came from the houses above from women peering over balconies as I entered the alleyways that would lead me down into the main square. I recall that Napoléon had visited our town nearly one century earlier; it was said people welcomed him with violets, his favourite flower. The imperial colour, the colour of princes of the church, the most expensive dye colour in the world achieved from a sea snail . . . but my world was flowers, and I needed to shake those beautiful petals from my thoughts. And still I had the image in my mind that they seemed to shower on me and stick as effectively as any enfleurage.

The flower – its colour, its ink, its letters – connected me to my lying father, his treacherous lover, my dead mother, my grandmother, my violent, arrogant husband, and now even Sébastien, who wrote with a nib dipped in violet. I rounded a familiar corner, smiled greetings at some women I recognised, but hurried on with intent . . . my thoughts forcing themselves away from all the sins of the past. Only Sébastien was blameless. He was pure in his intent.

I passed one of the fountains where children sipped from its spout, spraying water at each other. I smiled, ruffled the hair of one as he stepped back laughing, no doubt unaware of me or France's plight. I ruffled his hair. '*Bonjour*, Hugo.'

'Excuse me, Madame De Lasset,' he coughed out, cutting his friend an embarrassed glance.

'How is your mother?'

'She manages, Madame. I am on an errand for her.'

'Has she heard from your father?' Hugo's father was Georges, one of our best rose farmers.

Hugo shook his head. 'Not in a while. She cries a lot, Madame.'

I knew I had some stray coins in my pocket, which I took out now. 'Here, Hugo, run your errand and buy something extra for your sisters and brothers . . . perhaps some sweets.' I palmed off the equivalent of a couple of francs in nickel centimes. It wasn't a lot to me but it was plenty to Hugo and his family. His eyes widened as he glanced at the coins. I didn't want to linger over this and I made a shooshing sound. 'Hurry, don't keep your mother waiting,' I urged.

He touched his cap, still a little dazed, I think, and ran off at my nod. I made a mental note to do more for the mothers of larger families. I decided then and there that the Delacroix and De Lasset families could maybe provide some extra basics for these women who were no doubt in a desperate struggle for survival of their youngsters. Bread, milk, cheese . . . some staples. Yes, I would speak to Madame Mouflard later today and we would get some sort of program underway.

I arrived into the bustle of Les Aires Square and realised it had been too long since I'd seen its colourful architecture, painted mainly in orange tones to warm the quadrangle shaded by its tall buildings. Shutters were closed on this cold day but their pastel greens and blues added a sense of whimsy and joy to a wintry scene of barren trees and pinched expressions on the people moving within the frigid shadows below. Today the watery sun just managed to slant lazily off only the uppermost storey of the buildings, turning them a fiery orange. The town square was not nearly as busy as it might normally be if it had its population of men moving around it. The trees were naked, their limbs pointing skyward in an unadorned beseech to the heavens. They stood as stark sentinels around the square, echoing the poignancy of the Front and our men who kept watch against the enemy. Certainly not so many people were seated, sipping beverages: none drinking liquor, of course, or smoking or laughing with deep voices. No doubt it was the absence of younger men that made it so easy to pick him out.

Sébastien shuffled along, looking into shop windows, overly conscious, I surmised, that he was here and not at the Front, although his pronounced limp and his clearly injured arm pointedly answered any questions. He politely lifted his hat to passers-by and finally paused to stand at the fountain to smile at children floating paper boats and a couple of boys pretending to be soldiers shooting at each other. I sighed at the innocence – the idea that war was a game and that a winner would eventuate and everyone would cheer. That France would go back to its routine probably seemed feasible in their minds. The adults around them, however, were already counting the cost of lives in sons, brothers, fathers . . . lovers. I admonished myself at that last thought. Would I ever have a lover? Someone whose touch or even the thought of his touch would excite me? My gaze was lingering on Sébastien, whom I surreptitiously watched from the doorway of a draper's shop, and experienced the sensation that I was pilfering . . . as though by not announcing myself I was stealing something from him. A customer cut me a glance of irritation at having to push by me to enter but then realised whom she was glaring at and dipped her eyes. I had to look away from the dark stranger who was occupying far too much space in my mind and do the right thing by the lady before me.

'*Pardon*,' she murmured. 'Good afternoon, Madame De Lasset.'

'And to you, Madame Raineri. Forgive me, I was just wishing our square was populated by our men,' I explained, affecting a wince of sorrow. 'It strikes me sadly that for every man who has left us, there is at least one woman, potentially several, who grieves at his departure to war . . . mothers, wives, sisters, daughters, nieces, granddaughters . . .' I sighed.

'Monsieur De Lasset and your fine brothers will return as heroes, Madame, I am sure of it,' she confided, with a much kinder expression.

'Let's hope all the men of Grasse keep safe, including Monsieur Raineri,' I said. We both knew our hopes were wishful as news of the fighting intensified. We'd heard yesterday that one of Pierre's sons was gravely wounded, lying in a hospital somewhere helpless and likely dying, and there had been at least another dozen deaths that Jeanne knew about from the town. But we shared an understanding smile as she entered the drapery and I felt obliged to leave the doorway. My attention returned to Sébastien, who had shifted position and was now in the centre of the square, about to attempt a wobbling kick of a football to a trio of boys, impressed that he was joining in.

He laughed with them and I hadn't seen that open expression from him previously; it was as though, just briefly, he was one of them – a carefree child again despite his injuries. I imagined his lonely childhood; he must have spent plenty of it wondering about his father, his brother and why he had been ripped away from them. I should have felt a similar pang of regret for Aimery, but my husband did not pay sufficient heed when I'd told him that I didn't forget anything. It was a gift as much as a curse and unfortunately for Aimery I would not forget – or forgive – his viciousness on our wedding night.

Now that I had broken cover and Sébastien was facing my way, I could hardly pretend not to be aware of him, especially as he had just seen me. I felt a drift of annoyance with myself that his noticing me won a pang of pleasure. I lifted a gloved hand and smiled indulgently. He bade his playmates farewell and half limped, half skipped towards me.

'Be careful. What are you doing here when you should be resting?' I warned and then I saw his bandages oozing afresh. 'Oh, Sébastien.'

He looked embarrassed by the stain. 'Sorry,' he murmured.

'What for? Wasn't it re-dressed?'

He shrugged.

'Clearly not very well. Come on,' I said, now sounding like a wearied mother. 'My father always said to me if you want something done properly, do it yourself.'

'A wise man, but don't let me keep you from your tasks.'

'I was just on my way to the post office, beating the delivery.'

'Well, let me walk you to it. There may be some news.'

'I'm hoping for something from Felix. What about your hand, though?'

'Dear Fleurette, this is nothing in comparison to what is going on in the north-east to all our soldiers – I'm truly the luckiest of all of them.'

Something in his glance told me he was conveying more than his bare words said. 'But you were sent here to convalesce, so the least we can do is take the best care we can with you.'

He nodded as if to say 'Touché'. 'I'd offer an arm if I could,' he said, looking politely towards his elbow.

'I know.'

'And I'd enjoy walking with you on my arm.'

I cleared my throat and smiled. There was no easy or suitable response to that so I said nothing.

12

We strolled companionably without touching but still I was aware we were drawing undisguised interest from the women of the town. I found myself introducing Sébastien to many: some had heard already that my brother-in-law had finally come home, others were shocked to hear it. All were titillated by who he was, of course. The younger women were instantly interested because he was single, obviously rich and his surname was De Lasset. It was like unearthing gold bullion. Neither of us revelled in the notoriety and I couldn't get into the post office fast enough.

'Yes, Madame, there is a letter for you from Monsieur Delacroix.'

I couldn't help the small clap of glee I gave.

'I knew you'd be delighted to hear it,' the ageing and much-beloved postmaster assured with an indulgent grin. 'If he can write, he's safe,' he whispered as he patted my hand. He'd known me since I was a baby in my mother's arms. I wondered what the postmaster believed about my mother's death. I tried to imagine my father convincing everyone of complications after birth, which meant the physician was implicated in the lies . . . I would have marched straight to his clinic and demanded the truth had he not died last year. Did anyone know that my father was writing letters to my mother's best friend and that her best friend's son was his, not Monsieur De Lasset's? I felt the anger building again.

Nevertheless, I took the scruffy letter as if it was the most precious item in the world and felt the mood pass because I was too pleased to have news from my brother. I glanced at Sébastien, waving it.

'I'm so pleased for you,' he said, smiling.

'Thank you, Monsieur,' I called over my shoulder, kissing the letter to show the postmaster how much it meant to receive, and felt the previous irritation passing.

The letter from Felix felt as though it was burning a hole in my pocket but I was determined that we first stop Sébastien's bleeding. On our way home I gave some centimes to one of the town children and asked him to take a message to our family doctor to call on the house tomorrow.

'Repeat the message, please, Louis,' I urged.

He dutifully said aloud what I'd asked. Sébastien's face twisted in soft vexation. 'I shall be fine, Fleurette, please . . .'

'No. Blood loss is dangerous in so many ways – as a chemist you know this. Anyway, I want someone professional to look at your wound again. But he's probably out on calls now so let me at least change those bandages and keep the wound clean.'

We continued in silence up the hill, back to the villa, and I felt an unexpected sense of ease to be walking with Sébastien. I don't know why I had the feeling I did but conversation didn't feel necessary. Our quiet was an entirely comfortable one.

As we cleared the town and found ourselves walking into slightly more open vistas, he sighed. 'I can only imagine how beautiful Grasse looks in summer.'

'You must see it to believe it,' I remarked. 'This year was one of our best harvests.'

'What will you do with the product?'

I shrugged. 'I'm a woman, in case you hadn't noticed,' I said archly.

'As a matter of fact I had,' he replied in an understated tone.

I couldn't help but grin back. 'I don't do anything with it without a man's say so.'

He blinked at me with consternation. 'You're also a Delacroix at heart and a De Lasset in name. That alone takes you into a new status.'

'A new breed of woman?' I offered, trying for more levity.

He stopped moving, his expression intent. 'You have the Nose. You have the skill that most only dream of possessing. A perfumer, Fleurette, is what you are.'

I snorted. 'Tell that to Henri or, better still, try having a conversation about me being anywhere near the factory with Aimery. I've been effectively forbidden and the chemists at the De Lasset laboratory look upon me as an intruder they must bear but not permit any knowledge being shared with.'

'Then change it,' he urged.

I gasped. 'I'd like to see you try.'

'All right.'

'What do you mean?'

'Well, one good turn deserves another. You change my bandages and I'll change the world you live in.'

'I don't understand.' I frowned.

'Let's make a perfume.'

'What?' I realised we must look ridiculous perched roadside, looking down the valley, frowning at each other. Tongues would be wagging, surely. We were hardly hidden. Somehow, I didn't care. Sébastien's words were lighting something beneath me that had only ever needed one spark of agreement from a man.

'You heard. I don't know how long I'm here but perhaps a

week or two, so let's not be idle, let's work on something. You must have ideas?'

'Ideas? They're pulsing through me.'

'Then share one. What's going on at the moment . . . in the factory, I mean?'

'Not a lot. In winter it's mostly about cleaning and repair of equipment. But I think Henri managed to get through a shipment from the Far East before the world went mad.'

'What did he bring in?'

'Oh, the usual,' I said airily. It felt reassuring to be talking about my favourite subject with someone interested. He was listening attentively too, not at all distracted by the old couple approaching, to whom I flicked a hurried glance. When I looked back at Sébastien his attention hadn't wavered; his gaze had a disarming way of navigating a path to effortlessly close all distance between us. It didn't matter that we stood suitably apart with room for two others to stand shoulder to shoulder in that polite gap; we might as well have been pressed up against each other for the way my increasingly focused awareness of him made me feel. I was risking being rude and allowing the elderly pair to pass me by and I caught myself just in time to look away from Sébastien and find a bright salutation. They murmured theirs back and continued their shuffling, arm in arm, leaning against each other, dressed immaculately as they tottered into town.

'Aren't they marvellous.' Sébastien glanced with admiration at their backs.

'Monsieur and Madame Vence. She's in her early seventies but he's eighty-one. Used to refer to my father as the "Delacroix boy" when they spoke.' I smiled at the memory. 'He, and now his sons, are the best growers of violets in the region, although perhaps you could guess that.'

There it was again. That flower. It haunted me.

'Why should I guess it?' A gentle but quizzical smile puckered his cheeks.

I gave a soft shrug of embarrassment. 'I shouldn't presume everyone smells the aromas that I do.'

'No, Fleurette.' He chuckled. 'You should not. It's winter and you're smelling spring violets off that man?'

I pushed an invisible strand of hair behind my ear in a nervous gesture I was aware of whenever I felt caught out. But his tone was awed and that made me sigh a laugh. 'To tell you the truth, I'm likely smelling years of past springs on his clothes.'

'You're amazing,' he said, shaking his head. It was spoken beneath his breath and I only just caught it before the gentle breeze on the exposed position we'd paused at caught his words and buffeted them away into the valley. Our gazes met, held, and it felt as though a new link was made . . . a forbidden connection. I had the vivid image in my mind of Sébastien's battle-scarred fingers of his good hand intertwining with my pale, unblemished fingers. The mental picture spread a bright warmth that flashed in my face, I was sure, but far more dangerously low between my hips, and that only made me blush deeper.

'I'm sorry, I shouldn't speak so openly,' he quickly followed.

'No, no, it's lovely. I mean . . . it's charming that you . . .' I didn't really know what I was trying to say.

He helped me out by returning us to safer ground. 'I meant what I said about making a perfume together. It will give me something to occupy myself, help offset the discomfort from this,' he said, looking dejectedly at his bandaged hand. 'We've got two laboratories at our disposal and any amount of raw product, I'm guessing. And I'm your chemist and I am happy to take your instructions. Let's put your talent to use and stop you moping around a house that anyone can see you don't enjoy and get you doing something that helps Grasse, helps keep the spirits of the men up who are struggling to remember what home felt like.'

I stared at him now with a sense of wonder, unable to respond.

'I won't try to explain what the soldiers are enduring. This is not the polite war of yesteryear where leaders shared parleys. This is brutal and bloody. Death is swift and scores of men are cut down at once. Too many will die from time-poor doctors and surgeons who can't attend to the injured fast enough rather than from the wounds themselves. Men will die alone in feverish states in filthy trenches from disease rather than the glory of the battlefield. Snipers will cowardly take aim and slaughter men invisibly rather than face each other as our forebears did across an open field. This is ruthless, soulless, unimaginable suffering.'

I swallowed, watching his surge of emotion come at me, like an inexorable tide pushing to shore.

'And when the men of Grasse return, you won't recognise them. Apart from how they may have changed outwardly, they are going to be different in here.' He touched his chest and I found that gesture profoundly moving because in my heart I knew he spoke the truth.

'Let us make a perfume, then, that speaks to our brave men, and women can proudly wear it in their honour.'

He reined the passion back and the silvering glitter in his eyes dulled and he was quiet Sébastien again. He finally let me go from that hold and our invisible fingers unfurled. 'You will make your family proud and the men of Grasse will have their spirits uplifted to learn that all the women are tackling new skills and, yes, even down to making perfume.' Now he shocked me by suddenly gripping me by the shoulder. 'The world is ruled by men, Fleurette, who make stupid decisions to go to war and ruin the lives of those they are supposed to represent. But if this war does anything, it's going to prove to the world that women are casting off the shackles that men have put around them. Are you familiar with Emmeline Pankhurst in England?'

I glanced at his hand on my shoulder and he immediately let it fall away. I didn't mean it to be an admonishing look, I just wasn't sure such a display was seemly in public . . . or indeed anywhere. Nevertheless, I missed the weight of his touch as soon as it left and he reached to take his cane again, which he'd supported against his thigh. He leaned heavily on it as though bearing a new strain. I could swear I still felt the warmth of his palm against my overcoat, seeping through its thick wool, reaching through the lighter wool of my dress to touch my skin in a private, intimate scald. It was this notion that sent my mind foggy momentarily and I realised I was stammering a response. 'I . . . barely . . . yes, well, I know she is involved in political disturbance,' I admitted, trying to regain some ground.

'Oh, she's so much more than that. Her union will, I suspect, bring massive change not just to the women's movement in Britain but beyond, I'm sure. And whether you love or loathe her, she's fighting for the rights of women to be recognised.'

'I'm not sure what you want . . .' I began but trailed off, searching his face.

'I want you.' He said these words so urgently and emphatically that I froze. He saw the consternation – perhaps even fear – register in my face, no doubt, because I watched him run a hand through that ever-disintegrating parting in his hair as he hurried to explain. 'By that, of course, I mean that I want you to grasp that the people of this town look to their leading families. And if those leading families only consist of women at this stage, then the burden of responsibility falls to them.'

I blinked.

'Lead the way,' he urged. 'Your perfumer has gone to the Front. So you should step into his shoes.'

'Don't think I don't dream often on that.' I shook my head. 'But I can't follow through because when Felix —'

'When your brother returns, the world will be different. I know people can't imagine this but anyone who has been at the Front knows it. When Felix comes home, you may find him a willing ally in having a second perfumer at this side. The fact that you're a woman may cause less of a furore than you think. Women are already taking on much of the burden of keeping France going right now and I suspect Britain will follow in her footsteps once conscription starts happening . . . and it surely will next year.'

'Me . . . that has always been my private intention,' I breathed, as though a door was opening on my greatest dream.

It would have been hard for him to avoid hearing the wistfulness in my tone in the same way that I had clearly heard him say something else just moments previously. He'd covered it well with a blustering explanation but we'd both been astonished, appalled by what I suspected I was right in believing was a reveal.

'Is that a yes?'

With his wide-eyed, smiling encouragement it seemed so easy to cross the threshold. 'It is.' I knew by entering through that door I was walking onto life's quicksand – I could picture Henri's horror, Aimery's anger, probably, and no doubt Felix would feel only amusement. But I suspected even Felix might wonder about the brave and new vision that Sébastien was talking about for women in this future world he seemed able to imagine.

Back in my room, I sat on the bed, still in my coat. Only now, many minutes since lowering myself to the soft mattress, was I even beginning to pull at the fingers of my gloves to ease them off my hand. But I was doing this by rote, not concentrating, because all of me was focused on two topics – both of them unrelated, you could say, and both so deeply intertwined I couldn't separate them. And most disconcerting of all, both had flung my normally alert mind into a fractured state. Everything looked precisely how I'd left it. Jeanne worked hard to keep my surrounds ordered given that I was interminably messy, which no doubt stemmed from the lack of a mother in my life coupled with an indulgent father. What no one could see or touch, however, was my tidy mind. I was one of those people who could compartmentalise her life. Presumably this was a reflection of my vault-like ability to store information and particularly memories, but most especially smells, of course.

And in spite of that talent and in contrast to the neat and tidy atmosphere of my chamber, my mind was scattering. It felt like I had spilled a box of the ball bearings that were used in the factory. Glimmering thoughts, like those tiny silver balls, were rolling out of reach. The more I grabbed for purchase on the thoughts, the more slippery they became and the more determined they seemed to escape me.

Apparently I had agreed to make a perfume. This was no small commitment. Not only a challenge in itself, but it was as though I was shaking my fist at society and ignoring all the protocols we lived by. I would be throwing a spotlight on myself, something my father would have abhorred, but my sense of loyalty to him was so compromised I could push past that barrier, although there were a dozen more lining up behind it.

Far worse than this was Sébastien's revealing slip of the tongue. I heard it. So had he. We'd both recoiled from it as one would from a viper spotted in the grass.

'*I want you*,' he had said. And there was a full stop at the end of that phrase. It was a full sentence. The inflection as he'd spoken had fallen by the passage of the third word. He had completed what he'd wanted to say – even if it did sound involuntary, almost . . . a reactionary response to my query. And still I had glimpsed the raw honesty of his feeling. He'd quickly regained his composure, instantly adjusting what he'd meant as though he had been following a thought and paused after the third word . . . but our shared embarrassment – and yes, shared guilt – was plain.

My newly awoken awareness of a man and my particularly heightened sensitivity to this one couldn't have been more ill advised. Of all men to find myself holding my breath over, stealing glances of, eavesdropping from, even thinking about him right now so determinedly . . . he was about as dangerous a choice as one could imagine. My husband's brother! The brother Aimery cared so little about that he couldn't even be bothered to wait for his arrival at our wedding. The fact that war had stepped in the way was irrelevant; Aimery simply did not care for or about Sébastien.

But then my ranging fear began to pull itself together. As though by warming it up in my mind and melting all the scattered elements, I was drawing them together into a soup of anxiety. Sébastien was not my husband's brother, was he? Sébastien was actually my half-brother's half-brother.

I panicked inwardly. Minutes passed as I stared at the rug, focusing on a single sprawl of flowers at its edge, falling into the childlike game of trying to make out a different shape of the petals . . . a face, a dragon, an angel. Anything but focusing on the fear.

Finally I stood, pulled off my coat and paced. Why was I feeling like this? Why could I accurately picture and describe the feathered curve of Sébastien's eyelashes, which blinked in a dark swoop of half crescents and framed his smoky eyes with charcoal intensity? How could I do this so easily and yet I couldn't, in all truth, even picture the true colour of Aimery's eyes, let alone his more subtle features. Blue? Muddy blue like a dirty fountain, perhaps. Who cares? I suddenly thought with a vicious clarity. Aimery cannot be regarded as my husband. Having thoughts of another man does not betray him, or cuckold him. But even with this surprisingly clear-headed rationale, I felt guilt lining up like an army of soldiers down my gullet, all the way through my gut, and in charge of those soldiers were their captains, horror and shame, yelling loudly in my mind.

I had barely paused as I arrived in the house, lost in my disgrace. I had been in such a hurry to get upstairs and examine what I'd just agreed to, leaving behind a bemused Sébastien and maidservant, I couldn't imagine what he said to her about my flight. But as he seemed to possess the wit of Felix I'm sure he thought of something immediately appropriate and vaguely amusing to say that would alleviate any potential alarm.

I leaned my back against the door as I unravelled my scarf and tossed it to where my coat and gloves lay on the bed. My mind felt bruised with shameful thoughts of Sébastien, pretending our conversation and time together was innocent. It might have been coincidental to meet but there was certainly nothing naïve about our heightened awareness of each other.

Sébastien's bandages might have to wait until I calmed. I snatched at Felix's letter, thrilled to hear from him but equally thrilled to be distracted from my spiralling thoughts that suddenly felt pathetic as I was reminded of where in France this letter hailed from. I couldn't even wait to slice it open neatly with a letter opener and nearly tore the pages with my haste.

Fleurette!

What a surprise to hear from you again so soon. You must have been reading my mind, for I was thinking of you only this morning as we trudged along yet another muddied road. I am glad that you are so far from the noise of the guns. I played the game we used to as children, trying to guess what the other was thinking, and all I could imagine was the peace that you wake to. I helplessly envy you that but I know you won't mind. Your morning begins with the chattering of the birds. We, however, are woken by the rip

*and snarl of the Boche's guns. Dare I say our seventy-fives
are more melodious, even to a tone-deaf oaf such as I?*
    Anyway, I'm writing to tell you that Aimery is here!

My breath caught at that. All of them together, none of them wise
to the knowledge that they shared the same blood through our
father? I set the repulsive thought aside and focused on Felix and
my intense relief at knowing that he's alive, he's safe.

*To be truthful, I had no idea that his company was so close
until this afternoon when in he strolls while Henri and I
were making the most of our meagre meal. He must be
finding this war rather agreeable for he looks every inch the
dashing officer. I don't know how he manages to stay so
tidy and correct. Well, rest assured that the action and fresh
air are doing him no harm at all. I myself am noticing my
uniform is suddenly roomy; even podgy Henri has defined
cheekbones.*

I chuckled, even though I knew he was doing his damnedest to put a
happy slant on his situation. I knew just from the smattering that
Sébastien had shared that Felix's days were ugly and frightening.

*It's true my feet are interminably sore after relentless
marching. Can you imagine me – someone who rarely
walked further than a few kilometres while hunting
pheasant – now capable of completing dozens of kilometres
in a single day, as well as carrying all of my equipment?
Heroic indeed . . . I hope you're on your feet and cheering.*

I smiled again but not for long. He'd set up a cheerful introduction
so that talk of fighting might slip by me more easily.

The fighting has been harsh and for a number of days the enemy has had the better of us. We were forced to leave behind our dead on the field of battle without being able to accord them a proper burial, which hurt our hearts more deeply than most of us cared to share. All we could do for our wounded was to offer them some meagre aid but many of them must have fallen into the hands of the enemy.

Yesterday, though, despair was set aside and we not only returned to the offensive but have halted the Kronprinz's army. From the very moment that we left our positions the enemy's artillery tried to crush our spirits but we continued onwards, ignoring the crashes and eruptions of the ground before us as shells exploded here and there. The companies followed their orders as though they were on parade for the commander-in-chief. The Boche could not have failed to remark that a few shells could not dampen the ardour of the Chasseur when he is fighting in defence of his beloved country.

These Germans are good soldiers and their NCOs know their trade but once cornered they soon raise their hands and shout 'kamerade'. How do they know I am a comrade? I would rather like to think that I look far too stern in battle. Tomorrow I shall take a mirror with me. As I rush the enemy I shall pause and have a look to see if I am smiling.

I was tearing up helplessly; Felix was working so hard to amuse and I loved him all the more for his desperate need to shield me from the worst.

Oh, dear sister, would you be ashamed of me if I said that I have not bathed in at least a fortnight? I smell something awful. Perhaps that alone might frighten the Germans into surrender? Yesterday we captured an entire German hospital! Poor sods lying pathetically in their cots. We were gentle with the injured. The German doctors assure us that they look after our wounded with no less care than their own, which is heartening after having to leave many behind.

Our hearts go out to the families of those who have fallen. As their officer I have the arduous duty of writing to mothers and wives explaining how Louis or Maximilien met their fate, which is why I know you'll forgive me for being such a poor correspondent. It is a sad duty but I am sure that these grieving women will be comforted by the knowledge that their loved ones have died so that France might be free from the Kaiser's yoke.

I regret that it is not just our valiant soldiers that are paying the price of this barbarian invasion. The roads are lined with shuffling destitute citizens from those villages now occupied by the enemy. Their homes have been destroyed, much of their livestock killed and now they haunt the roads carrying their bundles containing whatever few possessions they could carry away.

The smallest of the children must either walk or add to the weight of their already overburdened mothers or elder siblings. I have seen so many of the little ones who have no shoes and what they have to eat will not last them for more than a few days. This desperate state of the innocents is the most heartbreaking sight of all in this ugly war.

Such sights as these only make those of us who defend our beloved country all the more determined to do what must be done. In the meantime my single greatest duty is foot inspection. Yes, indeed, I am the Lord High Lieutenant of Foot Rot! Now I can almost see you laughing, dear sister, but you should be apprised that foot inspection is

*the highlight of my day and a vital part of an officer's duty
and I take my role so very seriously. As you can tell, I am
being equally heroic to Henri and no doubt your strutting
husband, for – let's face it – no one else would get nearly so
close to so many feet, humming with filth and infection, as
I and my long-suffering fellow feet inspectors!*

He had drawn a stick figure of a man holding his nose and falling
backwards. Somehow, in that naïve rendition and with a few
strokes of his pen, he had managed to capture the comedy of his
unenviable duty. While I knew he was deliberately diverting me
from the horror, I couldn't help the explosion of private laughter
that dissolved into tears of empathy. I prayed that all the angels
that seemed to hover around Felix's charmed life would continue to
protect him, keep him safe, and bring him home to us.

I read his final line with a happy sigh.

*Some soap would be a most welcome gift for your horribly
grubby brothers.*
Both sending our love,
Felix

I folded up the letter, still teary, laughing gently to myself. I wondered if in looking out for each other's lives, rather than just their
livelihoods, Felix and Henri would cleave closer. We both loved
Henri – no question of that – but I suppose our being twins made us
a happy club of two and his determination to be pompous at every
turn fought against every inclination we collectively shared to
include him.

Reading between the lines of Felix's jolly take on his participa-
tion was the sobering reality of war and being reassured that both
of my brothers – and indeed Aimery – remained safe for now had

the welcome effect of pushing away the upheaval in my mind.

I found fresh perspective in the wake of Felix's letter and was able to remind myself I was a grown woman and in charge of myself and must search for my own solutions to my problems. Sébastien's attention and my shameful feelings towards a man I had only met this morning felt suddenly ridiculous . . . laughable, even. By tonight around the dinner table I would be in control of those feelings, capable of making sparkling conversation and able to divert his attention as much as my own and perhaps channel it into his idea for us to make perfume. I wasn't going to let that opportunity go. In fact, spurred on by Felix's tales of valour, I would make a perfume for the women of France to wear as a salute to their men. It would be proud; it would smell of victory.

I nodded, happy with the image of me triumphantly brandishing a bottle of something called *la Victoire*. It was a terrible name but for now it worked in my mind and I was mentally reaching for the first of the grand base notes that would be the platform for my heroic fragrance. I grinned.

'Ah, *Héroïque* . . . that's what I'll call it,' I said aloud into the stillness of my chamber. The title felt right and I could imagine thousands of French women patriotically dabbing the perfume on themselves daily in honour of their men. I frowned in thought. Even *Patriotique* could work. I couldn't wait to tell Sébastien now; the notion of making our perfume no longer felt gauzy, like a starry nightscape up high . . . untenable, and dreamy. Instead this challenge felt suddenly solid, anchored to the earth with every possibility of nurturing it to fruition, like a rose cutting being planted and cared for all the way to the maturity of its first bud bursting with colour into full bloom and fragrance perfection. Yes, I liked that metaphor.

Excitement glimmered through me to chase away the former guilt that now felt like a momentary girlish crush and nothing to be ashamed of. I would have my composure by dinner and present only the vision of the married woman, enchanted by the attention but not seeking for it to change beyond polite exchanges. My mind was now whirring with possibility for the perfume, and my new relationship with Sébastien feeling as though it could indeed settle into a working partnership, if I could just ignore his presence.

I don't think that, even as a girl, when all my friends were swooning over this fellow or that, I had ever felt the giddiness of attraction that I witnessed in them. I was always too sensible, perhaps, or, more to the point, I was usually distracted and lost in my own thoughts, playing with fragrances in my mind, combining them into harmonious whole 'scents' that were as individual in totality as each of its component smells were.

With my new sense of adventure, and me finally stepping on the pathway I had dreamed about through childhood to this day, the darkness of Aimery was pushed to the recesses of my mind. I would confront it, but not yet.

13

I couldn't be bothered waiting on the household staff; where did they all disappear to in the same moment around three in the afternoon? I had to stop myself flapping my arms with vexation. I now believed my father's claim that perhaps my middle name should have been Impatience instead of Severine, for within ten minutes I had assembled a tray of items and was standing outside Sébastien's room.

I hesitated to knock. Why was that? Somewhere deep in my throat I felt it catch with tension. I dismissed this all as purely connected with this being an unusual situation, of finding myself in a wing of the house I didn't normally walk into.

And then the decision to knock was removed because Sébastien opened the door and blinked in consternation at the threshold. 'Oh, it's you!'

The tray dipped alarmingly in my arms in my surprise at being caught like someone peeping through a keyhole. 'Er . . .'

As usual he rescued me. 'You've brought fresh dressings; you're the kindest of souls, thank you,' he said, and I heard the falsely bright note. He was surely as taken aback to find me on the other side of the door as I was to be found by him lurking rather than taking the lead. 'I really was quite happy to wait for one of the staff to help me.'

'I couldn't balance the tray to knock,' I said, digging up an inspired excuse.

'I heard something,' he said unnecessarily but at least it clued me that he was as ruffled as I was. 'Um . . . shall we put that down here?' he offered, pushing back the linen and crochet table runner.

It was high time for me to keep that personal promise to gather my wits and display easy conversation skills. 'Oh, I do like your room,' I said once the tray was secure. My voice was even and familiar, but not overly intimate. Just the right note, I thought. I wandered to the window. 'So this overlooks . . .?'

'The herb garden and that side of the valley,' he answered, again rather unnecessarily because I could see that for myself having arrived at the window. 'Strikes me as a lonely spot,' he continued.

'In winter, yes, it is,' I said, hating how polite we sounded.

I realised then that we hadn't sounded this awkwardly courteous earlier when we were discussing perfume. Then, we were both filled with passion and longing. I stumbled in my thoughts over that recollection. I think if I were honest, in this moment, I was feeling as though I was filling with passion again but this time I recognised it as being for him, rather than for perfume. The notion was freshly arresting and sent spangles of new alarm through me. I hadn't ever felt such an emotional surge towards anyone outside of my family but this tingling, cumbersome, throat-closing sensation that meant I wasn't able to speak fluently was novel. In my chamber, with that sense of perspective that Felix's letter promoted, I thought I'd imagined how Sébastien affected me. But now I knew it was real and I genuinely had no control over this. I couldn't exert willpower over something that was as reactive and yet wholly natural as breathing, it seemed.

I swung around, trying not to look at Sébastien, who still

managed to impress me as darkly beautiful in his despondency, despite his lame, injured vulnerability. I insisted my gaze rove past that snatched glimpse to take in the rest of the room, deftly avoiding the bed, which was draped in a heavy brocade of the palest blue.

'I wonder what they call this room,' I wondered aloud.

'I have no idea, although I was told it was decorated by my mother,' he said and lifted an eyebrow in a softly ironic way.

I laughed.

'Apparently one of her favourites,' he added.

'Well, she certainly possessed excellent taste,' I said, taking in the deliciously delicate grey and pale blue, with all of the additional fussy gold decor boldly left ungilded. The uninterrupted pale colour scheme achieved a calm, serene ambience that well suited Sébastien, standing in rolled-up shirtsleeves and unbuttoned collar. Oh, dear, my villainous gaze would not leave him be. Downy, dark hair traced around his forearm and led my attention away from the delightful paintwork of his mother's inspired palette to his wrist and the tri-quetrum that looked oddly fragile, sticking out as it did, alone and knobbled. The only reason I even knew such a term was because Felix had once damaged his hand in a fall from a horse and I recall repeatedly trying to pronounce that part of his wrist when the doctor was explaining his injury to my father. I liked the odd way the word sounded rolling off my tongue and had irritated everyone in the household as I practised it for days later.

I tore my attention from his wrist and with a nod to our cook's favourite saying, I fell out of the pan and into the flames, as I con-nected with the candle-smoke grey-green of his eyes.

'The colours, I'm assured by Madame Mouflard, are dove,' he said and I noticed again his excellent accent, with his pronunciation of *tourterelle* without trace of his English breeding. 'And it is set off with a colour Mother mixed herself and called china porcelain blue.' He looked chuffed for explaining this and I couldn't help but laugh at his slight bow at his fine performance. It certainly eased the awkward moment.

'*Bravo!*' I gave a single clap. 'Er, shall we?' I gestured to his injured arm.

'Yes, of course. Fleurette, are you sure about this? I mean, the doctor —'

'Nonsense. The doctor will come tomorrow. I possess a most unenviable dose of impatience to my character. I simply can't waste my life waiting for others, if I can do something faster and better myself.'

'Oh, dear,' he frowned theatrically. 'Headed for disaster with that attitude.'

His efforts to amuse were charming, well timed and, like Felix, he rarely missed his mark. I'd met enough men in my life who aimed for wit but fell short and their remarks became tedious when forced chuckling or smiles had to be dug from my boots. But with Sébastien it felt natural – effortless, even.

We seated ourselves conservatively across the small table in his room. Our knees were barely a handspan apart beneath it but I was glad of that gap.

'I'm just going to cut this all off, all right?' I said, picking up a huge pair of shears from the tray and waiting expectantly for his permission.

'I would never argue with a woman brandishing such a weapon.' His expression had shifted in that heartbeat, though, to serious. 'Fleurette, it's not very pretty beneath these bandages. Have you the stomach for it?'

'If you have, I have,' I remarked, wondering whether I did. I didn't give myself a chance to reconsider and the sharp scissors cut easily through his bandages. As they fell away, the malodorous smell that I hadn't mentioned pervaded his room, intensified, and we both reeled back.

'Bloody hell!' Sébastien gushed. His curse in English broke the spell and we both laughed. 'I'm so sorry,' he continued in French. 'This is awful.'

I shook my head, leaning in, already used to the sweetly foul odour. I was fascinated and horrified at once to see a weeping sutured wound that potentially needed resewing. I couldn't sew to impress anyone. My father had despaired of me, particularly as Felix could sew rather well and Henri could knit, for goodness sake, while their sister could do neither. I realised I'd been saying this all aloud, including my observations of the wound to Sébastien. Our heads were bent close now to mutually inspect his hand and I could feel his thick hair just touching my crown.

It felt exquisitely intimate and I didn't want the contact to end. I knew I was blushing but it didn't matter for we weren't looking at each other. We were both silently mesmerised by the sight of his mangled hand, pathetic and limp.

'Oh, you don't need to sew to impress anyone,' he murmured. 'Least of all me.'

His last few words hung tentatively between us.

He deliberately wiggled his fingers and instinctively I knew it was purely to amuse and predictably in a helpless release of tension I laughed. A tear took me by surprise and landed on his palm, glistening in a tiny puddle of regret and yearning.

'Fleurette.'

'I'm sorry. I didn't know I would feel so moved by your injury. You could be Felix or Henri. You are thousands of men, presumably . . .'

He nodded, understanding what I meant by the unfinished sentence. 'How is Felix? I'm glad a letter has arrived.'

I let out a breath. 'Just in the way you do your damnedest to amuse me, he does the same in an effort to keep me from the horror.'

'Because he loves you.' Our heads lifted and we both eyed one another but I quickly dipped my gaze again. Sébastien cleared his throat. 'I think we should regard me as one of the lucky ones rather than feel sad for me.'

'That's a wonderful attitude,' I murmured. 'I'm no doctor, but this isn't a smell of infection, I don't think.'

'Well, I did begin training as a doctor but found I preferred chemistry, and I can assure you that my hand isn't infected. That nasty aroma is just the decay of dead skin. It's a good smell despite its unpleasantness because it's trying to heal.' He pointed at the gap between his fore and little fingers. 'You'll see when you clean the dried blood away that the surgeon has closed that all up nicely and it's dry, forming scar tissue. Soon the dreadful itch of real healing will begin and I'll drive everyone mad as I reach for knitting needles to plunge down my bandages.'

I smiled at the image he'd prompted. A thought struck me. 'Are you left-handed?'

He shook his head and I sighed with relief.

'Hopefully you can handle a pipette and the like with normal dexterity.'

'I can assure you my pipette is always dexterous,' he said in the driest of tones, definitely designed to win my laughter. I rewarded him and he shook his head as he searched my face. 'Why did you wait so long?' he suddenly asked.

'For what?' I wondered as I poured brown antiseptic into the shallow bowl of water on the tray. The water turned a dark gold and instantly the pungent smell of iodine enveloped us. I immediately pictured the seaweed from where it was derived and I wondered if Sébastien saw the same image.

'To get married,' he replied.

I paused in my ministrations, all thoughts of the beach forgotten. 'What an odd question.'

'Not really. Surely there were suitors banging on the door, kicking it down?'

I grinned. 'Well, if there were, I didn't hear them.'

'Oh, come on. No earnestly lovelorn gents?'

'Not many. I had two big brothers.'

He grinned. 'It's a pity Aimery got to you first.'

I couldn't help it. My gaze flicked up to stare at him. 'Before whom?'

'Before the right brother.'

He'd said it. I took a silent slow breath. 'You mustn't speak like that, Sébastien.'

He withdrew his hand slightly to stop me working on it. It was cleaned anyway; I think I had just been going through the motions, enjoying touching him. What I said and what I did were clearly at odds and I was surely lying to myself.

'You mean I mustn't be honest?'

There was nothing coy about the glance we now shared.

'I think it's dangerous.'

'But you feel it?'

The words of truth were trapped in my throat. They thrashed to get out but I swallowed them back.

'Do you feel what I'm feeling?' he pressed. There was nothing amused in his expression now.

'What are you feeling?' I asked, trying to defend my position, poised with dripping linen and the smell of iodine in my nostrils. Perhaps a marine base note was required for *Héröique*. I blinked in irritation at myself.

Sébastien moved faster than I could react. Staggeringly fast, in fact, and in spite of his limp, he was suddenly out of his chair, around the table and lifting me to my feet. I let go of the linen dampened with bromine and with it my rationality, I'm sure, because I allowed him with his one arm to hold me. I should have expressed shock, pushed him away; at the very least I should have said something to exert my status in the house. Instead I stood in his embrace more surprised by how outrageously I was enjoying it than mortified by it.

'Let me show you instead,' he said, and before I could make even the weakest of attempts to deny him, his lips were on mine, soft but urgently demonstrating his answer.

He didn't force the kiss any further; it was more like tender sips rather than any sense of force. And yet I admit in my newly emboldened state a heat was simmering low in my belly again and my heart felt like a piston, pumping so hard its thump reverberated in my throat. He was not tentative in any way but he was gentle, and I couldn't work out whether I did indeed feel any shame because I did nothing to dissuade him. Internally it felt like I was on a horse at full gallop and I was yelling to the heavens with joy at the feeling of my true spirit being released.

This was romance. This was what it felt like to want someone in such a distracted way that you would risk being caught in a situation that would be deeply damaging to one's reputation. I knew Jeanne or Madame Mouflard could knock or step in at any time. And still I encouraged him, my arms no longer hesitant but reaching to drape around his neck like a scarf. And then my hands! I hadn't realised how desperate they were to touch his hair. It was obviously something that had been niggling in the back of my mind all day; this new intimacy clearly gave me permission and my fingers tousled the thick waves.

Sébastien suddenly pulled away and I had to catch my breath.

'Am I taking advantage?' he questioned.

I gasped a rueful laugh. 'It's a bit late to ask that now,' I murmured but I followed with a hopeless shake of my head. 'It's not as though I pushed you away, Sébastien.' I touched my lips, already lonely for his withdrawal. 'What are we doing?' I whispered, feeling awed and fearful at once.

'Falling for one another?'

'I barely know you.'

'Do you need to know much more? My favourite colour is green, my favourite food is —'

'Oh, stop, please.' I began to pace. 'What in heaven's name are we doing?' I repeated, distracted, suddenly coming back to the present and re-engaging my sensibilities. Now I did feel mortified. 'I'm married!'

'Yes, but to your own —'

'Don't say it!' I cried, swinging around to warn him.

He watched me silently as I paced and muttered to myself. Thoughts of Henri's horror and rage arrived, as much as all the Delacroix ancestors would be turning in their graves. Felix wouldn't say much but I could almost taste his inevitable disappointment in the sour fear gathering at the back of my throat – for if Felix was anything, he was a dutiful Delacroix.

'What is your instinct telling you?'

'To run!' I snapped, turning to face him.

He took a step forward but I backed away. If only he knew it was because I didn't trust myself. All I wanted to do was hold him again, have that feeling of discovery . . . of finding something that had eluded me, as though I'd just opened a hidden box to the secret of life. I don't even know what I meant as I thought this because I was beginning to sense a deranged quality to my mind.

But even though I was essentially a stranger to him, Sébastien caught my attention deftly, pushed it back on course in a way that only someone who understood me to the core might. 'Fleurette,' he urged in the softest voice, 'if you could describe it as a smell, what did kissing me feel like?'

I looked back at him, astonished, but it was as though all my scattering thoughts stopped in their tracks, turned around and headed home again. 'P – pardon . . .?' I stammered, collecting myself.

'You heard. Be absolutely honest.'

Instinctively I closed my eyes.

'Good,' he soothed. 'Now describe it.'

'When I was a child . . .' I began.

'Yes?' he encouraged and I could hear a smile in his voice.

'My favourite time of the year was May. It still is.'

'Why?'

'It's spring. It's rose harvest in Grasse.'

'Go on.' He sounded closer, as if he tiptoed nearer, but I didn't open my eyes; I was under his spell now and I liked this game. It was one I knew, one I felt so good at, that just playing it made me feel I was on safe ground, no longer with thoughts deranged.

'Rose petals from the fields of *Rosa centifolia* are coming in so fast we can barely tip the burlap sacks out fast enough,' I said. 'Everyone's ready for them – the whole town is ready for the harvest in May.'

'And?' He was closer still; I heard the floorboard creak softly from his weight.

'They arrive at the factory. It's a gloriously beautiful scene of small mountains of roses to be weighed. The days are warm but the roses, picked in the early hours, add the cool sweetness. Father allows me to lie down on a quilt of pink. He laughs. Felix flings them at me and I'm showered in confetti of roses. The colours are astonishing. From afar it's just pink,' I said, reaching to my happy memory of childhood. 'But up close the still-moist petals are everything from the vaguest blush to a dazzling cerise of twilight.'

Again I sensed him smiling, enjoying my vivid recall, but especially he was enjoying watching me. He'd stolen so close it was no longer the wheeze of his recovering lungs that clued me to his whereabouts. I could now feel the warmth of his nearness.

'And now describe the smell of that May day.'

He spoke this leaning close to my ear but without physically touching me. Yet the delight in his voice, the caress of his breath, the memory of his kiss combined to make as effective a cocktail akin to an embrace. A tremor shivered through me and sweet longing erupted; the secret I'd discovered was my own desire awakening prompted simply by the voice of someone, simply by his presence. I had never experienced this quickening in my body where just the mere thought of a man could make my pulse race. Felix used to laugh at me when I complained that I was the only girl I knew who had never had a crush on someone – I didn't even know what the other girls were talking about when they swooned about this fellow or that.

'It's because you're too distracted; you find your own mind too interesting,' he'd said, laughing at me.

'Well, no one has ever approached me formally.'

'Why would they? You're untouchable, Fleurette. Two brothers, one a handsome twin, the only daughter of one of the wealthiest, best-known families in southern France . . . Who would even risk making a pass at you?'

I remember feeling hurt. 'Well, just a whistle might be nice.'

He'd shaken his head at me. 'You have no sense of self.'

'You've just told me I'm lost in myself!'

'You are self-possessed, for sure. But your awareness of how others view you is limited. Not everyone sees you as fun and approachable, Fleurette. Your mind alone is daunting . . . your looks? Well, I'm going to say this only once so you don't get swollen-headed – there is no doubt you are Grasse's town beauty. You are probably the most eligible woman in all of the south and coincidentally your looks match your eligibility and your wealth . . . both at the highest end of the marriage spectrum. Now,' he said, his tone dry enough to make most cough, 'do you think that makes you easy to have a slap and tickle with, or do you think all of those qualities might just make you a daunting prospect and inhibit most poor fellows?'

I'd never thought of myself as plain but I'd also never considered myself radiantly attractive. I thought all the other girls were the beauties because they inherently seemed to know how to flirt, how to catch a boy's attention, how to behave demurely and yet sensually. I'd missed out somewhere, or so I had always thought. I didn't colour my cheeks or wear ribbons in my hair. I preferred boots to dainty heels; I was happiest in the lab rather than walking through the town square and being seen in my finery. I liked long conversations about perfume rather than the flirtatious talk of nothing of consequence.

But now here it was. The moment of awakening, a stirring of the previously dormant sexual need that I'd wondered if I would ever feel. I realised I wanted Sébastien in the same way that our flower pickers needed chilled water to quench a raging thirst. I could picture them tipping back their heads to drain a whole flask, not even worrying if the sweet water poured too fast and ran down their chins. They were parched, desperate for deliverance. That was me in this moment. I was desperate for Sébastien – and only Sébastien – to relieve my need.

'Tell me, Fleurette. I want to hear your vivid memory about your favourite day of the year,' Sébastien coaxed.

And I opened up my mind to the May harvest.

'It's hypnotic,' I began again, this time focused, as the desire for Sébastien's touch became one with the memory of my favourite perfume. 'I can't wait for when we distil and I can inhale the *absolute* . . . the very essence of my joy.' Before he could urge me to describe it, I was already there in my mind, keen to share. 'The cool sweetness of the petals has now been transformed into a dusky, sensual oil of deep complexity. It speaks to me of a sun-baked earth that sits between the salt of the ocean and the tumble from the alps of our Riviera. As I inhale I am reminded of the promise of raspberries in summer and blackcurrants of autumn but it's honey that I essentially taste, with a zesty citrus riding high above that.'

'And do you believe our kissing reminded you of that fragrance?'

'Yes,' I admitted.

'So now, just for me, describe our kiss and your rose memory in one word.'

'Intoxicating,' I said, without pausing to consider.

'Open your eyes, Fleurette.' I did. His gaze was soft and liquid from what I realised was the grey of his anxiety and that gaze held me as effectively as if I was pinioned. 'Good word,' he praised. 'And I am drunk on the essence of you.' I began to say something but he hushed me. 'No, you must hear this. From the moment you entered the drawing room I felt drowsy, as though I'd recently woken but was still caught in the remnants of a lovely dream. And even as I gave you the worst possible news that I think someone might receive, I was feeling guilty because in comforting you I derived a smug sense of satisfaction that Aimery could not have you. Seeing you for the first time gave me a dizzy feeling, like staring over the lip of a precipice and being disoriented momentarily. And this afternoon walking back from town with you I felt drunk; I'm surprised I wasn't bumping into the town walls. You see, I'd already jumped from that precipice – it's why you found me in the herb garden trying to sort out my warring feelings. I knew it wasn't right to take advantage of you in this way. I brought the most heinous news and I was in danger of preying on your vulnerability and yet I couldn't help myself. I have hated myself for hours, as though I were some sort of scoundrel and yet I am drunk on you, entirely addicted to your kiss, your laugh, your voice, even your ability to see everything and everyone as a smell. I've fallen, Fleurette, from the cliff top of sensibility into the perplexing, achey cauldron of desire. There's no way out. You are the one I've searched for.'

'How can you know?' I said, airing my thoughts aloud. I was embarrassed that I'd revealed my ignorance.

'Because I have been around enough women through my adult life.' His candour was unnerving. 'I won't lie to you: I have kissed and courted, bedded and moved on from enough women to comprehend when I have come into the presence of one I know I can't walk away from without it costing me.'

'Costing you?' I frowned as I repeated his phrase.

'A mortally injured heart, Fleurette.' He held up his wrecked hand. 'This is nothing in comparison to the blow you can wound me with.'

I shook my head, suddenly well out of my depth. 'I feel like I've swum too far out to sea.'

'I'll save you,' he offered, grinning sadly.

He leaned in again but paused as though requiring my permission. Again I didn't deny him and this time I learned about kissing in a way to make me feel that everyone who had gone before was simply a rehearsal. And perhaps it had been just that. The two boys who'd stolen kisses – when my father finally let me out to social galas with Felix on my arm as an escort – felt like fumbling adolescents by comparison, even though both considered themselves quite the young men about town.

But Sébastien brought a sexual assuredness that meant he was the one choosing to hold back; he understood my lack of experience, even my reluctance to commit a sin that would make all our parents shift in their graves, and yet he also knew I could be led . . . that I really wanted this to happen. In the back of my mind a thought bubbled that I must be transparent but it burst, disappearing, because by then I was pulling him close, and then closer again still, that he responded with fervour.

I was lost once more, mentally lying down in a quilt of roses, reminded of a truly happy time in my life that was now helplessly linked to a kiss that I never wanted to end. Skimming along a shared wave of passion, Sébastien gave me a glimpse into a future that wasn't about the despair of a loveless marriage.

The knock at the door and the familiar voice made us leap apart, startled as though we'd both been discovered naked and rolling around his bed. Wide-eyed and frantic, I watched Sébastien calmly take a seat, covering his lap with his jacket to make me giggle helplessly, soundlessly. He glared at me with a wry expression and offered me a seat as he called back.

'Who is it?'

'It's Jeanne, Monsieur de Lasset.'

He looked at me and I blew out a silent breath, seated myself again and restrained from fiddling nervously with my hair or clothes. Instead I picked up the linen again and nodded. It felt as though I took ten minutes or more to achieve that when in fact the ticking clock on the mantelpiece suggested it was only seconds.

'Come in, Jeanne. I'm here with Madame de Lasset.'

We both bent our heads again over his injured hand and as the door opened I was wringing out the antiseptic. The sound of trickling water accompanied us as we looked up at Jeanne in enquiry.

'Hello, Jeanne,' I said, amazed and disgusted with myself for sounding so innocent. 'Everything all right?'

She looked not only horrified by the sight of Sébastien's hand – odd that I had not experienced the same – but equally offended that her ladyship was messing about with bloodied water.

'Oh, Madame, please. One of us could have —'

I gave a gust of breath and a wave of my hand to suggest it was of no consequence. 'I'm happy to be useful for once,' I offered in a deliberate attempt to be self-effacing. I noted Sébastien didn't appear flushed and hoped I was giving off the same careless confidence.

'Did you want me?' Sébastien asked easily, his breath sounding wheezy but his illness couldn't touch his humour; he glanced at me in a wicked silent message as he spoke these words to my servant.

I blinked with disdain at him and returned my attention to Jeanne.

'Er, yes, sir. It was to tell you that the doctor will be calling in this evening instead of tomorrow and dinner will be served at seven.' She glanced at me. 'Madame has ordered a broth for you.'

'Excellent,' he said. 'That's very kind of you, Fleurette. Thank you, Jeanne. I may need some help putting my jacket back on,' he suggested.

'Of course. I shall have one of our men sent up.'

'Etienne will help,' I said, joining in. 'Tell him to see me, though. I'm sure we can find some more clothes for my husband's brother.'

Jeanne curtsied, then waited.

'That's all, Jeanne,' I said gently and with a smile. 'I can finish up here.'

'If you're sure, Madame?'

My answer was another grin and a nod. She closed the door and we both shared a look of amusement; like two children who'd got away with mischief. We waited but I lifted a hand to my lips and pretended to turn a key in it. He nodded, understanding that walls had ears in a house like this and who knew what Jeanne might report back beneath stairs. We would now have to be more than careful; we would have to be blameless.

'How does that feel?' I asked, genuinely interested in his hand.

Sébastien pointed to his lap. 'Well, there's an itch now that I don't think can be easily scratched.'

I had to cover my mouth and laugh silently. I'd never engaged in such flirtatious behaviour and I would be lying to myself if I didn't admit I loved how girlish and reckless it made me feel.

Perhaps the danger of us teetering on the edge of discovery contributed to it. When the truth came out – however it came out – I might be exonerated, but I knew it wouldn't pay to smear Aimery's reputation with his household staff. To publicly cuckold him would be an unnecessary cruelty, so I gathered myself while I assembled all my medical paraphernalia back onto the tray.

'Well, that's the same for any stitched wound, I suppose,' I said, trying to pull us back on track.

Sébastien mercifully followed suit for the benefit of any listeners, especially Jeanne, if she had chosen to remain paused behind the door. While I knew every other board in my wing of the villa, I couldn't rely on the floorboards at this end of the house to squeak and communicate, so I had no idea whether my maid had left us.

'Thank you for coming. Your special ministrations have done me a world of good.'

I gave him a look of soft despair and he rewarded me with a crooked smile to accept the admonishment.

'It was just easier and quicker for me to do it myself than wait for anyone else to help you.' I spluttered behind my hand again, struggling to keep the amusement silent. I would need to practise my innuendo if I was to play this game with him again.

14

We were in the Delacroix laboratory, pulling off dustsheets as Sébastien surveyed the equipment, nodding, making sounds of approval, and all the while his glance – if not his hand or body – making contact with me. Frankly, we couldn't keep our gazes off one another.

It was as though a vault had opened into a new world. I was like Alice on my own adventure in Wonderland, except there were only two characters – Sébastien and me, because I couldn't bear for anyone else to trespass into our story. Only making perfume had consumed me in the same way that Sébastien consumed my thoughts. Since yesterday afternoon I didn't believe I'd thought of anything or anyone else but him . . . the smell of him, the feel of him, his kiss, his confidence especially. That last sent trills of delighted anticipation through me. When would I feel his bare skin against me? I refused to permit the reality of my marital status to creep into my daydreaming. For now, the wistful joy of Sébastien's affection was my sanity.

'Why is no one here?'

'There are some of the older fellows in and around the factory and there are plenty of women around, just no one in the lab,' I said, squirming away from his encircling arm. 'This is off limits. My father was always particular about keeping the lab as free from cross-contamination as he could, so he set up a strict regime that we all adhered to.'

'Oh,' he said dryly, a new tone of mischief entering his voice. 'So we're all alone?'

I grinned. 'I wouldn't count on that, but —'

I didn't get to say more because in the next heartbeat he was kissing me and I was melting beneath him. I came up breathless from the deliciousness of the awakening of such passion but also the novelty of affection. 'Sébastien, we can't . . .'

'Why not?'

'It's . . .' I laughed. 'The ghost of my father still walks around here.'

He faked a shiver and pulled a face of horror. 'Do we have any Erlenmeyer flasks?'

I nodded. 'Oh, plenty of them. How many do you need?' I moved to reach up to some boxes on a higher shelf and with no shame at all Sébastien limped up behind me and cupped my breast. I should have been incensed. Instead I burst into helpless laughter. I was in an impossible position, balancing a heavy box.

'Oh, just the one for me,' he said, gently squeezing and setting off an explosion of sparkling tendrils of arousal.

I gave a soft groan. 'Don't,' I said weakly and he took his hand away.

'I won't. That really was most ungentlemanly of me.'

'It was,' I agreed, wishing he'd do it again, wishing in fact that we could walk into the Delacroix villa this moment, go upstairs to my old beloved suite and make love all afternoon.

'Then why don't we?' he said, and I startled with the realisation I'd shared my thoughts aloud.

Our playfulness was chased away by a new tension that suddenly held us in its maw. I could hear the tick of the clock on the lab's wall matching time with my heartbeat, both normally inaudible but now they sounded like a thundersome duet. No one inhabited the villa other than our old housekeeper, and she was presently away with her family in Nice; the potential for adultery was now disconcertingly real.

I knew I was blinking with consternation.

'May I tell you something?' he said, interlocking our fingers and kissing the pulse point at my wrist, a move so sensual that I closed my eyes and swallowed the powerful yearning it prompted.

'Yes,' I replied, making sure my voice was reliable before I answered, but then I held my breath, knowing I was now no longer on dangerous ground but about to tread into a landscape that had a huge sign posted nearby that warned me to *Beware of quicksand*.

Sébastien continued, his voice raspy with apprehension. 'I mentioned to you that I have been with many women in my time.' He paused but I gave him nothing back; we were both now emotionally naked and I needed him to feel as raw and vulnerable as I was. I was glad to see his Adam's apple bob. He too was swallowing hesitation. 'I have not truly loved a single one of those women.'

I held my nerve, made him finish his thought.

'Until a couple of days ago I might have allowed that I had very strong feelings for Alice; I could even have been pressed to admitting that losing Catherine to Jeremy Padstow two years back hurt me far more than I realised. But I've never felt like this. It's sudden. It's filled with anguish. I could almost wish it hadn't happened because there's some pain ahead for me, for us, for our families . . . but, Fleurette, I believe myself in love with you.'

Now I wanted to speak and took a breath to respond but he shook his head.

'Nothing you say can persuade me otherwise. If you denied

me, asked me to leave, told me it was impossible, you couldn't brutalise me more if you tried. But I would leave . . . today . . . if you don't feel the same way about me.' He pulled me close now and stroked my cheek so very gently. 'Tell me you don't love me,' he defied.

I was trembling. I couldn't be sure it wasn't purely from the provocative words – no one had ever spoken to me like this. No one had ever felt this way about me. Or was I trembling from my emotional response to Sébastien?

'I have no one to compare you to.' It came out baldly but at least it was pure . . . an entirely honest response.

A twitch of amusement fluttered at the edge of his smile but in his eyes I could see it had disappointed him that I couldn't gush back with words of love.

'If I limped out of your life this moment and you could never see me again, never hear from me again . . .' he encouraged, trailing off to leave the question in his expression of hope.

I searched my heart. It was easy. 'Anyone else who came after you would suffer.'

I watched the look of hope rearrange into elation.

'I would compare them to you and I would come up wanting because I don't want there to be anyone else.'

'Even if there could be?'

I nodded. 'I trust my senses. I am at one with Nature's perfection – her beauty, her colours, her fragrances – and she has allowed me to glimpse it in a man.'

'I'm not perfect, Fleurette,' he warned, looking instantly anxious.

'No, but your love for me is. My senses tell me that. I have no need to look for love elsewhere than in your arms.'

He kissed me and all thoughts of making perfume left me. 'Shall we go to the house?' I whispered, privately appalled at my brazen attitude but it was as if an invisible force now was in charge. It was love, desire, awakening – call it what you must – but it had taken away my free will.

He nodded. 'Is it far?' he croaked. 'I may not make it.'

I blushed, laughing, and cooled my cheeks with my hands. 'I'd race you there if it wasn't so close.' I pointed to a door at the back of the laboratory. 'That leads into a corridor that lets us into my father's old study.'

'The villa is connected?' he said, his tone wondrous.

It was my turn to nod. 'Shall we?'

We walked through the laboratory door into my father's study that even Henri had found hard to inhabit as his own. There were times when I could be so critical of Henri and yet at our query as to why he hadn't beaten a quick path to our father's desk, chair, private space, an oddly wistful expression had ghosted across our elder brother's face.

'Not yet,' he said. 'When I can no longer smell his arthritis liniment, then I'll know his spirit has finally given permission. For now, he's still in here.'

'Does that comfort you, Henri?' I recall Felix asking.

'Curiously, it does. I know you both think I wanted to take over the business promptly, almost wishing our father to an early death, but you've always had me wrong in this respect. I am daunted, to tell you the truth.' I remember how surprised we were by this reveal. It was a moment of fragile honesty we were not used to.

'Trust your instincts. You know what you're doing, Henri,' Felix had assured in his ever-generous way. 'Father trained you for this. He has groomed you for a decade for this very moment.'

I had watched my older brother nod, fighting back his emotion. 'Thank you for the faith.'

'You run the business, brother; let me and our sister worry about the product.'

Neither of us could be heartless enough to tell him that for us twins the pungent smell of our father's tumerol liniment, made from the curcumin rhizome that he imported from India, might never leave this room. Father had met an old Indian spiritualist man who spoke to him of the medicine of Ayurveda and had stared at my father's crooked fingers and recommended a paste made from the dried turmeric root. Father had laughingly told us the original recipe had called for cow's urine but he had since developed the paste with lime and saltpeter and believed it genuinely did alleviate the inflammation of his aching finger joints. The smell of our father's ointment was part of the very fabric of this room and obviously for Henri it had now faded sufficiently, but for me I could still taste its pleasant freshness at the back of my throat with a lingering camphorous odour that I recalled from the fresh root. Our heightened sense might always be able to pick up the faintest trace of our father's medicine. Henri was wrong; our father was still here and likely would never leave, even though we had.

I ran a finger over the dust cover that hid his desk.

'Memories?' Sébastien wondered, and I felt embarrassed to have locked him out of my thoughts.

I nodded but must have looked pensive because he reached for my elbow and made me turn towards him. 'Fleurette . . .?'

'Don't ask me again if I'm sure. I am,' I said, hoping the uncertainty I was indeed hiding would not push through my feigned confidence. 'Follow me.' I walked with haste now, not pausing for him as I moved over the elegant parquetry that lit golden when the sunlight cleared the roof and peeped in through the twin floor-to-ceiling arched windows that flanked our front door. I felt the rush of pleasure that this space always brought to me – it was the beauty of our house combining with that wonderful sense of security of being back in the home you grew up in. Father had allowed me to transform it from its sombre colouring of the previous century and bring into the twentieth century. It was now the palest of greys . . . like a summer's shower of rain that dissipates before it even reaches the dry earth. My all-knowing twin had once told me this liquid-to-vapour effect was called virga. And so we had always referred to this paint colour as virga in our household and it had stolen from the hallway into other rooms as a pastel palette from which to add decoration. I had used it in my bedroom but warmed it up with pinks and scarlets of the centifolia rose I loved so much.

I hurried up the stairs, noticing nothing now, because anxiety, perhaps excited anticipation, had turned everything familiar to a blur. I didn't look at the paintings that lined those two flights, I didn't glance out of the windows on the landing, I didn't register the pinks of the rugs beneath my tread. I passed the pedestals and busts covered in dust sheets and I definitely didn't linger outside the doors that led to my two brothers' apartments. No, I skipped up the final stairs to the third level of the house where my chamber resided and pushed open the door to my private space and immediately felt relief wash over me.

I was home.

I was safe.

It was not Aimery behind me. That alone brought me hope and a sense of my future no longer bleak.

Sébastien would take what Aimery felt was his – and could not be – and I had never been more sure about anything in my life than wanting this most private and precious of my possessions to be gifted to a man I loved. I wanted it gone now, though, before it could become a point of argument. I turned self-consciously to welcome him into my room and he stood at the threshold, waiting for the final invitation. I liked his hesitation – whether it was just good manners or his own nervousness, I didn't care. I was reassured by his politeness.

'May I?'

'You may,' I whispered.

He stepped inside and closed the door. Now everything in our lives – past and present – was excluded. Sébastien looked around, being careful, I thought, in not advancing immediately; maybe I did look like a deer being stalked who could startle at any moment and flee.

'You have good taste,' he murmured, angling away from me in the limping gait I now found helplessly attractive. I could see he was taking in the richer colours of my bedroom's palette. 'My, my . . . you actually do sleep on a quilt of roses,' he noted, glancing at the bed that was semi-enclosed by an exquisite timber-panelled alcove, replete with oval windows. 'You must have always enjoyed good dreams in that splendid niche,' he remarked in soft awe.

I shrugged, distracted by his tender approach, and smiled, my shoulders relaxing as he guided me past my apprehension. 'It replicates an eighteenth-century bedroom in the Louis Quinze style to imitate the architecture of the doll's house I'd played with in my childhood,' I explained.

'How spoilt you are!' he teased in gentle mockery. 'So, where is it?' He looked around for the doll's house of my early years.

'Er . . . in the attic, I believe.'

'Awaiting your daughter,' he said. 'A special heirloom.' It was a lovely thought and echoed my love for family and my desire to look forward to its future.

'I do hope so. My father designed it and helped to build it. I think he worried constantly that I didn't have a mother and so did everything he could that a mother might bring to a daughter's life.'

He turned and fixed me with a cool gaze of appraisal. 'He did a very good job. You are spoilt, clearly,' he said, waving a hand at the elaborate suite of rooms that I called mine. 'But it doesn't show in the slightest.'

I was taken by surprise. Compliments had come my way often but none that meant quite as much to me as this one. I had grown up hating the 'rich girl' label that followed me like a loyal servant and, as Felix had pointed out, had kept so many potential friends at a distance. Oh, I knew the town folk loved me because I was a Delacroix, but at a social level it was people's hesitancy that had served to make me feel something of an island, especially with no sisters or mother to gossip or laugh alongside about girlish things as I knew others did.

'He would be pleased to hear that. As the only female in the family, I often felt like an only child. He did worry about over-indulgence sometimes, though, I'm sure of it.' I felt embarrassed admitting this to Sébastien but transparency seemed important right now.

'You can never overindulge a child with affection. It costs nothing.'

'Well, affection and encouragement were like a fast-flowing stream from him . . . to all of his children . . . er . . .' I faltered as I realised we'd inadvertently brought up the sins of my father and Sébastien's mother. Here was the very shadow over our lives that I'd hoped to shut out of this room.

'Can you find it in your heart to forgive him?'

I didn't mean to narrow my gaze or clamp my jaw but both occurred anyway and he watched the gestures deliver him the unspoken answer.

'Fleurette, I realise the wound is fresh but you must find the strength not to judge.' He stepped closer now, throwing aside his walking cane to reach for me.

'Why?'

He leaned forward and kissed me gently, softly urging my

mouth to open and return it until my arms were around him and I could feel his need pressing against me. We broke slightly breathless and I was aware, even though I knew nothing firsthand about sexual union, that neither of us could wait much longer to share it. But he paused long enough to tip my chin and force me to look at him directly. I was aware of my breathing; I could see it creating a visible rise and fall of my chest. I wanted him. I felt light-headed at how delightfully reckless the need for the feel of his skin against mine was making me.

'What?' I searched his querying expression that was urging me to understand.

'Think about how this feels.'

'I am. I've never wanted anything so badly as this before.'

'Say it.'

'I want you to be my first . . . my last.' It was a series of words I'd never uttered previously and hoped I'd never say again to anyone.

But Sébastien's response was not what I'd hoped I'd hear in return. He did not speak of love or longing, or rather he did, but not of ours. 'This is how they felt.'

It was as though a pail of cold water had just been tipped over me. I turned away and moved to sit on the edge of the bed. The alcove embraced me into its safe, familiar hollow.

'Have I offended you?'

I shook my head in a lie. 'It was my impression that men whispered sweet nothings into the ear of the woman they were trying to seduce.'

'I'm not trying to seduce you. In fact, I think what we're doing here is dangerous.'

It's true that I sneered, but not at him personally. I knew he was trying to protect me from being rash, making a decision I might regret, and certainly couldn't retrace my steps from and pretend hadn't happened. But I needed to make him understand he wasn't forcing me to do anything. He was not in control.

'Sébastien, you can't imagine how much, on my wedding night, I wished I *hadn't* saved myself for someone special. I was naïve, I wanted my husband – who would be the man I loved with all of my romantic heart – to have the pleasure, the responsibility, the burden, even, of . . .' I shrugged, knowing he'd understand.

'Let's wait. Please. Let's not complicate an already complex situation. Do you really want to add adultery into your life?'

I gave him the respect of considering his question but shook my head. 'You and I both know I can't be accused of that.'

Sébastien looked at me with profound affection and I felt my heartbeat stutter. The feeling was wonderful, to be truthful; I loved this sensation of falling in love, of being so interested in one person that everything else paled.

'You and I know that, yes, but the rest of Grasse doesn't. I didn't come here to steal my brother's bride.'

'Too late,' I quipped. 'Anyway, I don't care about what people think. I will set any detractors straight when the truth is out.'

'The truth has a way of going askew. The purity of how you feel doesn't necessarily mean it can't hurt others.'

'Like Aimery?'

He nodded.

'You care about him?'

'I don't know him. But it doesn't change my opinion that none of this is his fault.'

'True. But you should know he has a mistress who I can tell is precious to him. She even visited me only a few days ago to strike a bargain with me that I leave them to their clandestine affair.'

He looked at me, aghast.

'Yes, it's shocking when I say it like that but she's actually immensely likeable and I admire her self-assurance, her honesty and her offer to protect me from my husband by providing what he needs.'

'You struck a bargain?' he said, sounding incredulous.

'The truth of Aimery's birth has given me my excuse for escape, but Sébastien, he makes my skin crawl. Graciela's offer was most welcome, I can assure you. Anything that might distract him from me is something I'd grab at. But now you've given me legitimate legal and spiritual reasons to annul my marriage, which was a sham anyway. And now I'm not going to talk about it any more. I will love whom I want and I will choose who shall be my first lover. I've chosen you. I cannot be dissuaded. So now it's up to you. If you deny me, fine, but don't do so out of worrying about the little virginal girl. I want this. I need it.'

He blinked, torn.

'I want you, Sébastien – I know we only met yesterday but I've never felt like this before and I like how it feels and I'm not scared and I want all of it . . . all of you.' I looked down from where I sat on the edge of the bed. I hated to beg. 'Please. My father's adulterous affair with your mother shouldn't be compared to this.' Even as I said it, I didn't believe it. The truth was that I was behaving exactly as they probably had – helpless, yearning for each other, her facing a loveless marriage, him a carefree bachelor with no love in his life. We were like a mirror image of them.

He limped a couple of strides and knelt in front of me with difficulty so he could look up into my eyes that were fixed on the rug. I didn't want him to see my fear of rejection at a moment of such vulnerability. I deliberately laid my palms flat on the coverlet too, denying him any chance to take either of my hands into his. I wanted him to know that talk of my father's adultery was still raw for me. I could count how long I'd known about it in hours – the wound was fresh, still bleeding. No, I wasn't offended in truth because Sébastien had come to save me from my father's sin but I wasn't happy either to be bringing the perfumer's secret into my bedroom, into our special moment. And just as Felix would snap me out of a dark passage of thought by distracting me, Sébastien instinctively knew to do the same.

'So you think I'm seducing you?'

'Aren't you?'

'No. Seduction suggests I simply want to have my way with you.'

'Don't you?' I said, realising I was teasing in the coy way those flirtatious girls I had so often wished I could behave like did.

'I do. Desperately,' he groaned and I smiled, though glad he couldn't see it because his attention was fixed on the hem of my skirt for some reason. 'But you see,' he continued, 'seduction, in my interpretation, is about lust, which can be thoroughly fun, I should admit. However, what is happening to me is unnerving because I've surrendered my power.'

'What does that mean?'

'Well, if I want to seduce someone, then I have the control. Whereas, where you're concerned, I cannot manipulate the situation because you're in charge. I've yielded because I've fallen in love with you. And what I'm doing now,' he said, raising my hem to reveal my legs and to make me gasp inwardly, 'is making love to you.' He reached under my skirt to run his fingers tantalisingly up my stockings to where they were pinned. 'There is a difference,' he finished, as he expertly released the first fastening.

I could no longer keep a cool head as his clearly well-honed skills in dismantling the fussy undergarments that we women wore were frighteningly speedy; and he was doing with one hand what I needed two for each evening. Before I could raise his head to look at me, my sensible day stockings were pooled around my ankles. Scarily, my first thought was not what would people think of such a delicate position the newly married Delacroix girl found herself in, but just how quickly could we get out of our clothes so we could both be naked and feel the full joy of each other.

But Sébastien had other ideas, for once again his head bent and now he began to kiss the revealed skin of my legs. In shock I thought I might cry out with the outrageous pulse of pleasure that vibrated through me. Instead I let out another gasp as he moved higher with soft kisses and I felt myself falling backwards against the coverlets.

'There's no rush for this,' he whispered, and then I didn't hear another word but I was sure the whole world could listen to my heartbeat.

———

This was it. I felt as though I had reached the summit of life and I was now basking with the gods on some imaginary mountain looking down upon the valleys where ordinary people lived. Except I didn't feel ordinary right now – what I had just experienced had been outside of all normality. Nevertheless, as I lay there smiling to myself, it occurred to me that just about everyone I knew in Grasse had been busy at this particular pleasure, but I allowed myself to believe what had occurred between Sébastien and me was rare and sparklingly precious.

He seemed to pick up on my thoughts as I lay in the crook of his good arm. His breathing had improved too and I no longer worried that our lovemaking was endangering his recovery.

'It will never feel like that again,' he wheezed softly, twisting a curl of my hair around his fingers.

I shifted out of my dreamy thoughts to regard him. 'Why?'

'First time? Oh, I don't know. It's like uncovering a secret that everyone else knows about and shares and you're finally let in on it.'

I nodded, amused. 'That's exactly how I feel. It makes me cross to think that buxom Madame Chaval has birthed eight children to prove how busy she's been at the secret.'

He laughed and coughed at once. 'Madame Mouflard too, don't forget.'

I cut him a look of mock horror, which widened his smile and kept it in place as he stared back at me. 'Tell me about your first.'

'A gentleman never reveals —'

'Oh, that's not fair. You are intimate with my first time.'

'This is true. You have me there. All right. Her name was Gabrielle.'

'Pretty name.'

'As pretty as she was,' he agreed.

'How old were you?'

'Fourteen.' Now my look of horror wasn't feigned and his body shook with laughter beneath me. 'So I began early!'

'I had my hair in plaits at fourteen!'

'And I bet you looked like a minx.'

I gave him a playful shove. 'How old was Gabrielle?'

'Ah, she was twenty-three, I believe.'

I gasped. 'Nine years' difference! Had she no shame?'

'None at all, and I was glad for it. She taught me plenty about pleasuring a woman. I owe her a debt.'

'Was she a —'

He put a finger to my lips. 'Gabrielle is one of the kindest, most generous people I've ever known. She was beautiful but poor and she earned her money the only way she could. She enriched my life, taught me skills, made me laugh . . . and especially she gave me affection when I most needed it. We were friends as much as . . . um, partners in a transaction.'

I smiled. 'Do you still see her?'

He shook his head. 'I came to a point where I didn't want to share her. She used to laugh at my possessiveness.'

'What happened?' I leaned on my elbow to look at him squarely. I was intrigued.

Sébastien shrugged. 'I grew up and realised she'd also taught me how to make love to a woman without being in love.'

'Is that possible?'

'Oh, yes. And that's when it is pure lust. Providing both people understand they're simply enjoying one another, neither needs to get hurt.'

'I see. So you don't think you've hurt anyone along the way?'

'I didn't say that, but I've always been honest.'

'Have you ever been in love before?'

'Once.' He grew more serious. 'It felt real at the time.'

'Tell me.'

'I was fourteen. Her name was Gabrielle.'

I grinned but he didn't return it and I realised I had finally found my way to the very centre of Sébastien. For all his jests, his gentlemanly manners, his carnal knowledge, his intelligence, his romanticism . . . this was the place where his soul resided. 'So she was your first and your only love,' I whispered, remembering how this conversation had begun.

He nodded.

'Nothing even close again?'

'Until now.'

I felt a surge of relief to hear this.

'But it's different.'

'How?'

'I'm older, wiser. More to the point, you feel wondrous. New and shiny . . . and mine.'

'And are you mine?'

'All of me. Every last inch!' He made his eyebrows dance at his remark and I had to cover my mouth with the quilt to stop my laughter resounding too loudly through the empty house. Walls still had ears, I reminded myself. 'Did I hurt you?' he asked, suddenly tender as I regained my composure.

'Yes.'

He opened his mouth in alarm.

'No more than I expected, and it wouldn't put me off doing it again and again . . . and again.' I shamelessly rolled on top of him, loving this new and reckless sense of freedom that a naked man beneath me brought. He coughed and I rolled back off, alarmed, but he ignored my worry.

'You are mine, aren't you?' he said, sounding uncharacteristically hesitant.

'From the crown of my head to my little toe, I am yours, Sébastien De Lasset.' And then a gust of sharp reality edged closer. 'Of course, that's our secret.'

'Only for the time being. As soon as we can, we are going to explain everything to Aimery.'

'I don't want to think about the ugly scene as Aimery learns of my adultery.'

'We can hardly hide it or we become like the very people you are finding so hard to forgive.'

His threat troubled me dimly somewhere deep where I didn't care enough to explore it. I knew I didn't want to ruin Aimery, and yet Sébastien's words suggested that's precisely what was likely to happen. Sébastien didn't know his brother as well as I did; reputation was everything to Aimery . . . everything!

'You don't believe me, do you?' he challenged, rolling me back so he could lean over.

I frowned. I didn't want to behave like my father and Marguerite. 'It's not that. We mustn't do this again after today.'

'Why?'

'Because it *is* wrong.' He wanted to dispute this but I kept talking over him. 'It is, Sébastien . . . maybe not in the eyes of the law, or the church, because you and I know the truth, but everyone out there considers me married to Aimery, including him. No, for the sake of reputation we must refrain from being anything but cordial as a brother-in-law and sister-in-law should be.'

'I doubt I can keep my hands off you.'

'Well, you've only got one that works easily for now, so keep it in your pocket or on the walking stick until we can make a plan and we'll be able to keep the two family reputations intact.' He started to say something more but I moved away, swinging my legs out of the bed. 'I insist. Until we sort this mess out, we mustn't do this again.' I walked around my bed, aware of him watching me, and the new bold girl I'd become over these last couple of hours enjoyed seeing his hunger roaming over me. 'Now, before we dress, teach me more about what this clever mouth of yours can do other than charm me with words.'

He smiled and shifted to let me sit so I could admire him.

'You're beautiful, Sébastien.'

He gusted disdain.

'No, truly, I love looking at you. You're sculpted. Michelangelo would have been mad for you,' I teased, a fingertip tracing the muscles that outlined his chest, and I followed the downy line of hair that led me past his belly in line with his pelvis. Brazenly, I let my fingernail track lower still and could feel his tremor of pleasure beneath my touch. I learned something in that moment: I learned that as strong as a man might be physically, women possessed inordinate power through their very presence. What he'd said earlier about surrendering and about how I held the power resonated now. I looked at him, weakening beneath my gaze, his arousal intensifying with each beat of his heart . . . amusing me with the way it was suddenly awoken from exhaustion and demanding fresh attention from me. And all I'd done to achieve this was allowing him to watch me move naked, to touch him lightly with a fingertip, to lick my lips as I was doing now. Such power!

'What have I created?' he cheerfully asked the universe as he pulled me towards him.

15

We had returned to the laboratory, slightly flushed but buttoned back into our clothes, my hair pinned neatly, while his was parted and combed precisely into place. No one was any wiser to our discovery of each other or the ferociously committed bond that had formed and fashioned itself invisibly between us. We were now helplessly manacled through love and longing. We even smelled of each other as we returned to our inventory in readiness for the making of a more visible perfume.

'So what is it to be?' Sébastien asked.

I told him about my ideas for a fragrance that could promote the notion of our nation's courage and determination not to be invaded by another power, greedy for domination in Europe.

He didn't look convinced.

'What's wrong?'

'Well, it's all rather patriotic and fist-shaking.'

'What do you expect?'

'No one wants to be reminded about the war. You might as well create something that prompts visions of twisted metal and charred bodies.'

I could feel my lips thinning with irritation at his disdain.

'I had something deliciously feminine in mind.'

'I see. Of Gabrielle maybe?' He blinked and said nothing but he didn't have to. I was disgusted that I was prepared to wound the person I had only recently been whispering words of love to. 'Sébastien, I'm sorry. I will never mention her again.'

'I shared that with you because —'

'I know, I know. . .' I glanced over my shoulder, checking we were alone as I felt we were more vulnerable now in the lab. 'And I will respect that memory from here on, even though I'm a stupid, desperately jealous woman.'

He watched me for what felt like a long heartbeat. 'You're jealous of Gabrielle? Who is now about thirty-five years old and her nipples probably trailing on the ground?'

I laughed helplessly, glad the tension had passed. 'Yes! You loved her. You loved her first. Whereas I've never loved a man as I do you.'

'You are your mother's daughter,' he accused and I felt myself redden at the truth. I was also my father's daughter in my wanton abandon with him in my bedchamber. What had I been saying about how I would never behave as our parents had? He understood, I think, where my thoughts were ranging. He lifted a shoulder. 'I can't help that I made love to women before you, but I can make sure that I never give you cause to love another man ever again. And I promise never to love another woman.'

'I want you to forgive me.'

He smiled. 'Love is forgiveness, my mother taught me.' He stroked my hair. 'Don't think on it again.'

I breathed out silently. 'So, how would you describe *deliciously feminine*?'

'Easy. I would picture you wild and uninhibited, your hair falling about your shoulders, tickling my skin. I want to be reminded of your soft mouth opening to mine, of our bodies cleaving in ecstasy.' I blushed to hear it but I was addicted to hearing him speak of me like this. 'I want to think of the taste of you, to smell the roses of your bedroom, to recall the frost of winter that delivered me to your door and for that coolness to be chased away by the warmth of you, the sweetness of a sunny harvest day in Grasse . . . an experience I have never had previously.' He kissed me. 'I want it to be you in a bottle.'

'Me in a bottle,' I repeated, transfixed.

He nodded. '*Allumeuse*.'

'You think I'm a tease?'

'I think you are entirely unaware of your own attraction. It is an endearing quality.'

'How about *Scandalous*?' I asked, dampening the mood.

Sébastien refused to bite. 'How about, then, something that combines both the spirit of you now in this moment and your hope for France?'

I nodded. 'Yes, perfect. But what is that elusive quality that sums it up?'

'*Libertine*,' he said, closing his eyes and then opening them sharply. 'Yes, *Libertine*!'

I liked it but he was already shaking his head again. 'That works,' I urged.

'Not nearly as good as the one I prefer most.'

'Which is?'

'Which is all about flowers, all about being a sensual woman, all about Grasse and love and sunshine.'

'Say it, then.'

'There is only one word that sums that up. *Fleurette*.'

I stared at him.

'Make your perfume. Let it be called *Fleurette* so no one can mistake the perfumer. It will be the first of many but it will be the benchmark by which all of France and indeed Europe will know the exciting new perfumer for the De Lasset brand.'

I swallowed. 'What do you mean? How can I make perfume for Aimery's —?'

'Oh, darling Fleurette. Never forget my surname. Never forget my true birthright. Never forget that France, unlike Britain, has a law of succession that no child can ever be cut out of a will. Aimery knows that. It's why he wishes me out of his life, away from the business. He was content to keep me at arm's length, content to pay me whatever my father's arrangement was while my father was alive. But our mother is dead, and now I no longer care about appearances or what is polite. I shall claim my inheritance.'

'Half the business?' I murmured in disbelief. I knew the French law of succession all too well.

He nodded. 'My due, that is all. So now Aimery can no longer have full say on who is "*le nez*" for our family's empire. If I want to bring a female perfumer into our organisation, I shall do just that.'

I could barely believe what I was hearing. 'You would do that for me?'

'I would insist upon it. It seems rather stupid, if you possess the skills and the creativity, that we wouldn't take full advantage of it.'

'I'm a woman!'

'And you still don't think I've noticed?' he said with mocking astonishment to make me grin and almost shake with delight at what was unfolding. 'Man, woman, what does it matter? Isn't it only the skill that counts?'

'Well, I think so, but no one in Grasse would agree with you.'

'Well, I was conceived here but I don't owe Grasse anything, least of all my support for its short-sighted attitude. Times are changing, Fleurette. Wealthy women can control their own assets these days by law and while Britain leads the way in this across Europe, it will come.'

'I can't,' I admitted.

'Well, start thinking about what this war is going to do for the causes of women and their demand for more independence. If the war continues, women are going to be running our countries effectively.'

I gave him a look of disbelief.

'Maybe not in title, but they'll be keeping our countries going, doing all the jobs previously handled by men.' He opened his arms expansively. 'It's happening right here in Grasse. You told me yourself about the harvest and how amazing all the women of the region were.'

I nodded; it was true.

'They can harvest, they can even do their own carpentry and make their own enfleurage boards; they can distil, they can be chemists and they can be perfumers.' He shook my shoulder. 'Believe it.'

He possessed the ability to fire me up, that was certain, because I was riding his confidence more than my own. I nodded again, purposefully. 'Then let's make this perfume.' I reached for a pencil and paper. I gestured to a seat around a desk and we both settled ourselves. 'It begins like this. Well, truthfully, it begins here,' I said, touching my temple, 'in my imagination. But you're the one with this vision so tell me the qualities you want and I'll dream up the notes for it.'

His smile warmed me as effectively as stepping out into a field of jasmine in the middle of July. I wanted to tell him that but he was already muttering, and I touched the lead of my pencil to my tongue and wrote down three headings. This is how Felix and I worked.

'How do we do this?' Sébastien asked. 'Teach me.'

I sighed and frowned at how best to describe this process for someone new to the concept. I sensed that Sébastien was a visual person, good with imagery, so I decided he would learn best if I could paint a picture in his mind of first the architecture of a perfume. 'Close your eyes for me.'

He did so.

'Now, imagine, if you will, a gathering of birds. All shapes, all sizes. They've all conveniently landed in an imaginary garden. Can you see them?'

He nodded obediently. 'Yes, elegant flamingoes like ballerinas, squawking parrots, proud peacocks, wise tawny owls staring down disapprovingly at the host of chirruping sparrows . . . um, blackbirds too busy to pause, magpies standing sentinel and watching their feathered companions. I know you want me to stop talking now,' he finished.

I grinned to his closed eyes, loving his imagery, loving him. 'Good. Actually, excellent.'

He opened one eye. 'Have you ever seen a flamingo?'

I shook my head. 'In books.'

'I've seen so many at once that they covered an entire lake in Africa, turning the whole vista the most glorious pink.'

I sighed. 'I envy your travels.'

'We will travel together one day and I'll take you to Africa and we'll discover new plants, exotic new fragrances for you to play with. And then we'll go to India . . . and on to Australia.'

'Promise me.'

Sébastien put his hand on his heart. 'I promise you.'

'That means if you are sent back into the war zone, Sébastien, you can't die and break that promise.' It was the first time we'd mentioned the war and his inevitable leaving.

'I will not break it,' he assured. He closed his lids and once again silky crescents of dark lashes dipped in the hollow of his eyes above his cheeks. 'Now, I've got this garden brimming with wretched birds, making a terrible racket and leaving droppings all over my carefully tended vegetable allotment,' he urged.

I laughed. 'Indeed. So, imagine now that you run outside and clap two cymbals together.'

He opened one eye again, affecting a suspicious expression. 'And why would I be running into the garden with cymbals?'

I forced myself not to show any amusement at the question. Instead I dug up a glare. 'Just picture it, would you – do as you're told.'

'All right, all right, I just want to be accurate. So, I'm rushing out onto the porch with the most enormous pair of cymbals that I can barely carry and I am clashing them together in a sound that makes my ears bleed.'

I was glad he couldn't see my face crumpling with delight – he was so reminiscent of Felix. 'So, now tell me, Sébastien, what is going to happen at the first sound of your clash of cymbals?'

'Well, I can assure you the first event is that my intolerant neighbours are going to open their windows and —'

'Sébastien!'

'Sorry.' He cleared his throat.

'Perfume is serious business,' I admonished with no real heat.

His eyes remain closed but he grinned. 'I shall be as sombre as the grave from here on. Let me see. I think what you want me to imagine is that the sparrows and the starlings, the iridescent wrens and scarlet-chested robins and their tiny companions are going to be terrified and fly away.'

I breathed out my pleasure silently. 'That's exactly what's going to happen. All the bright, chattering, tiny birds are going to lift into the air and disappear. They'll look beautiful as they leave and their speed will make them dazzling when they take flight together.'

'I'm presuming you want me to clash my cymbals again?'

'I do. What happens next to the birds in your garden?'

'Well, I suppose the magpies, crows, owls, et al, will put up with me for a while and then tire of my tinny percussion.'

'Yes, they'll linger but they won't stay. They'll fly too. Heavier, they'll be longer leaving.'

'I understand.'

'Do you?'

'I believe so. What's left behind are the more cumbersome birds that don't necessarily fly unless there's a purpose. They don't flap around a lot. They need a bit of run up to get off the ground too.'

I was nodding and he opened his eyes to see me doing so. 'What are these birds a metaphor for?' I asked, almost holding my breath.

'Molecules,' he answered correctly and I clapped.

'And so our heaviest birds, or molecules, are the base notes of the perfume.'

'Nicely done, Fleurette. Base notes being the scent or scents that are left behind when the other molecules have flown away.'

I stood, waved my arms with triumph and made him laugh with the pirouette I performed. 'Exactly! They're strong, they amplify and hold all the other smells in place, you could say, on their collective shoulders. And when it's just these heavier molecules left, they must linger with beauty too so we have to get their mix perfect. They may not be so lovely at first – or indeed in isolation – and they could be masked by the lighter molecules too but together they'll show their beauty in their lingering as they turn into deeper, richer smells. So we need to get the base notes of our perfume into perfect harmony because they're essentially what boosts the other fragrances but also the lingering scents that remain on the skin or clothes. The heart notes are those middle range of molecules . . . vitally important – the main thrust of the perfume, in fact – and they're there for a while, mixing beautifully with the base notes. They're mellow, often quite gentle.'

'Rose?'

'Yes, definitely rose! Jasmine too, nutmeg, lavender. Don't make me list them. We could be here for hours!'

He grinned. 'And our tiny birds?'

'Top notes? They're there for just a short time to dazzle us. They're bright, springy, busy, sparkly.' I could see his gaze softening with pleasure to hear me so passionate about the subject closest to my heart. 'Citrus is a fine example . . . fresh, fruity, sharp.' I took his hand. 'Come with me.'

I led my lover to a door that permitted us into a chamber that was not nearly as light-filled, with high windows and a high ceiling, but felt confined. I watched Sébastien's gaze roam with increasing awe.

'This is my favourite place in all of Grasse.' I inhaled, tasting a lifetime of familiar and beautiful scents of nature's incredible wealth.

'Better than your Louis Quinze alcove?' he wondered dryly.

'Until today I might have said yes, but now I have reason to love that alcove even more.'

He kissed my neck and I felt its effect like an arc of electricity shooting to points in my body that held memories of this morning.

'Don't distract me,' I warned, pointing to a chair and desk with shelving stacked in a curved shape around it and containing dozens of vials of liquid of varying shades of amber through to near clear. 'This is the Delacroix Perfume Organ.'

'A hallowed place, I gather, from your reverential tone.'

I nodded, serious now. 'This is where my father sat for years.' I touched the cracked leather of the seat and instantly could smell his liniment. 'I remember when I wasn't as tall as this chair, stealing in here to see him but really to gaze at all these tiny vials.'

'And now Felix has this seat.'

I smiled. 'Yes.' I didn't mean to sound as wistful as I did.

'Do you wish it were you?'

'Not in his place, no; but alongside him? Oh, yes, I would love that. And that's how it's always been, to be honest, Sébastien. Felix and I have made beautiful music with this organ and its notes.'

'Orchestrated by your father, though.'

'Yes. Now it's Felix's turn to orchestrate and I will gladly follow his baton's instructions.'

'And presumably De Lasset replicates the organ?'

'Of course,' I said, 'although I have not seen it.'

'What?'

'I haven't been invited into the chamber, nor will I be. The main chemist and his assistant who weren't called to the Front nearly blacked out the first time I strolled into the lab. Now they just look edgy should I visit so I've stopped calling by. Now they come to me and take coffee; it's all very proper and they give me a progress report. There isn't much to discuss right now, as you can imagine, but it provides me with something to write to Aimery about.'

'And makes you feel connected to making perfume?'

'You already know me too well.' I looked away.

'I hate how sad you sound. What about here?'

I shrugged. 'Felix is gone, all the laboratory workers are in the trenches.'

'Then we make your perfume here, where you belong, plus we can keep ourselves secret and it means I can kiss you often.'

I pushed him playfully but he'd brought back my smile.

'So,' I said, seating myself in my father's chair, loving the way I slid comfortably into his position against the leather rubbed smooth. I straightened, took a deep breath and confronted the sweep of vials.

'I'll bet you know every oil in each of those bottles.'

'To the last,' I confirmed. I swept my hand across one section. 'Base notes. Here you find a lot of the woody smells . . . cedarwood, sandalwood. It's here,' I said, reaching for a bottle, 'that you'll find patchouli; both bitter and sweet myrrh; amber, of course, and musks.' I pointed to another range. 'Heart notes. And over here, everything from grapefruit to bergamot, clary sage, berries . . . our top notes in the organ.'

'I'm frankly dazzled by how many there are!'

'And we're discovering new aromas all the time. Those exotic places you've promised to take me – I'm sure we've hardly begun to discover the scents that they can deliver. We group them, so as I said: woody, fruity, marine, musks . . . there's more, but increasingly Felix believes that one day we'll be able to replicate the smells in the laboratory.'

'Believe him,' Sébastien assured.

'I don't wish to be part of that progress. If it's not natural, it will lose the point.'

'No, it won't. Because tell me how much ambergris is?'

I shrugged. 'Very costly. It takes decades for nature to make it . . . for the sea to gather it, for us to import it.'

'Imagine that you could imitate it right here.' He gestured to the walls around us.

I swung around on the revolving chair and challenged him. 'I know it's occurring, but why should I want to do that?'

'Cost?'

'Perfume *is* expensive,' I said like a dismissal. I couldn't see where he wanted me to follow him with this conversation.

'Fleurette, right now only the wealthy can afford it. People like you.'

'So?'

'So, imagine a Europe where most women might have their own favourite bottle of perfume that they dab on for special occasions. Imagine Jeanne, for when she gets dressed up for her sweetheart.'

I stared at him, momentarily puzzled. 'Making it for the masses, you mean?'

His eyes had a fresh, shiny quality despite the dimness of the organ room. 'That's exactly what I mean. And only being able to manufacture fragrances with man-made notes might enable that. I'm not talking about a perfume entirely made from chemicals, but I can certainly imagine one that stands apart because it is made with a man-made fragrance.'

I shook my head. 'I can't imagine it.'

'That's because you haven't smelled it yet. It isn't in your fabulous three-thousand-smell-strong repertoire yet. I believe, however, that if you can describe it, I can make it.'

I stared at him uncomprehendingly. 'How do you create something that isn't there?'

'It is there. It's roses, for example, but synthesised in the laboratory. Grasse only has so many roses but imagine if you wanted to mass-produce a fragrance and sell it throughout Europe, throughout Britain, America, the world.'

I blinked at the notion.

'Yes, you could import rose petals but imagine what is involved, how to prepare them, keep them from damage, or maybe you set up a plant somewhere and distil from them overseas. But think even bigger.'

'I can't imagine bigger than that. An overseas distillation factory sounds large enough.'

He smiled. 'One day, and it's not far away, a perfume will be made entirely with synthesised compounds.'

'I will weep that day!'

'You might also be pleasantly surprised. For now, let's work on *Parfum Fleurette*. Are you ready?' He stood behind me.

I swivelled back to face the organ. 'Ready.'

Sébastien's voice floated over my head and I closed my eyes to lock out everything but that voice and his description so that I could float in my memory of smells to find each element. '*Fleurette*'s foundation is one of good grace . . . and charm.'

'Wait, what colour is she?'

'Oh, she's fiery deep down, a scarlet woman in private.'

I giggled. 'Amber it is,' I said, reaching for my first vial. 'What else?'

'Well, let's see, she's sensible, conservative and grounded – and yet there's a giddy quality to her laugh, her humour, her lovemaking.' I elbowed him for the last remark. He laughed, continuing. 'She has shades of melancholy, though, probably because she is politically aware.'

'Hmm.' I set aside that he was describing me and worked with the description alone as unembodied. 'I think that calls for some vetiver,' I said, reaching for the vial of the oriental oil. 'This is a bright scent but of a cool nature. It comes from riverbeds, did you know that?'

'No, but it sounds appropriate. From Asia?'

I nodded. 'India, Ceylon. Next?'

'How many base notes?'

'How long is a piece of string?' I replied unhelpfully. 'Four or five,' I added, lifting a shoulder.

'All right, let's see now. She's warm. She's sensual without realising it, and —'

'Musk,' I interjected. 'It fits the profile,' I said without having to check my smell recollections. I inherently knew musk was necessary. 'It is the perfect balance with the amber and vetiver.'

He bowed to my knowledge and then continued, following his train of thought. 'Sweet but not sugary . . . um . . . what am I saying here?' he said, beginning to pace. 'I can see her laughing as she takes a puff on a man's cigar simply to enjoy being scandalous and to thumb her nose at society and yet she knows how to behave, how not to let down those counting on her. And she's kind; yes, there's a generous sweetness that can't be ignored.'

I breathed out audibly, trying to assemble these qualities into a single aroma. 'Vanilla, perhaps?' I reached for it and then changed my notion, reminded of the cigar imagery, and suddenly I could smell Dr Bertrand's tobacco. 'No, it has to be tonka bean.'

'Does that work with the other notes?'

'Oh, yes, it's a beauty. It shares some of the traits of amber and it will work well with the floral element that I just know has to be in this perfume. You could now put in some moss to add a bitter note to complement the chypre quality of the bergamot that I really believe should be in the top notes.' I looked up at him and smiled at his puzzled expression. 'You'll just have to trust me on that – plus something woody, perhaps, or earthy to add strength and a greener quality despite its milky soft aroma,' I offered, warming to my role. I could smell those additions coming into delicious harmony with those already selected. I nodded. 'This is a beautiful selection. It's very different to anything either of our families have constructed previously.'

'Good,' he assured. 'On to heart notes, then?'

'Violet,' I said, without hesitation, thinking of the ink, which was the first part of Sébastien I fell in love with. 'Maybe geranium to travel alongside the floral notes because while they can be confused, it adds a herb-like green with an almost minty undertone. I can't explain it better than that. Hmm. I must think further on this,' I mused, frowning.

He laughed. 'All of those, then. Should we have any more?'

'I think we should. Give me your thoughts once again. This is your perfume as much as mine.'

He kissed the top of my head. 'What am I smelling in your hair? I've been meaning to ask. It's mesmerising.'

'Oil of Macassar. I use it to smooth my hair and it keeps it in shiny condition. It was a gift from my father from his travels to the

East. He was told it is famed for its uses in the Levant.'

'That's what it is. Of course, I've smelled this before. It was triggering memories of my childhood but I couldn't place it.'

'You see how important smells are? They hold memories . . . they travel our lives with us. We can use some ylang-ylang, if you wish. It's a main ingredient in the oil I use in my hair.'

'Perfect,' he said. 'Then it's not only reminiscent of you but smells of you too.'

I was having fun but a glance at the clock told me I was neglecting my duties. 'Oh, no, look at the time, Sébastien. Most of the day is gone.'

'Do you regret that?' he wondered, sounding injured.

I stood. 'Not a moment of it, but I have duties and responsibilities to others. Our priest likes to discuss his sermon with me. We have coffee together Thursday, early evening.' I was already putting back vials and gathering up my notes.

'What about the perfume? It's unfinished.'

'It will wait for us. And don't tell me I have to write it down because it's already in its early stages of construction in my memory now.' I leaned in and kissed him, lingering in the taste of him, and as I pulled away I had to reassure him. 'I love you. And I love what we're doing together here. But you must help me by being patient. We have a long journey ahead before we can be free of our families' secret and unburdened of the sin our parents have forced their children to commit.'

He nodded and we both knew as we left the perfume room that we had to return to our platonic relationship for the benefit of others. At the door to the lab I let go of his hand and stepped out into light snowfall.

I squealed. 'Look, Sébastien – the snows have arrived!'

Snow had never lost its fairytale quality for me, especially light and harmless as this soft drift would be. It wouldn't settle long enough to be of any threat but it was beautiful to behold and I tipped back my head and opened my mouth as I had as a child to catch some of its icy flakes. He didn't join my mirth.

'What's wrong?'

'Suddenly everything,' he said, allowing a gloom to fall around us. 'I hate pretending, even though I understand your concerns. And now I'm thinking of the trenches. If it's snowing in the south, imagine how the north is faring.'

My mood dampened but I refused to turn maudlin because I knew it didn't help anyone's situation. 'Let's do our best not to be sad,' I said, giving him a sympathetic smile as we stepped out into the late afternoon. I pulled the hood of my coat up. No one was nearby to hear me. 'You should know that not in all of my years, and despite the challenges ahead for Europe, for us, I have never felt happier. And that's only because of you. Until today I thought my life was going to be bleak, certainly unfulfilled and loveless. I can't predict the future, Sébastien, but it's because of you that I am looking forward to tomorrow . . . and the next day.'

He sighed and I realised that life outside of my bedroom's alcove or the security of the perfume room was painful to him.

And life, it seemed, didn't consider it appropriate that while the rest of Europe grieved I should be allowed to forget for a single day that we were at war. And as I walked back up the hill, with Sébastien limping beside me at a polite distance, me still capable of feeling the sizzle of our passion invisibly dancing between us, life was going to make sure it reminded me that my joy of today was not to be tolerated.

16

We dragged the cold air in with us as we arrived, shivering and stamping away the more stubborn crystals of snow that clung to us with glittering determination.

'Hello, Jeanne,' I gusted as she hurried to help me off with my overcoat. 'Brr, I love the snowfall but I could use a hot cup of something right now.'

'*Bonjour*, Madame, *bonjour*, Monsieur,' she acknowledged brightly, offering to take Sébastien's coat as well. 'Shall I bring some coffee into the salon?'

'Make that tea, please,' I said, imagining Sébastien might like some of his national brew. 'I went down to the Delacroix villa,' I added in a breezy tone, making sure that I skimmed as close to the truth as possible. Felix always told me if I was ever going to lie, to keep the lie as honest as I could. His play on words had made me scoff but I knew what he meant now. 'It's so lonely down there. But it was most agreeable to see it's coping without its family, waiting patiently and calmly for my brothers to return.'

'It is sleeping, Madame,' Jeanne offered and smiled.

'Yes,' I agreed, returning the gesture, and dared not look at

Sébastien for fear of blushing at my own disingenuousness. 'I think I must consider opening it up to help the war effort, perhaps as a hostel or even a hospital. We'll finish December and next year I will look into this.'

'France will thank you, Madame.' She curtsied. 'Oh, Madame!' she said, forcing me to spin back on my heels.

'What is it?' I felt immediate guilt. We'd been discovered and she was about to ask me why I'd felt it necessary to take my husband's brother to my bedroom and —

'There is a letter for you! It is from Monsieur Felix.'

'Felix! Again?' I gusted with delight. 'He must have sent them barely a day apart.' I skipped to the hall cabinet and the silver tray and picked up the letter and kissed it. Then I did blush, turning back to a smiling Jeanne and a bemused Sébastien. 'Sorry, I get very excited to hear from Felix.'

'So it would seem,' Sébastien noted. I heard a tug of jealousy swimming beneath his dry remark but Sébastien would have to get used to sharing me with family, especially Felix.

Jeanne had departed and I gave him a softly admonishing glance. 'Care to join me for some tea, Sébastien?'

'What about the priest?'

'Oh, he doesn't come until about six and I need something to warm my bones.'

'I could make some suggestions,' he offered innocently as we moved towards the drawing room and won a glare from me for his trouble.

I closed the door behind us and gave him another look – of admonishment this time.

'What?' he asked, limping over to one of the armchairs. 'May I?'

I nodded and he lowered himself. 'You can't keep up the innuendo. People aren't stupid, especially Jeanne, and what's more, if I laugh only once at your remarks, I'll give myself away.'

'I promise I shall behave,' he said, waving a hand in submission.

'Thank you.' I walked over to where a fire spat and crackled. It was small but effective – the De Lasset chimneys drew beautifully, allowing maximum heat to be pushed into the room. I shivered this time with pleasure at the warmth easing past the chill.

'Why don't you read Felix's letter while I wait? I am happy to sit here quietly and reflect on my interesting day.'

I slanted him a look of exasperation from where I stood in front of the mantelpiece.

'I promise I can be silent and not interrupt you.'

'Can you, though? I'll admit I'm desperate to read it. It ends a perfect day.'

He nodded and I could see the sincerity. 'Enjoy the letter. Actually, let me leave you alone with it. I may head upstairs and change, I'm a bit damp, and you know how long it will take me to limp up and down.'

I grinned. 'Take your time.'

Sébastien left quietly and I was already pulling up a chair close to the fire, filled with anticipation. Felix rarely gave news but he was always able to amuse with his observations. I couldn't have cared less, to be truthful, whether he just talked about plants, scents, our childhood, his hopes . . . anything. Just to hear his voice in my mind would be enough. Just to hold this letter meant he was still alive.

I withdrew the thin pages. There were only two but that was his way. He was concise, always left me wanting. I was smiling to myself as I began to read, distantly revelling in the smell of the wood burning; someone had thrown in some pine cones left over from our subdued Christmas festivity that began with midnight mass and the inevitable *réveillon*, although our feast was modest this year and I ate with the servants in the parlour. I picked out the smell of the terpene compound immediately emanating from the pine. It made me momentarily look into the flames as the idea of trying to recreate this cosy scene came to mind. Could I craft a sweetly scented aroma that hinted of a lovers' campfire in a coniferous forest? Perhaps I'd add cinnamon bark, something autumnal like apples, even herbs of sage and rosemary . . . Yes, that last one would echo pine. It would be a masculine cologne for a pomade. Tobacco and musk now leapt to the front of my thoughts. My mind was wandering but it felt safe and comfortable here near the fire, with images of Sébastien making love to me just hours earlier skirting my consciousness, plus I was in no rush now to consume Felix's letter. It would be finished all too soon and then the wait would begin again. I'd sent them warm socks, new underwear – all practical things for their Christmas gifts, observing the army's requests not to send anything knitted in bright colours, and I hoped they'd had some peace. Oddly enough, even though my brothers were far away, fighting a war, the fact was in this moment I was convinced that this was the most secure I'd felt since my father died. I was in love with a man who had arrived so unexpectedly into my life to change it dramatically and for the better; I had a letter in my hands from the other man I loved most in my life and I couldn't wait for the two of them to know each other. To add to my pleasure, I had hopes of making perfume in my own right as a perfumer. And it was snowing and we were about to turn the corner of a new year. Life was good and might be great. Let's hope 1915 brings peace and sanity to Europe with my brothers safe and sound and home . . .

I hunched my shoulders, letting them drop in a sense of happy anticipation, and I opened up the sheets of Felix's letter to devour the contents.

> *Darling Fleurette,*
>
> *We have been involved in some fearsome fighting and I am reminded of Cyrano de Bergerac; you may recall that in*

*1640 he took part in a siege. It feels like that, as though we
are constantly with our backs to the wall.*

Felix was telling me he was in the Arras region with that opening
statement. I knew he was not permitted to disclose the location of
his unit so he buried it in an apparent mindless sentence. I had never
visited Arras but I had heard it spoken of as undulating fields of the
richest soil; it was an ancient town, as I understood it, that grew
wealthy as a trading centre with banking as important. Wool and
cloth merchandising was its main trade and my recollection of
school history now reminded me it was renowned through Europe
for its tapestries. And, ah, that's right, Joan of Arc was imprisoned
in Arras during the Middle Ages. It tended to be one of those regions
that moved back and forth in ownership between the French and
Austrians as well as the Spanish Hapsburgs. My memory now
reminded me of the most marvellous belfry in this town that took a
century to build. Hmm, so they were in the far north-east of
France – could we have been further apart? I wondered with slight
irritation.

I read on.

*I am also not one for theatrics, as you know, but if you are
wondering at the crinkled patches on these pages, they are
not raindrops from the weeping skies but the result of my
helpless tears. Tears for our dear brother, Henri, who took
his final breath today, in my arms, symbolically in yours too,
because he demanded to hold your most recent letter close
to his heart as he gave up his spirit.*

I had to read that paragraph twice again to make sense of what
Felix was telling me, and by the close of the second read I could
hear only ringing in my ears. My lips felt suddenly numb and the

pages in my hands were shaking like the helpless fluttering of a trapped bird's wings.

Henri was dead.

I refused to believe it for the next few dark moments but how could I deny the man I trusted most in the world? He would not lie. This was not Felix jesting. I touched the splotch on the faded paper, and in my mind I tasted a salty tear just as my tears began to drip down my cheeks, run into and past those numb lips so that I tasted the salt of grief for real.

I wanted to fling the pages into the fire so I no longer had to read about reality. Instead I moved like someone in a trance to the window seat so the afternoon light would help me to see through the blur of my weeping and I felt the cold touch of winter through the glass. Winter was my companion now and reminded me that the sun of today was being chased across the sky of my dreams, behind the clouds of a blizzard of sorrow.

> *I refused to send a telegram, darling sister. I could not bear*
> *for you to read those harsh and halting words that could*
> *convey no love or warmth, only the naked truth. Our dear,*
> *bombastic, often ridiculous but beloved brother is gone.*
>
> *And despite all of his faults that we would laugh at,*
> *you must know that as a soldier he had none. Henri was*
> *courageous from the day we arrived at the Front. He has*
> *saved many a man's life, including mine, at risk of his own.*
> *He took that risk for the last time two days ago when even*
> *against my best judgement he refused to leave an injured*
> *man behind. A German bullet from a sniper rifle felled him.*
> *Still he crawled to the trench to bid me farewell. I had him*
> *only a few minutes more and in that time he expressed only*
> *his love for the two of us and for our future. He wished he*
> *had said farewell to you on happier terms and curiously*

his dying words were about regret at forcing you to marry against your will.

A deep animalistic roar rose from my body and escaped my throat as a sob of anguish. Like Felix, I wasn't theatrical. I wasn't prone to screams or overt displays of emotion, but in this I had no control . . . and even now the sob sounded muted, not nearly enough volume to convey my despair. It brought people running, though. Sébastien was first through the door, ignoring his pain, hobbling fast on an injured leg, his damaged arm hanging out of the sling.

'Fleurette!'

Behind him came others. Predictably Jeanne, looking anxious with a tray in her hands and clearly feeling helpless. Madame Mouflard pushed past her in a no-nonsense way.

'Madame, Madame. . .' she twittered.

I looked up at them. Sébastien knew. I could see it in his unguarded expression. He'd had too much experience already of war to not be able to surmise what I'd just read. I stared at them all, weeping silently. No more sound would come. My voice was lost to those clouds of winter. My expression must have been so ugly in its crumpled grief but I didn't care. I shook my head at Sébastien and he understood that he mustn't rush to my aid as a lover but as a member of the family.

'My dear Fleurette,' he said, arriving to painfully lower himself to one knee before me. He tentatively touched my hand, the one that was squeezing the letter, the one he'd kissed so many times today, and now he had to act like a relative stranger. I still couldn't speak. I was looking at him through a river of tears. 'Felix?' he whispered.

And I let it out. I realised as I found my voice that I was releasing my relief, hating every inch of myself in the process because I was privately grateful that it was Henri and not Felix. I shook my head, racked with grief. I knew Jeanne was weeping too, and

I couldn't imagine Madame Mouflard could be hanging on to her composure easily.

'A cognac, please,' Sébastien requested in a gritty voice, full of anguish for me.

I smelled the fumes of the liquor before I focused on the small balloon of golden liquid that he pressed into my hand. First came a fruity floral fragrance, reminding me of the vineyards of Provence, that danced above pear and apricot nuances and then, like the top and middle notes of a perfume drying off, I smelled the complex base that anchored the world's most expensive tipple. The aroma was similar to what I smelled when my father's cigar box lid was opened. He hadn't smoked those fat cigars from Havana but he loved to own them, offer them to guests, smell their tobacco. A bouquet of toasted spice with a hint towards old leather, withered plums and roasted nuts. I welcomed the distraction but I knew I could never now think again on making a man's cologne. It would always remind me of the smell of smoke I had been pondering together with the fumes of cognac in my nose bound forever with the misery of Felix's letter in my mind.

'Sip it, Fleurette,' Sébastien urged, snapping me back from the land of smells, which is where from my earliest years I had always escaped to when problems visited.

There was a terrible silence in the room. Only the fire snapped and popped. I sipped and felt the rich burn of Aimery's prized Bache-Gabrielsen, tasting intense apples but then feeling only the fiery passage into my gut.

'Again,' he insisted, tipping the balloon for me until I spluttered. 'May I?' he asked, pointing at the letter.

I nodded like a helpless invalid. Silence held us again as he read the first page swiftly. And then there was movement. The women were trying to move me into an armchair; I could hear Madame Mouflard barking orders at Jeanne about fetching my shawl and making a milky posset to help me calm and rest. I swam out from the mist of shock to shake off their helping hands.

'Madame? You have had a terrible shock. We must —'

'Leave me,' I commanded in a voice that was firmer than I thought possible at present. 'Leave me!' I repeated louder and the two women flinched, casting a worried glance at each other and then to Sébastien, who nodded. They departed in stunned silence and he followed, turning once to look at me. 'The priest,' I murmured.

'I'll take care of it,' he said softly.

He closed the double doors so quietly I heard only the vaguest click. And then I was alone with my grief and Felix's letter.

I looked at the crumpled second page still twisted in my hand and I laid it on the window seat to smooth the wreck of paper. If Felix could bear to write this to me in his trauma of loss, then I needed to be brave enough and strong enough to read about our brother.

It was only just past five but night had stolen across Grasse, closing around the villa like a blanket. I shouldn't have cancelled the priest's visit but his inevitable attempt to comfort with words of consolation would make me feel worse than I did now and I couldn't imagine feeling worse. I was a coward, obviously. I dabbed away tears, my eyes already sore, and moved to a lamp to read the rest of the letter.

Both our Chasseur battalion and Aimery's were reunited. We were fighting a bitter battle for a town near Notre-Dame de Lorette. Aimery's boys were at the Front, while we were held in reserve, and then we were sent forward to take over trenches a couple of days after Christmas Day and I lost a dozen of our fellow soldiers within moments to injury or death. The fallen remain unburied, lying out in the brown sea of mud stretching ahead of the trench, freezing rain adding to everyone's misery.

There was a young lad, still wet behind the ears but eager, Fleurette – so heartbreakingly eager to please us officers. Henri kept him close. He had a soft spot for the youngster – I think we all did, but Henri hated that so many bright young men were being slaughtered from our region. He kept saying to me: 'These are our growers, our pickers, our factory workers, our glass blowers, our artists.' He took it far too personally that he couldn't save the men of Grasse and surrounds from the German war machine. And this boy had a stammer – remember Henri's stammer? I'd forgotten it until we met Marcel . . . he's from a tiny town that grows the violets we use. And while we all teased, Henri reassured poor Marcel that he would teach him how to overcome his ailment in the same way that he had overcome his own stammer all those years ago when Father brought in so many experts. Marcel had taken a bullet but we couldn't see where he was injured. He was moaning, begging for us to help him, calling to his mother . . . it was traumatising because only hours earlier we'd been teasing him about her. I think it was when Marcel began to cry and called to Henri that he would work very hard at his stammer if someone would deliver him from no-man's-land.

I don't think our dear brother could take it much more. I tried to stop him but he was over the parapet faster than any of us could imagine. He nearly made it too.

I noticed another tear splotch at the end of that sentence. It had touched the ink, which had bled, and I knew those five words had been so very hard for darling Felix to write and I cried for them both now.

*In an Atlas-like effort, Henri somehow lifted Marcel onto
his shoulders and staggered gamely back towards the trench.
I could see the whites of his eyes through the spattered mud
on his face, Fleurette. Henri was close enough to touch
and he threw the boy off his shoulders into the trench but
bullets were flying everywhere and caught our brother
through his chest.*

*He waved us away, calling, 'Faire face.' But I couldn't
square up to it as he was insisting. I had to get to him.
I managed to reach him and drag him down.*

*He was on his way to the shadow of the valley of death
before I lowered him into the trench but I had time to tell
him that he was loved, and to place in his fingers your letter
that he had been reading earlier that day, and to feel me
kiss his forehead in farewell and to hear his final words
about you.*

I will write to Catherine today to inform her . . .

I had to stop. I couldn't read the words any longer. They had
blurred to illegible with my tears and the sobs rose high into my
chest and I wept aloud, biting against my knuckles to prevent a
scream of anguish. Henri was gone. Brave Henri, trying to save
someone else, being heroic, always wanting to be the leader, the figure that everyone admired and looked up to. We used to laugh at
those traits but now he had died in glory, leading his men with
courage and vigour, saving his men with his own life.

Did he save Marcel? I scrabbled for Felix's letter again that
had fallen to the carpet. Sniffing and heedless of my weepy sounds,
I scanned for the words that would tell me my brother had not died
in vain. I skimmed through the part about Catherine, desperate to
learn about whether Henri's death gave life to someone.

Marcel survived. He is in a hospital and I hope he will make a full recovery and defy this war by staying alive for its duration and making Henri's life count for something more than his wealth . . . or even perfume, because suddenly, darling Fleurette, it all feels like a hollow dream. All that matters is family and our love for one another. The money and status couldn't save Henri . . . he gave his life for a poor man's son, and whose family's life will be richer for our loss but not because of money. Does that make sense? Is my grief making me ramble into madness? My brother is gone. Your brother is gone. Our parents are dead. It's only us now. I will stay alive, I promise.

I am coming home. I have been given some leave. We all have, so prepare yourself because Aimery will be heading home too briefly.

I shall see you soon.

Your ever-loving Felix

I flung the pages down. Suddenly this cosily warm and fragranced room felt claustrophobic. The smell of pine was nauseating me now and I regretted it would forever remind me of Henri's death. I yanked open the door and fled from the chamber, taking the waiting staff and a worried Sébastien by surprise. I'd had the full intention of going to my rooms but seeing them lined up anxiously, I turned right and moved swiftly across the hall to pull open the front door and I was running outside, welcoming the blast of chill air.

It burned me on the outside as the cognac had burned my insides. I could feel the effect of that liquor now and I welcomed the cold that woke me, dragged me out of today's daydream, and with this new pain of loss into the reality of my new life of grief. My wet cheeks numbed first and I ignored my chattering teeth. I trudged heedless of direction, ignoring the snowfall that had charmed me earlier, moving without purpose. I couldn't outrun my sorrow but I needed to make sense of it, come to better terms with it.

I found myself back in the herb garden, using the soft glow of the indoor light spilling from the villa to guide me. I stood behind its walls, believing that if I could shroud myself, then I could escape those who wanted to fluster around me. I understood but I didn't want them. I watched the flakes of snow falling noiselessly but disintegrating within seconds of touching anything solid, whether it was my hands or the bricks of the wall. I tilted my head to blink up at the dome of darkness and I began to pray as silently as the snow that fell around me. I prayed for Henri's memory and Felix's ongoing safety. I prayed for my father's soul, for the secret that had permitted a sin to be committed, with the two innocents in that sin paying for our parents' greed for each other. I prayed to be forgiven for loving Sébastien, for breaking my vow taken in church and for not caring enough about Aimery.

Sébastien was right. I could understand our parents now because I had touched the same dizzy abandon and carelessness that surely my father and his mother had felt nearly three decades ago when they couldn't contain their yearning for each other. I realised as I stood, my shoulders glistening with crystals of snow, that I had behaved identically and yet I dared to judge them. *People in glass houses shouldn't throw stones* was one of Felix's favourite sayings but I never thought it could be levelled against me. I was as guilty as my father before me, and I was as much of an adulteress as Aimery's mother was before him.

And now Henri was dead. Taken from us.

The bile rose, met the grief of death and riding cognac and little else, and it spilled onto the frozen ground as I vented my rage, my despair, my guilt. I retched with closed but watering eyes until my throat burned.

A strong arm encircled me and the voice I loved offered

soothing words but still I shook Sébastien off. I hadn't heard him arrive but now I straightened and glared at him.

'This is our fault.'

I saw him sigh.

I shook my head angrily. 'I'm riddled with guilt.'

'Fleurette,' he began in appeal.

'It's punishment for my unfaithfulness!'

'This is doing you no good.'

I ignored his rational soothing. 'I'm being taught the ultimate lesson and Henri bore the full weight of my shame.'

'Stop it. Stop your ridiculous talk!' he snapped. I didn't think him capable of speaking to me in such a harsh manner. 'Do you really think you're that important that the course of the war is affected by your actions?' he demanded in a low growl. He pointed north into the darkness. 'Men are dying by the thousands every day, Fleurette, with or without your involvement. You are just one of the millions of women around Europe who clutch photos and letters to their breast and hope and pray that the men they love will return. And too many of those men – no matter which side they fight for – won't return, including Henri. I'm sorry. I'm desperately sorry for you,' he raged into the falling snow, as though finally finding an outlet for his own despair, 'but this is *not* about you and it's *not* about us . . . and it is certainly *not* about people from a previous generation with the most human of failings to fall in love. I'm guilty of it. Here I am, admitting it freely beneath the heavens that I am guilty of falling in love but I am not ashamed of it and we don't get punished for loving each other . . . we get punished for making war on each other by losing people we love.' He still wasn't finished with me. Now he shook me, not hard but firmly enough to force me to not ignore him. 'In the scheme of Germany's war with France and her Allies, it's frankly obscene that you think our involvement could influence the death of your brother by a sniper's bullet hundreds of miles away. Wait, I'll get you a horsewhip, you might as well flagellate yourself while you're about it!' Oh my word, he was angry. 'We didn't plan this,' he choked out in his efforts to not raise his voice. 'Our parents didn't either. They didn't know they were going to fall for one another. Yes, I wish they'd taken more precautions or even considered the potential repercussions; I could wish they'd come clean and that our families hadn't kept their dirty little secret, but nothing we say or do can change the past. And Henri is now the past. I know that's harsh but it's the reality of war. When all the pomp and ra-ra-ra is done, there are men dying because more powerful men are greedy and want more than they have. Don't you dare sully Henri's name or what we share by linking them. I love you, Fleurette, but I don't like histrionics. You're behaving like a little girl instead of a woman whom this household and, in fact, the region will look to for strength. Everyone in the town, I imagine, will mourn Henri. So lead that grief with your composure. Be sad, don't be hysterical and don't read signs that simply aren't there.'

I stared at him wordlessly during his tirade. Sébastien was furious; mostly he was disappointed in me. I could see it in the way he swiped his hand through the frozen air and the low hiss and growl of his voice that made sure no one else could hear. He was right, of course, and I was struck silent by his forthright manner. Somewhere past the grief, much deeper, more private, I admired him for standing up to me. He wasn't a bully like Aimery, or wielding his status as Henri might; he was an equal treating me with equal disdain that he might show towards anyone who was stupid enough to measure their unimportant – almost pathetic – actions against the machine of war sweeping across Europe. As he swung around to groan at the expanse of night, I thought I could imagine myself looking at me with a similar sneer of disappointment.

'Henri died,' he said, in such a final tone that a fresh eruption

271

of tears fell but they were silent now. 'I grieve with you because I love you with all my heart, Fleurette, and I know how much you love your brothers. But Henri died gloriously. He will be remembered for his courage. So many I've seen have died while they slept, while they ate, while on the latrines, or in pain crying for their mothers, the women they love. His name will be on the lips of his company as one of the heroes of France's war . . . for not only going back for someone but carrying that injured man to safety on his back and then dying for him.' He must have quickly skimmed the letter to know this. 'It's a triumphant epitaph to the head of one of France's leading families. He will not be forgotten. His courage and name will live long. Instead of blaming yourself, which is insulting, applaud his valour, know your brother acquitted himself heroically for all of France, for your family.'

I was crying harder now but this time for the stirring words that did make me feel proud. I stepped towards him in the night and heedless of who might be watching I held Sébastien to me. It was not the embrace of lovers this time but of family, of friendship, of shared grief and comfort. Of someone who brought perspective at precisely the time I lacked it. 'Thank you,' I whispered.

He held me closer with one arm and I shivered into his warmth as he did mine. 'Now, show your fine breeding and your own brand of courage,' he murmured. 'You are head of this household, head of the Delacroix household too in the absence of its men. Take control. Dry your tears. Rise above sorrow and indulge your personal grief in private.' He held me back so he could look at me. We had only the dull moonlight, partially hidden by clouds. His eyes looked black – I'm sure mine did too although no doubt down to slits because they were swollen. 'No one's saying you shouldn't be sad or shed tears. But this is a moment to show your maturity. It's time for Fleurette De Lasset to be the force she can be.'

I took a deep breath.

'Good girl. Lock it away now. Be strong for all of us. There are going to be a lot more deaths and you will need to comfort those who lose their loved ones. You will be their strength because you set the example.'

I nodded.

'Fleurette?'

I gazed at him.

'I love you now in this moment more than I loved you an hour ago and I didn't think that possible.'

'Which angel sent you to me, Sébastien?'

'A fallen one, called Marguerite De Lasset, no doubt trying to make amends for her own failings.' We smiled sadly at each other. 'Come,' he urged. 'Before we both freeze where we stand. Come and take control of your house – they need to see you composed and strong.'

I walked slowly alongside my lover's limping gait back to the villa to make my family proud. I smelled clean, white snow like virgin air, unbreathed, untarnished, nature's beautiful purity. I needed to harness that for my perfume.

17

Jeanne and Madame Mouflard spied us as we walked across the gravel drive.

'What is it?' I called into the thin air. My voice sounded brittle.

'Telegram, Madame, telegram! It's Monsieur . . . He is returning.'

My heart sank, but then I'd been forewarned by Felix.

'When?'

'Tomorrow.'

The women reached us, their excited breath steaming between us. I glanced at Sébastien.

'Was the telegram for me?'

The housekeeper blinked, embarrassed. 'It was to me to prepare for his arrival, Madame.'

I felt the sting of being slighted but kept my expression even – it was not our housekeeper's fault that Aimery didn't consider my feelings . . . ever.

'But there is this one too.' She held out a second telegram, this one clearly marked for my attention.

I ripped it open, read it in a few heartbeats and half cried. 'It's from Felix. He's at Nice, on his way to Grasse.'

'We are so sorry about your elder brother, Madame,' Jeanne said for both of them, glancing at her superior as though apologising for taking the lead.

I nodded, keeping the emotion at bay as I'd promised Sébastien I would. 'I can't talk about it. I'm sure you understand. Let's go inside. We have preparations to make for the living. I shall dwell on the dead later.'

I knew it sounded theatrical but it summed up genuinely how I felt in that moment; it was taking every ounce of personal will I could bring to bear against my own sorrow, my need to grieve and be left alone to do so. Except, as Sébastien had pointed out, this was not my time to do so. And so, proving to myself as much as to him that I could, I led by stoic example. He gave my elbow a squeeze that neither of the women saw but I felt its reassurance and his pride in me.

Sébastien melted back from the new burst of activity and I mercifully got lost in it, busily supervising the making-up of Aimery's bed, airing and scenting his room and heating it with a fire. We put a copper pan, loaded with hot coals, between his sheets to warm the bed. Madame Mouflard felt that the fire and the bed warmer could be done later but I wanted his room to feel cosy and welcoming after so long in the freezing trenches.

'And please make sure there is a fresh bottle of his favourite cognac in the salon and in his bedchamber.'

With that all happening to my satisfaction I accompanied a small team of helpers to our villa to make identical preparations for my brother, except I was determined to breathe some freshness of Grasse into the air trapped in the house since his departure. I couldn't imagine how he'd feel rattling around this huge old place alone and decided I'd take the precaution of making up another chamber at the De Lasset villa in case he could be persuaded to stay with us for a day or so. I didn't for a moment believe he could be tempted; knowing Felix, he would relish the silence and the shadows as much as the painful memories that would flood back on entry into our family residence. I had every intention of returning to the Delacroix home, anyway – I doubted I would have much choice once the truth of the marriage's sinister secret came out – but right now I didn't want any of the servants entering my rooms, where just hours ago I'd been discovering my love for Sébastien. I could change my own sheets, air my own chamber when the time was right. It occurred to me then that Sébastien would need to move out of his brother's house as well. I imagined him digging his heels in, reminding everyone of his surname, but I would cajole him into living in the Delacroix house until calm could be achieved.

I shook my head at all the various permutations – all of us in the big villa, some of us down here . . . I could almost hear the argument that would rage once the initial delight of seeing our men alive had dissipated.

For Felix's benefit I sprayed cologne around the rooms, misting them with a scent that would make him assured that he was home and that it wasn't a dream.

I sent Jeanne off with a list of groceries that I discussed with the cook. Our men would not have eaten decent food in months.

'Keep it simple,' I warned, on Sébastien's advice. 'Their bellies will not be used to any rich foods, I suspect.'

We'd settled on a warming meaty soup, with homemade *fougassette*, the orange-scented bread of our region that they had likely not tasted since they left. This treat would be followed by uncomplicated roasted chicken with simple fennel to accompany, perhaps some kale from the winter garden; there was nougat, dried figs, pears, some cheeses and walnuts they could also nibble on if they needed something more after that.

'I wish I could present the thirteen desserts, Madame,' the cook replied forlornly. 'They would not have got that on Christmas Day in the trenches.'

I gave her shoulder a squeeze. Even we hadn't made up the thirteen desserts to represent Jesus Christ and the twelve apostles this year. 'We can serve our epiphany cake properly now. Next year will be different. Hopefully the war will be won and our men will be home for good.' Not Henri, though. I refused to let that thought out, determined to impress Sébastien with my resolve to lead.

But all the while I was geeing up others and keeping myself busy as a result, I was trying to keep at bay the demons in my mind that were mocking me, desperate to win my attention so they could question how I was going to face Aimery knowing I'd cuckolded him with his half-brother. Frankly, Aimery hadn't cared then and likely wouldn't care now that our legal paperwork wasn't intact; his intention was to make it so now. Far more to the point was how were we going to explain that the spiritual marriage was to be immediately annulled?

Felix's telegram said he should arrive at dawn, and I'd learned that Aimery would not be here until mid-morning. I thought about all the other families of Grasse who might already know their precious Chasseurs had finally been given some respite from the explosions, bullets and bloodshed. There would be celebration all over Grasse tomorrow to bring smiles to the town as we turned the corner into 1915, filled with hope for the end to war. The timing was perfect but there would be no smiles in the De Lasset mansion.

There would be only fury.

I had learned last night that not all of the Chasseurs were coming home on leave. It seemed Felix and Aimery as officers were some of the lucky few, and there were many others, who were either injured or had drawn a lucky straw too, but the majority of the two regiments were heading further east. I pitied them and was surprised to see so many of the town folk at the railway station clamouring for a glimpse of the brave boys who so far had survived and were coming home.

Just like the electricity that had come early to our small but flourishing town, so important to the economy and pride of France, the railway had reached into Grasse two decades before I was born. The first train that chugged into Grasse had begun its long journey south from Paris to Lyon and then hugged the coast to Nice before travelling into the highlands. There had been a lot of anticipation that steam would give way to electric trains and I recalled my brothers being excited by the testing four years before, between Mouans Sartoux and Grasse.

I didn't know how word had got around so fast but clearly people were aware that my brother Henri was not stepping off the train when it finally wheezed into Grasse station. I had received glances of sympathy, sombre nods, misted looks of shared pain, but whoever it was that had begun spreading the news of the Delacroix loss, they had also advised to give me a wide berth. I was glad of it but I realised that I mustn't be a damper on what was a joyous occasion. I knew it should be quietly happy for me too but my emotions were at war, not helped by the fiery new feeling of passion that had been ignited. One moment I could feel the warming memory of being naked next to Sébastien and the next my imagination threw me down into the mud where I was lying and facing my dead brother as the rain spattered his face and I could hear only the angry words we'd shared on our last day together. I had to snatch away the tears that helplessly welled; I didn't want anyone to see me crying.

Fortunately, though dawn neared, the night sky refused to relent, remaining determinedly black. Not even the moon was permitted to show through a wintry cloud cover, so we waited as a crowd of dim silhouettes, some faces illuminated better than others as lamplight caught them. Mainly what I saw in them was an eagerness, an impatience to see loved ones – for some of us, this moment felt bittersweet.

My mind was loose, wandering free. I stood alone and it struck me as odd that I hadn't seen Graciela since our meeting of last week, but no doubt this day would be an occasion for her to glimpse the man she loved.

The word *bittersweet* lingered in my thoughts and it brought a moment of clarity. That's what was needed in the perfume I was building. Was it that cyanide-like quality of the bitterness achieved from soaking almonds that gave marzipan its distinctive taste? Or was I reaching more towards the brighter, sweeter note of bitter orange?

'What are you searching for in your mind?' said a familiar voice next to me. I even had my eyes closed in thought and I didn't need to open them to know who it was.

'Sébastien,' I breathed. 'Is this wise?'

'It might look odd if I didn't meet my brother-in-law . . . and if I didn't accompany my new sister-in-law.'

'Neroli,' I said.

'Really? Bitter orange oil? Instead of bergamot?'

'Maybe. Bergamot is beautiful but potentially might be too softly floral, now I dwell on it.'

'So bitter orange for a fresher sweetness?'

I cut him a brief smile of cunning. 'To bring a brightly honeyed element with a metallic trace and a spiciness that I believe is required.'

He chuckled in spite of our sadness. 'You make perfume fun, Fleurette . . . and the way you speak of it is like a different sort of lovemaking,' he murmured.

I didn't look at him because people would always be watching, but I cheered inwardly at his comparison.

I couldn't respond because the town of Grasse surged as one at the first shout that the train had been spotted. We held our collective breath and then it arrived in a loud sigh of steam. Men we recognised were already hanging outside of windows waving, and my sorrow aside, I felt as though my heart was leaping within my chest at the thought of seeing Felix again. We had never been apart for this long, not even when he did his officer training.

Doors were slamming and soldiers were toppling onto the platform in a spill of blue. Hands were being raised to the sounds of women's yells and cries of delight. Those who weren't welcoming back their beloved alive had still come to clap the soldiers who defended France. I suppose, if they felt as I did, that they would privately cheer on those who lived because it brought a special nobility to those who had already died for them. I realised this was an odd psychology but it was helping me; it meant I could feel proud of Felix and could honour Henri at the same time.

And there he was. Suddenly my gloom lifted. I saw my brother, my second self, as he jauntily arrived on the platform, being joshed along by his companions. He was a sous-lieutenant and so I suppose he had to keep some composure, set some example for the whistling, cheering men he walked with.

They brought new smells to me, none I particularly liked, of damp cloth with decay clinging to it and of unwashed bodies. Nevertheless, there was Felix – that was all that mattered – and he'd spotted me, given me a heartbreaking smile that told me everything would be all right, and still I felt my chin wobbling with the easing of my resolve not to cry.

By the time I had rushed into his arms, I was weeping freely and he was holding me close and no doubt shedding tears also, both of us thinking of Henri, as around us people sang 'La Marseillaise' and fiercely hugged their loved ones.

The two men I loved most confronted one another.

'I'd heard you were at the Front,' Felix said, shaking Sébastien's good hand. 'I didn't know you were injured, though, or that you'd come here,' he said, glancing at me, not yet making the connection that I hoped wasn't written all over us. 'What a surprise,' he beamed. 'How goes the healing?'

Sébastien grinned and once again I was reminded of how similar they seemed, even in build. 'Your sister has been most generous.'

I resisted clearing my throat. Was that a slip of the tongue or was Sébastien taking some wry amusement playing on words? I cut a look back at my brother, who appeared untroubled by the remark.

'I was taking up a valuable bed in the hospital. Seemed the right thing to do to head home when the medical team suggested I do so. Real home felt a voyage too far.'

'Yes, of course. You'd have been in poor shape to travel, although England would have been closer.'

'I'm a shocking sailor when I'm well. Trains were easier in my state.' Sébastien shrugged. 'When I suggested southern France, they couldn't get me down here quick enough.' He lifted his bad arm slightly. 'I'm one of the lucky ones,' he admitted. 'I'm, er . . . really very sorry about your elder brother.'

Felix and I glanced at one another and found strength in the gesture. It had always been this way between us. Suddenly I felt capable of rising above my grief that just hours ago had felt like an impossible mountain to scale. Now, shoulder to shoulder with Felix, he and I could lean on each other and cope as had done when our pets passed away, when our father took his final breath . . . and now in losing our brother.

'Do you know the expression we use that he died *"en beauté"*?' Felix asked. His manner was so gentle I could tell he was still in awe of the reality that Henri was gone.

Sébastien nodded. 'In England we often say "He died with his boots on". I suspect it means much the same. It's certainly a compliment to his courage.'

'Come on. It's freezing,' I reminded. 'You must be in desperate need of some real coffee, Felix.'

'Just hearing you offer it makes me feel weak at the thought,' he admitted.

'I've made up your rooms and aired our house but I hope you don't mind if we go up to the villa first where we have food laid on . . . er, just briefly.'

His gaze narrowed. I felt the compunction to swallow as if to deny my guile but my heart was telling me what my mind already knew: that Felix had picked up on my nervousness and was now suspicious.

'I'd rather go home, Ettie,' he sighed. 'I'm not up for —'

'No, of course you're not. But there's no one else there. Just us,' I said, glancing at Sébastien, who had fixed his gaze firmly on my brother. 'It's just that the servants are already there, things are prepared, the whole house is warm.' Yes, I could hear myself blathering. It was no good trying to cover my guilt any longer. Anyone else glancing over might think Felix was simply giving eye contact as I spoke but I knew him far too well and realised he was watching me in nothing less than astonishment.

'Ettie, what's got into you?'

'Ah, I think I might be able to help explain,' Sébastien offered. It was gallant but I denied him with an urgent and, I hoped, small shake of my head, but did I really think Felix might miss that too?

Of course he hadn't. He looked now between the two of us as people jostled past. We barely heard their salutations, hardly felt them shouldering by, smiling or touching their caps. It was a triangle of stares, a hideous sort of silence within that three-pointed space that shut out all other sound, except perhaps the whirring cogs of Felix's mind.

'No,' Felix finally uttered in a low growl of shock. This single word said it all and seemed in that moment to encapsulate the entire, dizzying height of how far I had fallen. 'Tell me it's not true,' he pleaded, his gaze darting between both of us, his expression a twist of disgust.

'Felix,' I began.

He shook off my hand. 'While our brother bled into the filthy mud of the trench with your name the last word on his lips, you were . . .? Making full mockery of our family name, and especially him as head of the Delacroix empire?'

I began to shake my head. I couldn't defend myself ably because he spoke the truth.

'Felix,' Sébastien tried.

But my brother's injured look contorted to an expression of such repugnance that whatever Sébastien was about to say paused in his throat.

'No, you treacherous Tommy scum. You don't get to explain or offer me any advice. Get away from me . . . both of you!'

My breath came in a shallow draught, shocked by his insult to Sébastien, an ally who worked for the same outcome as the French. I looked around, horrified that people might see this exchange, but no one was particularly interested in us this morning, plus we had the good fortune to be withdrawn from the main bulk of people, turning away from the platform and flowing out into the town proper. We would be alone soon, our voices echoing across the station if we were not careful.

'Felix!' I snapped, my anger and fear combining with hurt that he'd attack Sébastien so fast. This was not Felix's way and I knew it was the devastation of Henri driving this attack. I also knew I could tell myself this repeatedly and it wouldn't change the reality that I'd effectively spat on our family reputation. He rounded on me, dark eyes glittering in the dawn light and filled with his furious accusation. 'You need to hear something and it's not about us,' I said, pointing between Sébastien and me. 'It's about our mother and it's especially about our father . . . it's about a sin far greater than anything you can accuse me of.'

He shook me off again. 'I hate you right now,' he said in a low, mean voice close to my face. The tone made me tremble. I had never heard him speak this way. 'Whatever it is you have to say to me, you will say it in the Delacroix house so its ghosts can bear witness to your fall from grace.'

Sébastien squared up in front of Felix; they were of near identical height, both broad-shouldered and dark. I had a darkly comic thought that the wrong brothers had been mixed up and in fact I was Sébastien's half-sister, not Aimery's. But the tension between the two men was like that between two snarling animals being held back by handlers . . . in this instance it was simply their good upbringing that stopped them brawling in public. Even so I tried to pull them further apart but I was no longer relevant.

'Too late!' Sébastien said, barely inches from Felix's face and I was confronted by my lover's anger stirred. This was a day for firsts. I was appalled at the rage that simmered in his quiet manner.

'Too late for what?'

I think I must have known what Sébastien was about to spill in the heartbeat before he did and yet I prayed he wouldn't. My prayer was ignored.

'They've already borne witness, you smug *poilu* bastard.' I hissed my despair at the slang term for the French soldier that accused them of being hairy. 'You had your chance to save her from a repulsive marriage and yet money, family name and duty were more important to you two brothers than her safety or happiness.'

'Safety?'

'Ask her! Then ask your sister why her marriage has to be annulled.' He growled so close to Felix's face you'd have sworn they were kissing each other in salutation. 'Instead of insulting her, instead of leaping to conclusions, for heaven's sake, man, listen to her. Give her the respect she deserves.'

Felix's complexion, normally healthily tan but currently sallow, turned an apoplectic scarlet.

'You dare lecture me, you lecherous —'

Sébastien actually laughed in my brother's face and that's when I moved quickly to stand between them. 'Stop right now, both of you,' I snarled beneath my breath that snaked in angry curls around us. 'And I mean now! Sébastien, have coffee and food sent down to the Delacroix house. Felix, do me the courtesy to walk with me.'

Mercifully, Sébastien limped away after one cutting glance of warning at my brother. We watched him in a shared rage until he was out of earshot.

'How could you?' Felix said but didn't wait for me to answer. He picked up his pack and strode away.

I caught up with him. 'I'm going to give you one more chance to hear me out or, I swear, I am leaving Grasse never to return.'

That halted him. He eyed me dangerously. 'I don't believe you.'

'Believe me,' I pressed, my anger matching his. 'Because you have no idea what we're actually arguing about. Sébastien's right, you should at least hear me out because you're getting it all so wrong.'

People waved, called out to us, welcoming Felix home. We both feigned pleasure, lifting our hands together in salutation, returning their good wishes before we were back, glaring at each other.

'I'm not wrong about one thing, though, am I? Your lover confirmed it.'

I stood straighter. 'No, you're not wrong.'

He gave a sound of despair and stomped away from me.

'But it's not what you think,' I said, hurrying alongside. Fortunately the Delacroix house was downhill from the station so it was easy going for us. We walked without paying much attention – we knew these streets in the dark, blindfolded, no clues.

'To be honest, I can't wait to hear you convince me that your . . . your liaison with Sébastien,' he said, enunciating the word liaison as though it was a filthy utterance, 'is pure and permissible.'

'Far more pure and permissible than Aimery and me.'

He frowned at me, then lost patience. 'I'm going in. You can come in if you want but I'm not going up to that villa.'

'Felix, you don't give me permission to enter my own house.'

He swung around and in that moment I could swear I didn't know this man. He was a stranger to me. 'You're so naïve, Ettie. With Henri dead, this is my house now. I permit whomever I wish. I can also banish whomever I choose.'

I nodded slowly, the truth sinking in deep to a place of injury where it sat like a brooding bruise. 'Maybe I never want to be in this house again. This house of sin and secrets.'

He pushed into the double gates, his footfall crunching on the gravel drive. 'I hope you've left it open. Hurry up, if you're coming in,' he threw over his shoulder without looking at me. I watched him march ahead, fling open the grand entrance door and hurl his bag. He disappeared inside and didn't glance back.

I stood on our pathway leading to my home and curiously did not weep. This was a situation that even a week ago might have watched me crumple at the unfairness of it, or the heartlessness of my brother; instead, Felix had stoked the fires of fury more. How dare he cast me aside? How dare he presume? How dare he treat me as though I was less than he because I'd fallen in love – of course, he didn't know yet about my being in love; he only saw the ugly side of infidelity. And even as I thought all of this, I knew something was wrong. This wasn't the Felix I knew and neither was this about Henri. I had no doubt losing Henri had made him show his emotion more openly but I knew this man too well. My connection with

Felix was too finely attuned that my perceptive sense, like invisible antennae, was bending towards him, looking for clues for his oddly demonstrative behaviour. I was now convinced his outburst was connected with something I was yet to learn about, but he was using me as the target to blame, or at least to hurl his despair at.

18

With dread I followed the trail of cast-off cape and jacket and the sound of glass to my father's study where I found Felix, with a half-open shirt, muddy boots kicked off and a crystal glass of cognac being emptied down his throat. He slammed the glass down on our father's desk.

'Welcome to my study,' he said in a harsh tone laced with sarcasm and tied off with an ugly bow of anger.

I weighed up my options. He wanted an argument. I could see that. We so rarely argued, this was unfamiliar ground and I couldn't hide my nervousness. He ignored it and took my hesitation to fill it with more of his humourless baiting.

'Ah, yes, this is now my empire, Ettie. What do you think? The useless second son, the spare heir finally inherits. Winner takes all.'

I watched him and the pain in his heart was nakedly romping across his lovely face that was presently contorted into a sneering grimace.

'Do you think a second is wise?' I asked as he poured another slug.

'Second? This is my third,' he said, impressed with himself.

'*Salut!*' He threw his head back and gave a growling sound as he swallowed the fiery liquor.

'That's too strong,' I warned.

'What would you know? Or have you now added drinking to your slutty behaviour?'

I closed my eyes to shut him out. He's hurting, I told myself repeatedly and took a slow, deep and silent breath before opening my eyes. 'I know because I can smell it, like I can smell you.'

'Well, good for you, little sister!' It was a curious remark. He clinked his glass against the decanter and then raised it to me before he took the remaining slug.

'Are you planning to get drunk?'

'Hell, yes. Anything to escape. I thought coming home would help but no, you've made sure there's only more despair for me.'

'Felix, please . . . can we talk?'

'We are.'

'No, you're baiting me. What's wrong with you?'

He moved unsteadily and flopped into our father's leather chair. 'I used to love sitting in this chair,' he suddenly said, more like the Felix I knew, his tone now gentle.

I nodded. 'Me too.'

'We used to sit in it together when we were really small, didn't we?'

I smiled briefly with relief. Well, at least he could still tap into happier times.

'But now we're grown-ups and dealing with grown-up matters.'

'Felix, tell me about Henri.'

It was like a blow to his belly. He looked up at me as if winded, his expression bruised, eyes sunken and bloodshot. 'He was heroic. Took several bullets, to be honest with you. Waved away help, saved so many lives personally over the last few months and especially that youngster at the end. We can remember him with pride. He is one of France's finest sons.'

'Amen,' I said. He slanted me a look of the briefest amusement at one of our favourite expressions. 'And how has your war been going?'

He blinked at me. 'What do you mean?'

'You know exactly what I mean.' I sat down opposite him, on the other side of our father's desk, and I realised this was now indeed his desk, his salon. Poor Henri, his whole life he had been groomed to take over the family empire and he had enjoyed the status for just over one year. Felix had never wanted it. I pointed to my temple. 'What's happening up here, Felix? You're different.'

'So are you. Now you no longer respect the sanctity of your marriage vows.'

I bristled but held my vexation in check. 'Do you remember our discussion on the night of the wedding? Remember me saying I wished I'd ruthlessly slept with others? That I desperately didn't want Aimery to be the first?'

He nodded.

'My wish came true.'

'What?' He looked at me with disbelief.

I lifted a shoulder and quickly explained the captain's and mayor's interruptions, the mobilisation and how Aimery wasted not a second donning his uniform proudly and dashing off to join his company.

'He left your wedding bed when he had at least that night up his sleeve?' he said, aghast.

'I'm afraid so. Virginal me in a silken nightgown was still not enough to tempt him. Felix, this marriage is a sham in more ways than one.'

He frowned. 'I don't understand.'

'Yes, but you will. I need Sébastien here —'

'Sébastien can go —'

'Be quiet!'

My brother glared at my admonishment.

'And don't pull any "head of the family lines" with me. This is important. This is more important than any of us individuals because it *is* about the family and profoundly affects us all.'

'So why is Sébastien part of that? He's not our family.'

'Thank goodness!'

He threw me a puzzled glance. 'Am I drunk? What am I missing here?'

'Plenty. But you have to wait for Sébastien. He's the key.'

'I don't understand.'

'You will. Felix, if you're in any way rude to him, I will walk away from here and it will take more than you can imagine to persuade me to come back. I will find it harder to forgive you for treating Sébastien like an outcast than I did to forgive you and Henri for forcing me to take vows with Aimery.' He tried to interject but I spoke over him. 'Now, you can live a lonely life without your twin sister, or we stick together as we always have and we can make the best of what we have left . . . there's only us now.'

He impaled me with a stare that was so nakedly wounded that I looked away; he would not want me to see him so exposed. 'Or I could just do us all a favour and square up to it, and die like our brother.'

'Felix!' My voice sounded thin, whispered across the room like a misty Grasse morning. Even so I knew he must be confronting death daily. 'How could you say something so heartless to me?' Pain erupted in my chest. Was this what a broken heart felt like?

He shook his head, then rightly hung it. He should be ashamed for such a shocking suggestion. 'Forgive me. That was cruel and insensitive to our brother's memory.'

My hand was still covering my chest in horror. 'What would

prompt you to say such a thing? Every day, Felix, I wait for a letter from you. Every day! The staff think I'm pacing for the postal delivery because I'm so anxious to hear from my husband. I wish him no ill but I don't care if I never hear from him again. It's you and Henri I yearned to hear from . . . you are all that matters.'

'And now Sébastien,' he said, raising his gaze to meet mine.

'And now Sébastien.'

'I wish I were dead and Henri alive.'

I was not going to wait for any further explanation. I was up and around the desk and hugging him. It was all he needed, an excuse to let go of all that simmering rage and emotion. He wept in my arms. He wept for a long time; I smoothed his hair and offered words of comfort. I couldn't imagine what he'd seen or experienced; I didn't want to dwell on the notion that he had held Henri as he died and now would live with that memory forever.

He picked up on my thoughts as uncannily as he always could. 'They're dying horribly, Ettie. I have watched too much carnage. So much young life bleeding out into French soil.'

'Don't the Germans call the brave Chasseurs the Blue Devils?'

He gusted a humourless laugh. 'Apparently, yes. I know we have acquitted ourselves fiercely.'

'Yes, and I suspect you are, as usual, playing down your own part in the heroics.' He said nothing; I knew I was right. 'You could use a bath, you know.'

'Could I?' He shrugged.

I frowned at him. 'Well, surely you of all people can smell yourself?' I even chuckled.

But there was no amusement staring back at me in those eyes I knew so well – almost a mirror image of mine; all I saw now was the sense of damage they reflected. He held my look as I held his face and we stared at each other. I searched the darkness that normally twinkled mischief, and now reflected a broken man.

'Felix?'

'I imagine you smell really good.' He sniffed the air. 'I should be able to smell the remnants of Christmas in Grasse . . . cinnamon, snow, clementines, pine cones and the yule logs.' He shook his head.

'Of course, and any minute, some rich coffee,' I said, looking out of the window, wondering where it was.

'No, Ettie,' he said, and it was spoken so sadly, I forgot momentarily what I had looked out of the window for.

'What do you mean?' I said, refocusing, turning back quickly to him. I knelt down to look up into his face.

'I am no longer *le nez*. The Boche might as well have killed me alongside Henri. One of their hateful explosions has brought the worst sort of invisible injury to steal my sense of smell.'

In that heartbeat following his revelation, I felt an odd tingling in my lips as though in sympathy for his ailment. In fact I was sure my face was turning numb with shock and the deadened sensation was now creeping down my gullet to block my throat. I couldn't speak. All I could do was tremble as the enormity of his admission sank in while I physically folded in on myself like a sack emptied of its rose petals until I was on the ground and resting my head on his knees.

It was his turn to stroke my head. 'It's gone, Ettie.'

'Nothing at all?' I croaked in a pleading voice.

'Some, but only the obvious like blood and waste, and only when the air is warmed. I suspect in summer we might anticipate my olfactory expertise to win back some effectiveness but, Ettie, I can no longer make perfume.'

Was this worse than learning my mother had committed suicide? Or as painful as being gathered at my father's bedside when he smiled beatifically at me for the final time just before he slipped into a coma? Or was it even more shattering than learning I'd married a member of my own kind? Yes, I believed that this news, if I lined it up against the few terrible events in my life, was the most horrible of all, including losing Henri.

'What happened?' My voice sounded small and I felt inconsequential against Felix's revelation.

'Head trauma from a shelling session.'

'Why didn't you tell me?'

'Why would I?' he replied, exasperated. 'You can't fix me. No one can. This is it. The lottery of war. Henri dies, I lose the only gift I possessed. I think I'd prefer to have died heroically.'

'Stop it now. You have to stop thinking like that.'

He moved, helped me to stand, but I knew he was effectively pushing me away so he could prowl the room like a caged animal.

'There's no future in perfume for me. If I had done us the good turn of dying, this could all have been yours and I know you'd make something of it all. As long as I'm in the way it means —'

'Shut up, Felix! Just shut up! I don't want it. I never did. I just want to work with you as we always did. I want respect. That's all! I want the chance to make perfume and have my name attached to it . . . nothing more. I don't want to run a business, or have the status as owner. It's not about money, either. I've already got more than enough and use little of it. This is about achieving a lifelong dream but you're part of that dream.'

He had moved to the window to stare out of it.

'Felix?'

'I heard you. I've always found self-pity to be loathsome in others and here I am all but drowning myself in it. But, Ettie' — he swung around — 'I do wish I were gone. Not being able to smell the world makes me less than half the man I was.'

'You can't die, Felix,' I said firmly. 'Because I need you. And you're my twin and we need each other.'

'You hardly need me with a husband and a lover.'

'I have things to share,' I said, not meaning to sound as cryptic as I did but I could see over his shoulder to Sébastien and Jeanne arriving with another youngster from the main villa. 'And I need to tell you before Aimery arrives.' I nodded. 'Now Sébastien is here. Don't you dare abuse him; I need you to listen to us.'

Felix sighed as if in sharing his news all the bravado of coming home had been expelled, and I looked at the shell of the brother who had returned. 'Henri's death aside, I can't imagine you can share anything that feels more daunting than me learning I can no longer smell the scent of flowers.'

I stared at him, fixing his gaze. 'Imagine it,' I replied in a grave tone. 'Because I believe I'm about to.'

The two men had behaved cordially, me standing between them, my glare enough to warn them both against any further anger being exchanged. We had moved to the drawing room where a fire had been tended since the early hours to warm it for Felix's arrival. In any other circumstances, it should have been a jolly scene but we sat straight-backed and tense within an atmosphere that felt instantly brittle and as though it might shatter at any second. Even the coffee that brought genuine joy for my brother was short-lived in its effect.

Soon enough his hostile expression had withered into the shock of learning what we had to tell him, our voices finally petering out to a taut silence as we let him read all the correspondence between our two parents. I knew he couldn't doubt this: he would recognise our father's writing in an instant and his gentle, affectionate words to Sébastien's mother, to say nothing of the sharing of information about their son Aimery. He rubbed his chin distractedly as he read letters back from Sébastien's mother, a sure sign of his irritation, and he became as still as a marble bust as he read the letters from each of their lawyers, which formalised an agreement that while Aimery was their son, he would be regarded as a De Lasset so that he might live his life as the son of Arnaud and inherit accordingly.

Felix finally raised his head and looked between us both. His expression was haunted and he chased his incomprehension back and forth between our two pairs of eyes that gazed at him with searching expressions, willing him to believe.

'He's our brother?' he finally ground out, still incredulous.

We both nodded. The letters between our father and Sébastien's mother were conclusive. Felix had had a lifetime of trusting me when I was serious – as I trusted him. He didn't even waste the breath of arguing it but his overwrought expression told me plenty about the internal wrestle; I knew the feeling. If his complexion was sallow when he'd arrived, it was now the colour of raw pastry.

'I've had a few more days to get used to it,' I admitted as I watched him put down the letters with disgust. 'And if not for Sébastien, I think I would have gone quite mad with the knowledge.'

Felix flicked Sébastien a rueful glance. 'Quite the hero,' he said.

'I didn't take advantage of your sister, Felix.' He gave a crooked twitch of a smile. 'I was enamoured by her from the moment we met and I fought my attraction – you have my word as a gentleman. I tried to leave, get away from her for fear of my own weakness, but she insisted I remain in the De Lasset home and I want to say it would have been impolite to do anything but remain. However, I was already falling headlong for her and the truth is I knew she needed support in her shock and I couldn't have turned my back on her, even if you'd been running at me with a bayonet shrieking a war cry.'

I couldn't help the prickle of pleasure hearing Sébastien's

declaration prompted. No one had ever spoken about me like this; the novelty was like a drug I could easily become addicted to. I blinked away from my thoughts to pay attention.

'I might also add to reassure you that had your sister been in anything but this shameful wedding contract, I would have denied myself a moment's further time in her company. I am no marriage wrecker.'

'And I didn't mean for it to happen either,' I chimed in, eager to share the blame. 'Felix, this is the first time I've ever felt anything romantic towards anyone. In that carriage on the way to the cathedral to marry Aimery, I felt something dying inside and I genuinely tried to step away from myself. I wanted to live outside of the life that I was being forced into and when I took those sacred vows next to a man I detest, I resigned myself to a loveless life of misery. I was going to live without emotion and for someone who lives by her senses that was like a prison sentence. And still I had to be obedient . . . to Henri, even to you. But no more will I be servile to any man. Not even to this one whom I love,' I said, flicking a glance at Sébastien. 'You yourself told me the world is changing. Well, I'm part of that change now. I demand to be only with a man I love, respect, admire . . . I demand to choose whom I spend my life with – even if it has to be clandestine.'

Felix shook his head, incredulous, his features wrought with puzzlement as though he no longer recognised me. He stood, pacing at the hearth. 'Well, isn't this a pig's trough we find ourselves in?'

'This is why Father never entertained the idea of marriage into the De Lasset family. He let us believe it was because of an old mistrust that dated back decades.'

Felix leaned towards the fire, both hands placed on the mantelpiece, head drooping as though looking for guidance in the flames. I heard his soft groan of anguish. 'Why couldn't he have just told us?'

'I think both our parents rather hoped the secret would die with them,' Sébastien offered. 'Your father obviously hoped to discourage sufficiently all thoughts of linking the families through marriage.'

Felix swung around. 'Yes, but he didn't count on Henri's determination to blaze new ground. Our brother wanted to leave his mark, unite the two great names of Grasse. Now this has the potential to destroy both our families.'

'We can't let it,' I said, looking between them. 'We have to find a way to contain this.'

They both stared at me, for the first time united, both of them clearly astonished by my recommendation.

'How do you propose we keep quiet about something so explosive? The church alone would regard it as heinous.' Felix demanded.

'The church doesn't have to know,' I pleaded at their astonished expressions. I explained about Graciela, finally shrugging. 'We tell Aimery the truth and he agrees to leave everything as it is but he gets to enjoy his mistress, providing he leaves me alone. I can keep the charade up for the family's sake but I will not be denied Sébastien.'

'No!' Sébastien said. 'Intolerable for everyone! I want a life with you, Fleurette, not snatched hours. Besides, he wants an heir.'

Revulsion ripped through me. 'Well, he can't have one!' I snapped. 'He has to give up his dream as I must give up mine.'

Felix threw his arms wide. 'And you both find clandestine comfort in the arms of lovers?' His tone was so sarcastic I winced.

'Have you a better solution? I'm just trying to keep our two families' reputations intact.'

Sébastien struggled to his feet and limped to join Felix at the fire. They looked like twin sentinels. I loved them both so much and yet for all that love we faced only misery, all of us.

I watched Sébastien pull his injured arm out of its sling, vexed by the whole inconvenience of it. He turned to face Felix, his expression grave, frowning in thought. 'There is a solution, of course. I'm of the opinion now that we could just kill Aimery, Felix. No one need know the truth, if we take care of the ugly business here, perhaps in the wine cellars, and bury the corpse behind some fresh cement. I'm sure there's a small wall down there needing to be built. What do you think? The problem would then go away.'

I gasped in fright at the intensity and horror of his suggestion but then heard the rumble of laughter that had looped through my whole life like a bright ribbon. I loved Felix's laugh. It was spontaneous and bright, like a firework being ignited, and it colourfully lit everyone who was in its orbit. Genuine delight from Felix was hard to win and so it traditionally was unexpected, came from nowhere – as now – but when it did it arrived effortlessly and sincerely because Felix never bothered with deception. And it was always accompanied with that deliciously dry expression of his.

'Sébastien, you fool!' I gushed, relief draining through me. 'Don't jest.'

'Very good, De Lasset,' Felix said, still chuckling. It was a sound to lift the pall that had turned the room breathless and claustrophobic. 'Not many can entertain me and I didn't think I'd find much to ever laugh at again since leaving Grasse. But you give me hope.'

Sébastien nodded. 'Give me a chance with your sister and I'll try hard to remain entertaining and not let you down.'

Something passed between them akin to a loosening of their conflict, or maybe I was underestimating it. Perhaps it was respect; whatever it was, I felt my spirits lift. With Felix on side, there might yet be a chance for Sébastien and me.

'Felix, our mother loved —' I began, but he cut me off, swinging around with a finger raised in warning and all of that former lovely amusement was doused as if I'd thrown a pail of water over him.

'No, you won't make me feel guilty about her. She is a stranger to us, Ettie. If you let this eat at you, you're going to start feeling responsible for something that happened more than two decades ago that you had no hand in and no responsibility for. Anyone who takes their own life is clearly unbalanced.'

'But —'

'But nothing,' he snapped. 'If you could see what our men are coping with each day in the trenches, you'd wonder why more of us aren't blowing our dark thoughts away with our revolvers. We have genuine reason to, in what we see, in what constitutes life in a trench . . . and in the death and havoc we wreak on other people, on our beautiful lands. Northern France, so beautiful, so fertile, is now just a desert of thick, black mud. The fields have been scourged, the forests blown up to look like a wasteland. The devastation to our countryside is heartbreaking enough without the death of its men. It would be so easy to end it and still almost all of us resist, but don't think I haven't considered it.' I inhaled with shock at his admission. 'But I always hear you in my head pushing that bullet of peace away and your will for me to live is stronger than my will to die, so if they want my life, they're going to have to take it the hard way. I'm not giving it to them. Our mother was obviously weak. She gave in and gave up her life for what . . . a pair of lovers?' He gave a sound of disdain. 'With all due respect to your mother, Sébastien, and to our father, an affair before marriage is hardly worth our mother's tears, let alone her life. She would have achieved far more by financially destroying him, if she really wanted revenge. But she didn't, you see, Ettie. She just wanted pity because they kept something from her. I agree it was a heinous secret, but she was obviously too fragile of mind to fight back and let's not forget this was, at its beginning and end, about jealousy. She had every-thing to live for. Her nemesis, Sébastien's mother, even admits in her letter that our father loved our mother to distraction, plus Mother wanted for nothing. Imagine it: she had three small children, Ettie, two of them infants, and she put her obsessive love for a man and her jealousy about a liaison before he'd even met her above all of us. No.' He shook his head vehemently, pointing a finger at me. 'You will not martyr her in your mind, or try and make me feel guilty. What I am is angry. I could hate her memory now for her weakness.'

'Oh, Felix,' I began, a helplessly beseeching tone creeping into my voice.

He shrugged at me. 'Our father was not blameless, grant you, but he didn't push her off that rock, Ettie. That was her choice to be melodramatic and jump. But I do hold him responsible for fathering a child and then unwisely keeping that secret so it grew darker and had the capacity to do harm, to turn an innocent child birthed without knowledge of his blood into a potential walking sin – *that* I can't forgive our father for and neither should you. All it took was for him to be man enough to tell one of us; heaven knows I would have understood his romantic affair. I could even have kept his secret safe but at least he'd have had an ally beyond his own lifetime, for I would never – *ever* – have permitted the unlawful marriage to take place. He failed in not letting the next generation know how much his choices could so profoundly affect us.'

Sébastien had been frowning, as though reaching for something as Felix spoke. 'Well, that's it, isn't it?' he said, a dawning thought brightening his expression.

'What is?' my brother and I wondered together.

'Unlawful. That's the word you used, Felix. Fleurette' — he turned to me — 'you told me that the marriage ceremony was rushed into, despite your desire to wait for all the right formalities.'

'Yes,' I replied, 'but any day to marry Aimery would feel rushed.'

'No. I mean, you told me there was no civil ceremony.'

I opened my mouth first in awe, as understanding glistened like newly dug treasure. I could tell it had slipped Felix's mind too because he wore a similar expression of wonder. The comprehension turned to the release of wonderful relief; of course, the law of the land would prevail, as I'd warned months previous. But Felix spoke first. 'You're right!' he said urgently. 'There was no time for the mayor to preside over a civil ceremony and sign a marriage certificate. I remember when I mentioned this, Henri waved it off and said while it was unusual, so was the threat of war and the mayor would organise the paperwork as soon as he returned from Nice.'

'Except when he returned it was with the bells of the cathedral ringing the tocsin across the valley,' I continued, exuberance in my voice as I embraced what this now meant. 'And then it was too late. No one was thinking about much else except war, and Aimery departed soon after. There has never been a legal basis to this marriage.'

'I'm not altogether familiar with French law but I'm right, aren't I, that the church service is irrelevant?'

'Mere theatre,' Felix said, blowing out his cheeks with certain relief. 'Without that certificate from the mayor's office, the marriage isn't legal.'

My breathing stepped up with excitement. 'So I can just walk away?'

Felix frowned. 'Legally, yes, I believe you can. Your dilemma is now simply a moral one. But you can't save the two families the inevitable disgrace.'

'But at least no one needs to know the real reason that Aimery and I cannot live properly as man and wife. I would maintain the charade, if I were cornered, but this legal loophole is my chance to lawfully leave.' It was my turn to hold up a hand as Felix began to speak. 'No, listen to me. I'm sure when Aimery discovers the truth he will agree. We can devise some excuse that permits both of us our freedom. We could blame the war, for instance, and everyone would understand how it can change people. At least that way he could be with Graciela and I with Sébastien.'

'I think Aimery would already be married to Graciela Olivares, if that were his desire,' Felix warned, 'but I don't disagree with you that the legal platform does bring a new perspective. He will likely want to blame you in front of others, of course, as nothing must tarnish the De Lasset name, I suspect.'

I shrugged. 'I couldn't care less what excuse he uses, so long as it only humiliates me and not our family name, but knowing Aimery, I imagine he'll want to maintain his heroic profile and will cite my overwrought mental state at losing my brother as the culprit.'

'And there's truth in that,' Felix agreed. 'Right, I suggest the first —'

My brother got no further. The double doors of our drawing room were flung open to slam back against the wall and shudder on their hinges as Aimery strode in, cape sweeping grandly behind and bringing with him a chilling draught that made the flames of our cosy fire gutter with irritability and expectation.

19

I was so shocked by Aimery's arrival I was struck temporarily mute. Despite his travels he looked immaculate in comparison to Felix or Sébastien: he was shaven, cheeks pinched rosy by the cold, but there was that dangerous gleam in his eyes I had come to recognise.

'Why, may I be so bold to ask, is my wife here with you, Felix, when she should be standing on the steps of my villa to greet her heroic husband home from the Front?' His gaze reflected anger bristling so close to the surface I could sense him shaking beneath all that uniform. 'And who the hell is this broken individual?' he said, taking in Sébastien's bandages and walking cane. I found my tongue in time but as I opened my mouth to speak, Aimery forbade it with a cut of his hand into the former warmth of the room, its temperature descending fast. 'I did not speak to you, wife! I spoke to the man of the house.'

'Still, why don't you let her speak for herself, brother?' Sébastien answered for all of us. Clearly he was not cowed by Aimery's bluster or sense of power in Grasse.

'Brother?' Aimery snorted, his eyes settling with threat on Sébastien. 'And by what right do you term yourself thus, stranger?'

'By blood, Aimery. I am Sébastien De Lasset, your estranged brother.'

'Ah.' Aimery nodded, managing to look interested but sound uninterested. It was quite a trick to pull off, as he tugged at the fingers of his leather gloves with his teeth. 'Reports say you were one of the heroes at the chateau. I heard you acquitted yourself most courageously, saving several lives. Not bad for a civilian to show such pluck.'

Sébastien shrugged. 'A family trait, perhaps?' The backhanded compliment to Aimery aside, he'd not mentioned anything to me about saving lives, only his own. I didn't know in that moment if I could love him any more than I already did but I wanted to for his modesty, while his half-brother strutted like a peacock in full mating glory. Face to face with Aimery again and I knew, despite my earnest commitment, I could not live with him or keep up any charade. I would find it hard not to gag in his presence, and if not for Felix and Sébastien's presence, I would likely be looking for a way around him and out of the house.

'And why are you here instead of taking advantage of your escape from war, tucking your tail between your English legs and running back to Mummy?'

Sébastien didn't flinch. 'Because our mother is dead, Aimery.'

Aimery laughed. 'Good riddance, I say. What happy news indeed. So now what, you run injured from the battlefront in order to lean on our father's estate?'

'Our father?' Sébastien smirked. 'Mmm, perhaps my father; not yours, Aimery.'

I watched my husband pause, his gaze narrowing. This was not the way to tell him. 'Aimery,' I began gently.

'Shut up, Fleurette,' he hurled. 'The men are talking.'

'Don't speak to her like that,' Sébastien warned.

'Or what, little brother?'

'Or I'll destroy you.' He forbade Aimery a chance to debate. 'I can, you know. Legally I have claim on everything you believe you own. I can exercise that claim in a blink,' he said, clicking the fingers on his good hand, making a snap that sounded louder than it should in the horrible silence. I wondered if he could snap the fingers on his wounded hand, now that we'd re-dressed it so that his fingers were free to move and hold items again. My mind was wandering. 'I will demand precisely half of it all, which would surely ruin you as Grasse's pre-eminent perfume manufacturer . . . or we can be amicable.'

Aimery's expression darkened. Graciela had warned me of his moods and I'd had a small taste of them on the day of our marriage. I was fearful of witnessing them being so deliberately stoked, but with others present, what could he do?

'I owe you nothing, Sébastien Beaumont!'

'De Lasset,' he corrected. 'It is my real name, you know, which is more than I can say for you.'

I took a deep breath but was relieved that Aimery was too enraged by Sébastien's threat to focus on his subtle baits.

'People barely know you exist!' he spluttered. I saw the weakening of his composure and threw a glance at Felix using our mode of silent communication. The way my brother regarded me in return suggested that maybe Sébastien's confrontational tactic was indeed the way to go, even though it was not the approach either of us would favour.

'Well,' Sébastien continued in a dry tone, 'as we Brits say, it doesn't matter a jot what people think or even know. The law is on my side, brother.'

'What the hell do you want from me? My blood?'

'Certainly not. It's not nearly as pure as you imagine. Definitely not as pure De Lasset as mine – you'll be surprised to learn the truth.'

I mentally rolled my eyes and suspected Felix was doing the same.

'But let's just say that what I want from you will cost you nothing.' That caught Aimery's attention. I watched him swallow hungrily. 'Just one of your so-called *possessions* will do it.'

I breathed out, scared now that I could see where this was going, and I sensed it was not going to turn out well. 'Sébastien . . .' I tried, keen to dissuade him against this path, but he glanced sweetly at me, only affection in his expression.

'Hush now, Fleurette,' he warned.

Whether it was me murmuring Sébastien's name or the familiarity by which he responded, I couldn't tell, but instantly Aimery's demeanour changed. He halted where he had been moving from foot to foot like a child on a hot pavement. His expression shifted from haughty and angry to cunning; there was accusation in his eyes now. He was busily connecting clues. I would never make the mistake of accusing Aimery of being a dullard. Growing up around him had taught me his mind was agile, capable of speed and moving down sly pathways. I wondered if he had already made it to the right conclusion.

'Which possession, brother?' he enquired, intrigued, although his tone told me he'd already guessed.

Sébastien was not playing his games. 'Your half-sister.'

Neither Felix nor I was expecting him to sound the trumpets of Jericho so politely or quickly. We both gasped audibly.

'Sister?' Aimery looked confused, glancing at both Felix and me, and I couldn't blame him.

'Half-sister,' Sébastien corrected, unfazed and calm as a summer morning, willing Aimery's attention back to him. I had to admire his directness. He left little room for misunderstanding.

'I don't have one, you idiot. Is this a jest? Has the war made you simple?'

'No, but the war has made you a cuckold, although technically, given that your marriage is not legal, perhaps me falling in love with Fleurette is nothing more than normal for any man who lays eyes on her. It is also permissible, given the unlawfulness of your wedding. Plus, legalities aside, even spirituality set to one corner, morally you're on the shakiest of grounds to be marrying Fleurette . . . although I grant you, you were not to know.'

'What the hell is he talking about?' Aimery demanded, finally ripping off his cape with great swagger and threat. Instantly both my men stepped closer to me.

Aimery watched this instinctive move. He nodded as if accepting the challenge, although his voice clued differently. 'Felix?' One word. A question clearly posed while spoken calmly; the query in it sounded almost charmingly innocent but I wasn't fooled. The atmosphere felt splintered, as though it could explode at any moment into a million sharp pieces of pain.

Felix cleared his throat and obliged, telling our sorry tale in half the time it had taken us to relate it to him and a fraction of the time Sébastien had laboured over explaining it to me. I realised we hadn't offered Aimery a seat, none of us had moved from where we stood, close to one another in a tight trio as we watched him receive the dreadful news. But if we appeared still, Aimery was immobile; not even his expression twitched or gave anything back to us so that we might gauge his response. He stared at Felix with unnerving intensity and I helplessly found myself looking for Delacroix features. Now that I concentrated I found them with sickening acceptance. The shape of his head was like our father's, despite his colouring being wrong. He even tilted his head as my father used to – and just as Henri did so often – and the large blunt hands were achingly familiar. I wondered as I stared at him with this fresh insight whether he'd suffer arthritis in years to come and the ache of Heberden's nodes.

I could also smell him now. It had taken a few minutes for the air in the room to warm again and my keenest sense had reached out instinctively and tasted the angry air around him. On it I smelled liquor. He may have looked immaculate and held his alcohol well, but I had no doubt now that Aimery had been drinking. I didn't care whether the reason for it was to stay warm or to dull the memories of the trenches; I only cared that liquor did not make him a happy drunk, like Felix; it turned Aimery belligerent, argumentative and unpredictable. I felt the flutterings of fear, and my anxiety exploded like a swarm of bees taking to the wing.

I admired Felix, though. His voice was crisp and steady. He spoke in that calm, mellow tone that had always reassured me. Plus he was surprisingly concise with his language, speaking officer to officer in the way of the army – only the facts, no embellishment. He pointed to a small table. 'There are letters that confirm everything between my father and your mother . . . even from lawyers on both sides of the Channel. You are a half-brother to Henri, Fleurette and me. Sébastien is the only one amongst us who is not related by blood to a Delacroix.' He cleared his throat. 'I'm very sorry, Aimery.'

I stood and moved towards him with the bundle of letters. 'Aimery, would you like to look over —'

He batted my offering away and the bundle scattered on our rug. 'No, I would not,' he sneered.

I left the letters where they landed. I wasn't going to give him another chance to insult me while I was cringing near the floor. Now, more than ever, I was determined to press for freedom. There would be no compromise, no covering up for family reasons. I wanted my name separated from his. I would never agree to Aimery De Lasset having any say over my life again. I hated him more than I thought possible and yet . . . yet I could feel sympathy for him. For both of us, paying the price of the sin of our father.

Sébastien rejoined the conversation. 'That's rather childish, isn't it?' he noted, glancing at the fallen envelopes. 'But then our mother did say you were a needy infant.' Sébastien shrugged. 'You can't hide from it, Aimery. And your marriage to Fleurette is to be annulled as of today. I will speak to the priest myself this afternoon, if you force my hand, and I will tell him everything I know.'

'With your one hand?' Aimery sneered, raising and opening his palms. 'Sébastien, I will kill you with my bare hands if you so much as breathe a word of this to the priest, you dog!' Aimery's hushed warning turned the room silent, leaving it heavy with expectation of what might come next. I do believe I was holding my breath.

'Why don't you try?' Sébastien offered. 'Here I am. All bashed up and partly helpless. Yes, take years of growing up in my father's shadow out on his blood child, his true heir. Go on, Aimery, I dare you. Use your bare hands on the injured soldier – I'm sure your men would consider you even more heroic when they learn of it.'

'Enough!' Felix stepped between them. 'Aimery, you've had a shock, you need to go home, bathe, rest, and we shall all meet later and talk this out. No one will be speaking to the priest yet about anything, Sébastien,' he said, deliberately eyeing him.

Sébastien nodded.

Felix looked back at my husband. 'Can you do that for me, Aimery? I think we all need to take a deep breath. I myself only found out minutes before you. It's a lot to take in, a mountain of hurt to deal with, a lifetime of pain to forgive our parents for. I mean it sincerely when I say I am sorry for you.'

The tension broke as Aimery lifted his shoulders and let them slump. He shook his head as if to say it was indeed all too much to take in at once. His voice sounded wearied and placating when he spoke. 'May I have a moment with my wife, please, gentlemen?'

I didn't believe any of us expected such a polite request. He was suddenly calm and it appeared that the moment of potential violence had passed as a result of Felix's tenderness. I could answer for myself. I was tired of all of them managing me.

'Of course,' I acquiesced. Sébastien slanted me a worried look and I didn't need to glance at Felix to know he was probably asking the same question silently. 'I'm fine,' I affirmed. 'Aimery is fine too.'

Aimery shrugged. 'I think we should at least have a private moment to come to terms with this alone.' He gave me a searching look and I felt that sympathy rise – surely he deserved it, as he was in as much denial and shock as I had been a few days ago.

'All right, we can step outside. Come on, Sébastien,' Felix urged. 'We'll be on the porch. I could use a smoke, couldn't you?' he said to the man I loved, who hesitated to shift position.

'We shan't be long,' I promised Sébastien in a murmur; unlike my lover, I was embarrassed by this moment of awkwardness as Aimery watched us. Sébastien had none of the history to feel guilty and perhaps why he felt so free to goad this man's temper.

We waited as they left, Aimery glancing sideways but not even changing expression as he watched Sébastien limp past him. 'Hurry along, can you, brother? We don't have all day.'

Sébastien shot him a baleful stare. 'You're the one who should be quick, Aimery. All you've got is a few minutes before either you leave or I remove Fleurette myself.'

Somehow he managed to make talking about me while I was present not feel domineering. If anything, I felt protected by his threat. I gave him a tight smile that Aimery didn't see before the door was quietly closed and Aimery's head turned slowly back. He regarded me with a gimlet gaze, sharp and searching.

He moved casually and I resisted the urge to step back. Aimery walked to the fire so he was now behind me. Tense, I faced the door to where the others were; again, I resisted swivelling to face him like a cornered animal. This is *my* house, I told myself; stay calm, stay strong.

'You've been busy in my absence, Fleurette,' he said, his voice not much above a murmur.

I finally turned to face him and nodded. 'Yes,' I agreed, trying my utmost to sound amiable. 'I've supervised harvest, enfleurage and distillation; I've made sure all the De Lasset equipment is —'

'I'm not referring to *my* perfume business. I'm referring to a much shadier business of you and my brother.'

Take Sébastien's lead, I reassured myself. Be firm, be candid. 'I wouldn't say busy,' I deflected, lacking courage at the last moment to hurt him. 'I only met him a day or two ago.'

'Even worse – you wasted no time at all falling into the arms of a man you barely know. How would you term adultery of a newly-wed while her husband is away defending his country?' He blinked slowly to show his disgust although his tone was congenial.

I looked down and sighed softly through my nose. I couldn't avoid this. So face it! I could hear both my brother and lover urging me through the timber of the door to be direct. 'Aimery. . .'

'Yes, Fleurette?' he asked, his tone heavy with sarcasm. 'Spin your tale for me of how none of this was deliberate and how you had no intention of humiliating me and all the other callow placations while you ruthlessly demeaned me. I would love to hear them.'

'I cannot help who your father is, Aimery,' I said, finding my spine.

He flinched.

'I cannot help that you and I are related through blood.'

His lips thinned to a line so taut I was sure he could barely breathe. He wasn't going to let me have another chance to distance myself from the main issue. 'You did, however, have free will in choosing Sébastien. Did he take your virginity?'

'Is that what really matters in all of this?' I hissed.

'Did he?' he demanded. In one stride he was growling in my face and I will never know what prompted me to turn on him. No doubt just these last few minutes in his company again had reminded me what a selfish and arrogant brat Aimery would always be. I wanted him to understand that I didn't have to cower beneath his gaze as his wife any longer. I owed him nothing. All earlier feelings of regret turned in on themselves and became feelings of hot rage. Years of his bullying, from the day he made me watch him tear wings off butterflies to the night of our wedding, and hateful moments of childhood and teenage despair in between as our paths had so frequently crossed over the years, now welled up like over-boiled milk.

Months of pent-up emotion from the day of my unhappy marriage turned from the cauldron of fiery molten into a withering, cool rage.

I shook my head. 'No, Aimery. No, he didn't take my virginity. I wouldn't let him.'

Aimery stretched his neck against his collar as if it was suddenly so tight he was choking on his own righteous rage.

But I wasn't going to let him enjoy his moment. 'I wouldn't let him take it, Aimery, because I truly wanted the pleasure of giving it to him with my own free will. It was my special gift to him. Would you like me to describe where and when I gave it? I can count it back in hours, even you can guess that; and if I close my eyes, I can still conjure the feeling of him inside me. Would you like to hear how he made me feel so alive, my senses so heightened, that I spoke his name like a prayer? Or do you think that's a private moment I should keep to myself? Do you want to hear about his lovemaking, so tender and delicious, that I want that sweetness in my life forever, and your tobacco- and liquor-laden breath, your vile arrogance and —'

If I was honest, I didn't really know what happened next. One moment I was snarling, slightly out of control, at Aimery, and the next I was dazed, unable to focus properly and impossibly crumpled, most unladylike, on the parquet floor. I was suddenly and puzzlingly next to the mantelpiece, I thought. The only reason I could gauge this was the smooth marble feeling so silken beneath my fingertips as I struggled to lever myself back into a sitting position. I failed and ended slumped like a ragdoll at an awkward angle, as though flung from a child's hand towards the bed or toy box and missing the mark.

Dazed and confused, I was beginning to understand Aimery must have landed me with a boxer's punch to the side of my head. Were the church bells chiming again or was I imagining that? I shook my head. He was talking but I couldn't hear him properly. My left ear was clogged, as though stuffed with wadding. I think I must have been blinking rapidly too because I watched Aimery through the clouded haze of my mind reaching to his thick leather belt, jerking at something. In a moment of new panic, I wondered if he was going to undo his trousers and rape me to teach me a lesson. But no, Aimery was well beyond simple punishment, I realised now as my vision began to clear and my hearing tiptoed back through the mist that Aimery intended to punish me in a far more permanent manner.

' . . . dare to humiliate me in this way,' I thought I caught distantly but then my focus snapped to attention to the revolver he was waving drunkenly at me. So that's what he'd done: removed his army gun from the holster at his hip. He was going to kill me, if he could hold it steady. I wanted to laugh at him, dare him to, but instead the sound that came out was a scream. I didn't know such a noise could come from me but it wasn't just fear, it was formed almost entirely from bitterness and anger.

The double doors slammed open for the second time and my brother, my lover and a third person, someone I thought of as my new friend, Graciela, burst through. I didn't have the leisure to wonder at her arrival.

'You bastard!' Felix growled, looking for me instantly.

But Aimery had swung around to point the revolver their way, while I still helplessly languished on the parquet. He was no longer interested in me. They halted immediately at his threat, hands instinctively raised, palms facing him.

Only Graciela didn't comply with the universal gesture of surrender. I had to read her scarlet-painted lips because my hearing was still not up to it. 'Aimery!' I read, imagining her vermillion silks rustling as though they too were incensed. 'What are you doing? Don't be absurd.' Although sound was muffled, her perfume reached me in a glorious waft of angry spice, warmed by her wrath and the room.

'I told you to wait for me until I came, woman! I do not want you in this company!' he snapped, instantly dismissing the beautiful Spaniard as he turned to face Sébastien. My hearing was improving, I could hear him snarl now. 'You . . .' he accused. 'You said you wanted one thing alone from me but it seems you've already helped yourself to that, *brother*. So I think I should give a demonstration of what I do to scoundrels who steal my possessions.'

My head was clearing rapidly as his threat bounced off the walls and tensions increased. I sat up properly, didn't think I should risk standing and startling Aimery, waving a gun around. Sébastien wore a sardonic expression and gave no impression that he was perturbed to have a gun barrel pointed at his heart, but I was horrified and blurrily looked around for what I might use as a weapon. Sadly, the fire implements were on the other side of the mantelpiece or I would have at least made an attempt on Aimery with a poker.

Felix, however, looked as worried as I felt. He still had his palms raised to waist level in a soothing manner. I heard him call to Aimery gently. 'Put the revolver down, Aimery. I promised you we will sort this out, and we shall.'

'I heard you'd talked two men down from committing suicide, Felix; apart from those you physically saved, you're quite the hero.

Certainly silver-tongued, but you see I have no intention of killing myself . . . others maybe, but not myself,' Aimery scoffed. 'So don't waste your breath.'

'Just —' Felix tried again but Sébastien spoke over him.

'I didn't steal anything that didn't ask to be removed from your gloating. Let's be clear here, Aimery. Fleurette is no one's possession and you've all made a mistake in thinking she ever was one to be bartered with. She will carve her own path on her own terms. With the annulment of this marriage she is free to choose whom she wants and to choose life on her terms. The world is changing. The war alone tells us that. Apart from your unsuitability and indeed unpalatability as Fleurette's husband, you're a dinosaur and I'm glad your age is done. Now there's a woman right here, it seems, who loves you for who you are,' he said, turning and bowing his head at Graciela. 'We have only just introduced ourselves outside but she has been candid. She is surely the right woman to be married to, because if I understand this situation correctly, you have always admired her.'

Aimery gave a mocking laugh. 'I will never marry a daughter who is the product of Moorish inbreeding with Spanish thieves and Portuguese pirates. She is comfortable with our arrangement,' he threw at Sébastien, and even in my blur I sucked in a breath at the vile remark, and how arrogantly confident he was in Graciela's adoration.

'You won't marry a beautiful, wealthy woman who loves you but you'd rather bed your half-sister? What sort of reverse logic is that, and how much more inbred could you want a child to be?' Sébastien said, incredulous.

'Put the revolver down, Aimery,' Felix warned again, forceful this time, and I knew that note in his voice and that obsidian-like glare in my brother's eye. If I could caution Aimery, I would tell him to pay Felix's warning heed.

But it seemed Aimery was beyond all reason. He lifted his weapon, took unsteady aim at Sébastien, and I staggered to my knees to be on all fours. 'Please, Aimery,' I tried, reaching for him, my hand slipping off his trousers as I did so.

'You have no right to ask anything of me, you whore. Now, watch me make another whore's son pay for his sin.'

It happened fast. I leapt at him, knocking him sideways. I don't know which of us screamed – I thought it was me, but Graciela's mouth was open, so it could have been her. There was blurred movement, accompanied by a yell, but I couldn't see properly because Aimery was in my way, a second yell of 'No!' and then the loud retort of a gunshot. I saw Felix slump slowly to the ground, a bemused look of disbelief ghosting in his expression. And I was instinctively crawling on all fours, hoisting my skirts to my chest so I could move freely enough to drag myself over to where my brother lay. There was a moment's horrible silence draping itself around us all as Aimery gave a sound of disgust.

'Damn you, Felix. Now look what's happened. You shouldn't have got in the way,' he said conversationally. 'You can blame your sister for impairing my aim.'

A vase was hurled at his head as I pushed myself to my feet. In my mind I had the ridiculous thought that no one should be throwing Limoges around but Graciela's fine attempt bounced uselessly off Aimery's shoulder. She hurled a stream of Spanish at him. He ignored her but it had distracted him for a few precious seconds although I no longer cared at whom he fired; I had reached Felix to cradle his head in my lap and I think I was willing my husband to shoot me dead too so he would be executed for double murder.

But whether Sébastien thought Aimery might attempt to hurt me, he was not leaving it to chance. He stepped in front of us as surely as my darling Felix had stepped in front of him to take the first bullet, its effect now obvious as Felix's blood spilled across his shirt.

He was breathing shallowly, eyes closed. I kept trying to say his name but no sound would come past my shock. My screams were silent, my pain too immense to focus on sound. Sébastien opened his arms. 'Go on, Aimery, you cowardly, half-bred pig dog! Do it.'

And Aimery did, rot his soul. He pulled the trigger. Angels descended on us that morning, it seemed, because there was another explosive shot to deafen everyone but the bullet landed uselessly in the door, spitting wood splinters down upon me. He was not a great shot; the kickback from the revolver combined with the liquor roaming his body had saved Sébastien's life. I watched Aimery look at the gun with an expression of fresh disgust, tutting irritably as though he were simply involved in shooting practice.

I'm not sure what it cost Sébastien to move as fast as he did but I watched him whip his walking cane into the air before swinging almost in the same motion with all of his might at Aimery's gun hand. He connected with a sickening cracking sound against my husband's wrist. I welcomed that sound and I especially enjoyed watching Aimery's eyes roll dizzily and his body crumple slightly. More importantly I carefully watched the revolver bashed from his hand to skid along the parquetry and bump harmlessly into Graciela's laced boots.

Aimery recovered swiftly, certainly fast enough to have his large hands around the neck of Sébastien, who had flung himself awkwardly down on Aimery to shield us twins once again. Apparently a fractured wrist was no obstacle to a raging brute.

'I told you I'd kill you with my bare hands,' Aimery promised, the side of his head bleeding.

'And I told you to try,' Sébastien urged through clenched teeth, as he tried to peel Aimery's fingers back. It was slow; there were guttural sounds emanating from Sébastien and I knew I had to leave my groaning, dying brother and help my lover, if he were to survive.

There was a bright snapping sound as Sébastien surely found near superhuman strength in his one good hand to break one of Aimery's fingers. The shocking pain registered in his brother's face and he let go with his broken hand but this time had the inspiration to reach for his trench dagger, a crudely fashioned stiletto that was the French version of the trench knife that Sébastien had told me about at some stage in passing over the last day or two. He dragged the vicious triangular-shaped stiletto awkwardly from his belt, ignoring his cracked wrist and broken finger.

Sébastien seemed to react instinctively before the knife could wield full damage, raising his injured hand to take the first swipe, and the blade cut through his bandages easily.

'Ready to be gutted, British scum?' Aimery ground out.

I didn't think Sébastien, now sitting on top of Aimery, could fend off another determined blow and I was reaching for a matching Limoges vase that, though cumbersome, might just distract Aimery enough if hurled at his head. His sight was blinded by free-flowing blood from the wound anyway. I could see him shaking it away to see clearly as Sébastien used his last option, which was to lean all of his weight down on his brother in an attempt to crush his neck . . . if only he could reach it. His able hand was fending off the stiletto but not winning the struggle for the blade that was inching perilously close to my lover's neck.

Suddenly there was a swirl of scarlet before me. 'Go to hell, Aimery,' I heard Graciela say in a guttural version of her normally smoky voice. For just a heartbeat both men stopped struggling; Sébastien even straightened. She took that moment to gather some spittle and hurl it into her lover's face. Graciela let rip with another stream of angry Spanish that I didn't understand and yet my heart somehow understood it perfectly. His insult of earlier had been too much to bear. She had suffered enough humiliation from him and she had debased herself long enough to prove her love. But his dismissal and disdain had lit her volatile Spanish temper as though he had thrown fuel onto simmering flames.

I only realised when she pulled the trigger at near point-blank range that she had picked up the revolver. It seemed Graciela had taken a shooting stance in planting both feet firmly and using both hands to steady her aim and to ensure little recoil. I was in a state of amazed horror to witness Aimery's head snapping back against the rug atop the parquet and, although the hole in the middle of his forehead looked quite small and neat for the tremendous noise of yet another gunshot, I dreaded to imagine the state of the back of his head. His formerly angry, sore and streaked eyes stared unseeing at the ceiling with a look of dismay as his final expression. I agreed with him – who would have thought the one person who loved him in this world would kill him? Blood quickly spread from beneath his head, viscous and so dark it looked black against the oriental rug of our sitting room.

The flames that had witnessed death danced merrily on in the fire and the snap and crackle of wood was now the only sound in the room.

20

The eerie silence of shock was punctured by rapid movement as we all, in the same instant, left dead Aimery to his maker and gave full attention to my shallow-breathing brother.

'Felix?' I whispered and his eyelids opened slightly. He gave me one of his radiant smiles.

'Am I dead?'

'Never,' I said through helpless tears, although even I could tell it would not be long before he made a liar of me.

We heard urgent, scared voices approaching. Graciela moved first. 'I will get help and find the mayor.'

Sébastien grabbed her gloved hand. 'Graciela,' he snapped, pronouncing her name perfectly. 'Say nothing to incriminate yourself. Leave this to me.'

She frowned and shook her head slightly. 'I am prepared to take full —'

He made a hissing sound of disapproval. 'Listen to me now! Say only that you arrived to find this scene.' He shook her. 'I mean it. Repeat it!'

'I don't have to. But you also don't have to —'

'Let me handle it! Now go! And rub that powder off your sleeve.'

She held his stare a moment longer, then nodded and was gone, closing the doors behind her.

'Fleurette,' Sébastien whispered, touching my hand.

I moved at his touch as if burned and my anger surely showed but my attention was firmly on Felix and the dying light in his eyes.

'Fleurette, look at me,' he demanded again, softly but more firmly now. I raised my watering gaze. He shook his head deliberately to say what I was trying to deny in my mind. He was right; of course he was, for he would have seen wounds like this before. The bullet had done its damage, not killing my brother outright but it was claiming his life all the same. The angels could only save one life today and they had clearly chosen Sébastien's, protecting him twice, once with my brother. I gathered my brother's hands together in mine and kissed them.

'It's so cold in here, Ettie,' he murmured.

'It's winter, my darling,' I said, trying not to lose control of my voice. 'Think of spring, Felix. Think of the harvest and us lying down in perfumed petals.' He broke a fresh smile at the memory. His gaze was becoming unfocused, unable to hold on to me as it roamed across the patterned ceiling.

'Ettie?'

'I'm here.'

'You don't have to tell anyone now about the Delacroix–De Lasset sin. It ends here with us.' He coughed blood and I had to swallow not to scream my despair as Sébastien put his arm around me, urging me to stay strong for Felix.

'The sin dies with Aimery,' I agreed, my voice small and pathetic, but he heard me.

His smile widened to break my heart because he looked so like our father in that moment. 'Now you are free to marry the right De

Lasset, and no one's memory needs to be stained.' He suffered another life-draining spasm and his blood oozed through my fingers from his wound and dribbled from his mouth. The doors opened hurriedly and three people spilled in: Graciela, our local policeman and the mayor, but Sébastien forbade them to come any closer. The two newcomers glanced first at our trio and then Aimery's corpse and fell bleakly silent.

'Bring our two families together properly,' Felix said, only vaguely recovering from his exertion. His breathing was so ragged and shallow I knew we had only moments left together. He looked at Sébastien. 'Be very sure I'll haunt you if you don't take care of her.'

'I give you my solemn word that she will be treated as the most precious woman on earth,' Sébastien promised my brother and raised his injured hand to his chest as an oath. It too was bleeding again, bandages falling away from where Aimery had sliced into them.

'I am only half a person without you,' I said, openly weeping now.

'No, Ettie. Take it all,' he said, struggling on each word. 'I'm happier this way. I'll be with Henri and Father – we'll cheer you on and watch over you as you make your first perfume. What does it start with?' he said, his dying grin emerging. 'Talk to me of flowers – let me smell them in my mind once more.'

'It always starts with our May rose, the rose of one hundred petals,' I began, ignoring the tremble in my voice. 'Can you smell them? Dewy and honeyed?' I kissed his lips farewell, felt his blood cling to my mouth and I tasted its metallic sweetness.

His eyes shone with a strange clarity as his spirit prepared to disentangle itself from this life but it gave him a final burst of prescience that Sébastien and I witnessed. 'We have to run to the fields, pick our blooms on the morning they open so we don't lose their brilliance. I smell first the lemony-apple citrus before honeysuckle and raspberry sweetness, and there's the clove and pepper running deep.'

'That's right. We begin there, Felix,' I promised.

I had to lean close to hear his next words. 'Plant roses above me, Ettie,' he whispered, and the last breath of my beautiful brother sighed past my ear and I felt his fingers slacken beneath my grip.

'He's gone,' I warbled in a whispering voice to Sébastien. He nodded, his face a mask of sympathy, and I wondered in that moment how many last breaths Felix and Sébastien had witnessed, themselves still so young.

I felt new arms around me. I was being lifted, urged towards an armchair. A blanket was placed around my shoulder. From somewhere a glass of cognac was put in my hands and through no effort of mine the small tulip-shaped glass ascended to be tipped against my lips. It was a woman's hand guiding mine.

'This will help,' Graciela urged.

I smelled first the volatile liquor before the movement of the glass swirling the cognac released the vapours of linden flower and old grapevine, a fleeting sense of violets before I noted vanilla and tobacco. The syrupy liquid slid into my mouth and down my throat in a tiny stream of nut and caramel flavours that heated me.

'All of it,' my friend pressed, tilting the glass until I'd swallowed the entire slug to burn its way past my gullet. I hated it.

She squatted beside me. 'You must be very brave now,' she encouraged. 'For his sake,' she said, and we both looked at Sébastien. He was in earnest conversation with the mayor and policeman, who was already grilling him for details of what had happened. I glanced at Felix, now covered by a dustsheet someone had kindly picked up from the neat pile we'd folded earlier this morning but forgotten to pack away; his feet poked out and they wore a pair of wool socks I recognised that I had knitted for him soon after he and Henri had left for the Front. I had to look away and my gaze fell on Aimery, who was covered by his cape. The ooze of his head wound had crept beyond the cape's reach and I shifted my feet so that I didn't have to have any contact with him, especially that sticky stain that pointed towards me like a finger of guilt.

The cognac worked its fiery path through me to enliven and I found I was arriving back in the moment and paying attention to the conversation.

I watched Sébastien shaking his head in answer to a question. 'Well . . . I don't know, sir,' he said in his flawless French, although I could hear how disturbed he was in the soft tremor quavering in a tone that was normally steady. 'Aimery was making some wild accusations here.' He ran a hand through his hair, making it look especially unruly. I wanted to stand up and smooth it back for him, let him know that none of this was his fault, although I sensed he felt the blame was clinging to him like a bad smell. We'd both snarled at Aimery and helped his mood darken, no doubt. Don't go there, I told myself. There's a lifetime of blame down that path when it was Aimery who lost his temper, reached for a weapon and took deliberate aim twice.

'I don't know what was in his head to say all that he did,' Sébastien admitted.

'But to accuse you of being with Mademoiselle Olivares?' the mayor wondered aloud.

Sébastien shrugged. 'Mademoiselle will no doubt assure you that today is the first time we have ever laid eyes on one another; we were introduced by Felix when she arrived at the house moments before Aimery fired his fateful shots.'

Graciela had moved away from me to approach the men. 'This is true,' she said in her thickly exotic accent. 'I didn't even know Aimery had a brother. I was shocked when he was introduced to me by Felix Delacroix.'

The policeman frowned. 'So all of you were on the porch.'

Sébastien gave a soft sigh. 'I shall tell you again, shall I?' he offered in a generous voice.

'Please, Monsieur,' the policeman agreed with a slight bow.

'I had escorted Madame De Lasset to the station pre-dawn to meet the train. You are aware that her eldest brother was killed, died a hero just days before he was given leave?'

The policeman and mayor bowed their heads in melancholy. 'We were deeply saddened to hear of Monsieur Delacroix's passing, yes.' the mayor replied.

'And now this,' Sébastien added, gesturing at Felix. 'It's all a terrible shock for her.'

'Yes, yes, forgive us . . . er, Mademoiselle Olivares, would you like to escort Madame De Lasset to —'

'No!' That was me. I hadn't been aware I was paying enough attention because I thought I was still drifting in my thoughts, the smell of liquor strong around me. I had discovered it wasn't just my cognac, it was Aimery still strongly reeking of alcohol.

'Madame?' the mayor enquired, looking between the men with surprise.

'Aimery was drunk,' I said, not caring at my raw bluntness. 'Come over here. You can smell him from where I sit. Not just intoxicated, sirs, he was so soused he was seeing and hearing demons.' Even in my haze I had picked up Sébastien's train of thought and now I hooked my carriage to his engine. 'Aimery was making the most ludicrous charges. He must have arrived off the train drunk, although if I'm honest, I took it for fatigue initially. He barged in here, irrational, making the strangest allegations. You would be aware his train had arrived earlier than any of us had expected?'

The mayor nodded. 'Yes, I was there to meet both trains. I saw you meet Monsieur Delacroix.'

'That's right. And I was going to escort Madame back to meet her husband but it came in early,' Sébastien remarked.

'I met it,' Graciela added coolly. 'Let's not play coy, sirs. We all know, including his good wife, that I was Aimery's mistress before his marriage. And the truth is that I loved him and wanted to see him arrive home. However, he paid me little attention. I didn't expect any, frankly. I just wanted to see him safely back. Nevertheless, he spoke to me, perhaps you noted that?' She glared at the mayor.

He gave a sheepish nod. 'We did, Mademoiselle.'

'Would you like to know what he said to me?'

'No, Mademoiselle, unless it is relevant to his death.'

'He wanted to know whom I had been sleeping with in his absence, gentlemen.'

I couldn't know if this were true or not. But she was convincing, as both men blushed. Aimery's affair with the Spaniard was known but their embarrassment was for me.

'It's all right; I told you his wife knows and we have made our peace over this, as there was clearly no intention on Monsieur De Lasset's part to be unfaithful once he was married.' I admired her putting together the lie so masterfully. 'The point is,' Graciela continued smoothly, 'she also knows – as did Aimery – that there was never anyone else for me. His question was that of a man in his cups, not thinking clearly, acting jealously and out of character.'

I rejoined their questioning. 'I wasn't at the station because it had only been a short while since I'd brought my brother home. We were still sharing coffee, with at least an hour to spare before Aimery's train was due,' I said, pointing to the upended tray and its contents from Aimery's struggles. 'He arrived angry, unannounced and, as I've told you, drunk. I think he had seen too much on the battlefield. The letters home attest to his heroism,' I said, finding my stride now. I stood shakily and accepted the helping arm of

Graciela. 'But heroism comes at a price, gentlemen. You only have to look at Sébastien De Lasset's injuries, or to hear Felix speak of our brother, Henri. What Felix didn't do this morning was speak of himself but even in Aimery's single lucid moment when he greeted Felix, he admitted he'd heard of how heroically he'd acquitted himself. But these men had witnessed so much suffering, it is little wonder my brother reached for the cognac decanter within moments of arriving home, and it's clear Aimery had started much earlier and drank far too much on the journey home. I forgive him only that much, but not his accusations, and as he has killed my beloved and only remaining brother, be careful I do not spit on his grave,' I said, aware that my breathing was becoming more visible as my passion and bitterness moved from disguising the truth of events to describing the reality of Aimery's actions.

'He was going to kill Madame De Lasset, you see,' Sébastien interjected smoothly, surprising me. I hadn't thought of that scenario but it was plausible, and it certainly added weight to the claim of defence.

'You're sure of that?' the policeman said. Both men turned to Sébastien in astonishment.

He nodded, calm. 'Even Mademoiselle Olivares realised this – she flung a vase at him to distract him.' He pointed to the shattered pieces against the stone of the hearth. 'Felix knew when a man was serious about using his weapon and leapt in front of her to take the bullet. We all watched him fall and my brother, calm as you like, took aim again to have another shot. It was my turn to step in front of Madame De Lasset. I'm making this sound as though we were all thinking clearly. To tell the truth, I wasn't thinking at all – simply reacting to Aimery's next threat, and it wasn't as though we couldn't tell he meant to kill by now. His first shot had told us everything we needed to know about his murderous intention. Anyway, I stepped in front of his wife.'

I nodded, putting a hand to my mouth to stem the sob, as the memory flooded back. I wasn't acting either now. Emotion was taking over from the initial shock. I had to hang on before I began to fully understand that Felix had gone, had died in my arms as Henri had died in his – and all because of Aimery's hateful temper. I felt myself beginning to tremble. Hold on, I begged inwardly.

Sébastien was still explaining. ' . . . but his firearm bucked badly in his hand and that saved me a bullet to the body.' He pointed to the shattered timber in the door. 'I put his bad aim and lazy firing down to the alcohol.'

Both of the officials frowned, nodding their understanding.

Sébastien pushed the hair away from his face with a sigh. 'Either way, it was the only chance I had and I took it. I used my cane to bring him down but all I managed to do was enrage him. I might have fractured his wrist but it didn't even slow him. He tossed his revolver aside and before I knew it he'd drawn his dagger,' he said, nodding to where the trench-fashioned stiletto with its evil-looking triangular blade was still gripped in his dead fingers. Sébastien glanced at his slashed bandages and fresh blood. 'I managed to get my arm in the way of his strike but he was determined to kill me, to kill us all, probably. None of us can guess what was going on in his mind but his accusations suggest he was hearing demons as Madame De Lasset suggests. In the ensuing struggle I had no choice but to grab his revolver and use it on him.'

'A very clean shot, sir,' the policeman observed.

Sébastien shrugged. 'I could hardly miss.'

I couldn't look at Graciela, although I wondered if she was reliving killing the man she loved with such obsession.

'It was either him or me, gentlemen. I can only speculate at his intentions for the women, had he brought me down with that killing blade. There was no doubt he aimed to kill. Aimery had clearly gone mad at the Front.'

The two officials were silent. They glanced at the two corpses, back up at us; Graciela and I genuinely wore expressions of trauma as we held on to each other, and their shared gaze finally came back to rest on Sébastien, bleeding, collected, awaiting their instructions. The two most powerful families in Grasse were involved in this terrible event; I suspected neither of these men wanted anything more than to have an uncomplicated summary as fast as possible. I imagined neither would want to cloud the issue with more questions than necessary. If all of us were saying this is what happened, then that is what happened.

It was not that the mayor didn't believe us, I don't think, but he wanted to close this messy scene of death with a clear and concise judgement. 'Let me get this clear, Monsieur De Lasset. This was self-defence?'

'What else could it be?' Sébastien snapped, allowing his calm composure to slip. I was sure it was deliberate. The straight-backed, stiff-upper-lipped, tally-ho English side of Sébastien surely outweighed the more emotional and demonstrative French blood that ran in his veins. 'He may well have killed these helpless women and me in the bargain.'

The mayor made a clicking sound of despair with his tongue and the policeman shook his head.

'This is a dreadful business,' the policeman offered into the gloom. 'I'm so sorry for your losses, Madame De Lasset. Clearly a most sorrowful turn of events for everyone.'

'And Grasse has lost two of its finest sons today,' the mayor added in a mournful tone. 'Ladies, please, let us take care of the fallen.'

Graciela urged me out of the doors and I dared not look at Sébastien although I knew he would be willing me to hold my nerve.

We shared a collective lie now, but this was one I could surely live with in order to protect Graciela and, indeed, Aimery's memory for Grasse.

I was driven back to the house alongside Graciela by a carriage summoned by the policeman and deposited into the collectively stunned bosom of the staff, who fussed and covered me with shawls and rubbed my hands to get my blood moving less sluggishly around my body. I was definitely slipping into shock. I was vaguely aware of Graciela's explanation to the household that was met with gasps of horror, even some outright cries of disbelief.

'Dead?' someone queried as if Graciela was somehow having a jest.

Her deep voice assured them it was not one but two men deceased, both brave soldiers and, yes, one of them was definitely Monsieur Aimery De Lasset. People hovered, were encouraged to leave by the more senior in the staff and by Graciela, who appeared to have herself entirely in control despite her involvement in the morning's sorrows and her private grief.

Another cognac arrived. The vapours revolted me. I didn't think in that moment I would ever smell cognac again without the ugly scene of murder being conjured once more in my mind and I would now forever associate it with blood, despair and loss. I pushed away the offering without explanation.

'Warm milk,' I heard the housekeeper instruct, snapping her fingers, reminding me of earlier ... when Felix was still alive. 'And, Jeanne, stoke that fire higher.'

'We need some quiet time, please,' Graciela demanded as I stared into the flames as Felix had only an hour earlier. Like him, I suppose I looked for some sort of explanation to the horror but none came. Nevertheless, the flickering warmth helped to soothe me into a near trance. It brought peace; my breathing slowed even if my mind was jangling.

Into the silence we'd held I finally spoke. 'I don't know what to say to you.'

'What can you say?'

'Thank you is necessary. My brother's cold-blooded murder demanded retaliation.'

'I liked Felix, I always have. But I doubt that I killed Aimery for him . . . or for you. I feel sure now that I killed him to release myself.'

I wasn't surprised by this admission, only that she'd had the courage to follow her heart, for she had so much less invested than her three companions in the struggle. 'You were prepared to go to jail for such a few moments of release?'

She shrugged. 'I was prepared to murder the only man I've ever loved, perhaps ever will, in order to stop his abuse. I have never been more hurt than listening to him speak of me like dirt on his boots. In that terrible moment I realised that, though he loved me in his twisted way, he had always been contemptuous of me; it was as though he was disgusted at himself for needing me. I realised something else, as I watched your husband take your brother's life so callously, and that is I have fought back from a childhood full of darkness and abuse at the hands of a man. To continue accepting abuse at the hands of another who simply wears a different face and speaks a different language but essentially is the same cruel brute makes me hate myself more than either of them. I wish I could have saved Felix for you.'

'I cannot contemplate yet what I've lost.' My lips felt numb again as though a great chill was descending on me. I could taste his blood once more in my mind. 'Felix is . . . was the man I would be.'

'Then be the woman he would be. Don't let his death not count. He saved Sébastien's life for a reason. I only have to look at you both to know something has occurred between you.' She shrugged. 'Felix gave you permission. Felix saved the man you love, am I right?'

I nodded, licking my unfeeling lips now of the salted tears that had dripped silently down my cheeks.

'We are all going to be doing a lot more crying. This war will not end fast, I do not think, Fleurette. You will need to find deep strength, for the remaining man in your life is surely going back to face more battles.'

'Both of my brothers,' I murmured in escalating disbelief.

Graciela was at my side, crouching to hold my hands before she reached up to pull my face so that my attention focused on her. 'There's only weakness where your mind is headed, dear Fleurette. Your family, the two great households, and even Grasse need you to live up to your name of Delacroix. I need you to show me that the promising defiant spirit I sensed in you is going to rise now and carry you through the most difficult of times. You are a woman. Don't you know that women bear the greatest sorrows of all? You are not the only woman grieving in this town but you must set the example of courage and tenacity. Lead Grasse, live up to all your promise.'

Stirring words that summed up Graciela. Here she was bearing up under life's greatest sorrow of not only losing the person she loved most but her memory of pulling the trigger that brought his death would be a lifetime sentence of misery for her. It didn't matter that Sébastien had protected the truth of manslaughter. She was a prisoner of the truth from now on anyway.

'I'm sorry for you,' I whispered.

'Show me how sorry you are for me,' she goaded.

I frowned at her. 'What do you mean?'

'I know the shock is fresh now but don't be a slave to your sadness. Just promise me that. Let me be witness to your empowerment so that I can live with the knowledge that I killed Aimery to stop him, to free you . . . to free everyone from his influence.'

'Grieve alone, you mean . . . in private,' I qualified.

She pointed to my chest and nodded. 'Yes, in here. It's your pain. No one else's.'

It was tough advice and there was nothing easy about her demand but curiously her challenge did make me feel stronger, more able to take control. I couldn't really think on Felix, or on anything right now. It felt overwhelming: too much at once. I couldn't imagine how our men were coping with so many deaths, so much destruction and fear at once at the Front. It struck me then that even if they did survive, they'd all be damaged in one way or another. Demons would haunt any survivors forever. In time I would separate out the shock I was feeling now into compartments in my mind and examine each, better prepared for the pain or the guilt.

'And you?'

'I will wait to be told my outcome. If Sébastien has convinced them well enough, then it is purely self-defence. In this there is no lie, yes? If he ultimately shares the truth, then I too could claim self-defence. Potentially at worst I might be accused of a crime of passion.'

'Henriette Caillaux,' we both said together. It was a reference to an infamous case earlier that year when a wealthy socialite from a family we knew calmly delivered six gunshots into the editor of Le Figaro to stop him publishing incriminating letters of her affair with the man she later married, when they were both married to other people. I had admired Henriette's courage and fierce determination to defend the man she loved.

'It won't come to that,' I assured. 'Sébastien even convinced me of his version.'

She nodded.

'You're like Henriette,' I said.

Graciela shrugged. 'I can't see how; I killed the man I loved rather than his enemy.'

334

'I mean you share her passion, your ferocity, your lack of care for the consequences to you. In a way, I suppose you've done Aimery a favour and saved him from himself. He was his own enemy.'

She nodded. 'And now you've found me out,' she sighed. 'It went through my mind in those horrifying seconds that there was no way out for Aimery. I didn't think your dear brother would survive the gun wound and I realised that Aimery would be accused of murder . . . manslaughter at best. He could not hide behind self-defence as I might so he would surely be executed for murder or jailed for killing a man. By pulling that trigger on Felix, he was effectively taking his own life. I simply made sure of it.'

'And it keeps his reputation intact as a war hero,' I murmured, all of Graciela's rationale, which she had summarised in fleeting moments and under extreme pressure, falling into place now. I suppose, standing aside from the tense words of this morning, she'd had an opportunity to see the situation with greater clarity than the rest of us had. Even so, she'd thought fast and made a traumatic decision. 'Can you live with yourself?'

She took a few moments to consider my question. 'I can,' she finally replied. 'Because everyone is better off for it.'

'Except you.'

'I couldn't have watched him executed for murder. I couldn't have borne to visit him in jail for the rest of his life.'

I nodded. That was easy enough to grasp for anyone.

'This way was best. It protects his name, his reputation. Now he'll be remembered for being understandably drunk and making a terrible mistake, but his status as a war hero is not tarnished. His family name and business is secure.'

There was a tap at the door and Sébastien entered with Madame Mouflard in tow. We both stood, no doubt concern on our faces, and I had to resist running to him. He looked pale, his expression filled with grief.

'Thank you, Madame Mouflard,' I said. 'We need nothing,' I added, before she could ask. 'Except quiet.'

She bowed and withdrew.

Now I did hurry into his arms. I didn't weep, I didn't make a sound, I just held him and we communicated our despair and grief, our love, our pain, all through that embrace, finally parting to look at my friend.

'You appear more composed than either of us, Graciela,' Sébastien said, stepping aside from me to walk over and give the Spaniard a long hug, which she accepted without flinching.

'It's an act,' she said in a husky tone and found a brave smile.

'Well, you impress the hell out of me and would make a great soldier.' He kissed each of her cheeks. 'Thank you for saving my life.'

'I think perhaps you have saved mine, or at least your actions have brought some clarity to mine.'

He frowned.

'Fleurette will explain,' she added.

I was trembling, reality sinking in. 'Where is Felix?' I asked, shaking as I tried to keep myself busy, pouring Sébastien a glass of cognac, holding my breath to avoid the scented fumes. I handed off the glass and he swallowed the slug in a single gulp, closing his eyes against the fiery sensation of its swift journey down. I felt sickened, imagining its taste as it travelled his gut. It was the taste of death for me now.

'He's been taken to the mortuary; so has Aimery. I held Felix's hand for you until he was put into the carriage.'

I felt the tears prick but refused them. I nodded my thanks, not able to speak at that moment.

He turned to Graciela. 'I did the same for Aimery. He was, after all, my kin. And I know you loved him.'

'Thank you, Sébastien. You are a good man. You will make

Fleurette a good husband in time.' We both inhaled audibly. 'Well, don't deny it. The pathway is cleared. Walk it, or make a mockery of this morning.' She pointed at me. 'Your brother died for it – don't deny it.' She switched her attention to Sébastien. 'And, even if it does require you to ease the town into understanding, your brother's death makes it possible for you to love his wife.'

I didn't want to discuss this now but Graciela was confronting as ever. However, she didn't know the facts. We held secrets upon secrets but Felix had urged us that the truth need not come out and do any more damage. We could hold the truth back, keep our two family reputations intact, and still have each other. He was right. The reality of Aimery's parentage would remain in the safekeeping of Sébastien and myself. Graciela did not need to be informed; no one did.

I sniffed back tears. 'It will take as long as it must,' I said, recovering myself, and feeling surprised at how calm I sounded despite the tremor in my voice. 'Time must pass for people to accept.'

'Indeed. And, of course, I will be going back.'

'Oh, Sébastien, no!' It hadn't occurred to me that I might yet lose him to the bombs and bullets of war.

He took my hand and raised it to his lips, gently laying a kiss. 'I must. It's my duty. I can't escape what others are facing.' He waved his cane. 'I'm hardly much use with this but my language skills alone are needed. I'm a chemist; perhaps I can help in the medical tents. I can make up drugs, do paperwork, send messages, any number of tasks that can contribute. I certainly can't languish here, in all good conscience.'

'When?'

He lifted a shoulder with a rueful expression. 'As soon as the mayor and police clear me to return . . . as soon as I can.'

I swallowed. All of them gone.

'Fleurette,' Graciela said, arriving to squeeze my wrist with affection, 'anyone who survives a bombing and then a gunshot aimed directly at him twice is like a cat with nine lives. He's going to come back, this lucky black cat of yours.'

I had to believe her. I had to trust the angels to continue to watch over him and bring him back to me.

I stood alone in the mortuary, my dead twin laid out on unforgiving marble. Around the base of the plinth he slept upon was hung a black wool curtain, richly embroidered with gold fleur-de-lys symbols and trimmed with a glinting gold metallic fringe. Not so long ago our father had been laid out identically and on this same table with this same valance, for a similar visit when my brothers and I had come to pay our final respects.

I felt the emotion rise and clog at the top of my chest over the notion that he wouldn't have anticipated that both his sons would be dead within two years of his passing. I corrected myself – that his *three* sons would be dead in this timeframe.

I touched Felix's hand. It felt chilled and stiffly unfamiliar but I held it all the same, as if I might pass some of my living warmth into his lifeless cold.

Graciela had accompanied me to the mortuary. But I wanted to be alone with Felix.

'Remember, his spirit has flown,' she reminded me as I hugged her before turning away; she remained outside. I suppose her remark was a way of preparing me to confront the dead. She had also handed me a small tin of lanolin scented heavily with lavender. I had no idea of her use for it, nor did I care. Graciela pointed to her nose. 'It helps with the smell of a morgue.'

I took it but didn't use it. Smells were my life. And revolting though this one might be, it was part of the fabric of the life I was blessed with. I couldn't linger with only the beautiful scents of nature; she offered up unpleasant ones also. They were all part of her landscape . . . mine too.

Felix didn't smell. Instead I inhaled the disinfectant, the tang of formaldehyde, the vague and horrible old sweetness of decay from other corpses that were stored somewhere here. Aimery was nearby but I didn't look for him, didn't ask for him either, and no one would blame me, given that word would have got around at how Felix died. I switched off from all of that and focused on my brother and mercifully it was only he who was laid out for viewing.

His complexion appeared waxy pale against the black flop of his hair, like a perfect gardenia bloom sitting amongst thick, dark leaves but the image I conjured disintegrated swiftly. Felix *was* beautiful but there was no beauty here, only sorrow and damage. Someone had diligently combed his lustrous hair into a neat style but not in the right way. I dug furiously and absently in my bag for a comb, feeling offended that he looked wrong, and lost myself for a minute or two, gently adjusting my brother's hair so that Felix emerged again. And after my ministrations he really did appear as if he were simply sleeping. The act of combing his hair calmed me. He was an extraordinarily attractive man despite the abrasions of life in the trenches. I touched a slight cut above his brow and a small bruise high on his cheekbone. 'How did you get these, Felix?' I pondered aloud softly. Had they occurred from the same event or separate injuries? I knew I would not learn the truth but it kept my mind dislocated from reality for a fraction longer while I considered how the cut would never heal, the bruise never darken and develop through its odd palette of colours. Dark lashes curved above the bruise and I remembered how as a young child Felix would entertain our father and me with what he called 'butterfly kisses'. He'd lean in close and flutter those lashes to tickle our cheeks and make my father chuckle or me squeal with delight.

That's how our flowers feel when the butterflies dance

amongst their petals, he'd explain. It was only in this moment as my whole body ached with loss that I grasped what a romantic my twin had been, even from childhood. He'd hidden it through his sardonic approach to life but he had not been waiting for the right woman to fall in love with him. No, only now I realised that Felix had been waiting for the elusive woman that *he* would fall desperately in love with. And whether she was considered right for him or wrong by the family, I don't think now it would have mattered. His well-disguised romantic soul wanted that sort of helpless surrender; it's why, I now understood, that he forgave me for loving Sébastien and then threw his life away to protect that love – the same sort of love he aspired to. I'd never really pondered his romances; up to this moment he'd been my laughing, handsome twin but I'd not paid much attention to how women viewed him. I wondered at how many hearts might break to learn of his death . . . how many hearts he'd broken while alive. Many, I suspected. His conquests were his, though, and never spoken about, certainly not to me, and I had known not to pry. I doubted Felix shared his triumphs with other men, bragging about this woman or that as others might. He was far more private and soulful than most realised. Perhaps all that others saw was the jovial, entertaining side of Felix but I knew there were depths to him. In thinking back over our final conversation, I could touch his grief over losing his gift. I began to imagine how life would be if I didn't have my ability to smell the scents of life. It felt momentarily impossible to imagine and then the notion that each day would feel pointless and insurmountable struck me. Yes, I understood. Felix, like me, was a creature who needed to 'taste' life and needed his olfactory senses to call upon. I too would feel incomplete . . . no, I would feel damaged, half the woman I was.

This is what he was trying to explain to me that morning: why he wished he'd died in the trenches, rather than being injured in this cruel way. And it was why he gave his life so willingly to Sébastien, still mostly whole, and in a position to give me a happy life of love.

Strange that I wasn't weeping; I hoped this was how it was going to be for me now. Had I reached some high precipice from which I had new perspective – that of someone who could be entirely in control of her emotions, who might lead by example? I'd cried enough tears this last year. And people were weeping all over Grasse for their dead, all over France for our men; I wasn't particularly special in this regard.

Henri was buried in a mud field somewhere in the north. One day I would visit him, sprinkle some centifolia rose petals of Grasse at his grave unless they could bring his body home for me – we would see. But Felix was here. He would join our mother and father in the family vault and he would wait for me there. I couldn't plant roses above him as he'd romantically asked me to but I would plant new roses for him and in his name.

I spoke to him now. It felt important to say what I needed to aloud. 'My heart hurts, Felix, but perhaps you would tell me yours hurt more at the realisation that making perfume together was not to be our future. I understand that now. You were brave to the last. I know you hid your courage on the battlefield and let people like Henri and Aimery take the praise. Both of my brothers gave their lives for others when the question was asked of you . . . and for that I don't think our debt to you will ever be paid. All I can say is that you are loved and admired; your memory will not die. I will hold it close in the vivid recollections I have of every moment of our growing up . . . to this very moment now when I am forced to bid you a final farewell.' I wiped a single stray tear. I would not crumple now. I sniffed the weakness back. 'I'll live for both of us, for all three of us, in fact. I'll make a perfume that the Delacroix and De Lasset families can consider the sum of their combined knowledge. I'll channel it into an elegant but individual scent to excite women the world over. It will speak of independence and courage, of triumph and hope, of facing adversity and staying true to oneself. It will, above all, darling Felix, speak of love, of course, and its secrets. I forgive our father for I have sinned in the same way and I know it is a sort of madness that overtakes. Love when it comes is not rational or fair. I am convinced it chooses us rather than the other way around. That is love's greatest secret of all – it is a free spirit and cannot be controlled. Thank you for saving the life of the man I love. Thank you for forgiving me for loving him. I don't know how to go on without you other than to try to get through each new day a little easier than the last until I no longer have to try. Tally-ho, my darling,' I said, surprising myself at bringing our mother back to mind in this moment, but she did love us and it was appropriate she share this dreaded moment of farewell. I could almost feel the presence of my father and Henri watching us.

'Until we meet again,' I whispered, my voice quavering with choked emotion. I bent down to kiss his chilled, immobile lips, pausing to give his cheek a final affectionate stroke. I hoped it would be a long time before we were reunited.

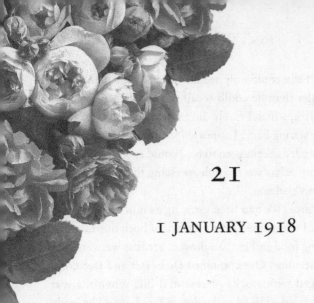

21

1 JANUARY 1918

Incredibly and with sinking hearts we moved into our fourth bitter year of war. It had ground everyone down to husks of our former selves as we all awaited the next telegram of grim tidings or the next distressing report in the newspapers or cinema. We'd begun gathering at the town hall for updates. I no longer considered it unseemly to be huddled alongside the womenfolk of Grasse, hanging on to every word. There was a sense of comfort in numbers and Graciela had urged me to be seen amongst the town's people, sharing their fears, walking with them, passing conversation no matter how bleak. These days the affection that came my way was not simply connected with my surname but with the person I was becoming.

I could feel it. I was growing into a woman with her own path to walk, her own take on life. I had suffered as much as any and they knew it; they saw my composure as strength, as something to adhere to, to look up to. Girls in their early teens would seek me out in the square, walk with me while holding my hand and speak of their concerns for brothers and fathers. They were looking for my assurance. I couldn't tell them that my heart ached for one man, so we talked about loss, about facing adversity, about finding inner strength. I felt if Felix could only see me now he'd probably say I was standing taller than he could recall me being. Although if I looked in the mirror, which I rarely did these days, I barely recognised the woman staring back. I appeared shrunken with a definite hollow where rounded cheeks used to be. I could count my ribs and the knuckles of my pelvis were visible, pressing through pale skin stretched across my skeleton.

Food was scarce. We had been growing as much as we could for all of France; I had turned over swathes of both our families' lands into growing food rather than flowers because we were simply not making perfume. Our combined De Lasset and Delacroix warehouses bulged with stocks of essential oil. When the war ended – if it ever ended – I liked to daydream that I would be ready to manufacture perfume from the day peace was declared. But for now I had opened up the family facilities into manufacturing much-needed soap and medicinal creams for our army. It felt to me as the least we could do, especially as in Grasse we had the know-how and access to product. For us it was relatively simple to transfer our skills.

At Sébastien's urgings I also opened up our chemical plants for the production of drugs for the medical corps and, walking around our once again busy laboratories, I wondered constantly whether Sébastien would handle the very vials we were producing here. I took to labelling them myself in case he did, as though each ampoule of painkiller was a private love note to the man I yearned I would never mourn.

I was supervising so many new duties now, down to signing out each cartload of our precious fruit and vegetables, especially during the busiest summer harvest season. I'd wave them off and watch the carriages rumble away down the hill into Nice to be railed from there to wherever our fresh goods were needed to feed our army, together with the medicines that would heal it.

At the De Lasset villa we were down to a sparse diet made worse by these winter months and now when I looked at our basic stews and painfully simple celebratory food on feast days, I could barely recall the decadence of that fateful Christmas of 1914 with its sugar and spice. But none of us complained. The new diet made us appear ghostly in our clothes that hung loosely but we needed to know our men's bellies were fed as best as we could manage while they fought for our freedom, and if that meant some hungry, lean times, so be it.

Thinking back now to the end of 1914, I saw that all of its trauma had shaped me into a woman. Before then I believed I was still simply a child in a grown-up's body. The New Year of 1915 was the beginning of a fresh era of my life when I left behind innocence in every sense of the word and I realised that life was not, and could never be, coloured with the black-and-white certainty of youth for me again. I now lived in a world where sometimes the dark to grey shadings of thought were my friend, often a comfort.

I understood now, as I quietly celebrated my twenty-seventh year over a sip of sherry and some simple orange-scented biscuits, that compromise was everything, especially in how we regarded one another. Over these desperately sad and challenging years I'd won myself some perspective on those last few days of 1914, and while I had not and never would forgive Aimery for murdering my brother, nor for his determination to kill Sébastien, I had not spat on his coffin in his family crypt. I had visited it many times, in fact, and placed fresh flowers in the vase, even dusted it so that the stone that enclosed him never appeared untended. I had come to realise that Aimery was as much a victim as any of us in the doomed affair of our parents. I wished I could have had more sympathy for him years ago; we might have avoided the outcome of that day. In my quietest moments, usually wandering a row of our roses or just before I turned out the lights for the night, I wished I could have shown some greater restraint that terrible day. I'd allowed pride, ego and my inflated confidence at finally discovering love with Sébastien to colour my approach to a man in pain. And he was like a wounded dog that day. In that blinded hour of his arrival I'd thought myself mature but a mature person would have known a wounded dog was always going to strike back at an attacker. However, the wisdom of years had also taught me that we can only act in the moment we stand, and that what I knew now or how I thought now could not be compared to a previous time. We evolve, we develop, we take fresh perspective, we feel less emotional about some matters, we become more intense about others.

I had needed to reach some plateau of clarity from which I could strip away all the emotion of that day and think objectively. And so, at some point, I don't know when, I'd taken on the full burden of both deaths and accepted my part that, while I didn't pull a trigger, I helped to enrage Aimery to the point of becoming a murderer. Even so, I'd made my peace with this. I had to, or risk going mad with guilt, plus I knew all the blame was not mine. Aimery was a brute, had always been capable of irrational behaviour and violence, would likely have pulled out his firearm and killed any one of us, even without my involvement. He was a tinderbox of anger at any given time but it was true I made it easier that day to light the spark into the volatile vapours that surrounded him. I couldn't change the past but I could shape my future, and so I'd reached the understanding – with no little help from my friend Graciela – that if I was to lead a productive life I must teach myself how to put that day away, lock it into an imaginary box and forget the key.

I spoke to Felix most days in the family crypt, although now, in spring 1918, my number of visits per week had slackened. It used to be daily, now maybe three times per week, sometimes two if I was busy in the lab or fields. Nevertheless, I always managed to find a single flower to pluck on my way to lay on his vault. Sometimes it was a simple daisy, other occasions I might lay an ethereal iris, a peppery geranium, whatever caught my attention. During these regular visits I told him what was happening in the war, I read him letters, I'd update him on our fields including those turned over to growing food now and I'd always spend a few minutes discussing the perfume I was mentally working on. Before I said goodbye, I'd tell him how Sébastien was, even if he'd already heard about him from a recent letter. It helped to keep Sébastien vivid in my mind – by speaking aloud of him like this and yet so intimately, he felt close and safe.

I had come to accept that Graciela had called it correctly. Sébastien possessed uncanny luck and remained gratifyingly alive, writing to us regularly. I'd read his letters aloud in the parlour, often to an audience of women as they knitted or crocheted, who would smile knowingly at his softly amusing remarks and sharp observations about men at war. While the business of a double death in our small town had stunned everyone initially, I had to admit that the sheer amount of death – and constant threat of it – that everyone was coping with did help to dilute the impact of two of Grasse's most prominent people dying suddenly and inexplicably at the Delacroix villa.

In peacetime the speculation and gossip might have raged for years. In the environment of war, it found its correct place as a tragic outcome for two brave men. Graciela had never been implicated and people who perhaps knew her as Aimery's mistress who saw us both together might have been perplexed at the beginning, but any idle chatter surrounding us had long ago lost its titillation.

The verdict of Sébastien having to bring down an intoxicated Aimery through self-defence was duly delivered and he was permitted to return to northern France within ten days of our sealing the coffins and placing our dead into their final resting spots. It's fair to say that word had moved like a grassfire up a hillside that my husband had arrived home drunk and angry over reasons we didn't understand, had forcefully cast me aside when I'd tried to comfort him and had been brandishing his firearm, killing Felix by accident when my brother had come to my aid. And then self-defence had prompted a third bullet. There was immense shock – of course there was – but people began to admit they'd seen Aimery De Lasset arrive intoxicated at the station. Madame Mouflard had confirmed he became belligerent and angry to discover that his wife was not at the house to greet him. Her statement – unsolicited by me, I might add – to police that she 'feared for Madame's life in his dark mood' was extremely helpful to our cause. Jeanne too had chimed in, saying she'd overheard him muttering as he'd left the De Lasset villa that he would 'choke' me for 'humiliating him'.

The mayor had visited two days after the funerals to explain, haltingly and with great embarrassment, that Aimery's and my marriage was not officially sanctioned because of the lack of a civil marriage ceremony and licence. I blinked sadly as he spoke, inwardly cheering, of course, as he gradually and tentatively built up to the words that I was not legally a De Lasset and thus I had no legal rights as his widow. He had struggled to get these final words out. I made it easier for him. I remember now how I'd sighed and stood, moving to the window.

'Perhaps it is for the best.'

I recall how he'd looked at me, aghast that I could be so accepting. 'Madame, I know this must be a terrible shock. I —'

'Nothing could shock me more than losing both of my brothers within a week of each other, sir. Actually your news makes it easier for me to come to terms with what Aimery De Lasset did. I do not wish to be his wife given his actions and so your news, though bleak, is not unwelcome.'

'I am humbled by your wise perspective, Madame.'

'Mademoiselle,' I corrected him with a rueful smile.

He had tittered nervously. 'It means no financial benefit. It all goes to his brother, Sébastien De Lasset.'

'I do not need the De Lasset fortune,' I had reminded him, ensuring I had not sounded haughty.

Everyone from Paris to Nice knew I was now the wealthiest woman in the region in my own right, perhaps in all of southern France. 'Still, it is a shame that our two families lose that special connection that the town so welcomed and celebrated,' I had said, airily.

He nodded. 'This is my deepest regret. It made our region more powerful. His brother . . .' His thought trailed off.

'Is a very fine man,' I picked up and continued for him. 'I've come to admire him immensely. We all have.'

'I hear that Sébastien De Lasset writes often to you?'

So the tongues were wagging. But this was good gossip – exactly what I had hoped to encourage. 'Yes, indeed,' I replied, without hesitation. 'The whole household waits on his next missive. I share them aloud to the staff and friends.' He nodded that he'd heard this too.

The mayor's subsequent shrug spoke droves. 'Maybe . . . who knows . . . after the war . . .' He tiptoed around what was in both our minds. He shook his head. 'Life must go on.'

I had beamed him a smile. 'We shall all do our best and the two families of Grasse will always keep her strong,' I said.

He'd held my gaze a moment longer than might be considered comfortable and a silent message had passed that I may well be open to being courted by another De Lasset . . . for the good of Grasse, of course.

I had never since his death spoken a bad word about Aimery, donning black – as a widow should – to mourn all those dead in our families and celebrating his heroic acts on the battlefield. However, I did nothing to dissuade people's admiration for Sébastien . . .

a true son of Grasse whom they were still to get to know, but his actions to seemingly protect me and Graciela did his reputation no harm.

And so I had continued to share his letters and Sébastien knew this, making sure he kept them general, interesting and as amusing as he could under the circumstances. Over the last three years they'd all come to know and admire him, and talked of him as though his returning to live here was the most natural progression for his life. Sébastien usually included a single-sheeted private letter just for me. These I did not read aloud, nor did anyone but Graciela know about them; in this she had become my ally.

These precious sheets I handled as a private treasure, forcing myself to wait all day to read them, busying myself with work in the fields or in the lab, allowing the tension and desire of hearing his voice in my head to build. And then after a meagre meal that I often shared with Graciela, now a regular visitor, I would light a spill and touch it to the candlewick so I could read by a naked flame in my bedroom; I knew it sounded childish, but it felt more romantic, for I know he would have likely written his letters to me aided only by a guttering candle or lamp.

I'd remained at the De Lasset villa, although there was no obligation or binding reason for me to do so. As much as I would have loved to return home, it was merely an empty shell and it held only bleak memories for the time being. Even three years on it felt raw in the drawing room and I swear I could still smell the fear and loathing of that tumultuous day.

To help banish those memories, by the autumn of 1915 I had turned the Delacroix villa into a convalescent home for injured soldiers. There were so many men in need of care it was one of the essential duties that many of the wealthy homeowners with empty houses provided and there were now numerous auxiliary hospitals in Grasse, including mine and Graciela's. The year 1916 was a terrible one for warfare at sea; I believe the number of allied ships lost was more than four hundred, and I don't doubt plenty of enemy ships and submarines were lost also. Our two houses seemed to be favoured for men rescued from sea warfare that the Allies, for a long time, seemed incapable of counteracting. And so we had many young men pass through our wards to recuperate; we got to patch them up and send them straight back into the fiery cauldron of war. In theory the role sounded sometimes pointless but the reality was exhausting, challenging and inspiring work that kept our morale high that we were contributing. They were all someone's brother or son, lover or husband, uncle or nephew. Behind them stretched so many women we felt connected to them all, and determined to help their beloved soldiers.

Each time we sent a man back, Graciela and I would say the words: *Somewhere a mother, a wife or a lover thanks us.*

Now and then as I passed through the main salon of the Delacroix villa that now served as a morning room for the patients, I could unhappily conjure the taste of Felix's blood, as though it were still fresh and glistening on my lips from kissing him goodbye. I needed more time. I needed life to be lively again, with the pall of death lifted from France, I thought, before I could confront banishing all the demons from that house for good.

Besides, I thought Madame Mouflard would not forgive me, should I leave the De Lasset villa. She cosseted me as the grieving widow in the first year and then when I'd cast off my mourning garments and had begun to introduce a touch of colour here and there, she'd make odd remarks that I couldn't and shouldn't remain a widow forever. She had begun to hint that the villa needed the sounds of children, of laughter, of life again in the future. She had also cunningly begun to rally her supporters so that other members of staff made similar comments about when the war was over and when the villa might have the squeals of happy children playing in the garden. I let it wash over me but always permitted it to gain momentum. If I let it take its natural course, I hoped that the staff might collectively feel it was their hope, even their idea, that Sébastien be the perfect match . . . to keep the De Lasset bloodline alive and strong in Grasse.

And so by candlelight in my bedroom of the De Lasset mansion that with each passing year had begun to feel more familiar, more like home, I would hear Sébastien's voice talking to me of love and longing. I yearned for his arms around me too. Watching him depart on that freezing day in January 1915 had been the second-hardest challenge I'd ever encountered. Four years ago I'd have said marrying Aimery was the greatest obstacle I'd faced, but now I knew that nothing would ever demand more of my strength, will, composure and discipline than closing the casket on Felix. After that, not being able to hug or kiss Sébastien openly but to simply accept three affectionate, polite kisses at the station in front of an audience of staff and wellwishers as he left for the battlefields again would be next in line as my worst day.

We'd avoided being alone together too over that fortnight of the New Year. We'd dined with Graciela or other guests. We'd gone to bed at different times, never headed upstairs together, and he had been deliberately accommodated in a separate wing of the villa anyway. If our shoulders touched or hands entwined for a heartbeat, it was in a stolen moment and we both tended to look around guiltily to see if we'd been noticed. And so even the simple passing of a teacup became a tense moment to savour as our skin might touch; salutations became loaded with deeper meaning and permitted us to lean together and to brush our lips against each other's cheeks lightly. Even laughter became threaded with romantic meaning – an amused look, a smile of pleasure, a throw-back of the head at a jest – each innocent gesture strengthened the bond between us as people moved around us, ignorant of the undertow of the hidden language being exchanged.

Most romantic of all were his letters. His absence and potential injury or death gave them a poignancy that ordinary letters in peacetime couldn't begin to match. Without touch or sight of each other, his words, the memory of his voice, became everything to me. Every word was gold. I would trace the words on the page with a finger as though I might reach across time and space and imagine that his hand, holding the pen that inked these thoughts, was mine to caress.

I didn't feel like making perfume in those two weeks he remained awaiting the police enquiry, or even talking about it. I certainly didn't feel in any mood for romance while grieving for Felix and Henri, so life made sure we were never caught in a situation that compromised our standing within the Grasse community. Still pretending with those perfunctory kisses at the station, not knowing if this was our only remaining touch, the final time we'd look upon each other, the last words we'd physically share, made my mood so brittle I was convinced the effort of stretching a fake smile might shatter the mask of an expression I was managing to hold. It hurt to let him go and still we had to cover the ache, talk and bid each farewell like friends, not lovers.

I recalled now how I'd made it through that afternoon by disappearing into the laboratory and begging off dinner, claiming I was feeling tired. I cried myself to sleep in such turmoil that I could admit to feeling quite demented for several hours as all the horrors of my losses swooped to roost at the end of my bed and stare at me.

But perhaps they did me a favour.

By the next morning, I'd packed my horrors away and as Graciela had once advised I made sure they remained mine, not anyone else's problem. In confronting them and then finding a private chamber for them in my heart, I alone controlled when they were exposed or scrutinised. I had control. Since that night I had never cried myself to sleep again; I had not, in fact, wept again and had no intention of feeling so weakened ever.

Trench foot, as it had become known, was one of the invisible enemies that stalked our boys along with artillery, wounds, disease and despair. I was busy reading another of Sébastien's letters to a group of women sitting in our parlour. We were knitting socks for our Chasseurs, still fighting bravely.

'The soldier is normally standing in a trench that is so awash that frogs live comfortably with them. The feet swell, turn numb,' Sébastien wrote and I read. 'I hear from the men that they could stick their bayonets into their feet and not feel anything. Some welcome it, of course, because it often requires amputation and that's a ticket home. Others who consider themselves unlucky enough to watch the swelling subside know the worst is yet to come with an agony that is hard to put into words.' I looked up, and watched the small audience collectively sigh.

'Good job we're knitting socks, then,' one of the older women remarked. 'How's your young man, Jeanne?'

'Alive. He had a bout of trench foot and survived and he said the pain after the swelling goes down is like a thousand hungry trench rats gnawing at raw nerves.'

The women shivered.

'I heard they're as large as cats,' someone said.

'With naked pink tails and evil faces; they dine on the corpses,' another offered.

Jeanne sighed. 'My fiancé says he waits for a rat to come crawling onto his legs at night and then he lifts his legs upwards suddenly, sharply flipping the horrible vermin into the air and out of the trench, providing shooting practice for the snipers on watch. It's the only time he hopes the Boche shoots true.'

We chuckled. The gallows humour always helped. She glanced at me and I indulged her with a 'keep your spirits up' smile, knowing she couldn't possibly know that I desperately worried about the man I loved too, even though I had to pretend otherwise.

Women bear the sorrows of men. That became my mantra. I would bear up. I would find strength in my own resilience. And so days became weeks that turned into months and ultimately the years ticked past and world events became far more pressing and important than my broken heart.

I was glad that Graciela had decided to stay in Grasse. There was a time when I'd feared my closest friend might return to Spain, although the fighting made it feel as though that journey would be impossible. Still, she often talked about 'going home' and I remained grateful she never acted on it. She too was finding a new level of acceptance amongst the community and had admitted to me that she no longer felt like the foreign interloper. Aimery's death had irrevocably and invisibly changed her status in their minds and her offering up her own grand home and grounds to the Allies for accommodation as much as a small hospital won her lots of hearts. There were occasions when we were both so exhausted that Madame Mouflard would find us slumped over the dinner table, far too tired to eat. Yes, they liked us both more for our frailties as much as our energies to help France's war effort.

I feared, of course, that one of the men who came into our care heavily bandaged, sedated or in a wheelchair would be Sébastien. I unconsciously scanned the battered and bleeding skeletal faces that came through but the lucky black cat within him kept him from crossing the Delacroix threshold and for that I remained grateful.

That was until his letters suddenly stopped.

22

MAY 1918

At first I permitted it was simply our postal service – there were such demands on it, we were lucky to get any personal mail. Plus I was so distracted by the demands of our hospital, which was now incredibly busy. Adding to this distraction was the cohort of loud and gregarious Allies now stationed in Grasse for a short while, some enjoying Graciela's generous hospitality.

Some more than others.

'Who was that I saw you walking with the other day near the fountain in the square?'

'Hmm?' she'd queried, all innocence.

I cut her a wry smile, which she did her best to ignore. 'Tall fellow, light-haired. I think he's a captain?'

'Is he?' she remarked. 'I have no idea. I can barely remember yesterday, let alone days ago.'

Now I laughed. 'Graciela! It *was* yesterday! I'm being deliberately polite. It was that lovely Australian captain. Carrying a picnic basket, clearly for two!'

She shrugged. 'He has worn me down with his charm. I agreed to try his eggs in aspic that he assures me has no equal, and he was determined to cook me his aunt's favourite blueberry jam cakes, he called them. He is a guest in our country. I could hardly be rude.'

'No, of course not. And I suppose the fact that he's extremely handsome has nothing to do with it.'

She gave me a slightly forlorn look. 'I must start the journey back to life somewhere.'

I felt embarrassed for making her feel even an iota of guilt. I put my arm around her as we walked, realising we must look comical at times, her so petite and me tall. 'Yes, you must, and I'm thrilled for you. He seems charming. Which woman wouldn't be happy to picnic with your dashing Australian?'

'He makes me laugh,' she admitted, 'and I wasn't sure I could laugh again with a man.'

'Then keep laughing with him, because it's been four years of grief.'

'I'm scared to like him,' she said.

I nodded. 'Because he may be hurt?'

She said it for me. 'Because he could be dead in a month, Fleurette. He's going back in a few days, as I understand it. To Ypres to rejoin his regiment.'

Sadness washed over me for her. There were quiet moments when I cursed my luck for loving any man right now after four hard years of war.

'Nevertheless,' she continued, 'he is like a bright song, a summer's day, a swim in the ocean. When I laugh with him I feel alive and, as dangerous as enjoying him is, I don't want to go without any longer.'

'Nor should you. Besides, with the arrival of the Americans, I don't think the battered German army will stand up to the fresh attack.'

'Let's hope not,' she agreed.

The presence of the recuperating men in our region had

brought a burst of gaiety that harked back to the good old days of life in Grasse, I had to admit. I too had welcomed their company but unlike Graciela had kept my distance from the helpless charm the smiling men oozed. Even so, in attending their various get-togethers I hadn't paid sufficient attention recently at the lack of news from Sébastien.

It only struck me today, as we busied ourselves in the make-shift hospitals at the Delacroix and Olivares villas, that we both now spent most of our days and nights in.

It was Graciela who asked. 'You haven't told me Sébastien's latest news,' she said as we stood on opposing sides of a cot, turning under sheets in a now well-practised manner. We had two more rows to do.

I frowned. 'That's because there hasn't been any.'

'How long since you've heard?'

'Oh, not so long,' I said matter-of-factly, but I didn't hide my darkening expression terribly well, it seemed, as I began to think back to just how many weeks it had been and was anguished at what I totted up.

'How long?' she asked again, smoothing the top sheet in a final flourish as her corner of the bed dropped back into place.

I attempted to shrug it away. It didn't work.

'Fleurette, it's May Day. When was the last letter?'

It was five weeks and three days since his last missive. 'A month, perhaps.'

'A month?' she gasped. 'But you two write to each other most days.'

I said nothing, lingering with my corner, folding it far more carefully and slowly than normal.

'Have you been writing?'

I nodded. 'Most days,' I said, unable now to hide my sadness or my anxiety. 'Come on, I don't want to think on it. You promised me he had many lives. He's going to make it, he's just found it impossible obviously to write.'

'Yes, of course,' she agreed.

But I caught her worried look and I held her gaze with a slightly defiant glare. I didn't want to be questioned about him any more; it was hard enough with all the demons raging around in my head mocking me that now Sébastien had been stolen from this earth too. All the men I loved died, they assured.

'We're done here,' I said, dropping my corner. 'I'm heading out into the fields. Are you coming?'

'As if I'd dare miss May Day.' Graciela smirked. 'You'd be unbearable to live around, should I try. However, we shall go via the post office first. Let's check for news of Sébastien.'

I didn't want to because I suspected the disappointment would ruin a favourite day – May Day with the fresh woodland smell of lily-of-the-valley scenting Grasse.

When the postmistress shook her head sympathetically at my look of hope, it gave me the flutterings of panic. Surely not . . . surely I wouldn't be punished in this way? Allowed to believe in his luck for nearly four years and then to have him disappear without any information?

I moved through our modest May Day celebrations like a marionette, as though a puppetmaster had to control my movements. I was polite, friendly, distant, but showed the appropriate delight when the sprig of our beautiful spring flower, muguet, was pinned to my shirt. I would wear it gladly, hoping the lucky charm would deliver. Felix would know this flower as lily-of-the-valley, with its pure white upside-down bells – like tiny scattered pearls – and wide green leaves. I wondered if he knew old lore said it possessed properties to strengthen memory and the heart – I needed it to do both for me now – and yet I also knew that all parts of this plant were poisonous. Wasn't loving someone like that? Love had the power to bring a ridiculous sense of joy and yet the higher one's emotions soared with happiness, the harder love could make you fall when she took herself away or felt threatened.

Still, the first day of spring did rally my spirits somewhat because it always meant new life, didn't it? And I was smelling the promise of life from the woodland surrounding Grasse in the creamy brightness of these tiny cups of spring purity. And their presence meant my favourite time of year was around the corner, when pale-blue skies would be sketched with light cloud and sunshine would be warm and mild, with lengthened days.

And a vow that Grasse would be carpeted in pink on this side of the hill. Vegetable fields would have to wait for us to distil our oil of roses. It was religion.

There was still no word of Sébastien by the May rose harvest another ten days later, and I had fallen into a gloom. But work kept my emotions anchored and I was glad that harvest had finally arrived and I could work until I dropped each morning and then spend from late afternoon through to the evening at the Delacroix hospital. These days we had qualified nurses and a doctor attached to the house so my role was mainly to manage the hospital and pitch in with the manual work. I was happy to do so; it made me feel useful but it especially embedded me in the hearts and minds of the townsfolk. The war had levelled us all out and it no longer mattered that my surname was Delacroix – we'd all lost loved ones or friends, we all needed to help the town survive without its men. I might have been a woman of means but four years of shared hardship had reduced me to another grieving sister of Grasse and, strangely, I was comforted by this notion as another rose harvest rolled relentlessly around, heedless of war, ignorant of our sorrows, uncaring of our losses.

There were roses to pick.

I was awake by three in the quietest hour of the night, pulling on a motley of layered clothes that could be discarded as the hours drew on. Right now before dawn it was chilly but the spring sunshine would ensure it felt like we were in Hades by lunchtime with the hard work we'd be doing. In fact no later than noon we'd need to be in the warehouses with our hundreds of sacks of vivid blooms safely harvested. Women had come from all over the south to earn through the demanding work and I had employed a new raft of women from the roaming workers' community that had caused a stir through the Grasse townsfolk.

'I'm not sure this is wise,' the mayor tried yet again as I strode through the town, symbolically gathering up my flock of labourers.

I was dressed like all the other women in a long, thick cotton skirt, long-sleeved blouse and apron with stout, laced-up boots. I was wearing a woollen shawl to protect against the fresh chill of the dawn but that would soon be cast off as the morning wore on. I clutched a huge straw bonnet as final armour against the sun we loved and needed but which could be such a villain to our work. This was to be the first of a series of exhausting mornings in the field and I welcomed the fatiguing toil; I needed distraction. I didn't want to think too hard, I simply wanted to work and needed the repetitive, often back-breaking nature of rose picking that would tear up my hands and scratch my arms no matter how care-fully I started out. I had begun to lose my faith that he might ever return. I'd seen it in other women around Grasse, comforted them even, as their families were eroded, losing husbands and sons. I was in danger of becoming one of those who dressed in only black, scut-tled amongst the shadows, no longer came regularly to church, and who might be seen shaking her fist at the sky or weeping to herself as she walked, not noticing anyone or anything any more.

That couldn't be my future and yet why not? I was no differ-ent. War was not choosy. The rich and entitled fell as easily as the poor. Bullets and bombs were neither caring nor discerning of status. Yet I clung to the notion of Sébastien's magical ability to dodge those bullets and bombs.

'Pardon me, Mayor?' I replied, suddenly aware of his remark that was still hanging between us.

'The new gypsies. It may not be wise right now, Mademoiselle.'

'The women prefer to be known as belonging to the Roma folk, sir.'

He blinked with irritation. 'I mean, Mademoiselle, if you'll pardon me, that this year I hear we are employing not just the Camargue gitans and some Basques but a new mix of Manouches. These are gypsies of German and Italian origin.' He whispered the last words as though he feared being struck down.

'Mayor, these women to whom you refer are simply travelling workers. They are all Romani and for my lifetime it's these people who have shouldered most of the back-breaking work of our harvest. I am not going to ignore them now.'

'But German and Italian!'

I sighed inwardly and schooled my expression to open and calm. My word, I'd grown up these last few years. Five years ago I would have shown my impatience. Now I smiled, adopting a kind voice. 'They are French through and through. Their ancestors may have hailed from Germany and Italy, even Spain, but I know these women – some worked for my father. They all carry the legal booklet that is required of all travellers. My manager is pedantic about checking their paperwork to keep everything legally correct to the law of 1912. None of these women have ever left France to my knowledge and most of their men are conscripted into our own army. At least half-a-dozen have lost their husbands or sons fighting for France.'

The mayor's lips pursed as my reasonable argument reassured him.

'They are simply travelling folk who move with the seasons and where the work is. Their men, like ours, bleed red blood.'

He cleared his throat, appropriately sheepish. 'I didn't mean —'

'I know you didn't,' I said, giving him a warm smile of friendship. 'I know your intention is only to protect us, Mayor, and we all thank you for that.' He puffed his chest up slightly with pride at my words. 'But there is nothing to fear from these women who will work hard for Grasse. I need help to bring in the harvest. Our town's women aren't numerous enough, even if we worked all day and burned ourselves to the colour of toffee. We just don't have the luxury of the transient workers of Camargue, whom we used to have in abundant supply. These Roma – they actually call themselves *Les Fleurs*, because they have become specialist pickers of roses in particular – will save our harvest, make sure we get it in on time and while the blooms are at their best. Trust me, sir, I have only Grasse's wellbeing at the forefront of my mind.'

'Forgive me, Mademoiselle Fleurette, for questioning your business practice.'

'Nothing to forgive,' I said brightly, relieved to have navigated us through the problem. 'Unless we get this harvest in, sir, there will be no enfleurage, no work for the women of Grasse who count on the income. I know you will trust me on this. Besides, I suspect the government likes to keep tabs on the travellers and Delacroix and De Lasset will now have a record of all of their papers, duly dated and stamped.'

'Yes, of course, that's true,' he agreed.

I had already lengthened my stride and was taking the steps two at a time that would lead me up to the church where my life had changed so dramatically. 'Good day to you, Mayor. Please remind your wife that I'm looking forward to seeing her at the villa for a coffee morning soon. I have really appreciated her help at the hospital,' I finished with a smile over my shoulder and moved quickly away from him.

I called to a group of those very women we'd been discussing, who were clustered at the top of the stairs to the church, tying on their bonnets. They were dressed in so many colours and I had to admit in the low light they added some much-needed cheer to our sorrowful town.

They raised their hands in salutation and before I was halfway up the stairs more were arriving at the meeting point. The tiny square where we were gathering was overlooked by the town hall, which had once been an episcopal palace, and the grand church itself with its tower of bells was now clanging the message that rose harvest day was dawning.

These were the only few days of the year when I felt reconnected with my old life; it was meant to be my favourite time of the year and I wore a smile as a façade for the workers, but May 1918 felt as though it was bringing unimaginable dread, especially as we were hearing about the fiercest fighting at the Front. Newspaper reports were signalling the most enormous peril for the Allied soldiers. I couldn't do anything to help that so I had to steel myself and do what I could to assist here at home . . . to help to heal the broken and bring in the harvest. Those were my two jobs this May.

I organised us to work in teams, walking the rows. No one in that field today held the sentimentality that I did for this toil. For all of them, other than Graciela –who turned up with the largest straw bonnet I'd ever seen, large enough to make me enjoy a much-needed gale of laughter – this was about a means to an end.

' . . . and this year the Delacroix family will be providing a bonus of double pay for every woman who can pick twelve pounds of blooms per hour on this opening day of the spring harvest,' I called out through cupped hands to help my voice carry to all.

They heard; the cheer was loud and appreciative.

'Let's do it, then, ladies,' I added. 'Good picking!'

'Good picking!' the words were echoed by all with a sense of triumph, and the women began to scatter.

Graciela sidled up, tying on her bonnet, and I began to laugh again. It made her appear even smaller.

'That hat is ridiculous, you do know that?'

'I care only for the impeccable quality of my skin, Fleurette,' she admonished. 'I had never picked roses in my life until you began dragging me out in the fields like a peasant.'

Her gripes only made me laugh more but then I thought that was her intention; I knew she was worried about me.

'And holding men's heads while they vomit, and cleaning up after they mess themselves, and washing floors!' She sounded so horrified by her own claims that it was like a piece of comedy, as though I was in an audience watching an amusing play. Her eyes had become wide with affront.

'We're all pitching in,' I said.

'On my noble knees, scrubbing floors!' she reinforced with great disgust.

'We have to keep the wards sterile,' I argued, enjoying the banter in spite of my hidden mood.

Graciela cut me a smirking look of loathing. 'And those nurses look down on me.'

'They do not! They tell me you're one of the most beautiful women they've ever seen.'

'I already know this! Tell me something I don't know.'

We both dissolved into laughter now as the voices of the workers lifted as one in a song about the harvest of flowers. The itinerant workers didn't join in but they smiled their appreciation.

We stared at each other, hands on hips. 'Let's get to work,' I said.

'Stay cheerful,' she said, moving to her place a few rows along.

I nodded and walked back to my deliberately chosen lonely

position at the end of one of the rows. But I had lied to my friend; remaining cheerful felt impossible. I sensed bleak news stalking me like prey, and the picking of the flowers, the repeated action, held no pleasure today although it did keep me occupied, preventing me from running down the valley and screaming my terror. All those months of schooling my composure – this was the moment when it must stand up to scrutiny, it must serve me . . . and save me. I had no choice but to open myself up to the pain of Felix not being in my life; the key I hoped I could forget would find me on rare occasions, whenever I felt unsure or threatened. Not hearing from Sébastien was deeply unnerving.

I let Felix out of my heart to roam free in my thoughts and I hoped we'd avoid talk of death, discussing roses and perfume instead. I enjoyed imagining him responding to my questions.

As I lost myself to the rhythmic plucking of my dewy pink blooms with their dozens of fat scented petals, almost drunk on the honeyed aroma, I told Felix about the perfume I had once again committed myself to. I had tried to find a fresh energy for it as a means of setting aside these new fears about Sébastien and his silence.

I want it to smell different.

In what way? he queried.

Not in the old way.

You mean not of roses and jasmine, our most famous flowers of Grasse? His tone was gently mocking.

Inwardly I smiled. He made me work for it. *I mean, definitely including them but using them in a way to make them less instantly familiar.*

More abstract?

Yes! That's precisely how I want it interpreted. Thank you, Felix. I want an abstract version of what our perfumes are always about.

So they will be there but not there?

A private chuckle to myself as I placed another prized bloom into the hessian sack at my side without touching the precious petals. *Their notes will be indecipherable at first and when they come, they will confuse because they'll smell fresh and new.*

Because?

Because, I began . . . wondering what I was reaching for. *Because I am making a scent for post-war. The woman who wears my fragrance will no longer be shackled to men. She will love men but she is newly independent in spirit. She has survived alone, tackled much that frightened and challenged her, but here she is – strong, decisive, she can rely on herself.*

Does she smell like a man now?

I actually burst out laughing alone in the field and had to stop myself from drawing attention. It felt good to loosen a laugh, ease the tension and thankfully a quick glimpse around told me that I was sufficiently isolated in my row. No one could hear me, nor indeed was anyone anything but focused on their own job in the low light and chill of a spring Grasse morning.

Somewhere far away, artillery was dropping and our men were being killed and injured. I prayed this was the last rose harvest that would pay a debt of blood. It was 1918 and I cast a wish to the universe that 1919 be the harvest of peacetime and that Sébastien be at my side.

I returned to Felix's question. *No, you fool, if anything she is more feminine than ever but she is not going to smell like her grandmother of straight roses and violets, of lavender and jasmine. She is the new woman, the modern woman, who is entering a new age of peace and prosperity. She wants recognition, she wants to achieve. She is complicated, diverse, at times contrary, sometimes whimsical, sometimes emotional, but always independent. She lives her life more on her terms.*

You make us men sound redundant.

Oh, you're good for some things, I replied wryly.

I thought I could hear echoes of his laughter across the rose bushes and wistfully hoped he was indeed laughing somewhere.

I'm going to add a metallic note too, I continued.

Whatever for? He sounded affronted in my mind and I smiled to myself.

It reminds me of you, Felix. Of kissing you farewell.

He waited, letting me go on. *There will be warmth and bitterness, there will be citrus and sorrow, there will be the brightness of hope, and the darkness of memory.*

Tell me about its formula, he urged.

I sighed inwardly. It had changed from the early structure but not so much I didn't recognise the fragrance I had built with Sébastien's descriptions. *Floral, of course, for Grasse. Tonka bean and vanilla that speak to each other of warmth and sweetness. And some musk – soft and subtle of the woodlands I love. These are what I'm calling my fond notes rather than base.*

I could feel him smiling within me, around me. He approved. *And the heart, Ettie?*

Peony, so it remains pretty and feminine.

And enveloping, he said.

I want pomegranate too.

Truly? For blood, I suppose?

You know me well. Yes, indeed, its fruit's colour symbolic of the blood shed for France, but we have both agreed, have we not, that our private notion of this fruit's distillation is akin to a freshly washed baby.

Floaty and fluffy, yes, he said, but with a query in his tone.

It's about rebirth, Felix. The blood of death, the blood of rebirth.

I like it. And I know the musk will work well against the

pomegranate – that's an inspiration, Ettie. What else? he asked with enthusiasm. *Wait, something spicy, perhaps?*

I felt relief that Felix could already smell it coming together and could guess at the elements to boost and balance.

Yes, I said with glee. *Ginger!*

The perfect balance of heat and citrus. It will give it an Eastern flavour.

It's what I want. The Orient is going to be more important than we can imagine for new aromas and for our business. I hope I'll travel one day to discover them.

You will. You and Sébastien.

I swallowed back the emotion that rose at the mention of his name. *And for the top notes, Felix, I want to use grapefruit.*

He laughed. *Only you would think like that. Gently sparkling citrus.* I could almost see his dark head nodding somewhere. *And it plays back to the citrus of the ginger . . . very good, Ettie.*

Now, I need you to trust me on these others, I warned.

Go on, then, he encouraged, *although I suspect you've already picked four pounds of roses. Do you need to rest?*

No, not until I have twelve. I must set the standard for every-one to follow.

That's my girl. Come on, then, surprise me with your top notes.

English tea to add a hay note . . .

And to give a nod to your English lover, I suppose.

I wanted to blow Felix a kiss for understanding. *And to our English heritage. I'm going to balance that out with . . . with green tea.* I knew I was right, I could smell it now.

Truly?

Yes! You know I love gunpowder tea, with its tiny rolled pel-lets of leaves. It speaks of the cannons of war and the explosions that have rocked Europe and hurt our lands, our men. Plus, it has again that Eastern note I want but also echoes the mint teas of

Morocco, where Sébastien has been and has promised to take me one day. But most of all because tea, like snow, smells untarnished, unadulterated. I was reminded of my grief in the snow.

He didn't say anything and I leapt into the pause. *Do you not agree?*

I love it, Ettie; so much symbolism in this perfume of yours. And you surprise me but you're right, the green tea will add that freshness and, while the citrus will sparkle at the top of your perfume, the two teas will give the clean notes like pure air.

Exactly! Like the air we all want to breathe again that is clear of smoke and gunfire and bloodshed.

And the fact that no one but us understands its complex story behind it, I think overall you are making a freshly floral perfume with a hint of oriental warmth. It sounds like no perfume I have never smelled.

It will be like nothing that's gone before, Felix.

What shall you call it?

I hadn't thought of a name until this moment because, having cast aside the notion of crafting a post-war fragrance that spoke of triumph and similar victorious sentiments, I hadn't considered what to name this sparkling and daring new perfume that I hoped women all over the world might want to wear once they'd smelled it or heard about it. In that moment of private enquiry I paused to consider and a soft breeze moved over the rows, gently tugging my hair and wafting our most famous fragrance around me in a richly pink splendour as though the smell itself had become a colour. Whichever way I crafted it, this perfume would always be about Grasse, its people, its life.

I shall call it Cachette, Felix.

He jumped to the obvious conclusion. *Why would you want to talk about our secrets?*

No, my darling, this is not about lies but truths.

Either way our family is damned even if you don't explain it. You'll know. I'll know.

I don't see it that way.

Tell me how you see it, Ettie.

I see Cachette about the fulfilment of love. Love is a secret, Felix. It creeps up on you. It doesn't announce itself. It can't be forced. It can't be helped, either. I mentally shrugged. *I fell in love with Sébastien without warning or desire. Our father fell in love with Marguerite and I'm sure if they could face us, they'd explain that they were as helpless as the butterfly that their son destroyed before us both.*

So love is cruel too.

Yes. In all of its guises love can be cruel because of how it weakens the lovers, takes away their control, removes their inhibitions. In our father's case, loving someone so much can have repercussions that damage for many years to come. Love can be bitter, filled with heartache. Heaven knows, there are days that I wish I didn't love Sébastien because it requires me to live with pain, and days that I wish I didn't love you so much and could let you go.

I wouldn't like that.

No, which is why love is also beautiful, uplifting, emotionally inspiring and can last forever if we nourish it. I lifted a shoulder. *I'm reaching for all of that truth about love through this perfume, and everything that binds our family is about us.*

It's about you, darling Ettie.

I suppose it is, as I'm all who is left.

Then forget our family and our dirty secrets. Make it clean and pure and call it . . . Fleurette! You will be the first woman perfumer of Grasse. Let your name be attached to this original scent that will spawn an industry of beautiful fragrances inspired by you.

His suggestion took my breath away because Sébastien had urged me to call my perfume after myself also.

Should I, really?

I shall be angry if you don't.

I'll think on this.

You haven't heard from Sébastien, he noted.

Is he with you, Felix? I asked, with terror in my enquiry.

Dead, you mean?

I couldn't say it. Felix hesitated, then sighed into my mind.

I do not know.

A sob, my first in years, escaped from deep in my chest, surprising me with its intensity because I didn't know I'd been holding that tension so tightly. I lifted a particularly beautiful bloom to my face and felt the cool dawn dampness of its petals. Here it was, my heart note of *Cachette*, clear and sweet at the outset, yet complex and deeply sublime as it lingered. It likely smelled slightly different to each who might behold it but to me I could reel off a dozen – no, two dozen – flavours within this one inhalation of Grasse's most precious flower.

'Don't take him,' I whispered into the petals that scuffed gently against my lips. 'Bring him home.'

A shout went up. Women straightened all around me, sighing at the easing of muscles, their spines clicking back satisfyingly into place. We shared a universal stance, one hand on hips, another hand to shade the eyes against the rising sun, bonnets pushed back. The chill of the morning was being chased away; it would be a warm day.

I looked across to Graciela. It was her voice I'd recognised.

'What is it?' I called across a few rows.

'Look who comes!' she cried, pushing back her huge bonnet and jutting her chin in the direction of the valley.

I was much further away and I squinted now to see a lone figure cresting the hill. I stared for a moment, my eyes adjusting to the light, taking in immediately that it was a man. I could see bandages around his head. He walked tall but his dark clothes hung off a hollow frame. And as he moved I noted his gait had a pronounced limp.

Sébastien! I screamed in my mind. *Felix, is it him?*

Be happy; be in love for all of us, Ettie, were his final words to me and it was as though the wind of Provence picked up the spirit of my twin that lived within me and carried him away, dislocating us properly from the dead and the living so that his soul could find its home and my heart could find its resting beat alongside Sébastien.

I ducked beneath the band of the sack of flowers that crumpled beside me as I threw it off and I began to run, pulling off the fabric protectors over my sleeves, untying my apron and flinging it aside. I dragged at the tortoiseshell comb that held my hair so that I could feel that lovely homecoming wind blowing through it as I raced towards my love.

I could smell my perfume streaming through my consciousness: all of its notes coming together as Sébastien's lovely features became more distinct, the perfume completing itself as I threw my arms around him and he lifted me into the air between the corridors of roses and spun me around, laughing and hugging me so close I could barely breathe.

This was the fragrance of *Fleurette* . . . love in its purest form.

ON THE SCENT
OF PERFUME

The Making of
The Perfumer's Secret

Often the hardest, most intensive, part about writing historical fiction for me is also the most enjoyable part – the research. This period is when I feel the story gathering about me like a cloud, but it's invisible at this point because there are no words yet. The best way I can describe my research is by suggesting that I'm like a marathon runner warming up on the sidelines. I can sense the long journey ahead, and all of my academic training is starting to come together as a more physical presence. Facts and stories, anecdotes, interviews, articles, images, memories, experiences and especially locations – these aspects all start sharpening in focus. At this point I can honestly say it's all about my gut instinct; I have a visceral and emotional connection with the era and my main characters who are going to lift the story up onto their shoulders and run that marathon with me. These characters may still be lurking in the distance but I can see their shape and I can hear their voices. Once I visit the locations of where they will move around, the story starts to take on a life of its own.

During my research I don't make a lot of notes. I shoot plenty of photos. I am a great believer in just watching and listening and that whatever will be important to the story will stick somewhere to me, for my memories to deliver that fragment back when I need it. That's how I'm wired. Not everyone would approach their research the same way and no two writers are the same. However, this works for me and I don't analyse it, I just go with it because I'm now thirty novels in and there's no point in wondering suddenly whether I should change my modus operandi. I completely trust my emotional response to places, people, stories and ideas. The research is a period of immersing myself in a world – whether it's on location or via books, the internet, conversations – and letting my instincts go to work and clue me and my storytelling. Most of what I read never finds its way into my novels but I certainly feel enriched for reading it all. It is usual for me to read a dozen nonfiction tomes, many of them written with dazzling story power.

Travel is the great educator and visiting all the locations that appear in my stories is my signature, I suppose. Coming from a travel background, it seems natural that all those decades of globetrotting would nourish my stories – and they do, especially my historical drama. For instance, for *The Lavender Keeper* locations include London, Hastings, Eastbourne, Farnborough, Bletchley Park in the UK. In France it involved so many of the towns and villages of the Luberon in Provence, including Gordes, Saignon, Bonnieux, Sault. Also Lyon, L'Isle-sur-la-Sorgue, as well as the Loire Valley, Mont Mouchet . . . and, of course, Paris. Its sequel kept me just as busy – back to many of those destinations again but widening my reach to Strasbourg in eastern France, Marseille in the south, then moving into Austria to Vienna, Switzerland to Lausanne, into Bavaria in Germany and ultimately to Poland, to Kraków and to Auschwitz.

Getting the locations bedded down takes up a lot of my headspace, physical energy and time in finding the right places that not only work seamlessly for the storytelling but also provide intriguing locales for the reader to visit during their time with the book.

There's always a seed to a novel and sometimes that seed can be buried deep, only emerging from the depths years on. This was certainly the case for *The Perfumer's Secret*, which has its roots in *The Lavender Keeper*, written back in 2010.

Researching and writing *The Lavender Keeper* focused my attention on plants and it was learning about the uses of the wild and beautiful *Lavandula angustifolia* that immersed me in fragrance. I also spent many months buried deep in books about lavender and other fragrant plants of yesteryear, World War Two and particularly the period of the occupation of France and its liberation a few years later. I learned a great deal about the famous maquisards of southern France, where the notion of freedom fighting began in that nation and perhaps the most fearless guerilla warfare was waged.

But throughout all that historical research it was the lavender that kept scenting my thoughts, and my credit card took a walloping as I ordered countless books about lavender . . . its cultivation, its myth, its uses, its botanical importance and so on.

Fiona McIntosh in fields of lavender, Provence, France

No doubt because I spent a block of time in Provence for *The Lavender Keeper* and its sequel, *The French Promise*, it was my experiences back then that began to squirrel themselves away deep in my mind. And here they are re-emerging again now. I am a firm believer that back of brain takes care of business, so when Penguin asked me in 2014 what might be coming next, it was from those stored memories of southern France and especially my visit to a perfume school in Forcalquier in Alpes-de-Haute-Provence that a new idea erupted in a cloud of fragrance in my mind.

I wanted to write about perfume. At first I thought it might be a follow-on novel to *The Lavender Keeper* and *The French Promise*. That seemed logical and the characters had even conveniently arranged themselves so that I could easily move them into perfume manufacturing in a third instalment of their story. Except this time I had an entirely new character calling to me from the distance. I learned her name to be Fleurette, a gifted perfume maker who resisted being the property of her family to be married off strategically to enhance their wealth. She belonged to one of the great perfume families of the early twentieth century and she possessed the near ethereal skill of being a 'nose' but, as she was a woman, it meant that her rare talent would be effectively overlooked.

Fleurette was all but giving me a story, but she was born before 1900. Decisions, decisions! When I forced myself to choose between this young, frustrated woman of the early twentieth century or Luc Bonet's daughter in the 1960s, I felt myself drifting easily back to 1914. I wanted to stay with Fleurette. So, when I set off on this adventure, I was convinced I was writing about Fleurette's struggle to be recognised as a perfume maker – but the keyboard refused to obey, and Fleurette wouldn't oblige either! I discovered I was writing about a young woman in complete crisis.

Fleurette was being forced to marry against her will to a man she loathed – the head of the pre-eminent French perfume manufacturer – and on her wedding day her beloved France announced war with Germany. With all of the men in her life marching off to the battlefields of northern France, she is left to juggle both families' empires. In their absence she discovers a most terrible secret that threatens to implode those wealthy empires from within. I simply had to sigh and let Fleurette take us by the hand and lead us through her tribulations.

Perfume weaves its fragrant miasma through all the pages of this novel and I realised I didn't have to be writing about an actual perfume to enjoy the crafting of this tale. Perfume became the theme of the story and thus demanded I research it thoroughly, which pleased me no end.

While researching *The Last Dance*, the novel I wrote before *The Perfumer's Secret*, I visited Marrakech in Morocco. Here I became even more embedded in learning about exotic extracts and their uses – from argon oil to frankincense, sandalwood and jasmine. I was in training for the next marathon novel! A few months after my trip to Morocco a timely visit to Grasse in southern France snapped me into full focus for the potential for this novel. I realised that I had to base it there, in what is accepted as the perfume capital of the world.

This town in the Côte d'Azur, fifteen kilometres from Cannes and even closer to Nice, might as well be a world away from the bustling cities, nestled as it is in the hills with forests, valleys and rivers surrounding it. The Grasse of today spills down the hillsides that were once a clutter of patchwork fields of the most extraordinary roses and jasmine. Like its more glitzy neighbours, Grasse too has been a tourist drawcard for centuries. Favoured for its fragrant plantations, the altitude of up to 400 metres ensures clear air and cooler climes in the hot summers of southern France. Queen Victoria spent several enjoyable winters in Grasse and Emperor Napoleon's sister recuperated in the town after an illness.

Back in the early Middle Ages, Grasse was a centre for leather. It smelled a whole lot different then, because tanneries stink. One of the most important and lauded tanners in Grasse was Galimard. It made a gift of a pair of beautiful leather gloves to Catherine de Medici and was inspired to perfume those gloves to ease the ugly smell when presented to the Queen of France. The story goes that the Queen was seduced, utterly, and Galimard grew into one of the prominent perfumers of the town as a result, especially as the leather industry faded. Emperor Napoleon visited in 1815 and was showered with violets, his favourite flower because his lover, Josephine, adored the fragrance. He covered her grave in violets and wore a locket containing the tiny flowers that later flourished around her grave. Grasse is now famous for violet and, incidentally at the time of writing *The Perfumer's Secret*, that fragrance is making a comeback.

I wanted my story set in my favourite era of World War One. This is pre-Chanel No.5, by the way. Chanel No.5 came into being in 1921 by Ernest Beaux for Gabrielle Chanel, a forward-thinking couturier. Legend has it the famous fragrance was achieved through an error of quantities of essential oil. The jasmine and tuberoses are still sourced exclusively from a fifty-acre field in Grasse that is guarded zealously. A tiny bottle (30ml) of the perfume is said to contain 1000 jasmine flowers and twelve of the exquisite May roses from these fields, which are of the highest quality in the world. I wanted my story to begin before the development of Chanel No.5 as I was writing about the creation of a fragrance. As it turned out, the era suited the story that strayed from its original arc.

At this time perfume had begun to take off around Europe but also in Britain and America, mostly with lavender, violets and roses as the key elements. It was the perfumers of Grasse, however, who looked further afield for new ingredients and began importing the spices, seeds, nuts, plants, leaves and even animal products that would provide fresh essential oils and aromas to mix innovative, daring perfumes for a hungry, modern society.

After reading every relevant reference book I could lay my hands on, I settled in to the town of Grasse in Provence during the summer of 2014 and began to inhale the history, its scents, its stories and its lifestyle. I interviewed perfumers, I visited museums, I walked its fields, explored all the narrow lanes, shopped in its weekend market, gorged on its local treats, worshipped in its grand church with locals and generally allowed a story to shape itself around me. As I've mentioned, I never plot a novel; so long as I have a couple of characters demanding their role in the tale, I leave it up to them to take the story where it needs to go. Essentially, though, *The Perfumer's Secret* was to be all about the smells of Grasse and I knew everything else would fall into place if I could get that right.

When I returned to Grasse that northern summer to write *The Perfumer's Secret*, I snapped numerous photographs to remind me of the sun-drenched streets. It helped enormously that a few days before shifting to Grasse I had spent a full week in Haute Provence inhaling the lavender in full blue roar as I took twenty-four Australians around the region to walk in the footsteps of my characters from *The Lavender Keeper* and *The French Promise*. We'd already had a week together in Paris but it was this colourful, scented, mesmerising week in the south of France that put me into the right frame of mind to absorb all the detail and texture that would layer itself six months later into the story of *The Perfumer's Secret*.

My final task in the research, I believed, was to learn how to make perfume and although I moved through a simplified, fast-tracked version, my days at Galimard – yes, the same firm – with a perfumer were enriching. I couldn't quite believe what a tense experience it was to sit before the vast perfume organ and to combine base, heart and top notes from dozens of choices, knowing that by mixing two oils, they would be irrevocably changed from the first drop. And then to add a third, a fourth, a fifth . . . and so on. Hours were lost in concentrated smelling and daredevil decisions, but I would urge anyone to give it a go.

Contemporary perfume organ in Galimard, Grasse

I do feel saddened that the majority of perfumes made today are manufactured by relying on a chemical process rather than on flowers, especially the delicate *enfleurage* process, which you'll read about in the novel. The ancient factories are now abandoned and the distilleries have disappeared but I can remember passing a crumbly old building with a tiny window on its cellar. I paused to sniff from the cellar that I knew had once been the storage for the raw perfume product and yes, indeed, one can still smell the potent, lingering fragrance of the essential oil. Amazing.

The three major perfume presences in Grasse today that particularly cater to international tourists are Fragonard, Galimard and Molinard. They offer free guided visits to their parfumeries so people can learn about the process of making perfume.

The result of my time in the laboratory with dozens of essential oils is 'Fleurette', the perfume I shall take on tour for this novel to share with readers. My intention was to retain in the perfume the integrity of the time I was writing about and to avoid anything notably modern while somehow trying to achieve a scent that could please a reader today.

A perfume almost identical to this is designed by Fleurette in the story and, true to her era, its most recognisable notes are May roses, violets and a touch of jasmine. I also added some of the exotics that were coming through to Grasse at that time, including tonka bean, ginger and green tea. The finished perfume is more gentle than the novel and the heroine it was inspired by, but hopefully you will find the tale just as intoxicating and uplifting, and find that it lingers long, like a well-chosen heart note.

fionamcintosh.com
facebook.com/FionaMcIntoshAuthor

ACKNOWLEDGEMENTS

Simon Godly, a Brit who lives in France, has an immense knowledge of the Great War. You can imagine with all of the detail I've been juggling in the research for *The Perfumer's Secret*, much of it in another language, that clearly someone's had my back. Simon cheerfully took on my story's twists and turns and showed me how to bend its shape to fit an accurate pattern of France's war. His delight in hunting down nuggets of information of what I considered pure genius to aid my tale cannot go without the highest salute. He enriched the story with the war minutiae that I so needed to make the involvement of an otherwise tiny town in the fabric of the Great War step out of history and I hope feel alive for the reader. The time we spent together in the northern battlefields of Arras remains memorable. Thank you, Simon.

Franck-Dominique Raineri and Monique Pawlowski from the Office de Tourisme de Grasse were filled with energy for this story and I'm grateful to Dominique Draghetti for her grand tour of the town. My thanks to the helpful folk at the Musée International de la Parfumerie, especially Marie-Séverine Pillon, who helped me to get a snapshot of life in this town dedicated to perfume. Thank you also to Philippe Massé, president of Prodarom, a perfume manufacturing syndicate based in Grasse, and his colleagues for their generosity of time.

My learning about how to make a fragrance began at the L'Occitane headquarters in Alpes-de-Haute-Provence while I was researching my novel *The French Promise* in 2013 but was fine tuned at the ancient perfume House of Galimard in Grasse during the northern summer of 2014, where I had my first attempt at perfume-making and produced a fragrance based on some of the main essential oils that were popular one hundred years earlier. I returned to Galimard in 2015, this time to meet perfumer, Caroline de Boutiny, who took that old-fashioned smelling recipe and helped me to improve it without losing the authenticity of the era. I called it Fleurette and am now quietly hooked on the pleasure (and tension) of mixing base, heart and top notes.

My thanks to Guy Bouchara, traditional perfumer in Grasse and fellow perfumer, Didier Gaglewski who is designing highly modern fragrances for men. Their discussions helped to inspire me.

The usual nod of gratitude to draft readers, Pip Klimentou and Sonya Caddy, as well as to all the fantastically enthusiastic gang at Penguin Random House Australia, especially my editors Ali Watts and Saskia Adams, as well as Rhian Davies, Lou Ryan, Sharlene Vinall and Clementine Edwards who keep me on track.

To the passionate booksellers of Australia and New Zealand – we can't do it without you. Thank you!

A big *mwah!* to my readers – surely the most loyal and affectionate group any author could hope to gather around her. And a kiss to the beloved trio of Ian, Will and Jack at home who put up with my obsession for smell and taste that raged during the writing of this story.

A special hug to you, Will, for hunting down a pristine, tiny bottle of my favourite perfume from 1970, no longer produced, that in its single impeccable ounce released all the hidden recollections and images of my teenage years and reminded me of how vital our sense of smell can be to love and memory.

Fx

AUTHOR'S NOTE

Being historically accurate is vital to my kind of novel and I do take every measure to ensure the correctness of my facts. There are moments, however, for the sake of story, that I bend the truth. For example, Fleurette and Aimery's wedding. In France marriage is only legal if it is first achieved as a civil ceremony and newlyweds then present their certificate of marriage to a priest if they wish to observe a holy union at their church. I have used this double service requirement for the story's advantage as you will have gathered if you've finished the book. It's law, so that means no marriage certificate, no church wedding. While in truth Aimery would have had a tough time convincing a priest to marry them without that civil certificate I am hoping the tension of war, the power of their names, their friendship with the priest and the sheer embarrassment of cancelling what is essentially a 'royal' wedding in Grasse because of a technicality – not to mention a hefty donation to the cathedral's restoration – helped the priest to overcome his resistance.

BOOK CLUB
DISCUSSION NOTES

1. Fleurette believes she is gifted as 'the Nose'. Given the era, do you think this is a blessing or a curse for a woman?

2. Fleurette describes her twin, Felix, as 'her second self'. In what ways do we see their special connection affect the course of this novel?

3. Sébastien asks: 'Have you ever been in love, Fleurette? The sort of love that makes you feel irrational, irresponsible, irrepressible?' In what ways does Fleurette act irrationally, irresponsibly and irrepressibly after meeting Sébastien?

4. Fiona McIntosh writes beautiful love stories but swears she is not a writer of romance fiction. What do you think are the key differences?

5. 'I am at one with nature's perfection – her beauty, her colours, her fragrances – and she has allowed me to glimpse it in a man.' In what ways does Sébastien's character typify her idea of perfection?

6. Could this novel be described as a tragedy?

7. Graciela admits that she feels sure she killed Aimery to release herself. Discuss.

8. Fleurette manages to find it in her heart to forgive Aimery for the gravest of crimes. Can you?

9. What do you think Fleurette means when she says 'Women bear the sorrows of men'?

10. Fleurette has a wonderful way of describing the fragrances she senses in her world, and the author had great fun concocting her own perfume for Fleurette as part of the research for this novel. If you had to formulate your own perfume, what 'notes' would it contain, and what would you call it?

Read on for a sneak peek of

The
CHOCOLATE TIN

Alexandra Frobisher, a modern-thinking woman with hopes of a career in England's famous chocolate-making town of York, has received several proposals of marriage, although none of them promises that elusive extra – love.

Matthew Britten-Jones is a man of charm and strong social standing. He impresses Alex and her parents with his wit and intelligence, but would an amicable union be enough for a fulfilling life together?

At the end of the war, Captain Harry Blakeney discovers a dead soldier in a trench in France. In the man's possession is a secret love note, tucked inside a tin of chocolate that had been sent to the soldiers as a gift from the king.

In pursuit of the author of this mysterious message, Harry travels to Rowntree's chocolate factory in England's north, where his life becomes inextricably bound with Alexandra and Matthew's. Only together will they be able to unlock secrets of the past and offer each other the greatest gift for the future.

From the battlefields of northern France to the medieval city of York, this is a heartbreaking tale about a triangle of love in all its forms and a story about the bittersweet taste of life . . . and of chocolate.

Brought to you by
Penguin Books

I

YORK – 1915

The argument had been tame, polite even, but there was no doubt in her mind that if she didn't make a decision, it would be made for her. Alex Frobisher gave a small clicking sound and nudged her coal-coloured mare to pick up its pace. The familiar noise of hooves on the road soothed, tried to take her thoughts back to a time when the summers seemed to stretch forever in a warm recollection of shared laughter and Scotland. Such happy days before that August afternoon of 1905 when darkness descended; it was this pain, she was sure, forever haunting the family, that was the root of her mother's urgency for a wedding . . . even an unwelcome one for Alex.

Blackberry didn't need guiding; she knew exactly where to turn left and enter the lush landscape of the sprawling green of the Knavesmire that flanked one of Britain's favourite racecourses. The canter turned to a light gallop and soon they gained speed, the land-scape melting into a pleasing blur of leaves. The glimmering late autumn sunlight that was toppling fast from its zenith of afternoon into that golden hour just before dusk, found the bluish hint of Blackberry's coat to make it shimmer. The breeze tried desperately to whip free Alex's hair that clung stubbornly to its pins beneath her riding hat; a few wisps escaped, particularly one determined strand enjoying freedom as much as she did.

Not only had her hair deepened to the colour of chocolate over the years, she felt her life had followed suit into maturity and this last year felt as though it had delivered her into a relentlessly dark mood.

She let the debate play out once more in her mind as she pulled gently on the reins to slow Blackberry's arrival at the entrance again. The horse obliged, finding an easy walk, steamy breath blowing in the fading afternoon as a chill crawled over the open plain of the park. Alex relived the uncomfortable, sometimes heated conversation that unfolded as vividly in her mind as if she were living through it for the first time. She replayed it now like a motion picture.

There was her father in his tweeds, sipping on his afternoon tea, unhappily ignoring the pikelets he so enjoyed in order to escape the shrill combatants of his wife and daughter. He'd moved to the bank of tall windows with their small squares of glass panes framed by heavy plum velvet curtains to look out across the grounds of the sprawling, champagne-brick pile called Tilsden Hall. This had been home to the Frobishers for decades and Alex knew he searched out the duckpond. She instinctively understood that her father was wishing he could stroll now to the pond and gaze out at the two swans moving peacefully across the glass-like surface. Instead, he was suffering through yet another debate between the women in his life.

Alex watched her mother lift her eyes to the garishly painted ceiling in the Arts and Crafts style that her elder had embraced so eagerly. Minerva had often claimed that it was a 'folk style' of yesteryear, but her daughter glanced now at the frantic circus of flowers and geometric shapes on the timbered ceiling and felt a familiar gush of embarrassment. Alex switched her gaze to her mother. Minerva Frobisher's pinched nostrils and pursed lips gave the impression they were shutting out the effect of something particularly putrid.

'Mother,' Alex appealed. 'I really must be allowed to make some decisions of my own.'

'You can. You may choose whether you wish to be formally engaged to Edward St John, Ashley Langdon-Smith, Duncan Cameron, or indeed courted by all of them.'

'Then if it's up to me, I choose none of them.'

Her mother baulked, gave a low gasp of indignance. Her father cut Alex a look of soft despair as though admonishing her for prodding an already enraged beast. She returned it with a tiny shrug of apology; they both knew he was about to be drawn into the discussion he'd aimed to avoid.

'Charles!'

'Yes, dear?'

'What do you have to say to that?' Minerva demanded.

Frobisher strolled back to stand near the fireplace where its blackened ironwork beneath the mahogany mantelpiece proclaimed its 1898 installation in bold relief. He turned his back to the gently dancing flames to pick up a warm pikelet that he folded neatly, careful not to spill a drop of the oozy butter or glistening jam. He bit into it deliberately to avoid speaking and nodded that he'd answer shortly when his mouth was no longer full.

Fresh exasperation was sighed out by Minerva. 'Alexandra,' she continued, 'you should have been married years ago. But as an only child we've indulged you. We've given you plenty of time, far more than most daughters, plus you've grown up in a world of entitlement –'

'I am aware of that, Mother,' she said, trying hard not to snap her words.

'Are you? Really, darling, are you? Because you show no indication that you're seriously taking on board your role.'

'Please . . .' Alex began.

'While I pray each evening that Cousins Hugh and George are spared, I fear daily that both could be gone from us in a blink. I know that men's lives are being cut down by the thousands, daily. Someone in this family has to be realistic about your future. Without Peter –'

Alex leapt in to cut off her parents. She didn't want to travel the whole emotional journey again. 'I know, Mother. You want me to marry and give you grandsons, retain Tilsden. I do realise this.'

'Both of us want this. But actually, Alexandra, I'm genuinely concerned that there is someone to look after you. Your father may not wish to press you but I know that women don't get nearly as much say as they would like. Now, we can rail against it and please don't misunderstand me,' she said, raising a finger. 'I am full of admiration for courageous women who wish to change the way of the world, but our way, darling . . . is to cling to the traditional. I know you don't want to hear this but I am going to say it one more time very clearly so you make no mistake about your job for the Frobisher family. And it is not any hare-brained idea of pursuing a career! You can't possibly contemplate working for wages – or you certainly wouldn't be considered marriage material. Besides, you know nothing about anything, frankly. Leave business to the men in your life – that's their role. Yours, my darling girl, is to marry. Most young women aren't given such a selection but we love you deeply and we do want you to be happy in your choice.' It was impressive how her mother could give offence even when her words were chosen to show affection. 'Each is ideal in almost every way.'

'Except the most important.'

'I barely knew your father when I was betrothed and I did not run from my duty to marry him, even though I was far younger than you are. I very quickly grew to respect him.'

'What about love, though, Mother?'

'Of course I love your father,' Minerva replied, with fresh indignance but conveniently missing the point, Alex thought.

'Well, just so that we're all clear, I don't respond to any of those three men.'

'Respond?' Her mother scorned. 'What on earth does that mean, child? In what ways don't you *respond*?'

'Myriad ways,'she sighed. 'Let's make this simple. Edward is pompous and has viciously bad breath; Ashley is scared of spiders and prefers to sleep with a lamp on. Hardly heroic! Anyway, I sense Ashley is easily persuaded by his London society friends . . . and Duncan . . . well, Duncan is Scottish.'

'He's next in line as laird!'

'Precisely. Do I really want to be lumped off to Ben Nevis, Mother?' She hated how dismissive she sounded. These men were at the front, fighting for their lives, fighting for her privileged life to continue.

'Duncan has a tremendous affection for you.'

'Of course he does. His choice is limited. It's me or a sheep, really, isn't it?' Sometimes her thoughts were spoken aloud before her mouth could capture them. Even through her shame she felt a helpless spike of triumph that her father guffawed over his second pikelet.

'Charles, really!'

Charles's amusement vanished as the tone of disapproval was now turned his way.

'I despair of you, Alexandra Frobisher. Duncan deserves better.'

'Mother, I know he's your first choice but be fair. Duncan doesn't want a woman to love. He wants a wife to show off, to run his household, to keep him warm in bed on those barren highlands,' she said, unable to hide her irritation.

'If it gives us heirs, so be it.'

She sighed, letting her shoulders visibly slump. 'You can imagine that the Camerons would consider any son as *their* heir rather than yours.'

'I don't care. The sooner you get going at the business of making family, the better. Then I know there are children growing up around you who will look after you in time to come.' Her mother raised her voice in deep exasperation.'We need grandchildren . . . grandsons would be lovely.'

'Any sons' surname would be Cameron, not Frobisher. How does this help us?'

'Don't be deliberately obtuse. I find it most vexing.'

'Minerva.' Her father finally finished his second pikelet. 'Don't, my dear. You know your blood pressure is high enough.'

'Charles, I need your support in this.'

He nodded, put down his cup and saucer and sat next to Minerva, taking her hand in a sweet show of affection. Alex loved her father for it, especially as she knew all he craved was harmony, his daughter happy, wife content.

'It's all very well for you both, Charles. You live in a tiny world of two sometimes, every inch a daddy's girl . . .'

Alex let her mother say her piece, congratulating herself that she didn't leap in and say unlike all the other spoiled daughters of her mothers' circle she didn't call her father daddy any more but the more modern and urbane *Dad*.

Her father smiled awkwardly and then finally nodded and turned back to address her. 'Alex, darling,' he began and she gave him her full attention because Alex knew his word would be final. 'This discussion began because you courageously shared with us that you wish to help out in the factory where they're calling for volunteers.'

'I do, Dad. And being around the Rowntree's business is a place to get ideas too.'

She watched the familiar crinkle of his eyes as he smiled at her, dimples deepening in his cheeks. In that moment she was a little girl again looking into the face of the only man she adored. She didn't glimpse his unguarded smile often enough . . . later this year it would be two decades of sorrow they'd be facing. She shook off the gloom, watching her father throw a look of gentle pride at his wife.

'And, of course, living in York, who could blame you wanting to be involved in its main industry?' he said.'What your mother is conveying rather baldly is that what we need you to do – as our only and much beloved daughter – is to follow through.' He nodded to himself, liking this choice of expression. 'We are not chocolate makers like the Rowntree family and –'

'We're not even Quakers,' Minerva observed as though tasting something stale.

Charles shook his head. 'There are many other ways to volunteer your time. And as for you dreaming of your own business, while I won't flatly discourage it because you've always been an ambitious child . . .' He hushed Minerva at her intended interruption. 'Let me speak, Min, dear. Alex has been an independent girl with strong opinions and I think we can both agree that she has firm morals. She won't let down anyone she loves, least of all us, so I think we have little to worry about.'

She thanked her dad with a nod and affectionate smile.

He lifted a finger of warning though and a pit opened in her belly. 'However, women do have responsibilities right now to their men, to family, to helping to keep the country safe and ticking over through war. Avoiding your responsibility as the only remaining child in this family is breaking your mother's heart.'

'You could, of course, marry a Rowntree . . . even a Cadbury would do, and make your father and I happy,' her mother interjected.

She ignored the remark.'Dad, I just think learning about business could inspire me. Please, I just want to do more than have the sum of my life being marriage.'

Her father took a deep breath to indicate that he understood. Alex opened her hands in appeal to hide her frustration, hoping it wouldn't show in her voice. 'Everyone we pass in the street is connected to chocolate, and anyway I can learn, Dad. Don't you see? Just being around it would be enlightening.'

Another gasp of horror from her mother punctured her thin balloon of hope and her plaintive statement died in her throat. Alex tasted instant bitterness instead of sweet joy.

Charles Frobisher looked back at her with tenderness in his gaze, making it worse, but she fought against turning sullen on him. 'No, my darling girl, you cannot. Association with the factory floor will not do – not for a Frobisher girl.'

Alex tried not to hear the clear dismissal. 'Give me a chance, Dad. I think I can build a career for myself, be a woman of independent means.'

'Career? Are you hearing yourself, Alex?' Minerva demanded. 'Because you sound deluded. Women don't have careers, for heaven's sake. This may be 1915 and you may well have modern ideas, but your job is to support your husband. You're going to be the wife of an important man, one way or another, and a mother to his children. We need to know your future is secure. That is your *career* as a Frobisher girl. We've never raised you in doubt of your duty, surely? Daughters from families such as ours have their part to play in the family's future. It's time to deliver on all your privileges and do your bit.'

Alex hated to disappoint either of them but why couldn't they understand she didn't want any of the entitlement to which they both referred? Her uncle's boys could have it all, if they lived long enough to take it on.

Alex let out an audible sigh and decided this was a battle best fought another day. She retreated, throwing appeasement their way to defuse the heat from her mother's glare and the disappointment in her father that the two women in his life were at such logger-heads. 'I cannot marry anyone right now because all our men are fighting for their lives, and ours, in Europe. Look, Dad, Mother, please don't upset yourselves; the trio you refer to are likely each in trenches. They may not be suitable in my mind but it doesn't mean they aren't good men, brave and patriotic.' She watched her mother's frown loosen and felt her own relief let go. 'We can't make important decisions on marriage while the potential grooms are fighting a war. You come from a different age, both of you; you were born when a queen ruled an empire and we've already moved through a king since. We're one quarter through 1915 and what is surely another year of war . . .' She lifted a shoulder. 'None of us knows what's going to happen but I suppose the modern woman in me knows that we can't halt progress no matter what. So, of course I will marry and of course I will give you grandchildren but I don't know who that will be with or when. Can we agree not to discuss marriage until we know there's peace?'

'Deal!' Charles said with a clap of his hands.

His wife turned her disbelieving gaze on him.

'Alex is right, my dear. This conversation is academic until those three jolly fellows are freely available. Poor old Cameron's being sent to Belgium or something, isn't he?'

'Well, they'll get leave, won't they?' Minerva queried.

Alex groaned.

'I'm sure they will at some time,' her father agreed.

'If they live long enough,' Alex observed.

'But I think our only precious child should make an informed decision when the world is in a less wretched frame of mind,' her father continued. 'Besides, it's no good her agreeing to marry a man who doesn't return from the battlefield. Imagine the trauma of that on all of us. What if she were married, pregnant, had a child?'

Bravo, Dad, Alex cheered inwardly.

'Enough, Charles.' The lower half of Minerva's face seemed to disappear into her neck as if desperately forcing down a new line of attack, but none of her pinched disappointment was masked. 'Right,' she said, finding her new path. 'So we're agreed, then? All of us? When peace is regained, within six months of it, Alexandra, please will you allow me to make an announcement of your engagement?' She eyed them both again, awaiting an answer.

'I think that's fair,' Charles remarked to the fireplace. He bent again towards the tray of cooling pikelets.

'You don't need another, darling. Remember your indigestion.'

'Yes, dear,' he said, stealing a wink at his daughter and another pikelet.

'Alexandra?'

She shifted her attention back to her mother because the tone was not to be ignored. 'I want to hear your agreement to this pact we're making as a family. Six weeks after formal peacetime you will be engaged. You will not break faith with this. I cannot have my daughter a spinster for much longer. This is a solemn promise you're giving us, darling, all right?'

'I agree,' she said and her mother nodded, seemingly satisfied. Alex glanced away to the tall windows that flooded light into this room each afternoon. It was still a couple of hours to dusk and she needed to take some air.

They could hear the phone ringing distantly. A tap on the door sounded. A woman with a familiar hangdog expression entered. The often sombre-looking arrangement of her features belied the genial, kindly person who lived behind them. She'd been at Tilsden since before Alex was born and Charles Frobisher had acquiesced to the housekeeper's insistence that no new butler was required since the war had dragged away so many of the men. She'd stepped up her role from housekeeper to shoulder most of the butlering responsibilities.

'Yes, Lambton?' Charles wondered.

'It's a gentleman, a Mr Britten-Jones, on the telephone, sir.'

'Britten-Jones? All right, Lambton, thank you.'

'Who is that, darling?' Minerva wondered.

'Do you remember the couple we met in Bath? He was involved in the expansion of the transport network in the west.'

'Vaguely.'

'Ruddy, built like a block of stone. Old money. New money too and lots of it – mind you, he'd need it. They had quite a crowd of a family, as I recall.'

'Wife thin as a waif and extremely short, I seem to recall.'

'That's the one. Well, I've been doing some work with him via the railways this past couple of years. He's a good sort. I like him. Excellent family. Strange he'd ring me at home, though.'

Alex followed her father to the door, smiling at Lambton, whose quiet yet somehow dominant personality she'd grown up to admire as close to a grandmother in her life.

'I'm going to take Blackberry out,' Alex announced to the room.

'Rug up, darling. It's going to be cold once that sun disappears behind those clouds coming in,' Minerva called after her in an entirely cheerier tone. 'Dinner's simple and a bit earlier at seven as Nessie is going to the play that's on at St Peter's School hall,' she said.

'Your mother chose a beef pie for this evening, Miss Alex, one of your favourites,' Lambton murmured as she held the door for her.

Alex looked back at her mother to see only affection in the smile, the row about marriage already forgotten.

It was the shivering chill that brought her out of gloomy recall of earlier today. She noted Blackberry had completed another circuit of the parkland, far slower this time, and they were again at the entrance near the main road that led from London into York via the fashionable and wealthy homes of The Mount where her family lived. She let the memory of the conversation dissipate, her breath coming harder for the cold ride, although the exhilaration of the gallop had helped to blow out some of the anger and gain some perspective. With her horse now still, she noticed her ladies' maid approaching.

'Getting a bit nippy, Miss.' Holly held a hand above her eyes to look up at Alex. 'You looked a bit sad?'

Alex smoothed her long black skirt, straightening it over the lace up boots, feeling the autumn chill finding its way through her thin jacket. She should have listened to her mother and rugged up more.

'Sometimes it's hard being the only child – there's just too much focus all the time.' She straightened her shoulders, instantly chagrined. 'Listen to me. I sound pathetic. Ignore that self-pitying remark, Holly.' She nimbly unhooked her leg from the side-saddle and easily slipped down to the ground. Alex pulled the rein over Blackberry's head to lead her. 'They want an answer on marriage.'

Holly's mouth twisted with sympathy.

'Is twenty-five really that old? Where is it decreed that I must marry by this age?'

Her maid cut her a sympathetic grin but Alex knew she couldn't blame Holly for likely privately considering her far too choosy as much as indulged. 'Lady Frobisher loves you to bits,

Miss. She worries about you, wants the best for you. She's not the enemy.'

'I know, I know,' Alex sighed. 'I am my own enemy. I assure you my mother is not the villain here. She's simply a Victorian trapped in this new age who believes every daughter is essentially a wife in training. That's how she was raised. She is determined I feel the same keen sense of family duty, especially since . . .' She didn't finish that painful thought. 'Well, anyway, according to women of my mother's ilk, their daughters should not have dreams that stretch beyond the front door of the household. There are times when I wonder why she bothered to educate me. Forgive me, Holly. I'm sounding horribly ungrateful.'

'Nothing to apologise for, Miss. We all have dreams. There's no harm in them.'

Alex was prodded into deeper guilt as she imagined Holly's life of endless work duties for the Frobishers and one day off a month, which she mostly spent travelling to and from Burnley to see her parents and siblings.

'What are yours? Marriage? Family?'

Holly lifted a shoulder. 'Yes, of course. I hope for both but there's not much time for romance with work the way it is.' She looked away immediately. 'I'm not laying any blame, Miss. I love my job with your family.' She frowned.

'What? Go on,' Alex encouraged.

'Well, I suppose I've always wanted to be a shopkeeper,' Holly admitted. Alex hadn't anticipated the honesty of Holly's choice and it must have shown in her surprised expression.

'Sorry, Miss. I've spoken out of turn again.'

'No, not at all . . . I'm intrigued, truly I am. A shopkeeper,' she repeated, sounding impressed. 'Really?' She nodded at Holly's self-conscious grin, happy for her personal maid who had slowly become a confidante since they were introduced five years ago.

Now you're eighteen, Alex, your birthday present is your very own maid, her mother had said in a hushed, impressed-with-herself tone. *Happy birthday, darling. Meet Holly.*

Alex remembered feeling instantly embarrassed for both herself and the new woman in her life. Holly was being passed over like a commodity and Alex had prickled with indignity so she'd set out from their first hour to keep their relationship as balanced as she could without drawing raised eyebrows. And she'd discovered that pragmatic Holly was wise beyond her years and it was often she who cautioned the young debutante about fraternising too closely with staff. 'One day you might have to sack me,' Holly had once jested but Alex had heard the truth riding beneath the humour.

'In all this time you've been at my side, why haven't I known about this?'

Holly smiled wider. 'Why would I mention it? It's just a silly daydream.'

Alex hid the soft blow of in injury she felt from being locked out of Holly's inner desires, especially as they'd effectively grown up together these past years.

Blackberry gave a snort of impatience and Alex obliged by leading her off the parkland. They paused again at the entrance.

'So what sort of shop did you have in mind?'

'Drapery, I always thought, but I like to daydream about a tea-shop now or a cake shop.'

'Oh, but that's wonderful.' She meant it.'Not even Mrs Morrison makes a pot of tea, or chocolate, as you can.'

Holly put a hand to the side of her mouth. 'That's because Mrs Morrison has put Tilsden on a permanent war footing and taken to re-using tea leaves, if she can get away with it.'

Alex laughed.'Don't tell my mother.'

'We do our best to protect the family from the outside world,' Holly admitted.

'Amen to that,' Alex muttered. 'How's your war going, Holly?'

Holly sighed. 'My youngest hasn't left for Europe yet. Both my elder brothers are in northern France, in a trench together, which helps us all to stay positive.' She shrugged. 'Sometimes I think it's probably easier not to have a sweetheart.'

'One less person to worry about?'

'I suppose. But I've got my man and I do miss a kiss now and then, though,' she giggled. 'We all need kissing, don't we?'

'Too right. And I think it's lovely you have your shop to dream about.'

'Is it, though?'

'Why do you say that?'

'Because I'm not in a position to act on mine.'

Alex blinked, took a second to fully appreciate the undertone of the challenge in Holly's words. 'But I am?'

'You have plenty of freedom, Miss. So long as you're not hurting anyone through it . . .'

Holly's words of daring made Alex feel as though she'd stepped out of a dark room into bright sunlight. 'Follow my heart anyway, you're saying?'

'I'm not saying that. It's not my place to encourage you to rebel against your parents, Miss,' she said, her expression clearly saying the opposite, as far as Alex was concerned.

She regarded the glorious racecourse they stood opposite stretching out verdantly and imagined that in a few weeks it would become boggy when the mire flooded. She'd seen people take boats out on it and in winter she usually joined the merry throng and skated over it during late January.

Alex could see a lone man galloping his horse in the distance on the far side of the course. She knew the figure to be Arnold Rowntree, nephew of the original Joseph Rowntree, philanthropist and founder of the famous confectionery label. Arnold was familiar to her father as they were both involved with the ever-expanding railway but she wasn't privy to how their work connected. Arnold was in his early forties, plump, with his hairline racing backwards at a frightening rate to leave a shiny dome and thickets of hair just above and behind his ears. Until recently and as a Liberal MP for York he was affectionately known as Chocolate Jumbo. As director of the family firm and a good Quaker, Arnold was also a conscientious objector, which had brought him the sort of notoriety in wartime that was far from positive.

Alex's gaze narrowed, thinking of her cousins and Holly's brothers and sweetheart, living in filthy trenches, potentially killed during every daylight moment, breathing mustard gas without warning while this chubby, jovial, prematurely balding man of immense wealth and privilege got to breathe fresh English air and ride his horse along the Knavesmire seemingly without a care in the world. And yet she liked him; everything her father said about him and his family's constant good deeds for the town was endearing, including his most recent assistance to open up part of the factory to becoming a hospital for injured soldiers to convalesce in. There were plans already underway to build a village to get their workers out of the slum areas and into clean, healthy, modern housing. The Tuke family, former owners of the business that the Rowntrees now owned, had even bought a vast tract of land on the rim of the city surrounded by patchwork of meadows and orchards and built a series of buildings to offer care and accommodation in friendlier, less sombre surrounds for the people of York with troubled minds. They called it The Retreat. According to her mother, the Quakers were spurred into this blitz to build a sanitarium of sorts after their collective personal horror that a Quaker woman died in the local asylum for lack of proper care. Alex shivered slightly. She knew the City Asylum to be a daunting hulk of brick and stone, built in the 1700s and where there were rumours of terrible treatments for the insane. She had to admire Rowntree in spite of others calling him cowardly.

'Penny for your thoughts, Miss?'

'Pardon? Oh, sorry. Arnold Rowntree over there. Apparently his stallion is called Business.'

'That's an odd name for a horse.'

Alex grinned. 'Well, the story goes that he detested the notion of lying to people in equal measure at having to entertain the constant stream of visitors he was receiving in a day on petty matters.'

'Go on, Miss.'

'My father said it eased Chocolate Jumbo's soul for his servants to be able to put their hands over their hearts and say to a visitor that the master was not in and that he was out on Business.'

There was not even a full second's pause before Holly had tipped back her head to laugh with Alex.

'Priceless, isn't it?' she added. 'I've always liked that story and it has endeared me to him knowing it hurt his heart to lie.'

'People say mean things about all the Quakers these days.'

'They don't deserve it because they've done so much that is good for York and let's not forget that Quaker sons have signed up for the Friends' Ambulance Unit serving at the front.'

Alex led Blackberry forward and Holly fell in step as they began to head up the hill. It was eerily quiet, given that the road to London was usually a steady movement of carriages, buses and even a few automobiles backfiring as they rolled sleekly down the main artery of the two cities. The ascent would take them to The Mount, a protectorate of the wealthy and powerful. This enclave resided on the edge of the York's dark, crowded medieval streets . . . beyond the slums and markets, the department stores and civic buildings all crushed together and encapsulated by the vast city walls . . . beyond all the dirt and drama of city life to a stretch of clean, cultivated beauty that opened onto the space and bright air of the Knavesmire to their backs. Alex didn't need to be told repeatedly about privilege; she lived it, accepted it, tried not to trade on it.

Holly switched them back to their original subject. 'So what are you going to do about your situation, Miss?'

'I just want to *do* something,' Alex groaned. 'Find something that fires my imagination and challenges me, and not just accept that now that I'm in my twenties I have to forget I have a brain or ambition.'

'So who can it hurt if you volunteer at the factory? I think it's something to be admired. Every pair of hands helps.'

'My mother could be hurt.'

'We can't have that. What if you balanced it out?'

'What does that mean?'

'You only sort of lied . . . you know, white fibs. Ones that can be forgiven.'

She smiled.'Go on.'

'Well, they always need volunteers at the factory hospital. Maybe you could do a hospital shift and then a couple of hours a day you could do some time in the chocolate factory.'

'Why on earth didn't I think of this before?'

'I'll bet my bonnet your parents agree with you that nursing injured soldiers is an honourable way to devote your hours.'

'They'd both consider it noble at the very least. I'll mention it tonight over dinner.'

'Dinner's at seven tonight, Miss. You'll need to get a hurry on if we're to re-pin your hair and get you ready in time.'

They'd reached the house. Alex looked down past the St Peter's School towards Blossom Street dominated by the convent, famous for its hidden chapel where the mummified hand of local martyr, Margaret Clitherow, called home. Well, if Margaret could defy Henry VIII's reformation and hold secret masses as well as harbour persecuted Catholic priests, then surely Alex could find the courage the defy her parents in such a tame way?

'Can you imagine the pain of Margaret Clitherow's execution by crushing against a piece of rock the size of a huge turnip?'

'Ooh, I don't really like to think on it, Miss.'

'Margaret Clitherow believed so wholly in her path that not even the fear of being killed so horribly beneath her own door loaded with heavy weights and stones could deter her.'

'They say it took a quarter of an hour of horror for her to die with that stone breaking her spine,' Holly offered, helplessly drawn into the conversation.

Alex sighed.'And yet my great achievement for today is to have my hair pinned up neatly for dinner and choose what to wear! There has to be more to life, Holly. Men are dying in Europe for my right to live a free life.'

Holly grinned. 'Too much soul searching for one evening, Miss. Come on, let's get Blackberry into her stable. I'll walk with you.'

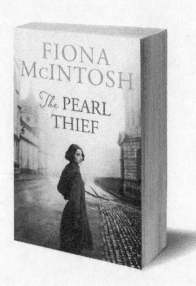

Her predator has now become her prey . . .

Severine Kassel is asked by the Louvre in 1963 to aid the British Museum with curating its antique jewellery, her specialty. Her London colleagues find her distant and mysterious, her cool beauty the topic of conversations around its quiet halls. No one could imagine that she is a desperately damaged woman, hiding her trauma behind her chic, French image.

It is only when some dramatic Byzantine pearls are loaned to the Museum that Severine's poise is dashed and the tightly controlled life she's built around herself is shattered. Her shocking revelation of their provenance sets off a frenzied hunt for Nazi Ruda Mayek.

Mossad's interest is triggered and one of its most skilled agents comes out of retirement to join the hunt, while the one person who can help her – the solicitor handling the pearls – is bound by client confidentiality. As she follows Mayek's trail, there is still one lifelong secret for her to reveal – and one for her to discover.

From the snowy woodlands outside Prague to the Tuileries of Paris and the heather-covered moors of Yorkshire comes a confronting and heart-stopping novel that explores whether love and hope can ever overpower atrocity in a time of war and hate.

'Fiona McIntosh is a prolific and superior writer in the genre, and if you enjoy popular romantic fiction, you'd be mad not to try her.'
THE AGE

Spirited doctor Isla Fenwick is determined to work at the coalface of medicine in India before committing to life as a dutiful wife. With hopes of making a difference in the world, she sails to Calcutta to set up a midwifery clinic. There she will be forced to question her beliefs, her professionalism and her romantic loyalties.

On a desperate rescue mission to save the one person who needs her the most, she travels into the foothills of the Himalayas to a tea plantation outside Darjeeling. At the roof of the world, where heaven and earth collide, Isla will be asked to pay the ultimate price for her passions.

From England's seaside town of Brighton to India's slums of Calcutta and the breathtaking Himalayan mountains, this is a wildly exciting novel of heroism, heartache and healing, by the bestselling author of *The Chocolate Tin*.

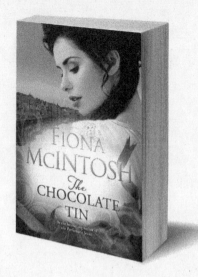

Alexandra Frobisher, a modern-thinking woman with hopes of a career in England's famous chocolate-making town of York, has received several proposals of marriage, although none of them promises that elusive extra – love.

Matthew Britten-Jones is a man of charm and strong social standing. He impresses Alex and her parents with his wit and intelligence, but would an amicable union be enough for a fulfilling life together?

At the end of the war, Captain Harry Blakeney discovers a dead soldier in a trench in France. In the man's possession is a secret love note, tucked inside a tin of chocolate that had been sent to the soldiers as a gift from the king.

In pursuit of the author of this mysterious message, Harry travels to Rowntree's chocolate factory in England's north, where his life becomes inextricably bound with Alexandra and Matthew's. Only together will they be able to unlock secrets of the past and offer each other the greatest gift for the future.

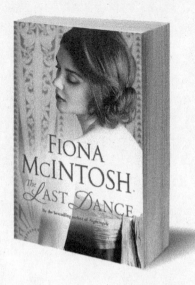

A highly romantic story about forbidden love between a young dance-hall girl and a mysterious aristocrat who leads a double life, by the bestselling author.

Impoverished Stella Myles meets the enigmatic Montgomery in a Piccadilly ballroom and he orchestrates a job for her as governess with the wealthy, secretive Ainsworth family at their country estate. Stella struggles to fit in – although nothing proves so challenging as restraining her emotions for the mysterious Douglas Ainsworth.

When they all venture aboard a cruise ship, tensions reach impossible heights. Stella finds herself in dangerous new territory, and in possession of an incendiary document that she must get to London at all costs.

From the rolling countryside of Kent to the colourful souks of Morocco, this is a heart-stopping novel of romance, intrigue and danger – and a passion to risk dying for.

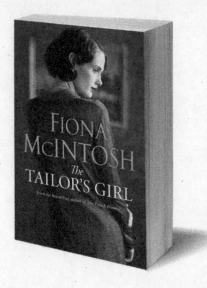

*A heart-stopping story of true love and
courage from a phenomenal Australian storyteller.*

A humble soldier wakes in a military hospital with no recollection of his past. Jones has only a few horrifying memories of the battlefield at Ypres, and his identity becomes a puzzle he must solve.

A stunning seamstress dreams of her own high-fashion salon in London. After a fated meeting with Jones, Eden Valentine is driven to help the soldier by something more than charity.

A mysterious and aristocratic man may hold the key to Jones's past – and to Eden's future. But the news that he bears will bring shattering consequences that threaten to tear their lives apart.